THE PLAN

THE PLAN

KIM PRITEKEL

SAPPHIRE BOOKS

SALINAS, CALIFORNIA

Editor - Tara Young
Book Design - LJ Reynolds
Cover Design - Treehouse Studio

Sapphire Books Publishing, LLC
P.O. Box 8142
Salinas, CA 93912
www.sapphirebooks.com

Printed in the United States of America
First Edition – February 2019

This and other Sapphire Books titles can be found at
www.sapphirebooks.com

Dedication

For Her

Acknowledgments

For all the women who came before us that had the courage to live their truth. We stand in your shadow.

Chapter One

Woodland, Colorado, 1956

Hello, teacher! I've been a naughty, naughty girl."

"Oh, yeah?" Eleanor Brannon muttered, her red pencil poised over the written page she was scanning. She paused at the stench of Anne's Lucky Strikes. "Please put that thing out."

"I know, I know," Anne murmured, painted lips pursed around what was left of her cigarette before she grabbed the ashtray Eleanor kept on the shelf just for her. "You're in a mood." She smashed the butt into the glass dish as she walked over to the small table where Eleanor had her work spread out.

"Yes, well, you know I hate those things." Eleanor waved her hand at the ashtray in Anne's hands. "I don't care what they say. I absolutely do not see how something can be good for you that smells so foul."

Anne smiled, setting the ashtray aside as she sat in the chair perpendicular to Eleanor's. "Yes, well, I'm a strong proponent of anything that can help calm my mother."

Eleanor smirked, glancing up at Anne. "Is it her cigarettes or the quart of gin she drinks in a day?"

Anne chuckled. "Touché. You know," she said, sitting back in the chair, a wrist dangling casually over the back. "My smoking didn't bother you like this when we first met."

Eleanor put her red pencil down and sat back in her chair as she let out a tired sigh. "Well, you didn't smoke as much as you do now, and over time, it gets old. Things change."

"As do people," Anne muttered. "What are you working on? And where's my hello?"

"The family tree project," Eleanor said and leaned over, accepting a lingering kiss, which she allowed to deepen a bit before pulling back, discreetly wiping Anne's lipstick away as Anne did the same.

"Can I help?"

Eleanor looked at her with raised eyebrows, her girlfriend of two years reaching up to tuck a strand of wavy hair in her ever-stylish hairdo behind an ear. She was ever the follower of anything Grace Kelly, and if the style was good enough for the beautiful blonde, it was good enough for Anne Sedgwick. Anne gave her a look of confusion.

"What?" she demanded, dark blond eyebrows falling in consternation.

Eleanor smiled and shook her head. She was surprised as Anne wasn't typically one to volunteer to be helpful. To be honest, she knew Anne had a rough day at the office where she served as the secretary for an incredibly demanding boss in Fred Gallant, who was anything but.

Eleanor shook her head and reached over to the artistic portion of the assignment. "Okay, go through these," she instructed, straightening the pile before sliding them toward Anne. "Each student had to create a family tree, minimum four generations, including them. See?" She tapped the pictures glued to the piece of brown sugar paper where the student had drawn a rudimentary tree. "See," she said again, her voice rising with excitement. "Here, the student used his own school picture on this branch, and then up a few are his parents and—"

"I get it."

Eleanor realized she was doing it again. "Sorry," she said with a sheepish smile. "I don't mean to go into lecture mode."

"No worries," Anne said with a sigh, gathering the projects before her.

"Anyway, so those that have either pictures or drawings of the four generations, put in one pile. If they don't have either or both, put those in a separate pile."

"Yes, ma'am."

Eleanor grabbed her pencil again and returned to grading the written portion of the assignment, where the students had to write a report on their family history. She spared a glance at Anne sitting a couple of feet away. "How was Fred today?"

Anne shrugged. "An asshole, as usual." She smirked. "He's lucky he pays decent, I suppose. But then, what choice does he have when it comes to women?"

"Anne!"

"Well, it's true! You've seen him…"

Eleanor studied the attractive blonde for a moment before she dropped her pencil again. She pushed back from the kitchen table in her small one-bedroom apartment and walked over to the icebox. She pulled it open and peered inside, relieved to see she still had the bottle of wine Anne had brought over the previous weekend.

"Want a glass?" she asked, holding up the chilled bottle.

"Please." Anne passed the project she was looking

at over to one of the piles she'd created.

"What did he do?" Eleanor asked conversationally as she dug out her corkscrew from a drawer that held random kitchen gadgets and utensils she didn't use.

"He's just so demanding. And," Anne qualified, "I'm not talking about demanding in expecting a good employee. I'm talking demanding as in an infant, replete with fits and tantrums."

"Sounds like he needs to sit through my War of 1812 seminar." Eleanor chuckled, pouring them both a glass of the sweet red.

"Isn't that the one you said the kids fall asleep in?" Anne asked, taking the offered juice glass.

"The one and only." Eleanor reclaimed her seat. "Sounds like he needs a good changing and a nap."

Anne smirked as she brought the glass to her lips, eyeing Eleanor. "I've missed you," she said before sipping the deep red liquid within.

"What are you talking about?" Eleanor asked, confused as she glanced up from the paper she was grading. "You're sitting in my kitchen."

"Yes, as I was last night and the night before. And like tonight, you were grading papers or working up a new project for your kids." Anne set her glass down as she divvied out a couple more of the family trees to the piles she'd created. "Why do you think I offered to help you tonight?" She snorted, tossing another family tree to the pile to her left. "So at least we can be doing something together."

Eleanor wanted to be irritated, but guilt immediately washed over her. She knew Anne was right. She knew she wasn't giving Anne the attention she wanted and deserved. She knew she wasn't giving what she needed to be. What bothered her the most, though, was that she knew she didn't have it to give.

Pushing her irritation and guilt aside, she reached across the short distance and grabbed one of Anne's hands, noting the perfectly painted and filed nails. "I'm sorry," she said softly. "You're right. I've been so busy."

Anne gave her a small smile and squeezed Eleanor's hand before pulling away. Eleanor knew she was hurt. *Damn.* "Who knows," she said, setting aside the newest project she'd been looking over. "Maybe we can go away this weekend. To that place in the mountains we went to last fall, remember?"

"The one at the lake? What was it, Taylor Lake?"

"Are you related to any of the students in your class?" Anne asked suddenly, glancing up at Eleanor from the green sugar paper before her.

"No, definitely not." Eleanor shook her head. "Why?"

"Well, if you're not related to this kid, I'd say you have a doppelganger, darling."

Eleanor accepted the stiff paper with the pictures glued to it. Her gaze immediately went to the picture where one of Anne's deep red nails tapped. She took in what was before her and felt her breath stolen from her as her mouth fell slightly open.

"Ellie?" Anne said softly, her hand lightly touching Eleanor's arm.

"Please don't call me that," Eleanor whispered, unable to take her eyes off the image, her own words not much more than a distant voice echoing in her mind.

"Eleanor? Are you okay? Do you know someone in that picture?"

Eleanor cleared her throat, desperately trying to clear the cobwebs out of the shadows of her memories as she did. She slid the page back across the table to

Anne. "Um…" She ran her hand over her dark brown hair, cut into a pixie cut. "Listen, uh…" She met Anne's concerned gaze, giving her a small smile. "Sorry. So we were talking about Taylor Lake?"

Anne looked down for a moment, her hand wrapping around her wine. "Someday, I hope you'll share your secrets with me," she said, once again looking at Eleanor. "I know we all have them, but yours seem to run deep."

Eleanor let out a heavy breath, grabbing her own drink, the glass rattling against her teeth a bit as her hand trembled. "Yes, we all do," she whispered.

❧❧❧❧

Eleanor removed the toothbrush from her mouth before she leaned over the sink and spit the minty foam into it. She turned on the cold water to fill the glass she kept in the bathroom for the purpose of rinsing her mouth as she did then, spitting once again into the sink before using the remaining water in the glass to rinse the sink bowl free of toothpaste residue.

She continued with her bedtime routine, washing her face and using the toilet before she stood in front of the oval-shaped mirror mounted above the pedestal sink in the small bathroom.

Studying her face, she let out a tired sigh and reached up to remove the pale blue cotton band she'd used to keep her hair from getting wet or mixed in with the cold cream she'd used to wash her face. She looked as tired as she felt, her eyes deeply shadowed. She studied those eyes, the ones that more than one person said she stole from Elizabeth Taylor. But because she was fourteen years older than the beautiful young actress, she figured she deserved the credit for having the unusual violet color first.

Smiling at her own thoughts, she placed the cloth band on the edge of the sink before grabbing her comb and running it through her short dark locks. Though disappointed, Anne had gone home at Eleanor's request. Eleanor had initially hoped the wine would give her the want for her girlfriend to stay, but seeing that picture, seeing *her*, she needed to be alone and had no desire to answer the many questions she knew Anne would toss at her. She did, however, agree to go away with her for the weekend, as promised.

Making sure the bathroom was tidy, she switched off the light and padded to her bedroom just across the hall, the light material of her nightgown flowing freely around her calves. The light was already on, revealing a small, rectangular room, not much larger than a prison cell with a full-sized bed tucked against the wall where the window was, its brass headboard polished to a shine. The quilt she'd made the year before was on it, which would be nice on a chilly late September night.

A chifforobe was placed against the wall opposite the bed, which left just enough room for a small bedside table where a lamp was perched, as well as her wind-up alarm clock, which she made sure was set for the next morning.

She covered her mouth as a yawn nearly split her jaw and walked over to the bed to pull down the covers and climb in. The mattress was a bit too soft and the springs squeaked annoyingly, but it was hers. She'd learned over that seemingly endless seven years, four months, and thirty-three days to never, ever again be ungrateful or take anything for granted.

The buttery hue of the lamp painted the ceiling

of her bedroom in the second-floor apartment—placed right above the pharmacy below—and her gaze followed the artfully done paint strokes.

She let out a heavy sigh as her body relaxed into the softness, the quilt and sheet pulled up just beneath her breasts. As she settled in, she allowed her mind to wander.

After Anne had left, she'd cleaned up the papers and family tree projects, stuffing them back into her work satchel from where they'd come. She hadn't looked at that picture that Anne had come across again. She couldn't, had promised herself she wouldn't.

Now she had nothing to distract her. Anne wasn't there demanding her time, and for a scintilla of a moment, she wished she'd let her stay the night. She clicked her tongue in a steady staccato as her fingers tapped against her stomach where they rested, so easily imagining pushing the covers back and leaving the warm cocoon of her bed to make the short trek to the kitchen table where her satchel sat, ready for a new day at school.

Inevitably, her mind drifted to that black and white picture. She had to smile as she remembered thinking that day that the photographer would never get the image he wanted.

"I think my face is frozen with this smile," she'd whispered.

"No talking, please!" the photographer had yelled out in frustration.

"Oops."

"I said no talking!"

Eleanor chuckled as she lay in her bed. "Always the rebel," she murmured.

Chapter Two

Brooke View, Colorado, 1933

August 1

Eleanor looked around her bedroom, making sure everything was perfect. She scanned over her perfectly made bed, her perfectly organized dresser top—her Bible centered. She opened the doors of her chifforobe to make sure all was hung and folded perfectly.

Certain everything was as it needed to be to pass inspection, she looked at her reflection in the mirror mounted to her dresser. Her long dark hair was pulled up into a tight bun, just as it was supposed to be. Her face was clean of any makeup—not that she had any to put on, of course.

She straightened the collar of her pressed white blouse, buttoned to the tippy top. She ran her hands down over the pleated front of her skirt, it too pressed and perfect.

She let out a breath and nodded. "Time to go."

She turned to her bedroom door and opened it, making sure it was pressed back as close to the wall as it could be, the brass doorknob touching the plaster wall of the old farmhouse behind it. Sure that it was steady and wouldn't swing away from the wall, she continued down the creaking stairs, her father refusing to fix the aging wood to prevent "anyone" from leaving the house at an inappropriate time.

Reaching the bottom of the stairs, she was met by her mother, dressed similarly, though her updo had streaks of gray in it.

"He's in a mood," she whispered, reaching up to straighten Eleanor's already-straightened collar. "Say nothing."

Eleanor nodded, butterflies battering her insides with nervous wings. "I thought he was supposed to be at the store already," she whispered back, reaching up to adjust what her mother had just done.

Emma Landry sighed, glancing over her shoulder in the direction of the kitchen. "He insisted on giving you a ride to school."

Eleanor's eyebrows drew together. "He knows I'm only going for the picture, right? It's not all that far and won't take long."

"Secrets are Satan's Scripture."

Both mother and daughter turned to see Ed Landry standing in the archway that led into the kitchen. "Eleanor, your breakfast is waiting."

"Yes, Father," she said, not giving her mother another glance before rushing by her.

The slap came quick and sharp by the stairs behind her.

The kitchen was small and furnished only with a round, simple table. No carvings, no embellishments, simple and made by her father before Eleanor was born, from what she'd been told. The kitchen was white and stark, only the bare necessities for her mother to cook simple, hearty food that was good with God, whatever that meant.

Her parents followed her in a few moments later,

her mother wiping away tears as she scurried to the stove where a pot of oatmeal simmered. The table had been set for three, small glasses of orange juice already poured and bowls waiting to be filled.

"Eleanor?" Emma said softly, emotion making her voice a bit nasally.

Without a word, Eleanor took the bowls to the stove where she held one out to be filled, ending up with two bowls filled and her mother's left at the stove. She walked back to the table where her father had already sat at his place, his back to the wall.

Ed Landry was a tall man, rail thin with the same dark hair as his daughter, worn short and smoothed back from an angular face. His round-lensed spectacles were in place, face clean-shaven. Today, his gangly lower half was covered by pressed black trousers, long torso and bony shoulders and arms covered in a pressed white button-down shirt with a thin black tie. Eleanor knew it meant he was planning to work at the store all day.

He said nothing as his breakfast was placed before him; instead, he removed his glasses and cleaned the lenses on the white kerchief he always kept with him. As Eleanor sat, he spared her a glance.

"Did you read your verses this morning?" he asked.

"Yes, Father," she replied softly, reaching for the bowl of brown sugar in the center of the table. She sprinkled in her allotted amount as she began to recite the Bible verses that had been left written on a page on her dresser overnight, just like they had been since she could read and comprehend in her fifteen years of life. Before that, he would read the verses to her and make her explain to him what she thought they meant.

As she spoke, her voice low and even, she was peripherally aware of her mother joining them with her own bowl of oatmeal. She noted that her mother brought a tissue up to dab at a bit of blood at the corner of her mouth. Anger filled her as she tightened her grip on her spoon.

"You're not finished," Ed said, mixing his own spoon into the thick goo in his bowl. "I left you with five."

Sighing internally, Eleanor shook off her ire and continued with her interpretations of what she'd read.

"Acceptable," he said when she was finished. "I expect not to have to ask next time, Eleanor. You should be excited and exuberant to speak of the Lord's word."

"Yes, Father."

❧ ❧ ❧ ❧

Ed pulled his 1927 dark green Ford pickup next to the lawn of the brick building with bold white letters across the front that read *Brooke View Senior High*. A few cars were parked out front, and a horse was tethered to the fence across the street.

Several of Eleanor's classmates—as soon as classes began in two weeks—wandered around the area while others stood in pockets chatting. There were fewer than fifty in her upcoming sophomore class, which was scheduled to have its picture taken for that year's yearbook at precisely ten fifteen in the morning.

"Your mother didn't explain why the class picture is being taken today, Eleanor," he said, glancing over at her from behind the wheel as he pulled the truck to a stop with the slightest squeak of brakes. "Can you explain how that makes sense?"

"From what the letter said," she began softly, "this was the only day the photographer could be here to get everyone." Expecting this question, she reached into her skirt pocket and pulled out the folded notification from the school. He took it from her and read it over.

"Very good," he said, tucking the note into his shirt pocket.

"Thank you for the ride," she said, pulling the handle to release the door latch when she hissed in pain, her father grabbing her left forearm with an iron grip. She was already bruised there. She met his hard gaze.

"The notification said this shouldn't take more than an hour. I expect you at the store in exactly one hour."

"Yes, Father," she whispered, wanting to pull her arm away, but she knew better. Finally, she was released and climbed out of the truck.

She waited until he drove away before letting out a long shaky breath. Even when he wasn't around, she felt as though she were being watched. Perhaps it was his God he was constantly shoving down her throat, or perhaps she knew her father was capable of anything. She personally struggled with the idea of such a vengeful God, so she figured her unease was far more grounded on Earth.

Shaking off her morose thoughts and fears, she looked around to see if there was anyone she knew who had arrived. Their tiny town of Brooke View was a farming community outside of Denver, though much of the land was owned by wealthy men, so the families were itinerant farm labor. Entire families—or single men—moved from town to town, working farms as they went, like locusts scouring the land as they headed west.

Since the big Wall Street crash in twenty-nine, families had become more transient than ever. The drought that continued to pummel much of the Midwest sent black blizzards up into the skies and dust storms across the Plains and even, word was, back East.

The acreage that the Landry farmhouse sat on had been in the family since Eleanor's great-grandfather Elliot showed up in Colorado after serving in the cavalry with the 13th Pennsylvania, under Colonel Charlie Redmond during the Civil War.

"Are you in the sophomore class?"

Eleanor was yanked out of her thoughts by a cheery voice. She blinked a few times before settling her focus on the most beautiful girl she'd ever seen. Her deep auburn hair flowed in waves of what looked like satin. She'd never seen such soft-looking hair before, so healthy. Her features were delicate and angelic with slightly arched eyebrows, a jaw line that was proud but not harsh and angular like her father's. The creaminess of her skin was incredible, and Eleanor could barely take her eyes off it. But what really got her was the aquamarine color of her eyes.

Those eyes were the only thing that seemed to put a bit of tarnish on this angel's halo, as their owner seemed to have the natural—and likely unwitting—ability to pin someone to the spot with their sheer intensity. Later in life, Eleanor would come to understand those were called bedroom eyes, which were staring back at her expectantly.

Clearing her throat, Eleanor looked away. "Excuse me, what?"

"Are you here for the sophomore class picture?"

the young woman asked again, seemingly unaware of how her presence was unnerving Eleanor.

"Yes," she said quietly. "I am."

"Then come on!"

Eleanor gasped as her arm was grabbed in both hands as she tried to tug her toward where the photographer was setting up his camera and the teens were gathering. She stopped and released Eleanor's arm.

Without a word, she gently took the arm in her hands again, fingertips smoothing a feather touch over the bruises, which were four perfect fingerprints. Eleanor was ashamed and began to pull her arm away, but the young woman gently wrapped her hands around the deep bruise as she moved to stand next to her. She gave her a warm smile.

"I think you'll be standing next to me in the picture," she said matter-of-factly.

"Um," Eleanor managed, her body stiffening at the proximity of this beauty who held her arm. "I think he goes alphabetically."

"I'm Lysette Landon," she said, holding out her opposite hand.

Eleanor smiled, briefly taking the hand. "Eleanor Landry."

"See?" Lysette laughed, such a wonderful sound to Eleanor's ears. "Meant to be," she said, getting them started toward their classmates.

"Okay, everyone, please gather around!" the older man called out, his box camera set up on a tripod. "If you are a sophomore, please come here, and I need you to get in groups based on the letter of your last name!"

"Come on, my fellow L," Lysette said with a grin, pulling Eleanor to stand over with her and another boy, who Eleanor recognized as Karl Lutz, the son of the barber. "Hello, Karl, my love," Lysette said, giving the boy a kiss to the cheek, which made him blush. "Do you know my new friend Ellie?"

Eleanor looked at her, never going by any shortened version of her name before. Seeming to sense this, Lysette met her surprised gaze.

"You don't mind if I call you Ellie, do you?" She wrinkled her nose. "You're too beautiful to be something so staid as an Eleanor."

It was Eleanor's turn to blush. "No," she near-whispered. "I don't mind."

"Yes, I know her." Karl gave Eleanor a quick smile and nod. "Hey, Eleanor."

"Hi, Karl."

"You see," Lysette explained, her fingernails lightly and absently trailing up and down the underside of Eleanor's arm, sending delicious chills throughout her body. "Karl used to go to Oakbur Academy with me in Denver." She looked from Karl to Eleanor. "It's this really ritzy, pompous school that I hated and finally escaped because my mother decided she wanted to paint nature this year. So," she concluded with a huge smile, "here I am!"

Eleanor felt exhausted by the energy Lysette exuded, her bright smile, piercing eyes, and torturous touch. "Um, welcome," she finally said.

Lysette giggled, hugging Eleanor closer to her side. "You're adorable."

Eventually, the photographer was able to get everyone standing on the three-tiered mobile stage that was usually used for choir concerts.

"All right, everyone," the frazzled photographer muttered from behind his large bulky camera. "Keep those smiles in place."

"I think my face is frozen with this smile," Lysette whispered.

"No talking, please!" the photographer yelled out in frustration.

"Oops."

"I said, no talking!"

After what felt like hours, they were finally finished. Feeling antsy, Eleanor turned to Karl. "Do you know what time it is?"

He pulled out his pocket watch and flipped it open. "It's eleven-oh-nine."

"Wonderful! Lunch and malts on me!" Lysette exclaimed, clapping her hands as she looked from one to the other.

"Oh, god," Eleanor gasped, her stomach in knots. "I have to go." Without so much as a second glance, she ran off, six minutes to get to the store.

Five and a half minutes later, she rushed into Brooke View General Store, out of breath and sweating. She saw her father helping a woman cut some fabric, his glare in her general direction pointed. She looked away, knowing she was still in trouble.

Chapter Three

These are my parents, Roger and Alice McKay, when they got married in 1921 in County Cork, Ireland, and then they moved to Nebraska." A hand flung out from behind the page the student was reading from in a staccato voice, pointing to the black and white picture of a couple dressed in their wedding best.

Eleanor sat behind her desk watching, trying to hide her smile as she watched her second-to-last student present his family tree project.

"And they moved into this house where my mom got pregnant with me, so they moved to Colorado and ended up here in Woodland where I was born." The page was lowered, revealing the freckled face of Benjamin McKay. "The end." The class of seventeen clapped politely as the boy hurried back to his seat.

"Thank you, Ben," Eleanor said. "And finally, Jimmy, would you please share your project with us?"

"Yes, Miss Brannon." Jimmy Vaughn pushed his chair back from his desk before he stood, his sugar board in hand, yet Eleanor noticed no prewritten remarks.

Eleanor studied him as he walked up the center aisle of desks headed to the front of the room where he'd present next to her desk. In the three months the students had been in her class, she'd always liked Jimmy. He was a bright kid with a spunky attitude.

He had confidence that she couldn't have dreamed of having at fourteen. He was a handsome young man, tall and lanky, though he'd likely fill out with age. His hair was cut short and slicked back from his face and was a rich mahogany in color. His eyes were an equally rich brown, but now she saw it: his smile. How on earth had she missed his smile?

"Good morning, ladies and gentlemen," he began, giving them a mischievous grin, a trademark of his. He set up his sugar board on the stand Eleanor had there for that purpose. "I'm James Vaughn Jr., otherwise known as Jimmy, and I'm here to tell you about those that I call family, and yes," he added with a wink, "I do think they're all out of their tree."

Eleanor smiled as she turned her chair to watch him, studying his profile. She'd intentionally waited to call on him last, needing to steel herself for whatever the gregarious teen might say.

"Let's start at the top," Jimmy said, turning to the sugar board. "My granddad Davis Landon fought in World War I, and it was in France where he met a firecracker named Adalyn Brodeur. Very French. Anyway, Granddad dragged Grandma home to Denver where the Landon family owned a whole bunch of land, including some farmland in Brooke View and over by Castlewood Canyon before it was trashed by the flood," he added with a grin. "So their oldest, my mother, Lysette…"

Eleanor listened, but as he went on, his voice became nothing more than an echo in her mind, details long known shared with his classmates. She pasted a polite smile on her lips, his words disappearing as random images danced before her mind's eye. He'd come back into focus with a gesture of his hands, the quirk of his lips in such a disarming expression, just like *her*.

She brought her hand up, resting her chin on her fingers and tilting her head slightly to the side, looking for all the world like she was the diligent teacher, paying attention to every single word Jimmy Vaughn was saying. The truth was, she was imaging her standing up there, presenting the very same assignment in Mr. Gleason's class, which she had. Eleanor had so much fun helping her put her presentation together, she'd decided to add it to her own curriculum when she'd become a teacher eight years before.

As he moved on to his father, she caught bits and pieces:

...James Vaughn Sr....

...met at a soda counter...

...local attorney...

"And so," he said with an exaggerated sigh, indicating himself with a large gesture. "You're stuck with me, the fruit of their love." A few of his classmates gasped at such language while others giggled. "Oh, and my annoying little sister, Bronte." He turned to Eleanor. "That's it, Miss Brannon. Would you like to give me my A now or wait until everyone else has had a chance to receive a grade?"

Eleanor burst into laughter, fully rooted in the present as she pushed to her feet and waved him away like an annoying fly. "All right, everyone. Excellent job on the family tree assignment." The bell rang its shrill end-of-class alarm. "Don't forget, we have the test on the previous four chapters Monday," she called out over the sound of scooting chairs, talking kids, and students rummaging through their bags and gathering their belongings.

"Miss Brannon?"

She turned where she'd walked over to the blackboard to erase the day's lessons. "Yeah, Jimmy?"

"Thanks for such a fun project."

She glanced at him over her shoulder. He stood a head taller than she did. "I'm glad you enjoyed it."

"You see, my mother told me she had an assignment like this once," he said, all grins. "She was excited to help me get it together. We spent all last weekend in the attic going through trunks to find family pictures and Granddad's medals from the war."

She smiled, arms crossing over her chest. "Yeah?" she said. "Your mom got into it, huh?" she asked, affection in her voice that apparently didn't go unnoticed by Jimmy as he eyed her quizzically. She cleared her throat and dropped her arms back to her side, the eraser clutched in her right hand. "I'm glad you enjoyed it. Also glad it gave you some time with your mother."

"Jimmy, come on!"

Eleanor turned to see a young girl, twelve or thirteen, standing in the open doorway of the classroom. She was the spitting image of Lysette, though her hair was more blond than auburn.

"Aunt Josie is waiting for us."

Eleanor's attention was instantly caught by the name, the smile of the woman behind it flashing across her mind's eye.

Jimmy glanced at the girl and nodded at her words before turning back to Eleanor. "Well, thanks again, Miss Brannon. See you Monday."

"Have a good weekend, Jimmy." She watched the obvious siblings leave, then returned to her task of wiping down the blackboard.

"Jimmy has a crush," she heard the girl tease in a sing-song voice.

"Shut up, you little insect."

Eleanor chuckled to herself.

❧ ❧ ❧ ❧

The leather strap of her satchel slung over her arm, Eleanor pulled the ends of her long wool coat closer to her body as she left the brick school building. It was a cool evening, though beautiful as the scent of autumn was in the air. She loved the fall, and as she headed down Coulson Court toward home, she tucked her hands into the pockets of the warm coat.

Woodland was a quaint town with fewer than twenty thousand people, and though so many knew your name, it was easy to get lost in it. It butted up to the foothills, so the views of the Rockies were breathtaking while it still possessed the charm of a valley town.

She smiled and waved as a car buzzed by, a student from the previous school year calling out a greeting from the open car window. Eleanor looked both ways before hurrying across to the tree-lined residential street that she'd walk along until she took a right onto Main Street, which was dotted with small businesses, including the pharmacy above which her apartment was located.

She smiled as Mr. Bowman, the postman who was walking his route, nodded at her. Nearing the Macon Theater, she slowed and glanced up at the marquee. The one theater in town was a place to find her nearly every weekend. She loved going to the picture show, but this week, she was disappointed as the sign advertised *The Last Wagon*, which had begun showing that day.

Not a fan of westerns, she continued on, only to stop when she noticed a man in his shirtsleeves with suspenders and tie standing outside a doorway across the street. He was leaning against the building smoking a cigarette. His dark brown hair was parted neatly on the side and smoothed back from a handsome face while his black-rimmed glasses were perched just so on his nose.

"Evenin'!" he called out, raising a hand when he spotted her. "Beautiful fall day."

"It certainly was," Eleanor called back, noting what was painted on the window of the storefront where he stood: *James Vaughn, Attorney at Law.* She did a double take and nearly burst into laughter. Looking back to the man, she wondered if that was Jimmy's father and her…husband.

He finished his cigarette and smashed it on the brick before placing it in a receptacle by the door for that purpose. "Have a good night!"

"You do the same."

Realizing she was now staring at the closed glass door with wood trim and slanted blinds, she shook herself from her surprise and continued on her short walk home. She'd tossed together some Jell-O salad that morning before work so it could chill in the icebox all day, and it would pair nicely with the tuna casserole she intended to make for dinner.

Reaching the pharmacy, Eleanor pulled out the key she and the other three tenants had been given to the outside entrance, a door set in the brick wall a few feet to the right of the main entrance into the pharmacy proper. The door hadn't always been locked, but they began having issues a couple of years ago with a drunkard who mistook the small entryway as a toilet.

The staircase was narrow, and it had been quite the feat when her furnishings were moved in. She didn't even want to think about how the appliances got there. She reached the top of the stairs and picked out the key to her door, which was second to the right, just beyond Marvell Walker's door, the community payphone mounted on the wall between their doors. She could hear his ever-present jazz spinning on his record player. Marvell shared with her that he'd been a jazz musician in Louisiana during the twenties and thirties.

One day the previous summer, she'd sat on the top step of the narrow staircase with the black man who was old enough to be her father drinking a Coca-Cola, his apartment door open so the music blared out. He'd told her all about his days playing with people he'd met on the road all the while his long dark fingers pantomimed playing the trumpet along with the music.

He reminded her of Samuel.

She unlocked her apartment door and let herself in, closing and locking it behind her. It was good to be home as she placed her satchel on the sofa table she passed before shrugging out of her jacket to hang it up in her bedroom closet. She had her own bathroom instead of a coat closet, a much better trade, in her opinion. After years of sharing a bathroom in Canon City, Colorado, and then in Wichita, it was a real treat to have her own. Now, if she could just get her own phone...

She glanced in the mirror above her dresser, grimacing at the state of her hair. From the breezy walk home, she looked as though she'd just woken up. Turning away, she unbuttoned her dress and let it fall to puddle around her feet as she stepped out of her high heels. Next, her nylons were unsnapped from their garters.

Eleanor nearly moaned as her legs aired out, her toes wiggling against the rug on her bedroom floor. Stripping down to just her bra and panties, she slid on a pair of capris and a top, glad to be comfortable in casual clothes. Slipping into some ballet flats, she made her way back down the short hall to the archway that led to the kitchen.

She blew out a breath and began to get her dinner together before clicking on the television set. She was looking forward to a quiet night watching some shows, as she knew it would be a rambunctious weekend with Anne at the lake.

※ ※ ※ ※

"Oh, darling! Look at this cabin!" Anne exclaimed, tossing her scarf onto one of the beds. "Absolutely lovely."

Eleanor bypassed the furnishings and fireplace to look out the two windows that faced the lake. "Look at those mountains," she murmured, pulling the heavy green curtains aside.

"Oh, poo," Anne said with a dramatic sigh. "Twin beds." She placed her hands on womanly hips as Eleanor turned from the window to see what the problem was. "How on earth do they expect two grown women to monkey around on two twin beds?"

Eleanor chuckled, letting the curtains fall back into place as she walked over to the other bed, shrugging out of her jacket. "Well, I think your answer is in the question, sweetheart. They're not expecting two adult women to monkey around at all, let alone on two twin beds."

Anne sighed again, sauntering over to Eleanor. She raised her hands and snaked them around a slender neck, long polished nails running up into the back of Eleanor's hair, making her shiver. "This is true and terribly short-sighted."

Eleanor grinned, moving to pull away from her as she knew they'd have company any minute. "We'll make do."

Not getting the hint, Anne pulled her in tighter, painted lips mere centimeters from her own. "We'll make more than just 'do.'"

"Annie." Eleanor froze, her hands on Anne's wrists as she had moved to cup Eleanor's face. They both turned to look at the door after a solid knock sounded on the other side. "It's the guy with our luggage and firewood."

"No, it's someone knocking on the wrong door. Ignore it," Anne insisted, moving in for a kiss.

"Anne, come on." Eleanor managed to get away from the woman-turned-octopus and hurried to the door after a second knock, unlatching it before pulling it open. "Hello."

"Hello, miss," the young man said, their luggage in hand and a wheelbarrow full of cut fire logs next to him.

Eleanor stepped aside, allowing him to enter. He hurried in, setting the two hard-shell suitcases at the foot of one of the beds before hurrying back out to retrieve the wood, two trips of armfuls of logs.

Eleanor moved back to stand by Anne, who stood closer to her so their hips and shoulders were touching. She felt a bit uneasy about the closeness in front of this man, but she knew what Anne would say: We're paying good money for this room, so he can deal with it.

Finished, he went through a well-rehearsed explanation of how to load the fireplace, how to light the fireplace and that by simply asking the operator to connect them to the main cabin, he'd return at any time to help or get a new fire started.

"Thank you," Eleanor said, reaching for her purse, which was on the bed. She fished out some coins when she saw him eyeing the two women, suspicion easily seen there, suspicion she'd seen many times over the years. She'd also learned that with a little extra heavy tip they'd be left alone and treated like everyone else.

"Thank you," he said with a smile, accepting the tip before scurrying from the room.

"Why on earth did you pay him for a job he's already being paid to do?" Anne groused once they were alone. Her desire obviously squashed for the moment, she lifted her suitcase to the bed and clicked it open to unpack.

Eleanor watched her and smirked. "We're only here for a night, Anne," she reminded.

"Yes, but I can't stand to be wrinkled." She lifted her dress out where it had been carefully folded. She walked over to the closet where wooden hangers waited to hold the garment for her. After that, she disappeared into the bathroom.

Left alone, Eleanor rolled her eyes. At times, Anne's nonstop energy—often negative—was tough to take. She grabbed her own suitcase and brought it up onto the other bed, intending to freshen up before they headed out for dinner.

"I'm going to shower, darling," Anne called from the bathroom. "I'd invite you to join me, but this stall is the size of the phone booth outside of my building!"

Eleanor smiled as she grabbed the outfit she would wear.

❧❧❧❧

"Thank you," Eleanor said softly to the waitress who dropped off their entrees. The pretty young thing smiled and wished for them both to enjoy, then scurried off.

"You never told me what your mother said in her letter." Anne glanced up at her from across the table as she unwrapped her flatware from the cloth napkin. "Is she still coming for the holidays?"

Eleanor nodded. "That's what she said. She's actually considering staying in Woodland for a bit, maybe into the spring."

Anne's eyebrows rose. "That's a good thing, right?"

Eleanor considered the question for a long moment as she cut up her steak before she nodded. "Yes. I'd love to show her around."

Anne smirked, reaching for her wine. "Well, that should take all of five minutes."

"Yes, well, it's about four and a half minutes longer than where I grew up."

"Is your mother still there? Brookeville or something, right?" Anne asked, holding her wine glass in elegant fingers as she studied Eleanor across the table. "You so rarely tell me anything of personal value, I forget the morsels you toss out," she quipped. The shimmering candlelight in the holder on the table between them made her eyes look sexy and dangerous, which pretty much described the woman behind them.

Annoyed at the snide remark, Eleanor decided to let it go. It was true, Eleanor did rarely tell Anne information about her life outside of them or her job, especially when it came to her mother. She was all she had now, and with the scare they'd had with her heart recently—no matter how much her mother tried to brush it off—Eleanor was very protective of that side of her life and her past. "Brooke View." Eleanor put the small speared bite of meat into her mouth. As she chewed the flavorful morsel, she met Anne's penetrating gaze. "What?"

"Why don't you talk much about your childhood or your parents? You never mention your father. Where is he?"

"Dead," Eleanor said simply, her tone flat. Her own gaze dropped back to her plate as she stabbed another piece of cut steak.

"Of?" Anne pressed, returning her focus to her dinner.

Eleanor set her fork gently on the plate and looked at Anne again. She knew Anne didn't understand, and how could she? Even still, this wasn't a path of memory lane she was willing to traverse. "Sweetheart," she said softly, just loud enough for Anne to hear. "Forgive me, but this isn't something I want to talk about, okay? Let's just enjoy our dinner and head back to the cabin and enjoy that wonderful fire waiting for us." She gave her as alluring a smile as she could, knowing that the direct way to distracting Anne was through her libido.

As Anne took care of the bill, Eleanor headed to the ladies' room. She reached the door, which was opening as a woman was about to step out. She started, obviously surprised by Eleanor's unexpected presence.

"Sorry," the woman said with a little laugh.

As she watched, the beautiful redhead's features softened, the lighter tone darkened and the startled eyes that looked back at her gleamed with mischief and love. Eleanor felt her entire demeanor relax as a slow smile curved her lips.

"Excuse me," the woman before her said softly. "Miss? Excuse me."

The smiling auburn-haired beauty in her mind vanished into the very attractive but annoyed woman trying to leave the bathroom.

"I'm so sorry," Eleanor said, stepping aside. The woman gave her a strange look, then hurried away.

❧❧❧❧

The cabin was slowly becoming darker as the fire burned down to embers. Eleanor had no desire to build it back up as she knew they'd be warm enough with their joint body heat on the twin beds they'd pushed together. Anne was asleep, her back to Eleanor after a long session of making love.

She glanced over at the woman whose behind was pressed against her hip as Eleanor lay on her back. She'd enjoyed their time together to be sure, but it had been a conscious effort to keep her focus, her mind constantly wandering off.

She brought a hand up, the back resting across her forehead as her eyes fell closed.

Chapter Four

August 2, 1933

"Crud," Eleanor muttered, dropping to her knees as she desperately tried to capture all the beans that had exploded out of the twenty-pound bag she'd moved that obviously had a hole in the burlap that she hadn't noticed.

Looking around the dim, dusty wood-plank floor, she saw some that had skittered under the long table she and her father used to unpack crates that arrived with merchandise for the store. There were too many burlap sacks filled with supplies. She knew, however, that what she was looking for was not under that table.

Using her hands to reach as far as she could, she shoved the pile of spilled beans toward the other makeshift pile before pushing to her feet. She'd have to get the broom, but first, she had to find those darn Buck Rogers Ray Gun stacks.

The toy section in the store was small, but her father always tried to have popular toys for the local kids, and they couldn't keep the space guns on the shelf. The mainstays were the ray guns and a few dolls for the girls. They were supposed to be getting some catalogs for customers to order from for the upcoming holiday season soon.

Bringing a hand up, Eleanor used the back of it to wipe sweaty strands of hair that had fallen free from her bun out of her face. It was hotter than blue blazes in that room, the early August sun beating down on a drought-ridden town. She would do anything to be able to wear one of the beautiful cotton skirts her mother had made for her—hidden in her hiding space under the floorboards with her diary—and a short-sleeved blouse. Her father would never allow it. At least he allowed her to roll up her sleeves when she was out of the sight of customers.

She walked over to the one window and with a grunt used all her strength to push it up, allowing at least a little fresh air to enter the stale space. The rooms above the stores were used for storage by some store owners while others had set the small, two hundred-square-foot space as homes. The one above her father's store was filled with crates, burlap sacks, the table, and a hidden countertop with sink and icebox that her mother and she used when they sold specialty food items they canned from what was left from the farm at home.

Eleanor waved her heavy skirt around her legs for a minute, glancing over her shoulder to make sure her father wasn't coming up the stairs as she lifted the skirt to her knees to get some air on her legs for a second before dropping the skirt back into place to get back to work.

She looked around for the broom before rolling her eyes as she remembered she'd left it in the small space at the bottom of the stairs. She'd come up before her father had called her back to carry up the heavy box of receipts he had for the previous month, which he'd go through later that night.

She quickly unrolled her sleeves and buttoned the cuffs and hurried to the top of the stairs, the clunky leather shoes she wore thudding on the wooden stairs as she trotted down them, slowing as she got closer to the main floor. She slowed further when she heard a voice that was familiar, but she wasn't quite able to place it. She stopped just before she'd round the wall to the small area where the broom was, so she was still hidden from the store population.

"It's so nice to see you again, Mr. Landry!"

"Uh, well, you've got the advantage here, young lady. Do I know you or your father?"

"I should hope so" was said with a little giggle. "I'm Lysette Landon."

Eleanor was surprised by the slight pause and change in her father's voice from polite curiosity to firm discomfort. She could almost see his tall frame straightening to a ramrod straight pole.

"Yes, of course," he said. "It's been quite some time then, Miss Lysette. Did your father need something? I'm certain I sent him the rent—"

"Oh, no! Not at all. I'm actually here to see Eleanor."

Another pause. "And why would that be?"

Indeed, Eleanor thought. She wondered the same thing as she eased down from the second step to the bottom.

"I met her yesterday at the school picture. Can you believe we're in the same class?" Lysette gushed, excitement in her voice. "Well, my friend and I invited her to lunch yesterday afterward, but she told us she had to hurry and get on to work here in this beautiful store. You see, Mr. Landry," Lysette continued, her voice dropping slightly, almost as though she were about to impart a special secret to him. Eleanor leaned a bit farther toward the edge of the wall. "She told me that, even though she wanted to join us yesterday, she was just too dedicated and committed to the work ethic that you personally instilled in her."

"She did?" Ed asked, surprise and—could it be—pride in his tone.

"Absolutely."

Eleanor shook her head, a bemused smile on her face as that conversation had never taken place.

"So since I heard she was working today, I decided to see if she could take a break. That is," she added, voice contrite, "if it's okay with you, sir."

"Well, I don't see—"

Eleanor didn't even wait for her father to finish his sentence as she nearly flew around the corner to grab the broom, then flew up the stairs, nearly tripping over her own feet in the process. She was out of breath by the time she returned to the little room and desperately tried to calm herself as she swept. She just hoped she looked natural and not like her heart was about to pound out of her chest.

She took a deep breath when she heard the firm, steady footsteps getting louder and louder until finally Lysette appeared. She looked even more beautiful than she had the day before with that soft, bouncy auburn hair and gorgeous eyes, which were fixated on her. Much like the day before, she was also dressed in an expensive dress, which looked cool and comfortable in peach and orange tones. Silk ribbon was weaved throughout the bottom of the skirt.

"Hi," Eleanor said quietly, wrapping her fingers around the handle of the broomstick and holding it in front of her like a shield.

"Hello, Ellie." Lysette's beaming smile erupted into an adorable bout of laughter. "Why are you looking at me like that? I'm not going to eat you."

Eleanor blushed, looking down as she brought a hand up to rub the back of her overheated neck. She wasn't entirely sure how much of it was from the oven that was the second-floor storage room or how much was from her nervousness of the girl standing less than twenty feet from her. Well, make that ten feet. When she looked up again, Lysette had cut their distance in half.

"What are you doing?" Lysette asked, looking around. "I always wondered what was up here."

"You've been in the store before?" Eleanor asked, grateful for a semblance of a subject to talk about. She knew she would have seen her there before. "And I'm… um…I'm cleaning up a mess I made. I was looking for those." She indicated the haphazard stack of ray guns. "And accidentally spilled those," she added, waving her hand around to bring attention to the messy bean piles.

"Oops," Lysette said, walking toward her, a saucy look on her face as she reached for the broom. "I'll sweep this up while you do whatever you were going to do with the ray guns."

"Are you sure?" Eleanor barely had the words out of her mouth when the broom was snatched from her hands. Deciding Lysette was, Eleanor turned and headed to the toys. Sitting on a shelf was a roll of blank price tags, so she grabbed it and peeled them off, sticking them to the boxes of the toy guns before scribbling the price on them with heavy pencil marks.

"I am," Lysette responded, the wispy sound of the broom whispering across the floor underlining her words. "I'm sure you're wondering why I just showed up, huh?"

Eleanor smiled as she continued with her pricing. "Yes," she answered honestly.

"Well," Lysette drawled, the sweeping pausing for a moment followed by the sound of a crate being moved aside. "I was terribly disappointed when you couldn't join us for lunch yesterday after the pictures."

Though Eleanor knew this from overhearing her talking to her father—regardless of the puffed-up version that was told to him—she played coy. She shrugged, unable to make herself turn to look at the beautiful girl sweeping mere feet from her. She felt ashamed. "Yeah," she said softly. "I guess I just have to deal with responsibilities." She cleared her throat softly and spared a glance over her shoulder.

She stopped, her mouth falling open when she saw boxes, crates, and bags had been moved and neatly stacked to clear space under the table, the wood plank below swept clean of runaway beans, dust, or scraps of paper that slipped behind.

Lysette stopped working and looked up at her, not a single hair out of place. "What?" she asked, a twinkle in her eyes. "Don't think us rich girls know how to work, too?" She reached out and quickly squeezed Eleanor's shoulder. "Your preconceived notion is forgiven."

Eleanor chuckled. "Didn't know I had one, but thank you," she retorted, returning to her task.

"Do you get a break of any sort?" Lysette asked conversationally.

"Essentially. My father lets me sit down and get a cold drink for ten minutes or so."

"Well," Lysette said, one hand holding the broom and the other on her hip as she met Eleanor's curious gaze. "Why don't I finish up here, then run down to the soda shop and grab us both a cold drink and bring it back? That way, you can finish what you're doing there," she added, indicating the stack of ray guns. That mischievous grin that Eleanor was beginning to recognize as an expression of a young woman who knew she'd get her way appeared. "That way, maybe your father will give you an extra couple minutes."

Twenty minutes later, the teens sat side by side on the stoop of the backdoor of the store, an ice cold Coca-Cola in hand. Eleanor's eyes slid closed as the sweet, carbonated liquid slid down her throat. She heard a giggle next to her and glanced over at her companion as she lowered the bottle from her lips, using the back of her hand to wipe away a little dribble that her tongue couldn't reach.

"Good stuff, huh?" Lysette said with a knowing smile.

Eleanor nodded. "Absolutely."

"Best dime I've spent all day," Lysette said, tapping her bottle against Eleanor's before taking a sip.

"So," Eleanor said, eyebrows drawing as she formulated the words for exactly what she wanted to know. "Earlier, you mentioned you'd never been upstairs before," she began, meeting Lysette's open gaze. "When have you been at the store? Customers aren't allowed upstairs."

"No, I don't imagine they are," Lysette hedged. "However, the daughter of the owner of the building is."

Eleanor blinked a few times before looking away, watching a stray dog rummage through some boxes left on the ground next to the trashcans before scurrying away. "So is that how you'd met my father before?" she asked, realizing too late that she'd just admitted she'd overheard their interaction.

Lysette smirked as she took another sip but replied simply with, "Yup." She lowered her bottle and let out a small burp from the carbonation that made Eleanor gasp, then giggle. "Do you ever get a Coca-Cola at the picture show?" Lysette asked, raising her bottle to emphasize her question.

Eleanor stared down at her hands, which were wrapped around the small glass bottle that rested in her lap. She considered fibbing but decided against it. She cleared her throat and shrugged. "I've never been to the picture show."

Lysette's eyes widened. "What?"

Eleanor let out a heavy breath, regretting she'd said anything. "It's frivolous and sinful," she said, repeating what she'd heard about so many things that she wanted to experience.

Lysette said nothing, simply gave her that same knowing smile and playfully nudged her shoulder with her own. "It's a hot one," she said softly at length. "Muggy too."

"Yeah," Eleanor agreed, looking up into the blue, cloudless sky. "Wish it would rain."

❧❧❧❧

August 3, early morning

Eleanor started, her body sharply moving away from something as she rose into consciousness. Her eyes opened and blinked several times. She expected to smell tobacco and looked for the source standing in his usual place when her body jerked again. A massive boom rent the world around her as it was lit with a blinding streak of lightning.

Sitting up in bed, she looked around as her bedroom was alight again followed by a deafening boom that seemed to unlock the heavens as rain poured down in a torrential deluge.

Pushing the covers aside, she swung her legs over the edge of the small bed and got to her feet, stepping over to the window. As she looked out into the night, the wind and rain pounded at the house, making her stumble backward as the front of her nightgown was instantly wet, and the long, loose strands of her dark hair hung in front of her face in tangled, damp tendrils.

She grabbed the window to pull it down, but it wouldn't budge. Gritting her teeth, she used as much of her body weight as she could while being lashed by the angry storm, the heavy curtains flapping around her head and slapping the wall.

Gasping, she looked up when she felt like someone had just poured ice cold water on her only to see water coming in from the corner in her bedroom. During a small lapse in the growing howling winds, she heard an unsettling creak.

"Father!"

"Go help your mother downstairs!" Ed barked as he ran into the room, long bangs hanging in his face and his hastily buttoned shirt—a couple buttons tucked through the wrong holes—saturated. His suspenders, which were still attached to the trousers he had on and had worn the day before, hung limply.

Without asking any questions, Eleanor hurried past him and down the stairs, her bare feet nearly slipping on the trail of water he'd left in his wake. She found her mother in the kitchen pulling out every pot and bucket she had to catch the onslaught of water that was coming in.

"Eleanor," Emma hollered out over the storm, "go grab the washtub. Hurry!"

Eleanor took off like a shot to the washroom, nearly taking a header on some freestanding water as it slowly seeped in from underneath the front door.

"My god," she murmured, glancing quickly at it before continuing on her mission.

The washroom was a small room that held the galvanized metal washtub. It was where they bathed, using the indoor water pump that her father had installed as an anniversary gift for her mother before Eleanor was born. The tub now was upended against the wall after the wash had been finished the day before.

With a grunt, Eleanor maneuvered the heavy tub to a position where she could drag it as quickly as she could to her mother. Panic struck her as she felt herself slipping and, with a loud cry, she went down. Somehow, she managed to roll away in time before the forty-pound tub fell right where her legs were with a deafening *clang*. She figured it would have broken her legs or shattered her ankles.

Heart racing and nightgown completely saturated, she gathered herself and began to get to her feet when the bathroom sounded like it exploded as another clap of thunder rocked the earth. Blinding lightning again ripped the night apart, as well as the tree that stood at the back of the house. Eleanor cried out again in fear and shock as half the sizzled tree crashed through the window, filling half the small space.

She gasped in surprise when she was grasped from behind, hands gripping her under her arms. Turning as she was almost dragged to her feet, she saw her mother, eyes wild.

"Let's go!" Emma yelled above the storm. "The storm shelter has been flooded, we're going to the store!"

Eleanor nodded in understanding, then followed her mother toward the front door, her father pulling around in the truck, which splashed to a stop in a wave. She gave the motorcar a dubious look before running out into the storm, trying to block her face from the punishing rain, which came from above but also bounced off the drought-hardened earth below.

The two women somehow managed to squeeze into the cab, her mother mostly sitting in her lap as Ed got the truck moving. He wrestled with the steering wheel and the gearshift as he tried to avoid the worst of the gathering puddles. Eleanor held on to her mother, her eyes wide as she brought up a hand to push wet, muddy strands of hair out of her face.

"God has spoken," Emma said softly. "Forgive me for my sin."

Eleanor glanced at her mother's profile, surprised at the soft words, which she suspected were meant only for Emma's soul.

The truck took on too much water and stalled out just outside of town, so they abandoned it and forged through the storm, which continued to rage. Eleanor was relieved to see all the windows were intact as they sloshed through the mud and gathering water in the street to the storefront.

"Eleanor!" Ed yelled over the wind, grabbing her arm to turn her toward him. He stuck the key into her palm. "Unlock the door! I'm gonna go 'round back!"

Nodding her understanding, she reached out and grabbed her mother's hand and yanked her along as she fought the storm the last handful of yards and struggled to insert the key into the lock. Victorious, she pushed open the door and nearly shoved her mother inside before following, both women working together to get the door closed again.

"Oh, my goodness!" Eleanor exclaimed, leaning back against it, her hand going to her chest as she tried to catch her breath.

"Not too bad in here," Emma said, walking around the main level of the store. "No water. Luckily, this part of town is a bit higher up than the farm."

"Do you think we lost the house, Mama?" Eleanor asked, her voice quiet and somber as she pushed away from the door.

"I don't know, honey. I just don't know." Emma put her hands on her hips and looked around. "Your father will be glad everything seems to be okay here. Let's gather some blankets to use tonight."

"No," Ed said, his deep voice resonating in the store. "Not wasting money for items to be sold." He walked over to Eleanor and held out his hand, the key placed in his palm. Without another word, he locked the store door and headed upstairs, the two women following.

Chapter Five

Eleanor raised her head from where she shivered on the floor curled up beneath the table next to bags of animal feed. She heard the front door of the store being unlocked and pushed open, though she was surprised there was no sound of punishing wind and rain entering with whomever was shutting the door, their wet, booted feet squeaking on the tile floor.

Confused, she looked around, nearly banging her head on the underside of the table as she went to sit up. It was only her back screaming at her that stopped her rise. Resting on her elbows, she looked around. It was still dark out, and the storm seemed to have receded to a mere mewl from the lion's roar earlier. She had no idea what time it was, but as tired as she felt and the fact that her hair and clothing were still quite damp, she assumed they hadn't been sleeping long.

Her focus turned to the stairs when she heard the squeaky footsteps ascending. The halo of light from a flashlight arrived before the silhouette holding it. Squinting at the sudden burst of light, Eleanor raised her hand to shield her eyes.

"Oh, sorry about that, young miss," a man said as the beam was lowered and partially shielded by a hand. The substantially dimmed light cast eerie shadows on the storage room around them and illuminated the handsome face of a man who looked around at the family of three, his gaze landing on Eleanor before it moved to Ed and Emma, who had found their own small space to attempt to sleep. "Lose your house, did you?" he asked Ed.

Ed was slowly sitting up, a hand coming up to push his hair from his face. "Roof went bad," he said, wincing as his neck popped. "First floor took on some water, too. Can't say I understand it. Bad storm but…"

The man walked in farther, his trouser legs covered in water with mud spots halfway up his calves. "The Castlewood Dam breached," he explained, reaching a hand down to help Emma to her feet as Ed picked himself up off the floor. After Emma was standing and steady, the man leaned down, extending his hand to Eleanor.

"Thank you," she said softly, crawling out from beneath the table with his help.

"What's got you out in this mess?" Ed asked, standing tall, hands on hips.

Eleanor looked from one man to the other. She'd never seen this new man before, though it was obvious her father had. There seemed to be tension between the two, particularly from her father. The other man— taller, larger, and stronger-looking—seemed more relaxed, even a small smile on his face. She glanced at her mother, noting that she was looking down at her feet.

"Well, with the dam going, Denver's got a few feet of water and rising. Came out here to check on Adalyn and the kids." He indicated the building around them. "Wanted to make sure everything here was okay, too." He looked at the three who had moved to stand in a small group at the center of the crammed room. "Listen, we've got room at the house. Why don't the three of you come on over and get a bath and a good night's sleep, hmm? We can fill your bellies with a good breakfast later."

"We're fine, sir," Ed said, taking a slight step forward. Eleanor was surprised to see her mother's hand reach up and grab his biceps. It didn't seem to be a move of support but rather one of warning. "I take care of my own."

The man, still unidentified to Eleanor, raised a hand and ran it through his short-cropped hair. "No doubt, Ed. No doubt at all. Well, listen, not sure what kind of shape your house is in or what it'll take to get it livable, but two stores down, I've got a little apartment you could use." He eyed Eleanor and Emma. "Only sleeps one comfortable, though. But it's got running water and a cook stove."

"We'll take it, Davis," Emma said, absolutely shocking her daughter even as she ignored a death glare from her husband. "But please allow Eleanor to take you up on your kind offer." She reached over and grabbed Eleanor by the arms and gently nudged her toward the stranger.

"Mama—"

Emma cut her off, again pushing Eleanor toward the man. "Please."

He met Emma's gaze, and if Eleanor didn't know better, she felt a silent communication, a softness pass between the two. He gave her an almost imperceptible nod before smiling at Eleanor. "Ready to head out?"

Ten minutes later, after Davis had opened the door to the tiny apartment, Eleanor sat in the front seat of his car beside him. She was terribly worried about her mother. The look on her father's face, the way his jaw muscle had bulged as she and Davis had walked away...

"She'll be okay, kiddo," Davis said softly.

She glanced over at him, noting the extremely kind smile he was giving her, his features visible from the lights of his dashboard instruments. She wasn't sure what to say, so she just gave him a small smile back as she tucked her hands into her lap.

He got the dark green Ford Cabriolet moving slowly, water parting in their wake in the double spotlight of his headlights. It made her think of the parting of the Red Sea. They passed her father's truck.

"Is that your dad's?" Davis asked.

Eleanor nodded before clearing her throat. "Yes, sir."

He took a turn past the truck, a slow wave of water washing up against the stalled Ford. Once they were headed straight again, he spoke. "Do you know who I am, Eleanor?"

She shook her head, again looking over at him. "No, sir."

"Well, I guess in fairness I haven't seen you in about thirteen years." He grinned over at her. "You and my daughter were just little things getting into trouble. The boys weren't even born yet."

Eleanor looked out at the world beyond the windows of the car. To her surprise, the flooding seemed to get less the farther into town they went. "How does my family know you, sir?" she asked, feeling slightly better to hear that obviously this man knew her parents to some degree other than the tension she'd witnessed between him and her father moments before.

"Well, nowadays, I own the building your father's shop is in, but I've known your mama since we were just a little older than you."

She searched her memory and couldn't ever remember a time when her mother had said the name Davis. She was putting together the bit of information he'd given her when he slowed the Ford and pulled off to the side of the road. Confused, she looked around, noting the man huddled beneath his jacket and fedora. His hands were shoved into the pockets of his baggy trousers as he hurried down the road.

"Samuel!" Davis called out, pulling the car up alongside the walking man. The man stopped and turned to look at them, the whites of his eyes bright against the darkness of his skin. "Any luck?"

"No, Mr. Davis. I think that dog done run off!" He whistled through his teeth as he reached up and adjusted the brim of his hat. "We'll find him come light of morning, though."

"All right, go ahead and get in."

Eleanor watched with surprise as the black man climbed into the backseat, sitting behind the driver. He removed his hat and nodded at her.

"Hello, miss."

"Hello," she said softly, baffled by the turn of events. She'd never seen a white person allow a black person into his car, even if he knew him, as this man seemed to.

"I really appreciate you trying, Sam," Davis said, glancing at the man in the rearview mirror as he got the car moving again. "Cisco is safe, though?"

"Yes, Mr. Davis. Miss Adalyn was holding him 'fore I left."

The two men grew silent, and Eleanor tried to wrap her mind around the very unexpected situation she'd found herself in. What she wanted was for the storm never to have happened and to be back home asleep in her bed. But as the car took a couple of turns down a quiet street, she knew that wasn't going to happen. They pulled into the long drive of a large home that she'd seen many times and had always found beautiful. The building material was sandstone with three floors of measured opulence, including a small turret. She'd always wondered what was inside that turret: was it a small room for reading? A closet? Or was it simply part of a spiral staircase to the lower floor?

The Ford pulled up and around into the circular drive. The large intricately carved wood front door opened, though nobody stepped out. Eleanor took a deep breath, relieved to be out of the confines of the car with the two men but nervous about what was next. She was startled out of her thoughts when her door was opened. She turned to look, and Samuel stood with a welcoming smile on his face.

"Miss…"

Glancing over her shoulder to find the backseat vacant, she wondered how on earth he'd exited the car so quickly and reached her side. "Thank you," she said, stepping out.

"Adalyn!" Davis called out as he too stepped out of the car. Eleanor again startled. She expected him to bark out orders to this Adalyn woman, but instead he said, "I brought you a surprise!" She was even more surprised when he smiled over the top of the car at her.

"Come on, miss." Samuel stepped up beside her and indicated with a large hand that she should walk before him. "Let's get you dry and warm."

She gave him a ghost of a smile before continuing on, hurrying up the rounded cement stairs that led to the rounded front portico that gave the already beautiful house a grand entrance.

As she stepped up the final stair, she saw a woman rushing down the circular staircase inside, lifting her skirt as she went. She was a stunningly beautiful woman with flowing chestnut hair, worn longer than most women Eleanor knew. Her delicate features reminded her a bit of those on a doll. Her smile was wide and welcoming.

"*Bonjour, mon amour*," she said, arms flung open wide as Davis stepped into them. "We missed you."

Eleanor was shocked at the display of affection and felt the need to shield her eyes. The most she'd ever seen her parents do was her father grabbing her mother's hand to redirect her where he wanted her to go. The hug and quick kiss on the lips these two shared brought a blush to her cheeks.

"What is my surprise, *chéri*?" she asked, her words beautifully accented with French. Her hands clasped behind his neck as he looked down at her with adoring eyes.

Eleanor stood near the opened door, not sure what to do and feeling awkward and beyond uncomfortable. She knew she looked and smelled like a drowned rat, and if she could have sunken into the marble floor of the entryway, she happily would have.

"Look who I brought you, my love." He released her waist, and with a hand on her lower back, he led her toward where Eleanor stood. "Baby Eleanor."

With wide eyes, Eleanor looked from him to her, her discomfort intensifying as the pair ascended on her, making her take a small step backward until she came into contact with the open front door.

"Look at you!" the woman gushed, her hands coming up to cup Eleanor's cheeks before her face was brought forward to receive a kiss to either side. "Beautiful girl."

Eleanor looked into her eyes, such a beautiful color and so familiar. She also noted the woman smelled amazing. Either she was wearing perfume at four in the morning or she was made of roses.

"Is your *maman* not with you?" she asked, looking past Eleanor to the early morning beyond.

Eleanor paused, the word the woman had spoken—sounding like mamaw—confusing her. "Uh—"

"No, darling," Davis said, stepping between the two. "She stayed behind with Edward."

The look that passed between the two, the shadow that crossed otherwise beautiful aquamarine eyes, wasn't lost on Eleanor. It seemed to be a flash of anger before that gaze was back on her, along with the warmth that had been in them a moment before.

"I am so happy to have you back in our home, Baby Eleanor." She smiled, her hands reaching down to take Eleanor's. "Not a baby anymore," she said with a wink, which made Eleanor blush anew. "Come, *mon cher*, let us get you into a bath." She put her arm around Eleanor's waist and guided her toward the stairs. "Samuel," she said softly to the man who stood nearby, as though waiting for instruction. "Please prepare the purple bedroom for our very special guest, hmm?"

"Yes, Miss Adalyn," he said, bounding up the stairs ahead of the ladies.

Eleanor was whisked off to the second floor and what seemed to be the area where the bedrooms were. They passed at least four of them before reaching the room at the end of an adjacent hallway, a bedroom and washroom off by themselves. For a moment, Eleanor wondered if she were being punished or hidden away.

"Here you can have your privacy," Adalyn explained, leading her into the washroom.

"Oh," Eleanor said, relieved if amused that Adalyn seemed to have heard her thoughts.

The light was switched on with the push switch to reveal a wonderland of purple and cream. The sink, commode and, to her delight, bathtub were all a vibrant purple while the tile and accents were cream. The fixtures were chrome and polished to a shine. Her gaze kept returning to the commode with its pull chain. At the farmhouse, they had an outhouse. She'd never used an inside toilet before and wasn't sure what she was more excited about—the commode or the deep, inviting bathtub!

"I will leave you to enjoy," Adalyn said with a smile.

A sudden wave of panic flowed over Eleanor as she looked at the very things that had been so inviting a moment before with flustered uncertainty. She could feel eyes on her and met Adalyn's gaze. "Um," she whispered, clearing her throat. "Okay."

Adalyn studied her for a moment before she reached out, running her fingers down a long strand of dark hair before she walked over to a cabinet, cleverly hidden in the wall. She pulled the panel open to reveal shelves. She reached in and retrieved a glass bottle with a rubber stopper. The contents inside were a light purple.

"Smell," she said, removing the stopper and waving the bottle in front of Eleanor's nose. "Beautiful, no?"

Eleanor's eyes slid closed at the wonderful lavender scent. "Yes, absolutely beautiful."

"Here." Adalyn handed her the bottle. "You decide what soap you want to use, okay?"

Eleanor took it and watched as the woman who looked to be around her mother's age made her way to the tub and placed the stopper, which was attached to the faucet with a chain, into the drain. She glanced over her shoulder as though to see if Eleanor were paying attention. Tub plugged, she turned both hot and cold spigots until the water flowed. After a quick, silent tutorial of how the commode worked, Eleanor was left alone.

Blowing out a breath, feeling slightly overwhelmed, Eleanor looked around. The steaming water waiting for her was so inviting. Adalyn had left towels for her, as well as a clean sleeping gown to slip into.

"Here goes," she said, slipping out of the mud-caked gown she wore, feeling very vulnerable as she slid her undergarments down her legs to puddle at her feet. She kicked them aside and scurried over to the tub.

Looking down into the scented water, she took a final breath before she tested the temperature with a toe. Finding it satisfactory, Eleanor stepped into the tub, lowering herself in as her eyes closed in absolute pleasure with an almost obscene groan.

Fully submerged, she rested her head against the back of the tub, the water rising to just above her breasts. She knew she didn't have long, as she did desperately need to get some sleep, and she had a few scant hours to do that before her father no doubt dragged her out of the bed by her hair, just like at home when she wasn't up when he felt she should be.

Allowing herself to enjoy it for a few moments

longer, she gathered her willpower and washed herself, scrubbing her hair and skin with the most beautifully scented shampoo and soap she'd ever smelled. At home and in the store, they had only the bare basics in products and toiletries. There were no pretty colors and fragrances. There were no perfumes and fancy powders, such as she'd seen Adalyn pour into her bath water.

Eleanor often saw her life and family in shades of black and white with a few grays in between. Her father insisted their home and beliefs be simple and his alone. But now, in this gorgeous home in the new experience of a formal bath in a tub, she saw there were actually colors to life, and not just the purple she was surrounded by.

She took a mental picture of her surroundings because likely she'd never enjoy the likes of it again.

❧ ❧ ❧ ❧

The sun was shining through the sheer window coverings as violet eyes blinked open. Eleanor was curled up on her side in one of the two twin beds in what was called the purple room due to the fine purple wallpaper and plush area rugs on the hardwood floor. As she lay there, she had the distinct feeling she wasn't alone.

Turning to her back, she immediately realized someone was reclining on the other bed on the opposite wall, book in hand. Lysette tore her focus from the story and rested her gaze on Eleanor.

"Good morning," she said with a welcoming smile.

Chapter Six

Eleanor sat at her desk in the empty classroom, the radio softy playing in the background as she graded a batch of tests. She wanted to go home and begin the newest novel she'd picked up and not have to take her work with her. A voracious reader, she'd been recommended Isaac Asimov. She was not particularly a science fiction fan, but she was willing to give anything a try in the literary world at least once.

"Hello, my darling doll."

She looked up and smiled as she watched Scott O'Shea waltz into the room—literally. She tossed her red pencil aside, as she knew any grading was finished while he was there, and sat back in her squeaky desk chair.

He reached her and, with a dramatic bow, leaned down and kissed her cheek. "Happy Wednesday to you."

"Someone has been watching their Fred and Ginger again, I see." Eleanor chuckled, reaching up and brushing a few strands of hair out of his eyes, falling there with his moves.

"But of course."

With that, he reached down and grabbed her hand, cradling it in his as his other hand found her lower back, and he led her gracefully around the small triangle of space between her desk, the wall, and the front row of students' desks. Eleanor was no Ginger

Rogers, to be sure, but he'd taught her enough to keep up and not step on him or get stepped on.

They ended their impromptu waltz with applause from the open doorway of her classroom, two other teachers standing there watching.

"So romantic!" home economics teacher Holly Sanders gasped, hand to her heart.

"When are you two going to get married already?" Holly's best friend and math teacher Martha Dooley asked, hand on rounded hip.

Eleanor and Scott glanced at each other and grinned before turning to their audience and giving them a small bow and curtsy, respectively. Left alone as their colleagues wandered off, Scott looked deep into Eleanor's eyes, mischief in the dark brown depths of his own.

"Yes, darling, when are you going to marry me?"

She playfully swatted him away as she walked back to her desk, slightly winded from their dance. "The day Ronnie gives me away as your bride," she said quietly, for his ears only. She smiled at the cackle that got. "You heading out?" she asked, reclaiming her seat.

Scott, the band and choir teacher, perched on the edge of her desk. "Actually, I was hoping you'd be up to letting me take you to dinner. I know, I know," he rushed on when she began to reject his offer. "I need to talk, Eleanor. I need some advice."

She studied him, his boyish features irresistible. Finally, she sighed. "All right."

❧❧❧❧

Eleanor and Scott sat at a table near the front window of the Woodland Diner, its dinner crowds thin yet. Eleanor sipped her coffee, watching as Scott made quick work of his meatloaf. She'd already finished her salad with tuna fillet, not in the mood for anything heavy.

"I finally spoke to my mother," he said quietly, using a knife and fork to cut another piece of the seasoned meat dish.

"And?"

He shrugged, sparing her a glance before scooping some mashed potatoes with his fork before using them as the glue to capture the bite of meat. "She said my friend is welcome in the house."

"Your 'friend,'" Eleanor said gently, shaking her head.

The loaded fork stopped halfway on its journey to his mouth. "What else am I to call him, El?" he asked. "My father—" He cut himself off as his voice had begun to raise. He cleared his throat and leaned forward slightly as he looked around to make sure nobody was paying them any mind. His gaze fell on Eleanor again. "My father won't even allow Ronnie because he's 'not like us,'" he described the black man using air quotes with pain in his voice, "into the house. What am I supposed to do?"

She smirked. "Your father would have a hissy if he knew I lived next door to a colored man."

He returned the smirk. "My father would have a hissy if he knew you lived alone, El."

She raised an eyebrow. "As you should be. Get your own place."

He looked at her like she'd lost her mind. "How on earth can I do that? I'm not married."

She rolled her eyes and set her coffee cup onto the provided saucer. "Scotty," she said with a heavy sigh, "you're a thirty-two-year-old man making a wage."

"But I'm not married…"

"Lordy, Scott." She sighed in exasperation. She held up her left hand, fingers spread. "Do you see a gold band here?"

"There could be," he hedged.

"No."

"Eleanor—"

No!" She softened her expression and her tone as she gazed adoringly at the man who she loved even as he drove her crazy. "I like my life. I'm not about to give up my freedom and sanity because you're too much of a mama's boy for your own good. At some point, you're going to have to become your own man. Especially," she added, "if you don't want to lose Ronnie."

He played with his food, his expression seeming to be a mixture of irritation and hurt. He reached for his Coca-Cola and drank before he met her gaze again. "What about Anne?"

"What about her?" she asked, reaching for her coffee again. She wasn't thrilled about the conversation turning in her direction.

"Do you think there's ever a chance of things getting serious?" he asked, his tone lightening somewhat, always an indicator that he was choosing to let his hurt feelings go.

She stared down at her fingers, which were wrapped around the delicate cup. There was no real reason to respond to a question he already knew the answer to. "Scott," she said softly instead. "Do you remember your first love?" Her gaze flicked up to meet his.

He took in another forkful of food, nodding as he chewed. "College," he managed around the food in his mouth. He shrugged. "Crushes before that, but it wasn't until Billy Everstein that I understood what it all meant." He grabbed his napkin and dabbed at his mouth. "Know what I mean?"

She nodded, a soft smile spreading across her lips. "I do. Where's Billy Everstein now?"

"He...he died," Scott murmured, focusing his gaze on his half-finished dinner.

"I'm sorry," she whispered, reaching across the table to cover his larger hand with hers, able to feel the sadness rolling off him in waves.

He cleared his throat again and squeezed her fingers before giving her a small smile as he slid his hand out from beneath hers and resumed eating.

"What advice did you want, Scotty?" she asked gently, deciding to get back to his initial reason for their dinner. "What are you trying to decide, hmm?"

"Well," he said after a moment, "all things considered, should I even pursue this with him? With Ronnie."

She studied his eyes for a long moment, her gaze spreading out to his open and honest features. "Do you love him?"

He glanced out the window next to their table to the bustling sidewalk and street beyond. Finally, he looked at her again. "Yeah."

"Then hold on to that," she whispered. "It's precious."

※ ※ ※ ※

Pulling her long jacket a bit closer to her body, Eleanor strolled, her high heels clicking on the sidewalk as she made the trek home after a relatively uneventful day at school. It was heading into the second week of October, and though there was a definite chill in the air, she absolutely loved the beauty of the change of the trees, their vibrant colors all around her.

She closed her eyes and inhaled the fresh, crisp air as she walked on. As per usual, she slowed as she neared the box office for the picture show. She was about to glance up at the marquee to see what the feature was when a car pulled up to the curb and stopped just past the theater.

She studied the deep maroon Chrysler New Yorker. A beautiful car, to be sure, and she certainly admired it, but as she was about to walk on, she gasped and ducked into the shadowed alcove of the box office. She watched as the driver's side door opened and a woman stepped out, dark auburn hair held in perfection by the sheer powder blue scarf wrapped over it. Sunglasses covered the beautiful eyes that she knew so well, but she'd know that air of confidence, that electrifying beauty and presence that made man and woman alike stop and stare.

She was dressed in the latest fashion, a petite yet wonderfully feminine body hugged by a midnight blue dress with tiny light blue polka dots all over it, from what she could see of the skirt portion of the dress, which flowed around curvaceous calves. Her upper body was wrapped in a cream-colored cape coat with satin lining, seen on the flared collar.

She closed her car door and looked both ways, waiting for a car to pass before her high heels clicked on the pavement as she hurried across the street toward the law offices of James Vaughn.

Eleanor stepped out of the shadows and into the afternoon sun, her gaze never leaving the woman who walked around a Chevy Bel Air and stepped up onto the sidewalk. She reached up and removed her sunglasses as she neared the door, which opened. The man Eleanor had seen several times standing outside smoking a cigarette or chatting with people stepped out. She'd come to suspect this was James Vaughn himself.

Stepping farther away from the building, Eleanor watched the interaction of the two, her hands absently coming up to wrap around a parking meter. She watched as the couple met a few feet from the door. He leaned in for a kiss, but she turned her head, the peck landing square on her cheek. Eleanor felt her stomach roil with the show of affection, no matter how brief and almost innocent. It was in that moment that her head turned, however, that Eleanor feared she'd been spotted.

Turning away, she quickly pulled her jacket collar farther up near her face and hurried away. She didn't stop until she got to the corner where she quickly hid around the side of the building, her back against the sun-warmed brick. Hand to her chest, she took a few deep breaths, trying to get the image out of her mind and, worse yet, all that her mind wanted to add to what she'd seen.

Her attention was grabbed by the sound of a car headed in her direction. She glanced over to see the maroon New Yorker stop briefly at the stop sign before continuing on. She watched it until it disappeared after taking a left turn at the next street.

Letting out a heavy breath, she pushed away from the wall and continued home.

❧ ❧ ❧ ❧

"Don't forget, guys, tonight are the parent/ teacher conferences, which means specifically teacher, which means *me*, and parents, which means *not you*." She gave her chuckling students a pointed look. "You can, however, take a cookie with you." She indicated the tin of homemade cookies she'd baked for the night's event but had made extras for her last hour of the day.

She watched as the teens gathered their things, some scurrying up to her desk to grab a chocolate chip cookie with a smile of thanks before ducking out of the classroom to join the sea of fellow students in the hallway beyond. She spotted Jimmy Vaughn making his way up to her desk, his usual swagger firmly in place along with his smile.

"Good afternoon, Miss Brannon," he said, reaching into the tin for his treat.

"Good afternoon, Jimmy."

"So, uh," he hedged, leaning a hip against the desk. "What does it take for a guy to get a good review from his teacher to his dad?"

She managed to hide her smile, but just barely. "Are you worried?" she asked, raising her eyebrows as though he had something to be concerned about.

"Hey, one never knows how he is perceived by those around him."

This time, Eleanor did laugh, shaking her head at his antics. "So just what kind of bribe are you looking at, kid?" she asked, both understanding she was joking.

"Well," he said, leaning in with his mother's cocky grin on his face. "My mother makes the most amazing lemon cake thing."

"*Gâteau de Mamie*," Eleanor said softly, remembering that cake well, as well as what Lysette and her mother had called it.

"Yeah!" he exclaimed before his eyebrows fell in confusion. "How did you know that?"

She merely smiled at him. "You think that would help what I tell your dad, huh?" she asked, entwining her fingers before resting her chin on them.

"It's really good cake…"

She shook her head and smiled, waving him off. "Get out of here."

Later that night, Eleanor filled one final glass of the punch she'd made for the meetings with parents and set it next to the open tin of cookies. She had one parent left, and her heart pounded and palms sweated as she waited.

"Miss Brannon, I presume?"

She looked up and saw James Vaughn walk into the room, still in suit and tie. His hair was just so, glasses just so, and his taste in fashion was impeccable.

"Hello," she said, standing from her chair and leaning over the desk with extended hand, which he took. "Eleanor Brannon."

"James Vaughn. I have the distinct pleasure of being Jimmy's father."

She smiled, able to see where one of her favorite students got his charm. He definitely had a double dose. "And I'm his teacher. Please have a seat and, if you like, here's some punch and cookies."

"Ohh," he said, fingers moving over the cookie tin until he chose what must have been the perfect one for him. Taking a bite, he shrugged out of his overcoat, keeping the suit jacket on, and removed his fedora before sitting. "Very good." He took a sip of the punch she placed before him before speaking again. "My apologies that I'm not very good at this. Normally, my wife would be here, but she phoned and feared she wouldn't be back in town on time. So," he added, popping the last of the cookie in his mouth. "Here I am."

She smiled, charmed. "Fathers are certainly welcome, as well, Mr. Vaughn. In fact," she added, getting settled in her chair and pulling the few pages she'd gathered for Jimmy, "I think it's important that fathers are interested and knowledgeable in their children's education."

He raised a heavy eyebrow. "Well, that's very modern of you. So," he said, slapping his hand on the edge of her desk as though bringing a meeting to order. "Is Jimmy passing? Is he doomed to be a jailbird? Any girlfriends I need to know about?"

She chuckled, shaking her head as she pulled out Jimmy's grades. "No, I think you're clear on the jailbird part. As for girlfriends, I don't get involved unless I need to pry them apart." They shared a knowing smile. "As for his grades, he's doing quite well." She turned the page for him to see. "His grades are overall good. He does have a few issues focusing at times, particularly if he sees an opportunity to get a bit of attention."

He nodded, rubbing his chin as he took the page in hand, scanning the handwritten grades and any attached notes she made at the time. "Yes, my class clown, to be sure," he said, sparing her a glance over the top of the page. "He certainly got his vibrancy from his mother."

Eleanor smiled at the accuracy of his statement.

"So anything else?" he asked, setting the grade report sheet back on the desk.

"He's been arriving a bit late in the mornings, but other than that, Jimmy is doing well. Treats his fellow classmates very well, and I have to say, I'm quite impressed by him. More than once, he's stepped in to protect a classmate that was being picked on or having some issue."

He chuckled as he grabbed his overcoat, flipping it over his arm as he pushed to his feet. "Again, the influence of his mother. To be honest," he said, placing his fedora on his head, "I wish he'd toughen up a bit." He winked at her and extended his hand. "Miss Brannon, an absolute pleasure. I can see why you're Jimmy's favorite teacher."

She smiled and rose to her feet. "You're my last parent, so if you'd like, feel free to take the rest of these to your family," she said, holding out the tin of seven or eight cookies.

He looked down at it, then grinned at her as he took it. "Excellent. The kids will love it. Have a wonderful night, Miss Brannon."

"You, too, Mr. Vaughn."

She watched him go, returning his smile before he left the classroom. Alone, she blew out a breath and ran her hand through her hair. She was glad that was over, though she had found him to be very charming and pleasant. To say it felt awkward sitting across the desk from Lysette's husband was beyond an understatement.

Shaking all that and the moments before out of her mind, she gathered the papers on her desk and straightened them into a pile to file the following day before class began.

She moved away from her chair, grabbed the eraser, and began to erase the day's lessons from the blackboard when someone hurried into the room.

"I'm so sorry! I got in much earlier than I

anticipated but worried I'd be much later, so I sent my husband in for me. I—"

Eleanor turned around, and her heart stopped. Lysette stood just behind the chair her husband had abandoned mere moments before, her jacket halfway down her shoulders. Her eyes were wide and her face frozen in midsentence.

"I," Lysette said softly, pulling her jacket back into place, her gaze never leaving Eleanor's. "I was looking for Miss Brannon. Miss Eleanor Brannon," she near-whispered, her gaze falling to the floor as though something had clicked into place in her mind.

"It's all right," Eleanor said quietly. "Hello, Mrs. Vaughn," she continued, Lysette's gaze rising to meet her own again. "Your husband was here. In fact, you just missed him. Delightful man. And you found her."

Chapter Seven

In a borrowed dress, Eleanor sat at the breakfast table, Lysette to her left and Lysette's ten-year-old brother Theodore to her right. She watched as Lysette's parents talked to each other, the kids laughed, joked, and even sent a rolled-up napkin flying across the table at the oldest son, thirteen-year-old Michael. But what shocked Eleanor the most was that handyman Samuel and cook Risa, a colored woman, sat down to join the family for the meal!

"Good, isn't it?"

She turned, still wide-eyed from her thoughts and observations, to see Lysette looking at her expectantly. "Huh?"

Lysette grinned. "The frittata. Isn't it fantastic?"

Eleanor looked down at her barely touched food. "Oh, uh, yes." She gave her a small smile, uncertain.

"What? You look confused."

"I've never had frittata," Eleanor said slowly, the word feeling strange in her mouth. She felt small and stupid, out of her league. What she wanted to do was run home and eat what she knew: oatmeal. It was bland glue that secretly she hated, but at least it made sense to her.

Lysette gave her an understanding smile. "Just try it," she said gently. "It's good, I promise. *Maman* brought the recipe back with her from Italy last year."

Eleanor gave her a small smile in acknowledgment

of what she'd said before looking back to the pie-like slice of egg dish sitting on her plate. She grabbed her fork and cut into it, bending her head to get a peek inside before carving out a small bite. To her surprise, it was amazing. The flavors that popped inside her mouth—egg, potato, sausage, seasonings—all mixed together in one delightful bite of food. Definitely better than oatmeal.

Lysette was looking at her with an expectant expression on her beautiful face. "Good?"

"Yeah," Eleanor admitted shyly. "Really good."

Breakfast was interrupted by loud pounding on the front door; everyone's attention focused on it.

"Everybody just stay put," Davis Landon said quietly. "Samuel, would you mind accompanying me?"

"Yes, Mr. Davis."

Eleanor looked around the table at those who remained, trying to gauge their reactions and any evidence of what they were thinking. Was this normal? Was someone expected? Were they as concerned as she was?

Her stomach fell immediately when she heard her father's voice booming in the entryway.

"I'm here to collect my daughter."

"Good morning, Ed!" Davis Landon boomed just as loudly, though cheerful, followed by the sound of a hand slapping a back in masculine greeting. "Why, Eleanor is eating breakfast right now. Why don't you join us? Got plenty."

Eleanor knew that though unintended, Davis had just angered her father. In his mind, he'd just been told he wasn't taking care of his own family. She gently rested her napkin on the table and pushed her chair back from it.

"Where would you like me to take this?" she asked softly, picking up the plate, prepared to clean up her mess.

"Just leave it, hon," Risa said, pushing up from her own chair and walking around the table to Eleanor's side. She touched her hand with her fingers before giving her a kind smile, taking the plate from her.

"Stay," Lysette said, reaching up and wrapping her hands around Eleanor's arm. "Please?"

"Lysette," Adalyn said. Though her tone was soft, warning was in it. "Leave her be."

Lysette looked from her mother to Eleanor and back to her mother. "But she's not even finished her breakfast, *Maman*!"

"Lysette." Adalyn's look was as hard as that single word.

Eleanor wanted to cry—in fear and regret—as she moved away from Lysette, whose hands fell limply back into her lap. "Thank you for everything," she said softly, then made her way toward the men's voices.

Ed Landry stood tall in front of the door. His gaze fell to Eleanor as she entered the entryway, his jaw muscles working.

"I'm here, Father," she said, head lowered in deference.

Ed placed a hand on her shoulder, moving her behind him. She squeezed her eyes shut, able to feel the tension coiled in his body. She listened as he said terse goodbyes, then she was roughly turned around and guided out into the sunny morning ahead of him.

During the ten-minute drive to the store to pick up her mother, Eleanor spared a glance at him before looking out the mud-splattered windows. The town she'd been born and raised in was a mess. The harsh rain had created deep rivets in the roads and yards, the mud quickly drying from the early morning heat that was already settling over the town.

The truck pulled up in front of the building, and Ed looked at her. "Make it quick."

Nodding, Eleanor was glad to escape his intense presence, his anger seeming to be simmering just under the surface.

"Mama?" she called, making her way up a back staircase that led to the second floor of the storefront.

"In the washroom, Eleanor."

She followed the sound of running water and found her mother in the tiny washroom that serviced the entire building. There was a commode, which wasn't much more than that in their outhouse at home, as well as a sink with cold running water.

Hurrying down the narrow hallway, as she knew time was short, Eleanor found the right door and peeked inside. There, she stopped cold. The other Landry woman stood before the small mounted mirror above the sink, gently dabbing at a cut on her chin with some tissue.

"Oh, god," Eleanor breathed, her paralysis lifting as she hurried to her mother's side, fingers to the uninjured part of her face to turn her to see the wound better. Instantly, tears came to her eyes. "I'm so sorry," she cried, easily able to tell that her father's slap or punch had sent her mother flying into something that had cut her. "I never should have left!"

"Shh, sweetheart, stop. Stop it now," Emma said, gathering the crying teen into her arms for a quick hug. "It's okay. Don't accept your father's sins as your own." She glanced over to the empty doorway before looking back at Eleanor, tears continuing to flow down Eleanor's cheeks. "Listen to me, honey," she said, voice low and serious as she reached up to brush loose strands of hair out of Eleanor's face before lovingly caressing her face. "We'll get through this, okay? I promise you, I'll never let anything happen to you. You let me take it all."

Eleanor shook her head. "No. I made it worse by going to the Landons' house. Why does he hate them so much?"

Emma let out a heavy sigh. "It's an old story, and we don't have time for it now. Don't you worry about that. Okay?"

Eleanor nodded, though she was absolutely worried about that. "Okay."

Emma left a quick kiss to the top of her head before returning to her reflection, turning her face this way and that before dabbing again at the cut. "Okay, this'll have to do. Let's go."

❧ ❧ ❧ ❧

The early afternoon was growing hotter and hotter, and the normally dry air was heavy and muggy from the deluge the night before. Eleanor had been stunned by the damage done to her bedroom, which seemed to get the brunt of the flooding on the second floor.

She'd found the wide-brimmed straw hat she used while picking crops in the fields and tied it on to block the harsh overhead sun as the three of them worked in concert to empty out the house. Her mother was mainly picking through what was being brought out to the front yard and tossing aside what was not salvageable, her father giving the final opinion, of course.

Left alone upstairs for a few moments, Eleanor knew she had to act quickly or get caught. Scurrying back into her emptied bedroom, she fell to her knees near the closet where her dresser had been and worked to pry up the loose floorboard she'd found years before.

"Come on," she growled under her breath, wincing when a splinter embedded itself deeply into her finger. "Darn it."

No time to deal with that, she continued to work on the wide plank until it finally lifted. Smiling with her success, she quickly reached inside until she felt the softness of material that she'd stitched around the cardboard she'd used to fashion a book. Pulling it free, she glanced over her shoulder before reaching up under her skirt and tucking the precious book into her panties before working the board back into place and hurrying from the room.

She ran down the stairs, mindful that the diary didn't dislodge from its hiding place before she could find somewhere to hide it. As she stepped out onto the front porch, she saw the glint of sunlight on glass before she heard the distant sound of a car engine.

"Who's that?" Ed asked, stepping away from the pile of destroyed belongings. He whipped his hat off his head and swiped the sweat from his forehead as the three watched the car approach.

Eleanor said nothing but felt her heart beat a bit faster as she recognized Lysette and Adalyn, who was carefully guiding the car around the larger ruts in the dirt road. She managed to keep the smile off her face, mostly because she was distracted when she saw a truck turn down their road a bit behind the car. From the distance, it looked as though the truck bed was loaded down with materials, and she saw a person sitting on the end of the bed, holding on to the side of the pickup.

"What the hell?" Ed muttered.

Eleanor made her way down the stairs to stand next to her mother. The two exchanged a look and small smile before looking back to their unexpected guests as the car pulled up in front of the farmhouse in a cloud of dust.

"*Bonjour!*" Adalyn exclaimed, climbing out of the car.

"*Bonjour!*" Emma replied, hurrying over to the driver's side where the two women met in a fierce embrace.

Eleanor watched, surprised. She couldn't remember her mother acting on anything with so much enthusiasm. She watched the interaction of the two mothers closely, noting a connection with Adalyn that she'd never seen her mother have with anyone else, outside of her own daughter. It was confusing but touching.

"The cavalry is here."

She turned to see Lysette walking up to her and was surprised when she was taken in a tight hug, which she returned, more out of self-defense than welcome affection. However, the feel of Lysette's soft body against her own and the enticing scent of her perfume drew her in.

"Are you okay?" Lysette murmured into the hug, her breath against Eleanor's ear giving Eleanor a shiver.

"Yeah," she said, giving her a small smile as they parted.

The two turned to watch the truck slow as it drew up beside the car. It was almost comical to see the poor man who'd been sitting in the truck bed hop down, covered in dust from head to toe.

"My goodness!" he exclaimed, sputtering with a chuckle. He used his own hat to slap at himself, the man nearly disappearing in a cloud of dust that flew into the air.

"I'm Ed Landry," Eleanor's father said, walking over to the newcomer, hand extended. "And you are?"

"Well, fella," the man said with a grin, "believe it or not, my name ain't Dusty. You can call me Gabby."

Eleanor recognized the man's accent as one she'd heard only once, and that man had been from Texas.

"Nice to meet you, Gabby. I'm Ed. I don't think I know you."

"Nope, you don't," Davis Landon said, pushing the driver's side door of the truck closed as he and Samuel headed in the direction of the two men, the women standing off in a group. Eleanor watched, the pit of her stomach in knots. "This here fella is new in town and has been asking around for work, from what I'm told. He's a carpenter." He slapped the man on the back, chuckling as a fresh cloud of dust wafted into the afternoon, making him cough. "Seems like a good man for you to have around right now."

Eleanor watched as her father ran a hand over his hair as he looked out over the seemingly endless blue sky, then back at their farmhouse. Nodding, he turned back to the two men, mostly ignoring Davis Landon.

"Yeah," he said. "I could use the help. I can't pay you right now, but if three squares and bunking in the out building over there will work for you, seems you're the man for the job."

"Great!" Again, Ed and Gabby shook hands. "Y'all don't know how much I appreciate that."

"Wonderful," Davis said, placing a hand on each man's shoulder, Ed visibly tensing at the touch. "Glad I could be of help. Today, you've got all of us, Ed," he said, stepping back toward his truck. "We gathered all that I think we should need today. Got building materials, tools, plenty of nails." He gave the gathered group a charming smile. "And my lovely wife and daughter brought us a hearty lunch, didn't you, ladies?"

Eleanor stood shoulder to shoulder between her mother and Lysette as they dished out fried chicken, potato salad, and corn on the cob to the men who went through their makeshift line before loading up a plate for themselves.

"Come sit with me, Ellie," Lysette said, taking Eleanor's hand and, without waiting for a reply, tugging her behind her.

They found a tree that, literally overnight, had sprung to life, green exploding from the leaves that stretched to the heavens.

"Is this okay?" Lysette asked, dropping Eleanor's hand.

As they got settled, Eleanor spared a glance at the young woman sitting across from her in the sparse shade. Her heart was racing, and her palms were sweating. Part of it was she was afraid she was doing something wrong under the watchful eye of her father, who sat alone on the upright log he used to chop wood on in the winter. He was watching her and her mother, who sat on the front porch with Adalyn.

Clearing her throat and her thoughts, she turned her focus to her companion. "Guess you got your lunch after all, huh?"

Lysette gave her an evil grin. "I usually get what I want, one way or another."

Eleanor chuckled with a nod as she used her fork to scoop up some potato salad. "I believe that."

"Did your dad do that to your mom's face, too?" Lysette asked softly, picking a bit of meat off the bone of her chicken leg. She glanced up and met Eleanor's gaze when there was only silence. "Like he did to your arm," she added, almost as though she wanted Eleanor to know it was no secret and lying about it was unnecessary.

Ashamed, Eleanor nodded, looking down at her plate, which was balanced on the palm of her hand. "He gets…exuberant at times."

"Interesting word for it, but I guess it'll do, all things considered."

They were quiet for a long moment, both lost in their own thoughts. Finally, Eleanor decided to voice hers. "It's so strange to see how your parents act around each other. It's almost like your father truly *likes* your mother."

Lysette grinned as she gave her a side glance. "He does. My mother hangs the moon for him. He once told me that when he first saw her while on leave for an afternoon in Paris, he knew he was lost and he would never leave France unless she was with him." She sighed wistfully. "They've been together since that day." She met Eleanor's gaze. "Can you imagine that? A love like that? A love that can last through anything, even war?" She shook her head as she sighed, tossing a bit of meat into her mouth.

Eleanor considered what she'd just heard and how otherworldly that sounded to her. "Not even the Bible talks about love like that." She smirked. "Well, I guess other than for Jesus."

Lysette's eyebrows drew. "What does the Bible

have to do with it?"

"Well," Eleanor said with a shrug of uncertainty. "I've heard people say they've read love stuff in books. I'm only allowed to read the Bible."

Lysette studied her for a long time before returning her attention to her lunch, not saying anything, though she looked as though she was having an entire dialogue in her head.

"What?" Eleanor asked, a bit uncomfortable.

Lysette smiled at her and shook her head. "Nothing, Ellie. I'm happy you're coming back home with us tonight."

Eleanor instantly lost her appetite, remembering the steep price her mother had paid for her perceived betrayal and disobedience. "No, Lysette," she said quietly. "I'll go with my parents."

"And stay in that cramped jail cell? No way. My *maman* is as good at getting her way as I am." She grinned. "Where else would I have learned it from?" she said sweetly.

❧❧❧❧

"Come in."

Lying in the twin bed, Eleanor was in the freshly washed and pressed nightgown she'd been wearing when she'd arrived the night before, about to say her prayers like a good girl before sleep.

The door opened, and a figure stood silhouetted in the doorway, backlit by a light on farther down the hallway. The unintended effect made her heart skip a beat as the beautiful young body beneath the sleeping gown was showed in perfect relief beneath the soft material.

She took a deep breath, shocked at how she was reacting to such a simple sight. That is, how her *body* was reacting to such a simple sight. She thought Lysette was absolutely beautiful, that she already knew. Beyond that, she'd not allowed her brain a full autopsy of the incoming visuals.

"Were you sleeping?" Lysette whispered, unaware of the state her sudden presence was putting Eleanor in.

Eleanor cleared her throat. "No. Is everything okay?"

"Yeah." Lysette softly closed the bedroom door behind her before moving in the dimness to the bed, perching on the side. "Here."

When her eyes adjusted to the darkness, Eleanor saw that a book was being extended toward her. She took it, the leather-bound tome cool to the touch. "What's this?"

"I figured you could start with something simple. You can't go too wrong with the Bronte sisters." She smiled, resting her hand on her knee after Eleanor took the book, bringing it up a bit closer to her eyes to read in the tiny bit of moonlight coming in.

"*Wuthering Heights*," Eleanor read aloud. She looked up and smiled at Lysette as she hugged the book to her chest. "Thank you."

"You're welcome," Lysette replied, her gaze never wavering and Eleanor unable to tear hers away for a long moment. "You can just leave it in here," she continued, her voice losing the soft, ethereal quality it had held a moment before. "Daddy said he figures it'll take two weeks at least to get your house habitable, so…" She grinned. "You can stay here."

"And read," Eleanor added with a chuckle.

"And read." Lysette leaned forward and placed a soft, lingering kiss to Eleanor's cheek. "Good night, Ellie," she whispered. "Sweet dreams."

For the second time that night, Eleanor's heart stopped. She swallowed, her heart racing nearly out of her chest as it began beating again. "Good night, Lysette," she managed.

Chapter Eight

How did this happen?" Lysette whispered, hands sliding off the steering wheel to her lap. "How the hell did this happen?"

She squeezed her eyes shut for a moment, trying to hold back the emotion she felt building. Taking several deep breaths, she glanced over at the house, several windows lit. Everyone was home, as she figured they would be. Times had certainly changed since they were all waiting for Jim to get home to eat dinner or watch the evening's television show.

She removed her key from the ignition, took a steadying breath, and gathered her purse before opening the driver's side door and climbing out of the New Yorker. The October night was cold, the smell of snow in the air as her high heels clicked along the stone pathway to the front door of the house she shared with her husband, two children, and Aunt Josie, who had moved in a few years before to help with the children while Lysette was off doing her work. Having Josie there also gave the retired librarian a steady, stable home after the death of Gerry.

The front room was quiet, only a lamp on to light Lysette's way, but she could hear the distant murmur of the television in the den, where no doubt Jim was lain out in socked feet on his recliner, tie undone and flung off into the bedroom somewhere for her to find and stow later.

Opting to head to the children's bedrooms to check on them, she made her way to the stairs, heels getting lost in the thick carpeting installed as an anniversary gift when they'd moved into the house. In truth, it had been a bit of a bribe from Jim to get her to agree to move back to Colorado and to the small mountain town from where he was promised to be handed over a flourishing legal practice from an old family friend. Though that was true and indeed things were going well for them, she'd liked their life just fine in Dallas.

If only she'd known.

As she made her way toward her daughter's bedroom, she had to laugh internally at the irony of it all. All that she'd spent so many years trying to escape had literally landed smack dab in the middle of her son's academic career.

Dropping her purse on the floor outside the closed bedroom door, she lightly rapped on the wood. Given permission to enter, she turned the knob and pushed the door open, instantly in a purple wonderland. At the old house in Dallas, it had been pink. Now, for some odd reason, Bronte had turned her world into a grape.

"Hey, honey," she said, an instant smile coming to her face at the first glance of the evening of her youngest. The twelve-year-old looked a lot like her, she was told, though she certainly had more of Jim's personality—the quiet planner—whereas she'd seen more of her own spontaneous nature and openness to talk to anyone in their son.

"Hey, Mom," Bronte said, looking up from the book she was reading.

"How's my little bookworm?" Lysette sat on the side of the bed, reaching out a hand to brush soft strands of auburn hair out of Bronte's lovely young face. She could see a lot of her mother in her daughter physically, which pleased her greatly. It had been four years since the stroke that ultimately took her mother far too young. It broke her heart that Bronte wouldn't get to grow up with such a wonderful grandmother.

"I got the award for reading the most books last month!" Bronte exclaimed, setting her current book face down on her lap. Her smile was bright, and pride shone in her eyes.

"Shocking," Lysette muttered with playful sarcasm, making Bronte giggle. She leaned in and placed a noisy kiss on the girl's head. "I'm proud of you, sweetheart."

"Daddy said as a reward I could go see a picture show with Lucy if you said it was okay…so, is it okay?" she asked, eyes wide with hope.

Lysette chuckled, leaning in until their noses touched, and she had an up-close and personal view of her child. "Yes," she said in a silly voice. "It's okay."

Bronte squealed and wrapped her arms around her mother so enthusiastically that her book went flying off the bed.

The two broke into laughter as Lysette stretched her body over the bed to snatch it with the very tips of her fingers, sitting upright again as she handed it to Bronte. "I'll talk to your father and see when is a good time for you girls to go, okay?"

"Thanks, Mommy."

Lysette was amused, knowing she'd definitely done well. That was the only time she got Mommy or Mama anymore, unless Bronte was sick, then all bets for her twelve-years-going-on-thirty were off.

With *I love yous* and *good nights*, Lysette closed

the bedroom door softly behind her as Bronte picked up her book again, trying to find the lost place from the flight to the floor.

"Hey, Bud," Lysette said, making her way farther down the hall to her son, whose bedroom door stood open. He sat at his desk with his tongue peeking out the corner of his mouth as he leaned over a paper he was furiously writing.

"Hey, Mom." He held up a hand in acknowledgment as the tip of his pencil danced across the paper. "One sec…"

She walked in, mussing his hair affectionately as she passed behind him to take a seat on his bed. She rested her weight comfortably on her hand as she looked around. It was as neat as she could expect from her eldest, just enough to keep her from complaining.

She saw his basketball shoes tucked into a corner, the floppy high tops fallen over to the side next to his basketball.

"So," Jimmy said, still working on his paper, back to her. "Guess Dad inherited my great taste in women."

"What?" she asked, bemused.

He sent a grin over his shoulder at her. "He thought Miss Brannon was kind of a dolly, too."

"Oh, he did, did he?" she asked, voice sounding slightly accusing, though they both knew she was playing with him. What he didn't know was, she was fighting tears again.

He put his pencil down, fully turning in his chair to face her. "He said it went really well. I'm passing everything and all that jazz. But," he said with an adorable crooked grin that had gotten him out of more pickles than Lysette cared to admit. "Mr. Barnes got on me today."

"Talking?" she asked, a delicately arched eyebrow raised.

"Talking."

"Tsk tsk, son," she said, eyeing him. It was a problem since he was little.

"I know. Miss Brannon is always telling me, *Focus, Jimmy. FO-CUS!*"

Lysette burst into laughter at both the fairly spot-on imitation of his teacher's voice and the fact that she'd been told that more than once by the very same person.

"Well," she said, pushing up from the bed and walking over to lean down to place a kiss to his forehead. "I'm proud of you for the good grades, and I know you're a good boy."

"Thanks, Mom."

"Good night, son. I love you."

"Love you, too, Mom."

Lysette mussed his hair again before walking past him to the door before turning at her name. "Yeah?"

"You're kind of a dolly, too, you know," he said with a grin.

She rolled her eyes and waved him off as she left the room, chuckling. Picking up her purse from just outside Bronte's door, she headed to the bedroom she shared with her husband of sixteen years. She tossed the heavy bag to the padded bench that sat along the foot of the bed and found a comfortable spot to sit during shoe and nylons removal.

Letting out a tired breath, she shrugged out of her jacket and laid it across the bench, intending to take the purse and jacket downstairs in the morning to be properly put away in the coat closet, which she'd bypassed coming in earlier. She held on to the footboard of the bed to balance as she stepped out of first one high heel, then the other, groaning at the relief to her feet, legs, and back. Next went her nylons and finally her dress, leaving her in her satin slip to walk across the room to the attached bathroom.

Snapping on the light, she studied her reflection in the mirror above her sink, the matching mirrors cut into a modern, wavy pattern. Looking into her eyes, she saw that she looked as tired as she felt. She'd been called beautiful her entire life, and yes, she supposed that was true. Good genes certainly helped in that arena. She grabbed her brush to brush out her dark auburn hair, wincing as she caught a snag. She'd need to get an appointment with her hairdresser Sonia soon. It needed to be trimmed and set.

After her hair was brushed out and shining, Lysette set the brush down and gathered her hair back from her face and held it back with a strip of cloth so she could wash her face free of makeup. So many of her friends refused to let their husbands see them "without their face on," something she never understood and thought absurd. From the beginning with Jim, it was imperative he understood what he was getting, both inside and out.

Well, all except one aspect of her, she thought, briefly looking into her own eyes.

Pushing that unwanted thought out of her head, she returned to her nightly ritual, expecting Jim to show up right about…now.

"Hey, honey. I thought you'd come down and watch Ed Sullivan with me."

"Sorry, sweetheart," she said, stepping over to where he stood leaning against the bathroom doorway and left a quick kiss to his cheek. "I'm so tired tonight and wanted to make sure I got to see the children before they turned in."

He nodded, entering the bathroom behind her and walking over to his sink, unbuttoning his dress shirt as he did. "Everything went well tonight," he said, turning on the faucet and rinsing his toothbrush for use.

"Thank you so much for going in my stead, Jim. I honestly appreciate it, and I know Jimmy did, too."

He looked over at her and gave her the boyish smile that she loved. "Of course." He leaned over, and this time, Lysette didn't turn her head and accepted a kiss to the lips to show her gratitude. "It was fairly painless, really," he continued, squirting some of the tooth goo onto the toothbrush. "She has her stuff together, that's for sure."

She smiled, following suit with her toothbrush. "Jimmy said you were taken with Miss Brannon."

He chuckled, looking at his reflection as he brushed his teeth. He shrugged, glancing at her reflection. "I've learned to appreciate independent women," he said around the toothbrush with a wink.

She rolled her eyes and shook her head with a smile as she finished up her own brushing. "Basically," she said, putting her rinsed toothbrush away, and squirting some Jergens lotion into her palm before turning and breezing out of the bathroom, "you've had no choice," she said over her shoulder. She heard Jim following, the bathroom light snapped off before he walked to the bench at the foot of the bed and moved her jacket and purse aside before sitting down. "Right?"

He spared a glance at her as he removed his socks, quiet for a moment as she rubbed the fragrant lotion into her skin. "Did Bronte tell you about her book reading award?"

"She did. I'm so proud of her. I told her we could do the picture thing with her and Lucy. In fact," she said, walking over to him and looking down into his eyes. "Why don't we make a date of it? You're always saying we should do more. So why don't we take the girls to the show and drop them off and we can grab some dinner, just the two of us?"

"When were you thinking?" he asked, second sock halfway pulled off his foot, the first tossed to the floor.

"Saturday."

He cleared his throat and looked away. "I can't. I have the Clarke case I need to do some work on."

She rolled her eyes and walked back over to the bed.

"Lysette," he began softly, glancing over his shoulder at her where she stood near her side of the bed. "Don't you miss...I don't know. Don't you miss the days when it was just us?"

She looked at him with drawn eyebrows. "Just us? Before the kids?" She smirked. "Because that was about exactly nine months."

He smiled, giving her a sheepish grin. "Yeah, a little oops on our wedding night for sure."

"So what do you mean?" she pressed, removing her wedding ring and placing it in the jewelry box on the dresser—she was always concerned with the diamond getting caught in the sheets and blankets—and turned down the bed.

He turned on the bench so he could turn his head and look at her. "I mean, and I swear, this has nothing to do with Aunt Josie. I love her being here and could never live without her baked pears. But," he scooted farther, resting his hands on the footboard as Lysette continued turning down both sides of the bed, fluffing first her pillow, then Jim's two. "Don't you miss when it was just the four of us? When we had dinner together—"

Hand on hip, she paused in her task and pinned him to the spot with a hard stare. "Reading between the lines," she interrupted. "What you miss is me waking you in the morning with a smile and kiss. What you miss is me meeting you with a smile and a cup of coffee, as well as a large breakfast. What you miss is me wasting my day waiting by the phone just *in case* you decide to call before you head out on a business lunch with a dinner request. What you miss," she continued, with a dramatic sigh, "is me waiting at the door with a smile and a rum and Coca-Cola. What you miss—"

"I get it, Lysette," he growled, pushing to his feet and walking to the closet as he stripped.

"No, that's just it, you don't." She walked over to him, standing with both hands on hips now and feet planted wide apart. "You miss having me here at your beck and call, full makeup and hair so you can come home to the perfect wifey who has magically created the perfect house with the perfect dinner and the perfectly washed and folded laundry, which," she said, finger held up in emphasis, "I would hang in the closet and put in your drawers for you. You miss me being here every second of the day for every need you may have, including going on a Fashion Week Easter egg hunt to find every piece of clothing and accessories you leave littered all over the house!"

He looked down at the growing pile of clothing at his feet, as well as his necktie, earlier flung to land on a lampshade and his socks by the bench. Without a word, he gathered his discarded clothing.

Lysette felt bad at the look of shame on his face as he moved around the room, gathering everything and making sure it all ended up in the hamper, even as a shirtsleeve dangled, almost as though sticking its tongue out at her.

"Honey," she said softly, very surprised that her emotions and temper had gotten completely out of hand.

Jim had been a good husband, a wonderful father, and good provider. For the most part, he'd given her latitude to follow her desires and dreams, far more than most men would with their wives. This had been a condition of their marriage, but still, he'd followed through on his part of the bargain as had she.

"Listen," she said, walking back over to the bed where he stood on the opposite side, giving her a quick glance that broke her heart. He looked like a puppy who had been caught messing on the floor and wanted a way to make it up to its owner. As much as she felt bad for losing her temper, she had to continue her point. "Jim, you've been good overall about my work with the underprivileged kids and getting them the supplies they need. And I didn't start my work outside of our local community until the children were a little older, able to do most things for themselves. And now with Aunt Josie here, she can be here that twenty percent that I'm not, or like tonight, the rare time you have to step in."

He nodded, climbing into bed, stacking his two pillows as he liked them. "I know. I just miss you, I guess."

Lysette switched on the bedside lamp before

walking over to the overhead light switch on the wall and pushing it off. "You can't have it both ways," she said, climbing into her side. "You can't crowd the plate on your weekends and then complain how I spend my weekdays." She again pinned him to the spot with her gaze, he holding it for a moment before looking away with a nod. Their long-standing mutual understanding reaffirmed.

"Good night, Lysette," he said, getting settled in.

"Good night."

⁂

"Okay, girls," Lysette said, a bucket of popcorn in hand to match those in Bronte and Lucy's hands as she stood at the entrance of the small theater with about sixty seats. "Decide where you want to sit." She glanced over her shoulder to see the two girls standing behind her, looking out over the darkened cinema. They'd arrived a little late as Lucy's mother was late dropping her off at the Vaughn house.

"There's three open down there," Lucy said, a fat kernel of popcorn between her fingers as she used that hand to indicate the general direction.

Seeing the empty seats, Lysette hurried toward them, murmuring apologies and excusing herself as the three had to sidestep in front of those already seated to reach their seats.

She chose the seat closest to the wall with Bronte sitting next to her and Lucy on the other side of her. Setting her popcorn on the floor between her feet, Lysette shrugged out of her jacket. She turned around in the hard wood seat as best she could to try to place it against the back portion when something a few rows up caught her eye.

Eleanor sat in a chair about midway down the aisle looking relaxed and ready to enjoy the show. She was not alone. Sitting next to her was a pretty blonde who was talking to her, her hand reaching out to brush or touch Eleanor's hand where it rested on the arm of the theater chair from time to time.

Lysette quickly turned back around in her seat, her heart racing. Yes, Eleanor could absolutely be there with a friend, but it was obvious there was history of some sort between the two women. There was intimacy either currently or at some time in the past.

"Mom?"

Lysette was…angry.

"Mom?"

How *dare* she!

"Mom!"

"What?" she snapped, glaring over at Bronte, who was glaring right back. She looked away for a moment to take a steadying breath, then turned back to the girl. "I'm sorry, sweetheart. What is it?"

"Will you please hold this so I can take my jacket off?"

"Of course."

Lysette took Bronte's popcorn and held it in her lap; her mind returned to where it had been headed moments before. Again, she could see Eleanor sitting there, looking so calm, so smug. She could see that *woman* sitting next to her. How dare she flaunt that in here? There were children present, for crying out loud!

"Mom?"

The blonde wasn't even that pretty, she thought angrily.

"Mom?"

As a teacher, effectively a servant of the community, Eleanor should—

"Mom!"

"What?"

"Can I have my popcorn back?"

Lysette looked down into the bucket, which was a third eaten. She hadn't even realized she'd been stuffing her mouth full with each angry thought. Without a word, she reached down and grabbed her untouched bucket, handing it over.

Chapter Nine

"Heads up!"

Lysette brought her hands up to instinctively cover her face, watching in shock between her fingers as Eleanor's hand shot up and, like a magnetic pull, snatched the flying barrel lid out of the air. Huge aquamarine eyes met equally large violet ones.

"How did you do that?"

Eleanor laughed while holding the lid. Michael ran over and grabbed it from her before running back to his brother where they'd been tossing it back and forth through the air to each other.

"No idea." Eleanor lifted up from where she'd been lying on the grass beneath the shade of a tree to watch the boys play. "What are they doing? They're going to kill someone with that thing."

Lysette chuckled, still lying on her back next to her friend, hands tucked beneath her head. "They call it the plate game. They picked it up from some kids on the beach last time we were in California."

"The plate game?" Eleanor turned her focus to Lysette as she also lay back down. "Tell me they don't use your mother's good dishes."

Lysette burst into laughter, her hand automatically shooting out to touch the soft skin of Eleanor's forearm. "You've been staying here for almost two weeks. What do you think?"

Eleanor grinned. "True enough."

The two grew quiet for a long moment, Lysette's fingers continuing to absently trace patterns on Eleanor's arm, something she'd grown fond of doing during their time together as unexpected roommates. She loved how soft her skin was. With very little hair on her forearms, Eleanor's skin was nearly as soft as a baby's bottom.

"Okay, so you were saying a turtle," she said, gaze searching the clouds above for the object Eleanor had pointed out before the runaway flying disc had interrupted them.

Eleanor's other arm raised, and she pointed a finger. "There. See it? Over by those trees? But…well, crud. Its legs fell off."

Lysette laughed, moving her head to rest against Eleanor's so she could try to look where she was. "Yeah, and its arms and its tail and its head…"

"Yeah, yeah," Eleanor grumbled. "So it's just a shell now."

"It looks like a boob," Lysette said absently, glancing over when she heard a shocked gasp. "What? Not like you don't have them, too." She was utterly charmed by the bright pink stain that worked its way up from the opened button collar of her dress. "Ohh," she purred, snuggling up to her and giving her an exaggerated hug to get her giggling as she was pushed away.

"Stop it!"

Lysette grinned and moved slightly away, though she stayed on her side, resting her cheek into an upturned palm. "What did you think of the chapters we read last night?" she asked. Somehow, over the past week and a half, the girls had migrated into sleeping in the same bedroom, the purple room, each in her own twin bed. But before sleep, they stretched out over the bed to laugh and giggle, play card games, or take turns reading out loud to each other.

Eleanor tucked a hand behind her head, her gaze still locked to the sky above. "I liked it, but I wasn't sure why on earth the sister would end up going off with the lumberjack." She scrunched her face up as she looked at Lysette. "And then when they kissed…"

A bark of laughter escaped Lysette's lips as her head fell back in amusement. "It wasn't that bad, Ellie."

Eleanor looked at her with a raised eyebrow. "Did the author ever once mention Richard bathing after cutting down half the forest?"

"Somehow, I think Harris was more concerned about telling the story than pleasing a picky sophomore who would be reading his book thirty years after he wrote it."

Eleanor chuckled. "Yeah, well, maybe he should have taken that into consideration."

"Have you ever kissed anyone?" Lysette asked casually, smiling at the expression that earned her.

"Have you met my father?"

"Touché. Have you practiced?"

Eleanor's eyebrows fell in confusion. "I essentially just told you I'd never kissed anyone before."

"No, I know. But like on the mirror or on your arm. You know," Lysette brought her arm to her face so the bend was at her mouth, leaving it there for a moment to give Eleanor the idea before dropping her hand back down to the grass beneath them, a bit scratchy as it wasn't thick and lush like usual because of the drought.

"Ew! No!"

Lysette gave her a mischievous grin. "I have. I

think my mom caught me by default one day. I was running late for school and forget to wipe my mirror off. She looked at me funny when I got home."

"Can't imagine why," Eleanor said dryly.

"Stop!" Lysette swiped playfully at her. "How else are we supposed to learn? I mean, I tried it once with a boy, and trust me," she said, making a face, "so not worth the price of admission."

"Well," Eleanor said stubbornly, "I'm never getting married, so it doesn't matter."

Lysette felt a little stab in her stomach, and she wasn't sure what it was. Was it happiness that maybe she'd never lose who was quickly becoming her best friend to a man and the life of a wife and mother? Or was it disappointment that Eleanor never intended to let anyone get close to her heart?

"Boys! Get your gear into the car!" Davis Landon boomed, stepping out of the house carrying his fishing pole and a large tacklebox.

Lysette sat up fully, attention taken from the beautiful girl lying next to her. It was the last weekend before school started—and the last weekend Eleanor would be staying with them. Ed Landry and his handyman William Gabford, who everyone called Gabby, worked night and day on the farmhouse when not manning the store. Gabby had been extremely helpful, but there was something about him that made Lysette uneasy. She couldn't put her finger on what it was, and though she wanted to talk to Ellie about it, she didn't want to make her feel uncomfortable around the guy who was around her family so much.

Their plate game abandoned, Lysette's brothers booked it to the house as their father walked over to the large tree.

"There's my girls," he said, giving the pair a wide, welcoming smile. "Your *maman* has a surprise for you two in the house."

"What is it?" Lysette asked, bouncing up to her feet and accepting the warm hug he offered her. She adored her father, and when she saw the way that monster Ed Landry treated Ellie and Emma, it made her blood boil.

"Well, it wouldn't be a surprise if I told you, now would it?" he asked, reaching up to tweak her nose. "Your brothers and I are heading up to Big Bear, and hopefully, we can bring back dinner for tomorrow. So," he continued, glancing over at Eleanor, who had also stood. "You think you ladies can manage to not burn down the house for a night?"

Lysette glanced over at Eleanor, lips curling into a saucy grin. "I don't know, Ellie. What do you think?"

"I don't understand that concern, Mr. Landon," Eleanor said sagely. "I'm just a good church-going girl who does nothing but read my Bible." She punctuated her statement with an exaggeratedly innocent smile.

Davis Landon burst into laughter as he slung his arm around Lysette's shoulders. "Oh, yeah, maybe a month ago, I would have believed that."

"Yes," Lysette added. "My little angel with a tarnished halo. A little crooked, too." She reached over to pantomime straightening said crooked halo.

"Hey, at least I have one," Eleanor quipped, sending Davis into a new burst of laughter.

"You two be good," he said after calming, which took several moments. He left a fatherly kiss on the cheeks of both teens before striding back across the yard where his two sons had appeared with their fishing gear.

Lysette watched him for a moment before turning to Eleanor surprised to see her entire demeanor had changed. She was looking down at her clasped hands and her shoulders were slumped.

"Hey," she said, placing her hand on Eleanor's shoulder. "What's wrong? Was my dad too touchy-feely? I can talk to him. He doesn't mean anything by it, just his way—"

"No," Eleanor said softly, shaking her head as she raised her head and met Lysette's gaze, her own filled with such sadness. "My father has never kissed my cheek." She gave her a sheepish smile before her gaze dropped again. "Sorry. I don't know why that hit me. I guess I just never realized it could be that way with a father, you know?"

Lysette felt her heart break for her friend. She'd been blessed her entire life with wonderful parents, and it wasn't until she'd met Eleanor and her mother that she truly realized what she had.

"Come here," she said softly, pulling Eleanor to her, a hand coming up to cup the back of her head as she urged it to rest on her shoulder. She smiled as Eleanor relaxed against her, their bodies flush as Eleanor's arms wrapped around Lysette's back. "I'll share," Lysette whispered, stroking Eleanor's long, beautiful hair, which she kept down when at the Landon house.

"Lysette! Eleanor! Come in, please," Adalyn yelled from the open back door.

Lysette glanced in the general direction of the house, then gave Eleanor a tight squeeze before loosening her hold. "Are you okay?" she asked softly, bringing a hand up to brush a few long strands of hair out of Eleanor's beautiful face. At Eleanor's nod, Lysette smiled. "Come on. Let's see what the surprise is."

Arm in arm, the two made their way to the house, Adalyn standing in the doorway watching their advance, a curious expression on her face.

"What?" Lysette asked, glancing over at Eleanor to see if her mother was seeing something she wasn't. "Why do you look so smug?"

"Come, come," Adalyn said in lieu of a response.

They entered the back door, which led directly to the kitchen, a bottle of wine and four glasses on the large prep table and an array of ingredients.

Lysette's eyes lit up. "*Gâteau de Mamie!*"

"*Exactament.*" Adalyn grinned, walking over to the table and popping the cork on the bottle, steadily pouring two full glasses of wine and two half-glasses, which she handed to the teens. "*Apprécie, mon amour,*" she said, giving Lysette a kiss to the cheek, then Eleanor. She gave them a devilish grin. "Let's bend the law a bit, uh?" she said, indicating the wine.

"*Merci, Maman.*" Lysette was excited, not given wine very often. It was essentially only on special occasions. A glance at Eleanor made her laugh. "It's okay. It's good."

"I, uh…" Eleanor stared down into the dark liquid before meeting Lysette's excited gaze with fear. "My father would kill me. I can't." She was handing the glass back to Adalyn when someone else entered the room.

"Then I guess we won't be telling him, will we?"

Eleanor's eyes saucered at the sight. "Mama?"

Emma gave them all a radiant smile. To be honest, Lysette thought that beautiful expression took ten years off her face.

Emma accepted the full glass Adalyn offered her,

as well as the kiss to the cheek, then took Eleanor in a tight, one-armed hug, careful not to spill either of their wine.

"What are you doing here?" Eleanor asked, her tone breathless after the hug ended. "I thought Father made you go to that revival."

"We were going to go, but Gabby invited him to some meeting or something. I don't know, some stupid group he belongs to."

Lysette's eyebrows shot up at Emma's flippant language regarding her husband and his activities. She could tell Eleanor was just as stunned. "So you get to spend the day with us?"

Emma grinned at her. "The day, the night, and the morning." She put her arm around Eleanor's shoulders. "Ladies, we are free for an entire day and night!"

"This is one heck of a surprise, indeed," Lysette said, nodding as she sipped her wine, looking ever like the little adult. "Let's get to baking, ladies."

※ ※ ※ ※

"Can I just say I had more fun this afternoon than I've ever had in my life?"

Lysette smiled from where she sat on the bench of her vanity table in her bedroom, painting her fingernails. She glanced over at Eleanor, who lay across her bed. "Yes, yes, you can."

"Oh, thank you so much for your permission," Eleanor teased, moving from her back to her side, head resting in her palm. "I had no idea my mom could be so feisty."

"I know, that was amazing," Lysette agreed,

pinky sticking straight out as she carefully twisted the cap onto the small glass fingernail polish bottle before spreading her fingers out and blowing on the tacky nails, painted light pink. "Your mama has some serious spunk, that's for sure." With both hands up and all ten fingers spread, she made her way to the bed, Eleanor scooting over to make room for her. "How did she end up with your father again?"

"Well," Eleanor said, pushing up to a sitting position, pulling her bare feet in to sit cross-legged. "My father's younger brother, Earl, was actually supposed to marry my mom. I'm not sure how they knew each other. I think a family friend or some such. But Earl was killed in the war, both of his brothers were."

"Oh, no," Lysette breathed, pausing her motion of waving her hands around to dry the nails faster. She felt heartsick. Both her parents had lost so many they loved and cared for in the war, but she couldn't imagine if both her brothers had been lost like that. "So was it romantic? Your father swooped in and took his place?" she asked, hopeful.

Eleanor met her gaze, her tone flat. "He swooped in and demanded to take his place."

Lysette let out a heavy sigh, carefully leaning on her hands on the comforter to try to get more comfortable without making a tacky mess. "You know," she said softly, "I try, I really try to find a reason to like and respect your father." She met Eleanor's gaze. "For the sheer reason that he *is* your father." She shook her head. "I just can't."

Eleanor gave her a small smile. "Trust me, I understand."

Lysette was about to say something when she hesitated, glancing toward her closed bedroom door.

She heard it again, wild laughter coming from down the hall. Turning to Eleanor, she saw it had caught her attention, too. "Is that your mother?"

"I think she's had a bit more wine than she's used to," Eleanor said with a small smile.

More raucous laughter and excited talking followed. "They sound like a couple hyenas." Lysette laughed. She and Eleanor exchanged a quick look before, as if by silent command, they began an exaggerated imitation of their mothers.

"Shut it, you two!" Adalyn called out, making the teens dissolve into laughter.

Fallen to her side, Lysette tried to calm down, her stomach muscles sore. She looked over at Eleanor, who was also coming down from the fit of laughter. She was sitting back against the headboard, legs stretched out in front of her, covered by the skirt she wore, bare feet crossed at the ankles.

She slowly sat up, mindful of her nails as she curled her knees up beside her, resting her weight on one hand. She studied Eleanor unobserved as those beautiful violet eyes were focused on her own hands, which sat in her lap. She thought Eleanor had such a natural beauty to her, something she hadn't seen before, at least not to the degree she did in her best friend.

It was as though the best features had been taken from her parents, the best features that were associated with femininity: full lips, perfectly proportioned nose and eyes that were not just a beautiful color, but were so soulful and deep, they nailed you to the spot with a single glance. At times, Lysette found herself needing to look away, feeling as though Eleanor were looking inside her, learning all about her deepest, darkest secrets, desires, and fears. She made the normally confident redhead feel unsure and awkward at times.

She was drawn to her, had been from the very moment she'd laid eyes on her. "Ellie?" she heard herself saying.

"Hmm?" Eleanor responded, meeting her gaze.

"I think we should practice." Lysette was shocked inside by what she'd said, her mind reeling as she tried to find a way out of her proposal.

"Practice?"

"Yeah," she said, changing her position as she sat up straight and crossed her legs in front of her. Though her heart raced and she knew deep down it was wrong or unfair, she forged on. "*You* may never get married, but I plan to fall in love someday. So why not help a girl out?" she finished with a quirky grin.

Eleanor pulled her legs into her body to mirror Lysette's position. "I still don't follow."

Lysette looked into Eleanor's confused eyes before taking in those full lips and finding her gaze again. She knew in that moment she could call the whole thing off. Eleanor wasn't fully understanding what she was saying, so she could laugh it off, call it a joke, or tell her she wanted to practice the Charleston. But the truth was, she didn't want to dance, and what she was feeling was no joke.

In lieu of an immediate verbal response, Lysette scooted around so she was seated directly in front of Eleanor, their knees touching. She spared a glance to Eleanor before reaching out and taking her hands lightly in her own.

"Now," she finally said, taking a silent breath to try to calm her racing heart and nervous stomach. "I need to know what to expect or what I need to do for future situations, right?"

Eleanor nodded slowly. "Right."

"So," she drawled, giving Eleanor a teasing smile. "Why should I bother with a mirror or my arm when I have a living, breathing guinea pig here?"

She was relieved when she saw a deep blush color Eleanor's cheeks as realization hit and not offended repulsion. "Oh," she breathed. "Practice."

"But only if you want to," Lysette said softly, not wanting Eleanor to think she had no choices with her. "You know, no big deal."

"No, no," Eleanor said, shaking her head. "It seems to be important to you. Besides," she added with a small smile. "We wouldn't want your future husband disappointed, now would we?"

"Never." Lysette winked at her, grateful for the slight bit of humor that had been brought into the situation, one which she'd created and now felt a bit like a cad for.

"Okay, so uh…what do I do?" Eleanor asked, gaze filled with her uncertainty and discomfort.

"Stay still so I don't miss my target," Lysette responded, trying to keep the lighter tone. "Close your eyes," she whispered, the butterflies in her belly intensifying as Eleanor did as asked. Taking a deep breath, she leaned in.

Lysette's eyes slid closed as she moved into Eleanor's personal space, able to feel her shallow breaths against her face, mingling with her own. The first touch of Eleanor's lips was amazing.

"Your lips are so soft," she murmured with a smile, never opening her eyes.

"So are yours," Eleanor whispered.

Lysette went in again, pressing her lips to

Eleanor's for a bit longer, familiarizing herself with the feeling, the softness, pleased when Eleanor didn't open her mouth and try to suck in as much of Lysette's mouth as she could, like the boy she'd kissed the year before.

As their lips moved lightly against each other in small, tentative movements, Lysette felt Eleanor's fingers tighten around her own. In response, she intertwined them, bringing a bit of intimacy into what they were doing. Essentially having no idea what she was doing, Lysette allowed herself to go off instinct, allowed her lips to feel what they wanted, her bottom lip to brush against Eleanor's, which to her delight, brought a soft sigh from the very lips she was exploring.

She felt Eleanor's body relax, less stiff as their kiss continued, Lysette's head tilting slightly. By accident, she sucked Eleanor's bottom lip into her mouth, her tongue brushing against it. Lysette backed up slightly when Eleanor gasped and started. Their gazes met.

"Sorry," Lysette murmured. "Want me to stop?"

Eleanor shook her head. "No, it's okay."

Lysette slipped a hand out of Eleanor's, about to place it on her knee for better leverage when there was a soft knock on the closed bedroom door. The two quickly backed away from each other, Lysette nearly falling ass over appetite off the bed.

"Come in!" she called, steadying herself. She glanced over at Eleanor, who had pulled her legs up, arms wrapped around her shins. For a moment, she was truly worried that she'd crossed a line that never should have even been flirted with, but the quick look and smile Eleanor gave her stilled the heavy lump of dread in her gut.

The door opened, and Emma peeked her head

inside. "Eleanor, honey," she said, looking ever the tired, heavy-hearted woman who Lysette had always known her to be before that afternoon. "It's getting late, and we have to be up early for your father."

Without a word, Eleanor scooted to the side of the bed and got to her feet. She walked over to her mother but turned and looked at Lysette over her shoulder. "Thank you for such an amazing day, Lysette," she said softly, the look in her eyes soft and filled with an emotion that Lysette couldn't quite interpret.

Chapter Ten

In Scott's borrowed Packard, Eleanor waited for a boy to pedal by on his bicycle before she turned left onto the dirt road that would lead to her mother's two-bedroom house that sat on five acres of land, much of it taken up with the endless flowers and garden she planted every year.

Eleanor smiled when she saw the white house with the black roof and the chimney with smoke billowing up into the overcast November day. She slowed as she approached the long drive that ran along the side of the property and house. She'd lived on the property for years, and though Eleanor often worried about her mother being out there all alone in such a rural area, her mother loved it, and it truly was beautiful. In any given direction, the Rocky Mountains could be seen, their white-capped tops evidence of the sometimes harsh but always stunning Colorado winters.

Pulling the car to a stop, Eleanor smiled when her mother came running out of the house, apron still tied in place and arms held out wide.

"Hey, Mom," she said, climbing out from behind the steering wheel.

"My little girl!" Emma crowed, gathering Eleanor into her arms almost painfully tight.

"Not so little anymore," Eleanor laughed, returning the hug and leaving a kiss on her mother's cheek. Pulling away, she looked her mother over, making sure she was taking care of herself and eating properly. Her mother had survived the Depression and Ed Landry, so she had been conditioned well in caring for others before herself.

"Come in, come in! I was so excited when you called, I made your favorite!"

Eleanor mirrored her mother's affection by placing her arm around her shoulders as they headed into the house. "Stuffed peppers?" she asked, hope in her voice even as her belly growled in anticipation. At the smile she got, she nearly giggled in girlish delight.

"I thought Anne would be with you," Emma said, dropping her arm from Eleanor's shoulders to push open the front door, a wave of warm, wonderfully scented air hitting them.

"Oh, my, that smells *so* good." Eleanor grinned, closing her eyes. She let out a happy sigh as her eyes opened again, following her mother through the small front room to the kitchen where a metal pot sat on the stove, the meat sauce she knew her mother had been cooking all afternoon simmering. "No, just me," she said, finally responding to her mother's earlier statement.

Emma grabbed the dish towel that rested on the counter as she walked to the stove, using it to keep her fingers from getting burned as she opened the door and peeked inside.

"Just about ready."

"Mind if I put some music on, Mom?" Eleanor shrugged out of her jacket and hung it and her purse in the closet off the kitchen.

"Go for it," Emma called from the stove.

Eleanor wandered through the front room where a warm fire was popping in the fireplace. She had mixed emotions when she saw the old rocking chair sitting near it, an unfinished book lying on the seat. It was the only thing in her mother's house from the old farmhouse as far as furniture went.

The story was, her grandfather had made it for Emma when she found out she was pregnant with her first baby, a boy, who was stillborn. There were a lot of secrets around that situation that Eleanor didn't understand. She'd heard a whisper that the child had been lost due to a beating her mother had taken, but she'd never dare ask about it. Six months after the baby was lost, her mother was pregnant again, and Eleanor was the result.

She ran her fingers along the top of the smooth carved back of the rocker and headed to the corner where the record player rested on a small table. A wire rack next to it held all her mother's favorite albums, which she fingered through until she picked her favorite Billie Holiday record. Carefully slipping the vinyl from its sleeve, she put it on the machine and set the needle in place.

About to turn back to return to the kitchen, a framed picture caught her eye where it sat on the mantel. Grabbing it, she brought it down to study the young faces grinning back at her, caught in an eternal burst of laughter. She remembered precisely where they were when that picture was taken, and she remembered precisely what it was that Lysette had said to make her laugh right as the picture was snapped.

"That was such a wonderfully fun day," Emma said softly, coming up behind her, a hand resting on Eleanor's shoulder.

Eleanor nodded, unable to take her eyes off Lysette, so young, so beautiful. "Our trip to Denver," she said softly. "I didn't know you had this." She looked back to meet her mother's gaze for a moment before returning her attention to the picture.

"Yes. Adalyn gave it to me a few years later, before they moved to California."

"Why do you have this out?" she asked, setting the framed picture back where she got it and letting out a quiet, centering breath before turning to face her mother, trying to let a wonderful memory go. "It was so long ago."

"It's my favorite picture of you girls. You were both so happy that day, like children bouncing all over the place." Emma smiled.

Eleanor nodded, giving a small smile as her emotions were equally bouncing all over the place. "It was a good day."

Emma studied her for a long moment before squeezing her arm and turning to head back to the kitchen. "Dinner's ready."

Food eaten, plates pushed aside, Eleanor sat at the round kitchen table across from her mother. Her stomach was utterly sated, but her mind was troubled. She sipped her second after-dinner cup of coffee as her mother prattled on and on about getting the property ready to sell come spring.

"But you love it here," she reminded her. "You've been here for so long now, all set up how you want it." Eleanor's eyebrows fell as worry wormed its way into her heart. "Is there something you're not telling me? What has the doctor said?"

Emma rolled her eyes, waving off Eleanor's concern. "Stop it. It has nothing to do with anything like that. And you're right, I do love it here, honey, but it's just a lot of work for one person." She let out a tired sigh, looking around her kitchen, mug of coffee in hand. "I love this little place. But," she added with a shrug, "I want to be closer to you, too. Without a car, it's harder for you to come out this way, and you don't have room for a visitor. It just makes sense for me to get a little place of my own in Woodland." She grinned, bringing a hand up to run her fingers through hair gone gray before its time. "I'm old, honey. I need simplicity in my life."

Eleanor looked at her mother's hair, cut shorter like her own. She hadn't thought about it, considering her hair had been almost stark white for so many years, but it seemed overnight she'd aged. It had been a night long ago, but overnight, all the same.

Rolling over something in her mind, she pushed back from the table and walked to the counter to refill her coffee, topping off her mother's before sitting back down. Stirring in some milk and sugar, she eyed her mother.

"Do you remember that student I mentioned, the one I get a real kick out of?" she asked.

"Oh, yes, the Vaughn boy, right?" Emma asked, pulling the sugar bowl toward her. "The little charmer, I believe you called him."

Eleanor smiled and nodded. "That would be him. Jimmy Vaughn." She shook her head as she finished stirring her coffee and set the spoon onto the saucer plate before bringing the fragrant brew up to her lips. "Great kid. Met his parents at conferences a few weeks ago."

"Oh?" Emma responded, an eyebrow lifted as though waiting for more.

Eleanor nodded, setting the cup down after she sipped. "His father actually came in," she began, not entirely sure why she was dragging her news out.

"His father?" Emma asked, eyebrows shooting up in surprise. "They do that?"

Eleanor chuckled. "Apparently, that one does. His mother, Lysette, wasn't supposed to return to town in time."

"That was so wonderful of him to come in—"

If it hadn't been such a personally moving situation, Eleanor would have burst into laughter at the look on her mother's face when realization clicked into place.

"Lysette? Landry?" Emma almost yelled. "*Your* Lysette?"

Eleanor nodded. "The very one." She grabbed her coffee again. "And she hasn't been my anything in a very, very long time, Mom." She looked down into the creamy depths of her cup. "She belongs to James Vaughn."

"How do you know it's her if he showed up?" Emma asked, leaning forward in her chair, almost as though she were hearing some super secret plan.

"She showed up after all," Eleanor said with a sigh, sitting back in her chair. "He was my last parent, so I was cleaning up, and she rushed in." She smirked, shaking her head as she thought back to that night. "She looked like she'd seen a damn ghost and ran out of there as quickly as if she had."

"Do you think she was surprised? The husband didn't tell her?"

"I don't think he knows. Really pleasant guy, I have to say. But yes," she added with a rueful grin. "I think I startled the hell out of her."

"You girls haven't spoken in all this time, have you?" Emma asked gently, sipping from her coffee.

Eleanor shook her head, bringing up a hand and running her fingers through her hair. "Nope. I sent her a few letters, but they were all returned," she said softly, looking away. She knew if she looked into the understanding, loving eyes of the woman who had supported her through it all, she'd break. "So," she continued after a moment and a few calming breaths. "I decided to leave her alone." She looked back to her mother, who seemed so sad as she returned her gaze. "Figured it was best."

"The last time I saw her was about four years ago at Adalyn's funeral."

Those words hit hard. Eleanor could only stare for a moment. "Adalyn died?"

Emma nodded. "Cancer."

"Why didn't you tell me?" Eleanor asked, hurt.

"I'm sorry, honey. I honestly didn't think you would want to know. In all this time, you never once asked about Lysette or her family. I truly figured you'd left that part of your life behind."

Still hurt, she understood her mother's reasoning. After all, she'd done her level best to eradicate that part of her life from her memory. "Did she say anything to you? How's Mr. Landon?"

"The funeral was huge. Lysette never saw me, and I didn't stay long. Just long enough to pay my respects and to see…" Emma's voice trailed off, and she brought her cup to her lips, waving the topic away. "I'm sorry I didn't say anything. Now tell me about you and Anne."

Taken aback by the sudden change in subject and total one-eighty in her mother's tone, it took her a moment to redirect. "What about us?"

"Are you happy?"

Eleanor let out a heavy breath, giving the question some thought so she could give a succinct answer and not a knee-jerk one. "I have fun with her," she began, sparing a glance from her cup to her mother. "We can talk, she's intelligent, that sort of thing. She's certainly beautiful, but," she shrugged, "I know she's not what I want for the rest of my life." She smirked. "To her chagrin. I think she knows deep inside that I can't give her what she wants."

"And what is that?"

"Stability, security. A promise that I'll always be there."

"Well, honey, doesn't she deserve those things?" Emma asked gently.

Stung, Eleanor's eyebrows fell. "Whose side are you on?"

"I'm on yours completely, but it's not that you don't have it in you to give those things, Eleanor. Anne obviously isn't the right woman for you or you'd want to give her what she wants and needs. Don't you think?"

Eleanor studied her for a long moment, mulling what she said. Finally, she nodded. "True."

Emma reached across the table and took Eleanor's hands in her own, warm from the coffee cup she'd been holding. "Honey, don't settle. Trust me on this." Her gaze bored into Eleanor's. "Don't waste your life on someone who doesn't have your heart. It's not worth it."

❧❧❧❧

After a leisurely breakfast and a walk around the property on the mild Sunday early afternoon, Eleanor headed home. She pulled the Packard to the curb in front of her building and killed the engine, pulling the key from the ignition and climbing out.

Smiling at the young man who lived across the hall with his beautiful wife, she accepted his gesture of entering the door that led to the stairs ahead of him. "Thanks, Richard."

"Man, what a peach of a day, huh?" he asked, closing and locking the door behind them before following her up the narrow staircase to the second floor.

"It was. Did Gwen get the job at the newspaper?"

"She sure did. Excited as a kid in a candy store, she is," he exclaimed, a smile in his voice, which landed on her lips.

"That's truly wonderful, Richard," she said, reaching her door and sorting out the correct key. "Tell her I said congratulations."

"Will do." He gave her a broad smile, his light brown hair sticking up at odd angles from the removal of the paper cap he wore as the cook for the local diner. "Have a nice day."

Taking her time to unlock the door to make sure he'd entered his own apartment, she tapped lightly before letting herself in. To her relief, Scott and Ronnie were fully bathed, dressed, and sitting casually on the couch watching television. She closed the door behind her and walked to the kitchen table, leaving her overnight bag and purse there before shrugging out of her jacket.

"Afternoon, boys," she greeted, smiling as Scott pushed up from the couch and walked over to her, taking her in a tight hug. "You guys have a good time?" she asked into it, keeping her voice low.

"We did. Thanks so much, doll," he said, leaving

a loud kiss on her cheek. "Means the world to me that you let us celebrate our anniversary together here."

"Not a problem. It worked out since I was headed to my mom's, anyway." She smiled up at him before raising an eyebrow. "You changed the sheets, right?"

He gave her a devilish grin. "Brought my own."

"Even better." She gave him a return smack to the cheek. "Honestly, I'd rather you guys spend time together here where you're safe than parked at some lover's cover somewhere." She turned to Ronnie, who watched them from the couch. "Hey, Ronnie. It's so nice to see you again."

"You as well, Eleanor. Thanks for everything."

Scott returned from the bedroom with his own overnight bag slung over his shoulder. "I hope you won't be mad, but we drank that bottle of red in the icebox." He handed her two dollars. "I think you said that was Anne's, so…"

She took the money and grinned at him as she handed him his keys. "I stopped at the filling station on the way home, bad boy. Get outta here."

He returned the grin before he and Ronnie left, peeking out the door to make sure the hall was empty before, with a flamboyant air kiss, he disappeared, closing the door behind him.

Chuckling, Eleanor walked to the door and locked it.

Chapter Eleven

Already shivering as the blast of blowing snow hit her, Eleanor pulled her wool coat closer to her body as she locked the door to the building. Finished, she pocketed the key and shrugged her purse strap higher onto her shoulder as she headed out into the cold morning for work.

She'd made it to the end of the building when a car rumbled up to the curb.

"Hey! Miss Brannon."

Stopping, she glanced over to see Jim Vaughn rolling down the driver's side window of his large luxury car. "Jim Vaughn, Jimmy's dad."

"Of course, I remember," she said, walking over to him. "Nice to see you again, Mr. Vaughn."

"You too. Listen, believe it or not, I was actually on my way to see you at the school before my eight o'clock client meeting. Why don't we both get something out of this and I get you out of this messy weather by giving you a ride to school and I get to talk to you?" he offered with a charming grin.

As much as she didn't want to, Eleanor liked Jim Vaughn. "All right," she said, returning his smile. "It's a deal." Hurrying around the purring car, she let herself in on the passenger side, and he got them moving, making slow progress as the snow overnight had frozen, creating an ice arena for automobiles to navigate. "What did you want to talk to me about?"

she asked, getting settled with her purse and satchel resting in her lap.

"Well, you see, December is just around the corner, which of course means Christmas," he said, sparing a glance at her from under the brim of his fedora before returning his focus to the road. "Every year, my wife and I have a party at the house. Nothing major, just a little get-together with friends and such that we're just too darn busy to see much during the rest of the year, you know?"

She nodded, butterflies batting at her stomach. "Sure."

"Well, the first part of the party is essentially kid-friendly. We let the kids invite whoever they want, school friends, whoever. So my wife and I spoke to them about it over the weekend and, wouldn't you know it," he said with a chuckle, shaking his head in amusement. "Jimmy asked if you could come."

She felt every single one of those butterflies fall dead and heavy in the pit of her gut. "I see. Isn't that a little inappropriate, Mr. Vaughn?" she asked, only able to see Lysette's shocked and horrified face that night in her classroom again. Somehow, she managed to keep her voice calm and reasonable and not reveal the panic she felt.

"Well, that was my first thought, but I know Lysette would love to meet you, and," he added with a shrug and another quick glance. "We've only been in town a short time, so it would be nice to extend our social circle a bit."

Eleanor swallowed as she saw the school looming just ahead. "I'll consider it. When and where?"

He gave her the date and address, which she wrote on a piece of paper she had in her purse. "Oh," he added, pulling to a stop in front of the brick building. "Jimmy says you and Mr. O'Shea are close. Feel free to bring a date, if you like."

She managed to hide her smile at that, instead nodding as she met his shaded gaze. "Thank you and thanks for the ride. Have a nice day, Mr. Vaughn."

"You do the same, Miss Brannon."

She steeled herself to face the cold blast before pulling the door handle and pushing the heavy door open. She stepped out into the blowing snow and pushed the door closed. With a returned wave, she made her way up the long pathway to the school, noting they hadn't put the flag out due to the weather conditions.

Her mind was reeling with the invitation she'd been extended. She was flattered, for sure, but there was a huge part of her that had no desire to get any more involved in Lysette's life than she already was as Jimmy's teacher and would likely be as Bronte's teacher in a few years. And from Lysette's reaction to seeing her, it was obvious Eleanor wasn't exactly a welcome surprise.

As she entered the building, her entire body shuddered as the warmth hit her. She unbuttoned her coat as she made her way to her classroom, dodging students and faculty as they crammed the halls. She flapped the ends of her jacket quickly, trying to get the snowflakes that had gathered on the short walk into the building to fall to the floor, her high heels clicking on the tile. She tried to be mindful of the wet footprints, not slipping or sliding her goal.

She waved to a few teachers and stopped to answer a couple of questions from students who were worried about upcoming semester finals, but finally, she reached her classroom. Once inside, she closed the door behind her and flicked on the light, letting out a heavy breath.

As she shrugged out of her jacket, the door opened, and Scott stepped in, hair perfectly greased and his bowtie slightly crooked. She smiled, hanging her jacket on the coat tree in the corner behind her desk before walking over to him, straightening it.

"Much better." She gave it an affectionate pat for good measure. "You're here early," she said, turning away to unpack her satchel for the day.

"Well, I have an exciting invite to give you. I was going to call you last night, but Mother was on the phone with my Aunt Gilda for an hour."

She smiled and shook her head as she removed her lunch to place in her desk drawer.

"Hold the judgment on the side with the pickle there, cook," he admonished. "Anyway, Jimmy Vaughn asked me yesterday if I'd escort you to the Vaughn family Christmas party. Isn't that a trip?"

She looked at him with surprise, though he seemed to take it as interest as he continued.

"Yeah, can you believe it? The Vaughns are famous around here for their shindigs, and if you're invited to one, well..."

She nodded, pulling out the family tree projects her students had done weeks ago. As a surprise, she'd done a bit of research for each of them and had added some fun family facts onto each project to hand back that day. "Mr. Vaughn asked me this morning."

It was Scott's turn to look surprised. "You've made quite an impression on young Master Vaughn, I see." He chuckled.

Rolling her eyes, she walked over to him and

pushed him toward the door as the bell for first period would be ringing before they knew it. "I'll tell you what I told Jimmy's father," she said.

"That you'll dress up all pretty and I can get my father's tux out of the moth balls and we can act all heterosexual for an evening of fun and dancing?" he said with a goofy grin.

"Out!" she exclaimed, unable to hide her smile as she pushed him out the door.

҈ ҈ ҈ ҈

The Vaughn house wasn't as grand as the Landon house in Brooke View or Denver, but it was impressive, all the same. It was decorated for the holidays with large festive wreaths on the double front doors and red bows on the myriad windows. The curved drive was filled with cars, as well as the curb in front.

"Quite the digs," Scott muttered as he found a place to park along the curb across the street. "But then, I guess that's not hard if you're a pricey attorney, huh?"

Eleanor could only nod, afraid if she opened her mouth to say anything, her lunch from several hours before would fall out. She glanced over at her date for the evening when she realized it had gotten quiet in the car. "What?"

"Why do you look scared to death? You can pull off straight better than I can," he added with a lopsided grin.

"It's not that," she blew out. She took a deep breath. "I look okay, right?" she asked, enduring his once-over.

"You look absolutely beautiful. There isn't a

woman in that house that's going to be able to compete, doll."

"Well," she smirked, "I'm not trying to compete with anyone. I just want to get this over with." She gathered her clutch and gripped the door handle with a white-gloved hand. "Let's go."

As they walked across the street, Scott glanced over at her. "You never said how I look tonight."

"Oh, sorry, Scotty," she said, taking in his black tux, which fit him well enough, and shined shoes, and took a whiff of his cologne. "You look extremely handsome." She wrapped her hand around his arm, resting it in the crook. "We make quite the dashing pair, don't you think?"

He smiled, though it was small and short-lived. "Do you think people like you and me will ever be able to go to a Christmas party like this without being a fraud?"

The words hurt her heart, as she'd wondered the same thing more than once. She pulled him a little closer as they continued toward the house. "I hope so, Scotty."

The house was filled with people dressed in their holiday best, good-looking or beautiful and all intimidating. Eleanor knew they were the elite of the small town, folks like the mayor, lawyers, doctors, and city council members. She took a deep breath and did her best to mingle, even as she saw the confused looks from the other guests. Of course, Scott was all over the place, chatting, shaking hands, and charming the women with a kiss to the knuckles.

She was there an hour before she saw one of their hosts, and it was Lysette. Eleanor was standing near the doorway that led to an out-of-the-way hallway, which she believed led to the kitchen area, just trying to become a wallflower. As she nursed her cocktail, she saw Lysette enter the room, Scott at her side.

With a gasp, Eleanor ducked back a bit into the hallway, eyes wide as she watched the two on the other side of the room, both holding a drink in their hand and seemingly engaged in a lively conversation. At one point, Lysette seemed to stop midsentence and looked around, obviously searching for someone. Eleanor couldn't help but wonder if Scott had told her they were there together. Perhaps she was looking for her.

She pushed the thought out of her mind as she focused on the woman herself. She had never seen Lysette look as stunning and gorgeous as she did that night. Her dress was form-fitting but incredibly elegant. It was a deep red color and looked to be velvet or at least a matte material. The off-the-shoulder dress showed off the creamy skin of her décolletage with just a hint of cleavage. Her rich auburn hair was pulled back into a chignon, revealing her tantalizing neck, delicate diamond earrings dangling from her ears.

"Jesus," Eleanor whispered, barely able to breathe.

Though they were an entire room apart filled with many chatting people, she needed some space and distance. She ducked into the hallway where she was relieved to find a powder room just before the kitchen. Hurrying inside, she closed and locked the door, flicking on the light before setting her cocktail on the sink basin.

She blew out a loud breath and looked at her reflection in the mirror above the sink and below the three mounted bulb lights that cast shadows over her eyes. She and Scott had seen and spoken to Jimmy when they'd first arrived, and she had told Scott after the teen left so the "adult" party could start, they should have, too. Scott had insisted they stay, feeling it would have been rude to go.

Now she was hiding in a bathroom, her stomach in knots and wanting nothing more than to be at home in her nightgown buried beneath her comforter. It had been stupid to accept Jim Vaughn's invitation. She'd known it the day it was offered, and she'd known it every day over the past week and a half since.

Eleanor paused in her self-recrimination as she heard footsteps go by the bathroom. The quick, almost aggressive clicks of high-heeled shoes made it seem their owner wasn't too happy. That theory was validated when Eleanor heard the owner speak.

"What were you thinking, Jim?" Lysette hissed. "Why on *earth* would you let Jimmy invite her here?"

"Really, Lysette?" he hissed back. "Do we have to discuss this here with a houseful of people?"

They stopped near the closed bathroom door, Eleanor taking a step back, almost worried that somehow the couple would figure out she was listening.

"It is entirely inappropriate to have her here," Lysette said, her voice low but angry, ignoring Jim's question.

"Why? Jimmy wanted her here. I had a pleasant encounter with her, and forgive me for being silly here, but we thought you might like to meet this woman we talk about, too." There was silence for a moment before Jim continued. "Good lord, Lysette. The way you're acting, you'd think I invited my goddamned ex-girlfriend or something!"

"Don't be ridiculous," Lysette muttered, her voice a bit closer to the bathroom door.

"It's not me being ridiculous, dear. Now I'm returning to our guests."

With the sound of a quick kiss, everything went quiet until Eleanor nearly had a heart attack when the doorknob was tried. When the lock held, a soft knock sounded.

"Is someone in there?" Lysette asked softly.

"Oh, my god!" Eleanor breathed, looking around for any kind of escape in the tiny room, equipped with only a sink and commode. There was a small window that, with the help of a small crank, opened inward. She rolled her eyes at the thought of attempting to squeeze through a tiny window in a thirty-dollar dress and heels with her mother's pearls. No choice, she gathered her courage and reached for the knob, unlocking it before pulling the door open.

Coming face to face, Lysette gasped and took a step back, a hand coming up to her chest in seeming surprise.

"Excuse me," Eleanor said softly, brushing past her as quickly as she dared.

Chapter Twelve

Eleanor was glad she was lying on her side facing the wall, so she didn't have to worry about him seeing her eyes open just a bit. The bittersweet stench of his tobacco wafted over her. He said it was sinful, tobacco, like everything else. Guess that was for other people, not her father. She hated that smell with everything in her, always terrified if she reacted, if she moved or let him know she was awake, what might happen.

Nearly holding her breath, Eleanor waited until she heard the footfalls of his heavy boots move away from the bed. With what ended up being nearly the rebuilding of the second floor of the farmhouse, the floor and stairs no longer squeaked. She had to rely on any sounds he made or the smell of his damn rolled cigarettes now.

Once he was gone, leaving just the bitter ghost of tobacco behind, she squeezed her eyes shut and let out a slow, shaky breath.

⁂

Sitting at the table, it was quiet as Gabby scooted himself in, the fourth at their breakfast. Ed had insisted Eleanor help her mother that morning to prepare a full breakfast with their guest in mind. She was fine with helping, in fact wished she was allowed to help her more often, but she was unsettled about Gabby's presence.

Ed said grace.

They'd been back in the house for little more than a week, and everything was essentially the same footprint as it had been before, though some of the kitchen had been taken to create a space for Gabby, who had been hired on as a full-time handyman, both on the farm and in the store. Her mother had been less than thrilled on so many levels, but like Eleanor, she had said nothing.

"Thank you, ma'am," Gabby said as he was passed a plate fully loaded with eggs, country potatoes, and a thick slab of bacon.

"Thanks, Mama," Eleanor said, accepting her own plate while her father remained quiet as he dug in, not everyone even served yet.

"This is mighty fine, ma'am," Gabby muttered around a mouthful of food, nodding to emphasize his point. "Mighty fine."

"Thank you, Gabby," Emma said, giving him a small smile as she served herself.

"So you mentioned at supper last night that you moved around Texas quite a bit," Ed said, sipping from his coffee. "Why'd you leave?" He emptied his cup and, without a glance to her, extended it in Eleanor's general direction. "Get me more. You don't mention your time there much, fella," Ed continued.

Eleanor set her fork down and took the cup, pushing back from the table, only halfway listening as Gabby told his story.

"Well, it's a sad story, really." Gabby glanced over at the other man before focusing on his plate. "Lost my wife and baby son and lost myself in the booze for a bit," he explained, continuing to eat. "Got myself in a little trouble with the law, so I decided to get on outta there and start over."

"I'm sorry about your loss," Emma said softly.

Eleanor sat down, placing her father's refilled coffee cup in front of him. She eyed the man with the sandy-colored hair that flopped down into his eyes. They were a light blue, and though a beautiful color, there was something in them that didn't sit well with her, an emptiness of sorts.

"Well, now you're here with us." Ed reached over and gave Gabby a slap to the shoulder. "Eleanor, after school today, I need you at the store. Gabby and I will be on deliveries for a bit."

"Yes, Father," she said, focusing back on her breakfast. She had wanted to stay after to talk to Mrs. Lawrence about extra help on her math, but she knew there was no way she could tell her father that. With him, options need not apply.

✦✦✦✦✦

"So what'cha studying?" Gabby asked, maneuvering the truck from the store, where Ed had been dropped off, to the school.

Eleanor, who wanted to hug the door, swallowed before responding. "Um, just the basics, I guess."

He nodded, turning off the main road to a side street that would lead in the general area of the school. "I wasn't too good at school. Ended up leavin' when I was thirteen. But then," he added, "Daddy was off fightin', so I had to help Mama and my sisters." He glanced over at her. "No real reason for me to keep going for book learnin' no more anyway, you know?"

She nodded. She'd heard so many similar stories to his regarding parents of classmates and some in her own family. When the United States had finally entered the Great War in 1917, a lot of young men marched off, leaving their families in dire straits back home.

"Yes, sir," she said in response to his question.

"Your daddy go fight?"

"No, sir. He stayed to man the farm while his younger brothers did."

He nodded, guiding the truck up to the curb. "Well, here ya go."

She murmured a quiet thanks, then climbed out of the truck, greatly relieved to be out of his presence and away from her father for the independence of a handful of hours at school.

Standing on the sidewalk in front of the building, she sucked in a cleansing breath, readying herself for a day of classes. Her eyes closed and focusing on her breathing, she didn't hear anyone come up behind her and pinch her behind, sending her nearly jumping into a nearby tree.

Whipping around in a somewhat hunched position to protect herself, she came face to face with a laughing Lysette. She blew out a breath, standing erect and bringing a hand up to her heart.

"You, beautiful girl," Lysette chuckled as she reached up to undo the top two buttons of Eleanor's buttoned collared shirt, "need to loosen up."

"No!" Eleanor hissed, trying to bat her hands away, even as she tried not to get lost in the smell of Lysette's perfume or her presence so close with an almost intimate touch. "My father will kill me."

Lysette made a show of looking around, including behind Eleanor before meeting her gaze as she continued with her task. "Do you see your father here?"

"No," she admitted grudgingly.

"Come on," Lysette said, hitching her school bag a bit higher onto her shoulder as she hooked her arm with Eleanor's and the two girls walked toward the building. "So I spoke with my mom the other night."

Eleanor grinned. "I should hope so. You do live in the same house."

Lysette sent a playful glare her way. "Smart aleck. I know it's not for a couple months, but for winter break, we want to take you and your mom to spend the day with us in Denver." A little hop was added to her step in excitement. "You've never been out of Brooke View, right?"

Eleanor's jaw tightened as her spine straightened with a very strange mixture of pride and shame. She cleared her throat and looked away, watching as two boys tossed a baseball back and forth in front of the building.

"Hey," Lysette said softy, stopping their progress with a hand to Eleanor's arm.

Eleanor stopped walking but couldn't look at her. She felt the weight of her heavy, uncomfortable shoes that were so cheaply made they made her feet blister. She felt the scratchy material of the plain white button-up blouse that made her break out sometimes. She felt how greasy her bound hair was because after the farmhouse was flooded and damaged, money had been used that was normally tucked away for extras, such as soap, toothpaste, or any special seasoning her mother may want. Bathing was only allowed twice a week, and one of those had to be Sunday for church.

"Hey," Lysette said again, the hand that had

stopped Eleanor's forward movement now gently squeezed it. "I didn't mean to upset you or embarrass you, Ellie," she said. "I may have been born here, but most of my years were spent in Denver, so," she added with a quirky little smile. "Kinda hard for me to *not* leave here, huh?"

Though obviously Lysette had a point, Eleanor was having a hard time letting go of her shame. All she could do was nod.

"Listen, most of these kids have never been out of here," Lysette pointed out. "How could they be? Times are so hard right now, have been for a while. Shoot," she said with a shrug, reaching up to run a hand over her perfectly coifed hair. "Some folks are just trying to make sure dinner is on the table, right?"

Feeling those beautiful eyes on her, finally Eleanor met them, nodding in agreement. "Yeah."

"Yeah," Lysette said with a soft, understanding smile. "So since we can do something for you and your mom, we want to."

Eleanor nodded, swallowing her pride and meeting Lysette's hopeful gaze. "That's really sweet, but my father would never allow that, you know that." The slow smile that spread across those soft lips gave her a knot in her stomach. "What?"

"Well, see, I have a plan for that."

"Oh, lord." Eleanor rolled her eyes.

"Yes, exactly!" Lysette once again hooked their arms and got them moving toward the school, their classmates wandering around talking, some boys chasing each other with a teacher yelling after them to stop. They ignored it all. "Now your father is a Bible thumper, right?"

"Absolutely. Although, I do have to say now

that Gabby has been joining us more and more for breakfast, he's stopped making me talk about the stupid scriptures." She felt Lysette's gaze on her. Looking over at her, she saw the confusion and waved her hand in the air. "Never mind. Why do you ask?"

"Because. We'll tell your dad that there's a teen revival that you'll be attending with me."

Eleanor shook her head, reaching out for the large metal handle on the front door to the school. She pulled the door open and held it for Lysette, following her inside.

"But see, here's the brilliance that involves your mom." She weaved them around a girl and a boy who were arguing in the middle of the hallway. Eleanor thought it looked like a lovers' spat. "You see," Lysette continued, unwittingly pulling Eleanor out of her thoughts regarding the assumed couple. "We tell him that it's only for us teen girls, and all of us have to be chaperoned by our mothers. It's a mother-daughter revival."

Eleanor mulled what she'd just been told, tasting the words and ideas before she gave her friend a small smile. "It might work. Darn, you're good."

Lysette chuckled as she grabbed her school bag and unlatched it. "I can't take full credit for it." She reached inside and pulled out a sheet of paper. It was a flyer for said teen revival. Handing it to Eleanor, she grinned. "Exhibit A of how we can pull this off."

Eleanor took the flyer and read it. Sure enough, everything that Lysette had espoused was true, except this said the revival was in a small steel mill town more than two and a half hours by car away.

"But this is in Pueblo." She looked up at Lysette, who met her gaze looking rather proud of herself. "You said we'd be spending the day in Denver."

Lysette chuckled as they stopped in front of the door to her first class. "Silly. Those are simple details your father doesn't need to know about. After all," she said, her voice not much more than a purr as she snatched the flyer from Eleanor's hands and backed away toward the classroom. "It's just for us girls to handle all the details." With that, she was gone, a little giggle following.

Eleanor stood there for a long moment, trying to get her heart to start beating again after the look Lysette had given her and the low, sultry tone of her voice. She honestly didn't even think her friend was fully aware of the effect she had on people half the time, but lordy did she.

Ever since they'd "practiced" that last night at the Landon house, Eleanor had followed Lysette like a little lost puppy. Even if Lysette didn't know she was there lurking close by, Eleanor was drawn to her like a honeybee to the most beautiful and fragrant flower.

She watched Lysette with other people; she was kind and made everyone feel special. She made Eleanor feel special. Sometimes, it was hard not to feel sad, not to feel that the special attention Lysette seemed to give to her was no different than what she gave to everyone she came in contact with. She had a way of making a person feel like she was the center of her universe in that moment, like nobody else mattered and only that person could make her smile.

That was certainly how she made Eleanor feel.

Reaching up, she was going to rebutton the two buttons, but in a moment of rebellion, she let them be and hurried to her own class, knowing she'd see Lysette again in math class later.

"Here you are, Mrs. Holdstead. Don't forget your fabric. Should make a real pretty dress for your granddaughter," Eleanor said with a smile, handing the older woman her bundled purchases.

"Thank you, honey. You have a nice day and tell your mama I said hello."

"Will do." She watched one of their regular customers leave before turning back to what she'd been doing before helping cut the length of flower-printed fabric that was requested.

"All right, Eleanor, I got that other delivery to make, then y'all are done with those," Gabby said, hurrying to the front of the store with a box filled with collected goods off the shelves. "Check it?"

Eleanor took the written list from him and checked the listed items with those in the box. Gabby was just this side of illiterate, so her father had mandated someone double-check his order before he left for delivery after a few mishaps.

"This is all good, Gabby, except you forgot the beeswax," she said, folding the page before handing it back to him.

He nodded and sent her a salute before disappearing to grab the tin, tossing it into the box and picking up the box, hugging it to his body. "Shouldn't be long."

She gave him a small smile and wave before returning to the opened ledger that lay on the counter where she'd been recording the numbers her father had counted that day for inventory.

"Let me get that for you, Mr. Gabby," a deep,

friendly voice said as the bells above the door jingled.

Eleanor glanced over, recognizing the voice. Samuel held open the door, Gabby giving him a long look as he passed him with the box of goods, never saying a word to the tall black man, though he offered a greeting to someone else outside who Eleanor couldn't see.

Samuel entered the store, Lysette strolling in behind him, though she had a strange look on her face as she glanced over her shoulder for a moment, her focus outside. Eleanor glanced out the front window to try to see what had so caught her friend's attention. All she saw was Gabby loading the box into the back of the truck before climbing in behind the wheel. She turned back to Lysette, who was headed her way, a smile sprouting on Lysette's lips.

"Hey," Eleanor greeted, unable to stop her own smile. "Hello, Samuel. How are you today? We got the new pipe tobacco in."

"You spoil me, Miss Eleanor," he said, waggling a finger at her. "I come to pick up a new watering can."

Eleanor pointed to the aisle where that sort of thing was. "We've got a few to choose from."

He nodded and tipped the flat cap he wore, then headed off, leaving Lysette behind.

"Hey," Eleanor said again, her voice quieter, meant only for Lysette. She leaned on her forearms, which rested on the open pages of the ledger, pencil tapping nervously between her fingers. "How are you?"

"I'm good. I stole a ride with Samuel." Lysette grinned, leaning her forearms on the counter, then leaning slightly over them.

It was hard for Eleanor not to notice it pushed her breasts up, almost putting them in her face. She forced herself to look into Lysette's eyes, so they wouldn't stray downward where they had no business.

"No, actually, I drove us here," Lysette was saying.

"Wait, your father lets you drive?" Eleanor asked, aghast. "Wait, never mind. What he doesn't know…"

"No, silly!" Lysette waved her off. "Who do you think taught me?"

Eleanor shook her head, amazed. "Wow. That would make my life so much easier, but Father will never allow that. He says a woman has no place driving."

"Of course he does," Lysette muttered, grabbing a nearby pack of Black Jack gum. "This stuff is heinous," she said, putting it back. "To allow you or your mama to drive would actually mean admitting you had a brain and ability to have freedom."

Eleanor felt panic as she looked around the store. She knew full well neither her father nor Gabby was there, but she couldn't help the fear that Lysette's words—no matter how true they were—would be overheard. Retribution would be swift and harsh.

"Please don't say things like that here," she whispered.

Lysette gave her a contrite smile. "Sorry. So did you talk to your mom about what we talked about the other day?" she asked, her voice remaining quieter.

Eleanor shook her head again, glancing around the near-empty store. "I haven't had time."

"What? Ellie, I talked to you about that four days ago!"

"Yes, and my mother isn't allowed to work in here, and when we're at home, *he's* always there." She tossed the pencil to the counter and stood straight, running a hand over her tightly bound hair. "I think he has one of those meeting things with Gabby this Saturday night. I planned to talk to her then."

"Okay. You promise?" Lysette asked, a single eyebrow rose in a doubtful expression.

Eleanor smiled. "I promise."

"And I promise to help you with your math," Lysette said sweetly.

Chapter Thirteen

Okay, wait. Let's try this." Lysette grabbed a fresh piece of paper and scribbled the equation down as it was written in the textbook.

Eleanor lay on her stomach next to where Lysette sat cross-legged on the redhead's bed, their textbooks for Mr. Barnes' algebra class between them. She was getting frustrated, which meant she was getting cranky, which meant no doubt Lysette wanted her to go home already.

"Look," Lysette said gently. "If you do it this way," she said, writing out the steps of the equation on the page, ending up with the correct answer.

"But wait, that's not what Mr. Barnes showed us," Eleanor grumbled, her frustration evident.

"I know, but obviously, the way he's showing us isn't clicking with you. Besides, he's doing it the long way. This way," she said, tapping her style with the tip of the pencil, "is shorter with fewer steps, so it's less confusing."

Eleanor studied it for a long moment, slowly nodding as it began to "click," as Lysette had put it. She glanced at the textbook and jotted down the next problem on the page and tried to use the method Lysette had used on the previous problem. It took a moment and a few pointers from Lysette, but ultimately, not only did she get the problem right, but she also understood how she'd come to the correct answer.

Shocked, she lifted herself to her elbows and looked down at the page. "Wait, did I do it?" She looked at Lysette, who was grinning ear to ear. "I got it right?"

"You got it right."

With a whoop of victory, Eleanor slammed her textbook closed, thrilled that torture was over with. She grinned at Lysette, rather proud of herself. "Thank you. I really appreciate your patience with me on this."

"Of course, silly." Lysette laughed. "Besides, I'm only good at math. You help me with everything else. She closed her book and stacked the loose-leaf pages atop it with her pencil. "So I want to show you something." She climbed off the bed, setting her school supplies on her dresser before leaving the bedroom.

Pushing up from where she'd been lying on the bed, Eleanor also cleaned up her mess, putting it all in her school bag before sitting on the bed again. A few moments later, Lysette returned, closing the bedroom door behind her and returning to the bed. She had a photo album tucked into her arms.

"Okay, these are pretty neat," she said, getting settled next to Eleanor, the teens sitting thigh to thigh. "So you know my dad and his twin, Josie, went to school with your mama, right?" she asked, flipping open the cover of the leather-bound album.

Eleanor nodded. "I knew about your father. I don't know anything about a sister, though."

Lysette's smile was sweet and loving. "Aunt Josie is wonderful. She lives over in Gunnison now." She flipped the stiff, picture-filled pages until she found what she was looking for. "Look. That's the three of them when they were about our age."

Eleanor accepted the half of the photo album that was being laid across her thigh, the other half on

Lysette's. There were two teenage girls and one teenage boy, all standing in a line arm in arm. The little bit that could be seen around them seemed to be a parade or some sort of festival, complete with someone in the distance dressed like a clown talking to a group of kids, their excitement forever frozen on their faces.

Her gaze returned to the grinning teenager in the center of the trio. The basic features belonged to her mother, but the joy in her smile and life in her eyes did not.

"God," she breathed, slowly shaking her head, unable to take her eyes off the image. "She looks so happy."

"They were all so young," Lysette added, resting her chin on Eleanor's shoulder. "That's my dad," she said, bringing a hand into Eleanor's view, lightly tapping the old picture where the young man stood grinning to Emma's right. "And," she continued, tapping the young woman to Emma's left, a very pretty thing who looked to be caught in the middle of a laugh. "Aunt Josie."

"The three of them were close?" Eleanor asked, turning her focus to the siblings. "Honestly, before meeting you at school that day, I'd never heard about your family." She turned and met Lysette's gaze, so close to her own as her chin still rested on Eleanor's shoulder. "Never heard of Josie, either."

"Yeah. From what my father says, they were all three best friends, inseparable." Lysette, sitting to Eleanor's right, reached her left arm out, her hand resting on the bed next to Eleanor's left hip, which made her breath hitch slightly at the proximity of Lysette's body to her own.

Eleanor swallowed several times as she watched

Lysette flip a few pages to settle on two adorable toddlers, looking as though they were caught in a moment of waddling around in cloth diapers. She was able to forget about the butterflies that were dive bombing her nether regions as she smiled. One toddler had dark curly hair while the other had blond hair—looking nearly white in the black and white tone of the photograph only to darken to red—both with the same bow in their hair at the top of their heads.

"They're absolutely adorable," Eleanor said at length. "Who are they?" When she got no answer, she turned to see Lysette staring at her like she was crazy. "What?"

"These two are us," Lysette responded, tapping the picture. "*Maman* said we were about a year and a half in this one."

"Us? But how?" Eleanor asked absently, looking back at the picture. She didn't recognize the room at all where they were, including a beautiful grand piano and expansive fireplace. "Where is this?"

"Our house in Denver. I guess early in your parents' marriage, your mama worked for us. After the war ended, your father was really struggling with the farm, so Daddy gave her a job with us. She brought you with her." She grinned. "Guess we were meant to be best friends."

Eleanor returned the smile. "What did she do for you?" she asked, studying the picture to take in the room and exquisite furnishings. She could only imagine what the house must look like in person. The one they were sitting in was grand enough.

"Cleaned, cooked with *Maman*. But I think mostly just spent time there, both of you."

"Escape," Eleanor murmured.

"Yeah," Lysette agreed softly.

"How long? And what happened? It seems my father practically hates your parents now."

Lysette let out a heavy sigh. "I don't know. They won't tell me that. I'm not sure how long it lasted. A year or so, maybe."

Eleanor sat back, staring off into the distance as she considered all that she'd been told. "You know, it's really shocking to hear things about your parents that you had no idea about. I'm close to Mama." She shook her head. "I wonder why she never told me this." She indicated the toddler picture.

"I know my parents really care about her," Lysette said, moving slightly away from Eleanor just enough to be able to grab the photo album with both hands and gently close it, hugging it to her chest. "That's why we really want to give you both a fun day in Denver in October."

"Well," Eleanor said, watching as Lysette pushed up from the bed to set the photo album next to her math textbook. "I told you that I was finally able to bring it up to her last Saturday night."

"Right," Lysette agreed with a nod as she sat back down. "And? Last you told me, she was going to think about it."

Eleanor nodded and took a deep, steadying breath. She wasn't sure why she was nervous to give her friend the news. "Well, she told me as best she could this morning that she wants to try and make it happen."

"Really?" Lysette squealed, nearly tackling Eleanor to the bed in her excitement.

Eleanor laughed, trying to push her away. "She just said 'try'!"

Lysette grinned, moving away from where Eleanor had been pushed back across the bed to scoot up against the pillows at the head of the bed. She patted the space beside her in silent invitation.

Eleanor sat up and turned to crawl the short distance to turn again and sit next to Lysette, both leaning back against the large pillows that sat against her headboard. The two got settled, Lysette turning to rest on her side with a hand cradling her head. She studied Eleanor's face for a moment before her gaze dropped to her ever-present white blouse buttoned to the top.

With a dramatic sigh, she brought up a hand and began to undo the first two buttons. "I like you so much better when you loosen up," she said, sparing a glance up into Eleanor's eyes, unaware that the brunette was attempting to keep her breathing even and calm. "How many times a day do I have to halfway undress you, hmm?"

Eleanor took a quiet, steadying breath. "My father's just weird."

"No kidding." Lysette chuckled, finished with her task. She brushed her fingers over her handiwork, leaving the blouse opened just a bit to show the pale skin beneath. "Why the white blouse and dark skirts and crazy bun?"

"I honestly don't know, it's just always been that way. Like, I remember one time, I had to have been maybe five. Mama bought some fabric, it was pink with little white flowers all over it. I guess she'd gotten enough to make me a dress and herself an apron. He absolutely lost his top. Father was so angry, he took the fabric from her and made her watch him as he burned it, she told me."

Lysette shook her head, reaching a hand up and scooping out the tiny gold cross Eleanor wore on a simple chain around her neck. She brought it out into the light of the bedside lamp. The feather-light touch of her fingertips against her skin made Eleanor's heart skip a beat.

"This is beautiful. I don't think I've ever noticed it before."

"It belonged to my grandmother," Eleanor explained. "I didn't really know her, but Mama says I'm a lot like her, so," she added with a shrug, "I guess I wear it to feel close to her somehow."

"How long do we have until your father is set to pick you up?" Lysette asked, gently zipping the cross pendant back and forth on the chain.

Eleanor grabbed Lysette's wrist, taking a peek at the delicate gold watch she wore before releasing it. "Twenty minutes."

"Well," Lysette said in a teasing voice, "we can work on more equations or we can try that practicing thing again. As I recall, we got interrupted last time, and I didn't get my money's worth."

"Not worth the price of admission?" Eleanor managed to say without her voice squeaking. It had been many weeks since that night, and it came back to her often. To her immense surprise, a deep blush colored Lysette's cheeks.

"Oh, definitely a price I'd pay time and again."

Eleanor wasn't able to hold Lysette's gaze and had to look away. Something changed between them in that moment, but she honestly wasn't sure what it was or what to do with it.

"You ready?" Lysette asked softly, pulling Eleanor out of her thoughts.

Ignorance and naiveté on her side the first time, she was even more nervous the second, as she knew how it would make her feel, but still she didn't know what she was doing. An awkward feeling, to be sure.

Moving to her side in the nest of pillows, Eleanor closed her eyes as she felt Lysette move in, her lips brushing against her own before pressing lightly to them. A bolt of sensation shot through her body, beginning with her lips and shooting straight down south. She let out an imperceptible sigh as Lysette's hand rested on her shoulder as their lips pressed together again, this time lingering.

As Lysette moved her lips lightly against Eleanor's, they scooted slightly closer together. Eleanor's hand found its way to rest on Lysette's waist; the tiny sigh shot another bolt of sensation through her.

Eleanor gasped slightly when she felt the slightest touch of a soft tongue swipe at her lip. She felt Lysette begin to pull away, but her tightened grip on her waist stopped her retreat. Eleanor returned the favor, not sure what she was doing, but knowing she liked it when Lysette did it.

Lysette's hand slid from Eleanor's shoulder to cup the side of her neck as their kiss continued, deepening from timid and awkward to exploring freely, their bodies moving just a bit closer until their breasts grazed each other.

Eleanor gasped again, pulling away from the kiss as she nearly bolted out of her skin at the touch.

"I'm sorry, Ellie!" Lysette exclaimed. "Did I hurt you?"

Eleanor shook her head, chest heaving with her excitement and arousal. She managed to shake her head as she caught her breath. "No," she said at length, sitting up fully. She blew out a breath and ran a hand over her hair, brushing back a strand that had been pulled free from her bun while resting against the pillows. "No. I'm sorry, I'm okay."

Lysette sat up, also seeming to be affected by what they'd done. After a long moment, they shared a long, knowing glance. "I think I like practicing."

Eleanor grinned. "Me too."

Lysette glanced at her watch. "Oh, your father should be here soon. Maybe enough time for you to… freshen up?" she offered, reaching over to wipe a bit of her lipstick off Eleanor's lip, showing her the bit of color on her fingertip.

"Oh, yes, definitely."

Nearly fifteen minutes later, they stood together in the entryway of the house, Eleanor glancing out into the darkness every few seconds, looking to see the head lamps of the truck pull up the drive. Only the darkness beyond met her every time.

"He's usually not late, right?" Lysette peeked outside over Eleanor's shoulder.

Eleanor shook her head. "No. I figured he would have shown up half an hour early, to be honest." She turned away from one of the tall, narrow windows that lined the door on either side. "It was one heck of a fight to get him to let me come here in the first place."

"Ellie, it's almost twenty after," Lysette said, concerned eyes meeting Eleanor's.

"Crud," Eleanor muttered. "He forgot, it's the only thing I can think of. I'm going to go, Lysette. If he's just late for some reason, I'll run into him on the way. Otherwise, I've got to get home."

"I'm so sorry *Maman* has the car, or we could just drive you," Lysette said, pulling her into a tight hug. "Are you sure you'll be okay?" she asked into the hug. "I can send Samuel to walk with you."

"No. No, really. I'll be okay." She hesitated for only a moment before leaving a quick kiss on Lysette's cheek before grabbing the front door handle. "Practice," she whispered with a grin, leaving Lysette laughing in the foyer.

It was a little unnerving making her way home in the dark, Eleanor had to admit. Though she knew the entire town and every back road like the back of her hand, the moonless night from an overcast sky left a chill in the air. She hadn't brought a sweater with her when she'd gone to Lysette's house, not figuring she'd need one.

As she walked, she thought back to her time with Lysette, not just the kissing, but their time in general. A smile came to her lips, thinking of the easy way they could talk and laugh together. It had been such a long time since she'd had a close friend who was a girl. Some of the boys in town who were her age were sweet, but she got tired of being asked to get a soda with them. Why couldn't they just be friends?

She had left the more condensed area of town and was walking along the country road she knew was R19, which stood for Rural 19, a long stretch of dusty road before she hit Mudd Forest. She could go the long way and keep following R19 or she could cut a mile off her walk and head through the forest, which would deliver her almost to her backyard. Well, it would get her to essentially her block, anyway.

Whistling softly to dispel the discomfort she was feeling, her eyes grew wide in the evening chill, the sounds of the night critters alerting her to their presence as she veered off the dirt road and into the forest. No more than a few minutes in, and she began to think it was a real mistake.

She could feel sweat building between her shoulder blades, and her hands reflexively flexed as her palms became clammy. She knew she was getting close to the clearing that she could cut across, which would mark the halfway point. She reached out to see if she felt the thick trunk of the two trees that had grown together and was always a visible—in this case, tactile—cue that she was close to the curve in the path, which was impossible to see without the help of the moon or the stars.

Feeling what she expected to on the tree, she hurried forward. Confused, she slowed as she heard the snap of twigs perhaps twenty feet ahead. She had mere seconds for that to register before, with a *WHOOSH!* a massive tongue of flame licked upward, and within seconds, Eleanor was staring at a ten-foot wooden cross, fully alight.

Mouth open and eyes wide in horror, she backed up a few feet. It was only then that she noticed a group of about fifteen figures stepping out of the shadows and into the ring of light. They were all dressed alike in white robes with pointed white hoods, circular cutouts for their eyes. Absolutely nothing of their faces could be seen.

Fear and panic gripped her as they gathered around the cross, and she backed up another step, crying out in surprise when she backed into something. She whipped around when she felt hands on her shoulders. Another of the hooded figures loomed over her. In her fear, her school bag fell to the forest floor at her feet.

"This ain't no place for you, little girl," a man's voice said from behind the hood. "Thinkin' y'all should be runnin' home now."

Eleanor began to hyperventilate, eyes feeling as though they'd bulge out of her head as she stared up into the soulless depths of the shadowed cutouts in that hood.

Turning, she was about to bolt when she froze, feeling eyes on her. One of the hooded figures across the fire was staring right at her, the angry flames reflected off the round lenses underneath that hood, making his gaze that of fire, burning right through her.

He said nothing as he stared at her. He didn't have to.

Chapter Fourten

J ames Mathew Vaughn!" Lysette waited at the bottom of the stairs, arms crossed over her chest and high heel tapping on the floor.

"Hey, honey, got home as soon as I could," Jim said, surprising Lysette as he approached her from the direction of the kitchen. He'd obviously parked by the detached garage and entered through the back door. He was still dressed in his suit and carried his briefcase. "How long do I have?" He shrugged out of his jacket and draped it across the bench where Lysette's attention had initially been focused on. With the clearing of her throat, he looked down. "What is all this?"

"Your son felt it was perfectly all right to run in from school and drop everything here." She indicated where Jim had just tossed his jacket, followed by his briefcase, and he was working on his tie. She glared at him.

Without a word, he gathered the growing pile, revealing Jimmy's school bag, basketball shoes, and the family tree project that he'd finally brought home, a large red "A" scrawled atop it.

"Let me get changed, and I'll help round up the gang." Jim left a kiss to Lysette's cheek and was about to head to the stairs when he stopped.

Lysette watched him, curious what had caught his attention. Reshuffling everything he held in his arms to one arm, he reached out and grabbed the piece of sugar board.

"What's this?" he asked, eyeing the pictures.

"Oh." Lysette walked over to him and waved his question away as she tried to grab it from him, but he held on. "Just a project Jimmy had to do. I had to gather some old pictures so he could make his family tree." To her relief, the pounding sound of shoes on stairs interrupted the moment.

"I have been beckoned by the master," he said with a dramatic bow.

Lysette managed to hide her smile, but just barely. Long ago, her oldest child had figured out that his charm and adorable nature would get him out of just about any bind. Steeling her resolve to get her point across to him, she eradicated any humor out of her expression and heart.

"What's my name?" she asked dryly.

The smile froze on Jimmy's face. "Uhh, Mom?" He blew out a breath. "No, okay. Mrs. Vaughn?" He took a step back at the look that one received from her. "Okay, super no. Um, Lysette?"

"Very good," Lysette said, her voice syrupy sweet. "Now," she said, taking a step over to him and tapping the end of his nose with a perfectly manicured fingernail. "In that little list you gave, did the word 'maid' pop up anywhere?"

Jimmy looked at her with utter confusion on his handsome face until she sent out an elegant hand waving over the mess he'd left behind. It was comical as he gave her a huge grin before he was off like a shot, gathering up his school bag and sneakers and ripping his school project out of his father's fingers, and bolted up the stairs.

"And remove those photographs from that poster

tonight when we get home!" she called after him. "I do *not* want to find it under your bed in a month!"

He stopped so quickly on the stairs that he nearly fell back down them. "Wait, back from where?"

"Your sister's dance recital is tonight," Jim said, continuing to loosen his tie.

Jimmy turned and looked down at them, hand resting on the banister. "Why do I have to go?"

"How many basketball games of yours has Bronte sat through?" Lysette asked, irritation in her voice.

He looked away as though doing some sort of mental calculation. "All but two," he said victoriously. "So can tonight be one of *my* two?"

"Do you have tonsillitis like she did?" Jim asked.

"You know," he hedged, "I'm going to have to go with a 'no' on that one, Daddy-O." He let out a sigh. "I'll go get ready," he grumbled, continuing up the stairs.

❧ ❧ ❧ ❧

The small theater was dark, curtain still closed as all the young dancers prepared for their first recital of the year. Lysette sat in the second row with Jim to her right and Jimmy on the other side of his father.

She read through the small program they were given at the door, listing the dancers' names, what school they went to, and what productions—if any—they'd appeared in. The house lights hadn't been dimmed yet, and she glanced to her right when she felt a bit of pressure against her right shoulder. She met Jim's gaze as he leaned toward her.

"Who was that girl standing next to you in the picture?" he asked quietly, so as not to disturb those getting settled in around them.

Lysette felt her heart rate pick up and stomach knot in a nervous tic. "You mean the entire class I was surrounded by?" she asked, trying to hedge.

"Obviously you were, but who was the one you had your arm intertwined with? You two were close, I'm guessing."

"Jim, we were fifteen. I haven't seen or spoken to her in decades. What do you care?"

He shrugged, glancing toward the stage as the lights flashed, alerting the audience that the show would begin soon. "I'd never seen that picture before. What's her name?"

Lysette wanted to argue further but knew that would simply get him even more interested. "Ellie Landry."

He nodded, uncrossing the left leg from her right to reverse the position. "How long were you close?"

She eyed his profile as he seemed to be studying the red velvet curtain that hid the stage. "We were friends for about a year," she said, keeping her tone nonchalant. She knew him probably better than anyone on the planet, and she knew that his questions were because either he recognized Eleanor for who she was or because he thought he saw something he didn't like.

"Have you seen her since?" he asked, equally nonchalant; however, she saw the trial lawyer peek his head out. She had to be careful not to perjure herself on the stand.

"Jim, I'm not sure why the Spanish Inquisition, but I haven't been friends with Ellie since I was sixteen. End of story."

He nodded as he began to applaud, the curtain rising.

Lysette sat nervously at the table waiting. She'd shown up early on purpose, giving herself time to settle in and settle her nerves. She hadn't seen Danny in almost a year, and it had been two years since their one and only intimate encounter. But they'd remained in touch, not her usual behavior with a woman she spent a single afternoon with, out of the small handful she had in twenty years.

She heard the bells jingle above the door in the small diner and glanced over from the booth she occupied at the back of the establishment. It wasn't hard to make out Danny Felts. She was a statuesque woman with the confidence of a Paris model and looks of any Hollywood starlet. Her black hair—longer than it had been when they'd met—was shoulder-length and tucked behind an ear. She wore wide-legged slacks and a button-up blouse underneath an unzipped bomber jacket.

As Danny made her way down the aisle toward where Lysette had waved at her, she caught every eye in the place, male and female. Danny, meanwhile, was oblivious.

"Hey," she said, sliding into the booth across from Lysette. "Glad you could have lunch."

"I'm glad you called," Lysette said, waving over the waitress. Drink orders taken, Lysette studied the onetime intimate partner who had become a friend. "What are you doing in town? You're still in Nebraska, right? Working on your new company?"

"Yes. My business partner, Allison, and I formed F&H Industries last year. I think we were still in the talking phase last time I talked to you about it."

"What do you guys do again?"

"Well," Danny said, pausing as the waitress dropped off their iced teas and took their lunch orders before jetting off again. "With my history of construction work back on the farm where I grew up, then with the Navy during the war, we're getting contracts with the government to build projects for them, that sort of thing. Plus," she said, adding a bit of sugar from the canister into her drink, gently stirring it with a spoon. "I have a bit of a business on the side." She met Lysette's gaze. "Building furniture, which I have a surprise for you."

"A surprise?" Lysette asked, squeezing the wedge of lemon brought with her tea, the juice mixing with the light brown liquid. "I love surprises."

Danny grinned. "I know. We're donating the rocking chair I made for you to auction or raffle off to raise money for your cause. Allison and I think it's pretty great what you're doing."

"Oh, Danny," Lysette breathed with a smile. She reached a hand across the table and lightly touched the other woman's before retreating. "Thank you."

Danny gave her a smile. "Of course." She sipped from her drink before setting it back down, eyeing Lysette. "How are the kids?"

"They're really good," Lysette responded, beaming. Any mention of her babies filled her with such pride and love. Truly the best decision she'd ever made out of a sea of bad ones. "The other night, Bronte had a dance recital." She laughed. "Poor thing got a split in her leotard, but like the little trouper that she is, she kept on going. Perfect pirouettes across the stage," she added, using her finger to make little circles across the table. "Right off into the wings," she concluded, her pirouetting finger disappearing off the table.

Danny joined her in laughter. "And," she said sobering, "how's Jim? How's the law office doing?"

"You know, it's finally really picked up. He's extremely busy, good for me." Lysette snickered. "But seriously, I'm happy for him. He loves what he does. I've been doing the accounting for him. In fact, I'm headed to his office after we're done here. Taxes are coming up, so..."

"Lord, don't remind me. So," Danny said, blowing out a breath as she sat back in the booth. "You mentioned on the phone you needed to talk about something. What's up?"

Lysette studied her friend for a moment, trying to figure out the best way to approach her thoughts and musings. Finally, she said, "When's the last time you saw Kate?"

Bright blue eyes went from mild curiosity to surprise to guarded. Danny looked down at her hands, which rested on the table. "Not since I left the Navy," she said. "It's been about seven years now, I guess." She cleared her throat and grabbed her glass of iced tea, playing with the straw, seemingly needing something to do with her hands. "Why?"

"I'm in an interesting situation right now. Well," Lysette qualified, "I guess it really doesn't *have* to be a situation, but..." She gave the woman across from her a sheepish grin. "You're the only person I know of who could possibly understand my potential predicament."

"Sounds mysterious." Danny moved her iced tea glass out of the way to make room for the waitress to set down their lunch plates. She smiled at the older woman before returning her gaze to Lysette. "Do tell."

"Well, I just feel you're uniquely qualified to understand and hopefully give me some clarity," Lysette muttered, feeling somewhat awkward in her question, which she felt was basically regurgitating what she'd previously said.

Danny cocked her head slightly to the side. "Which part of your situation am I uniquely qualified for?" she asked quietly, ensuring nobody around them would overhear. "Being in the Navy during the war? Or that I lived in the bottom of a vodka bottle for a few years to try and forget the immense betrayal by the woman I love more than my next breath? Or," she added gently, "the part that it's been seven years since I've seen her and her daughter, Megan, and her husband, George?"

Lysette was about to bring her spoonful of cheddar broccoli soup to her mouth but stopped, returning the utensil to the bowl. "My goodness," she said softly, sparing a glance at Danny. "I feel positively foolish worrying over my situation."

Danny shook her head. "No. We all have our crosses to bear, and they're not comparable. What is a walk in the park to one person is traumatizing to another. In any case..." She sat forward in her seat, eyes boring into Lysette's. "What's her name?"

"Eleanor Landry." Her smile was soft. "Though I called her Ellie." She felt a small thrill race up her spine at those words and the memories that fueled them. Unfortunately, they all landed in her heart with a painful thud.

"How long has it been since you've seen Ellie?"

Lysette let out a breath before forcing herself to resume her lunch. "Let's see...twenty-two years."

"Damn," Danny muttered. "Guess I shouldn't

complain about seven." She gave her a sweet and understanding smile. "That long ago, you two were young."

"Yes," Lysette said with a nod. "Too young, perhaps. Too young to realize that it all meant far more to me than to her." She felt the sinking disappointment and hurt that she thought was long buried. "I guess the plan didn't mean anything to her," she whispered.

"Ouch," Danny groaned. "Sadly, that scenario is far older than a mere twenty-two years ago. I'd go at least to the times of George Washington for that one."

Lysette returned the small smile she was given. "Either way, a long time ago."

"Yes. So why has it all come home to roost in your mind now?"

"It's come to my attention that she's in town," Lysette said, crushing a few crackers to put into her soup before scooping out another spoonful.

"Oh? Another George and Megan situation?" Danny asked before taking a bite of her burger.

Lysette smirked. "No, a Jim, Jimmy, and Bronte situation. Though that came after."

"Is Ellie part of the reason there *is* a Jim, Jimmy, and Bronte?" Danny asked gently.

Lysette sat back in her booth and considered the question for a long moment. She ran a nervous hand over her perfectly coifed hair. "Yes. No." She smiled and shook her head. "I don't know."

"How do you know she's in town? Did she reach out to you?"

This earned a full burst of laughter, a couple of nearby patrons glancing their way. "Sort of. She sent home a notice with time and date for parent-teacher conferences for my son."

Danny's eyes grew huge as she stared at her, burger at her lips. She lowered it and tilted her head. "No way."

"Yes way. She is none other than the woman my fourteen-year-old son has been talking about since the first day of school, Miss Brannon."

"Brannon? Did she marry at some point?"

Lysette shrugged. "I have no idea. I didn't notice a ring when I saw her, but I honestly don't know."

"Oh, so you've talked then?" Danny asked, finally taking her bite.

Lysette gave her a shy grin. "Not exactly. I've seen her twice now, and to be honest, the first time I was shocked as hell and ran out of there like a spooked rabbit. The second time, I just felt…" She searched for the word. "I felt angry. Really, really angry." She met Danny's gaze. "Does that make sense at all, or is that crazy?"

Danny also seemed to be taking her time to respond as she finished chewing her food and used the napkin to wipe her mouth and fingers. Finally, she sipped from her iced tea and spoke. "I don't know the details of what happened with you two when you were young women, but obviously, you carry a lot of hurt to this day. I know how I felt when I saw Kate that day standing on her front porch and looking at her with her two-year-old daughter in her arms, a daughter that could never have been mine, but it was a life that *should* have been mine. Does that make sense?"

"Makes more than sense," Lysette said, looking down into the depths of the creamy soup before meeting Danny's gaze again. "Absolutely."

"So in telling you that story, then no, I don't think it's crazy at all that anger was the emotion that hit you. Not to get all Freud on you, but my guess is that sixteen-, seventeen-year-old girl who is still inside you is who feels the anger. The one who likely feels abandoned." She reached for her glass of iced tea, lifting it to her lips. Before she drank, she said, "I know I did."

Lysette considered that for a moment before she asked, "If you were back in California and Kate was close by, even married to George, would you want her in your life again?"

"Oh, what a loaded question. Being that I'm available and she's not," Danny said softly, chewing on her bottom lip for a moment, "I'm not sure how wise that would be."

❧❧❧❧

"Okay, here's the remaining invoices," Jim said, setting the small stack on the edge of the desk where Lysette sat, presiding over the financial paperwork of the law office. "That was it, right? All you needed?"

"I think so." She looked over some of the paperwork he'd brought her. She looked up at him and smiled. "Thanks. I'll let you know if I need anything else."

"All right. Thanks, honey." Jim gave her a quick kiss to the lips, then scurried back to his office.

At the front of the office was Rita's desk. She was a kindly grandmother who worked for Jim as his receptionist and was a holdover from the attorney they'd taken the practice over from. As far as Lysette knew, she'd been there since the doors had opened in the thirties. She was currently out on lunch, so Lysette was responsible for double duty should someone stroll in looking for an attorney.

She blew out a breath as she settled in for a long afternoon. She'd ended her lunch early with Danny so she could get as much done as she could before it was time to get the kids from the respective friends' houses they'd spent their Friday night with into this beautiful, mid-January Saturday. Her Aunt Josie wouldn't be available to pick them up because she had a book club to attend with some local ladies of her age.

As if on cue, the door opened, and someone walked in. "Hey!" Lysette greeted, smiling as her aunt walked in, a covered plate in hand. She wore the overalls Lysette had seen her wear for years, the shirt beneath changing in color and style. Her hair, once golden blond was now gray with a few streaks of blond here and there. The long strands were pulled back into a messy updo, as usual.

"Hey, kiddo," Josie said, walking over to her desk. "Brought you and Jim some of those orange cookies you both love. Left some at the house for the kids, too."

"Ohh," Lysette groaned, lifting the towel covering the plate and snatching one of the warm treats. "I really shouldn't, considering I just had lunch, but…"

Josie chuckled, hugging the plate to her stomach. "How'd it go?"

"It went well." Lysette leaned back in her chair as she nibbled her cookie. "It was nice to see her."

"She's the really beautiful one, right? Tall?" Josie asked, raising a hand above her own five-foot-two height.

"That's the one," Lysette muttered around the bite in her mouth.

Josie nodded. "Gotcha. Okay, I better run. Last time Eloise got there before I did, we had to read the goddamn Bible for our book of the week."

Lysette chuckled, pushing up from her chair to walk her aunt out, accepting the plate and setting it on the desk. The two women walked to the door and shared a quick embrace.

"Thanks for stopping by," Lysette said.

"Sure. See you later, kiddo."

Lysette held the wood and glass door open for Josie to pass through, stopping her by calling her name. Josie turned to glance at her over her shoulder from where she stood on the sidewalk.

"If you could do it all over again, knowing what you know now, would you have done things differently?" Lysette asked softly.

The softening in Josie's eyes broke Lysette's heart. A slow smile spread across her lips as she nodded. "With all my heart."

Lysette watched her walk toward her old Chevy pickup truck until she drove away with a wave, which Lysette returned. About to turn back into the office and let the door close, she stopped, something catching her eye across the street.

Eleanor, dressed in casual capris with ballet flats and a winter jacket, scurried down the sidewalk to the box office. She stood there for a moment, her back to Lysette, who assumed she was buying a ticket. She heard a distant *thank you* float on the breeze just before Eleanor moved on to the door to the theater, which she pulled open and disappeared inside, the door slowly closing behind her.

Chapter Fifteen

I ncredible, isn't it?" Lysette asked softly, her voice not much above a whisper in reverence for what they were looking at. She felt her heart swell at the look on Eleanor's face as she took in the huge structure that loomed high above them. It gave her the greatest joy to introduce her to such wonders.

"I can't believe that was a dinosaur at one time," Eleanor whispered, her eyes huge and mouth falling open. She slowly made her way around the exhibit, her gaze never leaving the giant bones.

Lysette followed along, more enamored by Eleanor and her awe to everything she saw than by the Paleolithic history. They'd been wandering through the museum all morning, after a hearty breakfast cooked by Emma at the Landon Denver house. A self-guided tour that honestly shouldn't have taken more than an hour had been three, Eleanor looking at every single thing, reading every single placard, sometimes out loud, regardless if her audience was listening or not.

"Did you know that this museum opened the first of July, 1908?"

Lysette was pulled out of her thoughts by Eleanor's sudden words. She turned and shook her head slightly to clear it. "Uh, no. I didn't."

"Yup," Eleanor said with a nod, a huge smile on her face as she led the way over to a case full of Indian arrowheads. "The first president of the board here,

John Campion, said during his dedication address that day, 'A museum of natural history is never finished.'" She glanced over at Lysette, who stepped up beside her, a look of pride in her eyes. "He's exactly right."

Lysette shook her head, never taking her gaze off her friend. "How did you know that? I didn't tell you we were coming to the Colorado Museum of Natural History until we were on our way."

Eleanor's eyebrows fell, her expression that of confusion. "Didn't you see that on the plaque coming into the building?"

Lysette stared at her, feeling rather stupid. "Uh, no. I didn't."

"Girls, come on," Emma said, hurrying over to them. "Your *maman* left to get the tickets for the picture show. We have to hurry or we'll be late."

Eleanor looked around, a panicked look on her face. "We have to leave? But, but we just got here!"

Lysette wanted to hug her. "We've been here for hours, Ellie," she said with an affectionate smile, a hand on her friend's arm. That hand slid down the sleeve of the borrowed dress until Eleanor's fingers were tucked within her own. "We'll come back, I promise. But where we're headed now is…" She paused as she thought of the word. With a wide smile, she said, "Magical." She chuckled at the look that got her. "Yes, I said magical. Come on, you'll see."

Tugging her by the hand, Lysette guided them to follow Emma, who hurried across the highly polished floor of the grand building. As they stepped out into the mild, mid-October day, Eleanor stopped them, turning back to look at it.

Lysette took in what was, yes, a gorgeous building with all its grand columns and stairs, but was at a loss at what had Eleanor's attention. "What? What are you looking at?"

Not taking her eyes off the museum, a sad smile passed over Eleanor's lips. "I'm committing it to memory," she said softly. "Likely I'll never get to see this again. I don't want to forget a single detail."

Lysette pulled her hand free of Eleanor's only to take her in a comforting hug, right there on the stairs of the Colorado Museum of Natural History. "I swear to you," she whispered into the hug, not caring who saw them or who heard her. "I'll bring you back here someday." Her fingers ran through the long, free strands of Eleanor's dark hair. "You'll have your freedom, I swear it, Ellie." She left a small kiss on Eleanor's neck. "Let's go."

They caught up to Emma, who was about to turn the corner and get them on the street where the picture show would be. As they hurried by, the three were stopped by a man who removed his hat, addressing the trio with a warm smile.

"Ladies, I'm an out-of-work photographer, and I'd be honored if I could snap a picture for you to remember this day for all time," he said, hope in his eyes as he met their gazes. He indicated his camera, which was set up in a tripod with a camera case setting against the side of the building, just off the sidewalk. "I'll give ya a good price, most honest you'll get today," he added.

Lysette glanced at Eleanor, who stood to one side, Emma on the other before turning back to the man. "How much?" She could tell by the quality of his equipment and lack of that of his suit, which was worn with a hole beginning to work its way into the elbow of his jacket, that he was certainly on hard times. There were so many that were, her father told her. Her family gave as much as they could to those struggling, and this man was no different.

"A nickel and your home address will buy you a glossy, miss, that I'll develop and send off to your home," he promised, eyes brightening as she opened her purse and reached inside.

She glanced at her companions. "Will you two take a photo with me?"

"You two go ahead," Emma said, taking a step back. She gave them a wide smile of encouragement. "I want you two to remember this, always."

Lysette met Eleanor's gaze, a question in her own. When she got a small nod, she handed the man two quarters. "Here you go."

The man looked at the two coins in his palm, then up at Lysette. "Thank you, miss," he whispered. "Thank you."

"Come here," Lysette said, a goofy grin on her face that, not only did she get to make a perfect stranger's day, but she also was getting to immortalize the closeness she had with this person she was growing to adore and could not imagine her life without. She put her arm around Eleanor's waist to pull her closer before dropping her arm.

"Okay, ladies, beautiful, just beautiful," the photographer said, looking into the view finder of his camera. "Go ahead and stand a bit closer together," he suggested as he got his camera ready.

Lysette yanked on Eleanor's skirt until Eleanor bumped into her, nearly causing them both to trip. She grinned at the indignant look that move earned her. She stuck her tongue out at her friend.

"Okay, ladies. Over here, now. Say cheese!"

Wanting to make Eleanor laugh, she yelled out, "Practice!" She heard the gasp and looked over just in time to see Eleanor looking back at her, laughing in shocked amusement.

After leaving a very bemused photographer who was given their address scrawled on a piece of paper, Lysette felt Eleanor's gaze on her. "What?"

"Why did you do that?" Eleanor hissed as they neared the theater. "You could have gotten us in trouble!"

Lysette snickered. "By what, saying such an innocuous word as 'practice'? She giggled at the blush that colored Eleanor's cheeks. "And I paid for the picture, so it's not like my mother could be annoyed."

"All right, I got our tickets," Adalyn said, meeting them outside the theater where they stood on the sidewalk. "Here you go," she said, doling out the small paper slips.

"Is this it?" Eleanor asked softly, looking up at the building that looked like it belonged in Morocco more than Colorado.

"Yup. This is the Aladdin Theater," Lysette explained, then indicated the busy street packed with beautiful theaters and businesses around them. "You see, Curtis Street, where we're standing, is known as 'Theater Row.' You should see it at night, Ellie. All lit up like a birthday cake!"

Eleanor looked around, eyes wide as she cradled the ticket close to her chest. "It's beautiful," she murmured, looking back at the large theater before them.

"Adalyn, they made a mistake," Emma said, holding up the two tickets she held. "They gave you one too many tickets." She looked at Lysette and Eleanor.

"Girls, do you both have your—"

"Emmaline Brannon."

The smile was instant as she heard the voice and turned to see her. Her hands went to her mouth and her eyes got huge.

"Josephine Landon," she whispered.

"Aunt Josie. I didn't know—" Lysette began but stopped herself as she watched Emma and her aunt slowly walk toward each other until the last bit of distance was eaten up in excited steps and the two met in a desperate hug. She turned to see a satisfied smile on her mother's face and an equally shocked and baffled look on Eleanor's. "That's my Aunt Josie," she explained softly. "I don't think they've seen each other for quite a while."

"I guess not," Eleanor said, meeting Lysette's gaze. "Look at them. I've never seen Mama so excited before. I mean, she's crying." She brought her own hands up, fingers nervously fidgeting. "What do I do?"

"Just let them be, *chérie*," Adalyn said, walking up to the teens and putting her arm affectionately around Lysette's shoulders. She called something out to them in French, which was answered in French by the woman whose short, blond hair was in need of a trim and whose ill-fitting dress was a bland shade of light purple.

"What did she say?" Eleanor asked as she was shepherded toward the theater by Lysette.

"She told Aunt Josie we'd meet them inside and we're in the balcony."

Eleanor's eyebrows drew. "Balcony?"

Lysette grinned, leaning into Ellie as she wrapped her hands around her arm. "You'll see." As they were about to enter the building, she glanced back at the two women still standing on the sidewalk. She saw Emma bring a hand up and lightly touch Josie's face, then her hair, almost as though to make sure she were real. But what got her was the look in Josie's eyes. The only other time she'd seen a look like that was when her father looked at her mother.

"Are you coming?"

Lysette turned to Eleanor, who was still looking at her, her question hanging in the air. Without a word, they hurried inside.

Tickets given, treats bought, the trio headed into the theater proper, Lysette leading the way. She nearly had to drag Eleanor, as she wanted to stop and look at every single glittery detail of the opulent theater. She knew, however, what would really get her was the sheer size. The theater, which produced stage plays and picture shows sat more than nine hundred eager souls.

"The man who built this place a few years ago was called 'Mr. Movies,'" she explained, arm still linked with Eleanor's as they made their way inside the huge auditorium.

Dark blue velvet curtains, wood accents painted gold, and the Moroccan style of the outside of the building flowed through in the rounded curve of the archways with a pointed tip.

"Beautiful, isn't it?" Lysette asked Eleanor, who looked around wide-eyed and open-mouthed.

Eleanor turned her head and met her gaze, looking into Lysette's eyes for a long moment before she gave her a soft smile and nod. "Beautiful."

Lysette felt a wave of heat flow through her as she saw that violet color soften every time Eleanor looked at her. She gave the arm she clutched a little squeeze before tugging lightly so they could continue to the stairs that would lead to their balcony.

Lysette felt giddy as they got settled. She sat between her mother and Eleanor. Emma and Aunt Josie's seats were in the row behind them. They were the only ones in the balcony so far, and she wondered if it would only be them. For now, her attention was on Eleanor. She could feel the excitement coming off her in waves. She nearly vibrated in her seat, and Lysette found it adorable. She was so pleased she was able to be the one sitting next to her to witness it, to be part of it.

"Comfy chairs," Eleanor remarked, looking around. She raised a hand to wave.

Following her focus, Lysette saw Josie and Emma hurrying down the aisle far below. Emma returned the wave, and the two women rushed toward the stairs, the seats below beginning to fill as people filed in to see the show.

"Hey, ladies," Josie said, squeezing the shoulders of the three in front as she passed them before taking her seat, Emma beside her.

"Ready for the show?" Adalyn asked, turning in her seat, extending a hand. "So glad you could join us."

Josie took the hand, the two exchanging a look that seemed to communicate something only between them. "Me too."

Lysette met her beloved aunt's gaze. "Hello, Aunt Josie. I'm glad you're here."

"Hey, kiddo." She leaned forward and left a kiss to Lysette's cheek before turning her attention to Eleanor. "And it's certainly a pleasure to see you all grown up, Little Eleanor!"

Eleanor smiled shyly back at her. "Hello."

Lysette's attention went to the blue velvet curtain far below as the lights began to dim, the murmurs of the large seated crowd quieting down. She leaned into Eleanor. "Are you ready?" she whispered.

Eleanor took a deep breath before letting it out slowly, sparing a glance to Lysette. "Yes. I think so. I'm nervous." She grinned sheepishly.

"Don't be. This will be amazing." As the auditorium went dark, she reached down and grabbed Eleanor's hand, smiling over at her when their fingers entwined. Something caught her attention, and she glanced behind her just in time to see her Aunt Josie leave a light kiss on Emma's lips before they turned forward to watch the show.

Chapter Sixteen

Eleanor was humming, she knew she was, as she sat at the bright pink table, ice cream cone in hand. She'd had ice cream before, of course, but somehow, vanilla had never been so sweet, so smooth, or so perfect, just like her entire weekend, which she didn't want to face was ending.

The five of them sat at Wilcox Creamery enjoying a sweet treat before four of them would head back to Brooke View and Josie would head back to Gunnison. As Eleanor sat next to Lysette, who seemed to be thoroughly enjoying her sundae with extra cherries, she couldn't have imagined a better day. She felt so close to her friend, and in the small bit that she'd allow herself to fantasize, she could almost imagine it had been a date for them. Yes, others were with them, but she only had eyes for Lysette.

"Hurry with that, I want you to come with me," Lysette said, snapping Eleanor out of her thoughts.

Eleanor nodded and quickly finished her ice cream without question. She saw the empty glass dish that had held Lysette's dessert, then Lysette as she reached into the bag her mother had been carrying, digging through it and pulling something out. Hugging it to her chest, she pushed back from the table and reached down to grab Eleanor's hand.

"Wait," Eleanor said, about to wipe off that hand as it was sticky from holding the cone.

Apparently, Lysette didn't mind because she wove their way through the busy ice cream shop until they reached the ladies' room at the back. As they passed the side counter from the main one where ice cream treats were created and served, a soda jerk stood behind it in striped attire waiting on his customers. One of whom was a man standing there with a young girl.

Eleanor's eyes grew wide as she recognized him as Mr. Miller, the postman in Brooke View and a regular at their family store. She stopped their momentum, nearly yanking Lysette off her feet.

"What are you doing?" Lysette asked, irritation in her voice.

Eleanor nodded toward the man who handed the child with him a malt. "We can't be seen here!" she hissed.

Lysette smirked. "Then let's go so he won't see us!" she stage-whispered, tugging at Eleanor's hand again.

She spared a glance back over her shoulder at Eleanor before giving her one of her wicked smiles and pushing the door open, tugging Eleanor in after her.

The bathroom was painted a light mint green, which Eleanor felt likely belonged more in an institute of some sort than the bathroom of a sweet shop. Once inside, Lysette instantly went to look to see if anyone was in the bathroom stalls, but all three were empty. She stood by the door of the one farthest from the door, waving Eleanor over.

Eleanor stared at her. "What? Do you want me to wait out here while you—" She was nearly pulled off her feet as Lysette hurried over to her and grabbed her hand, yanking her to the stall and pushing her inside. It was quite cozy once she closed the door behind them, the two standing nearly breast to breast in the narrow space. Eleanor grinned. "What are you doing?"

"*Maman* got this for you," she said softly, backing up as much as she could, her back pressed against the wall so she could bring the item she'd snagged from Adalyn's bag into view. It was a Bible.

Eleanor's eyebrows drew in confusion. "Lysette," she said softly, meeting her gaze. "We have an endless supply of these things at home."

Lysette chuckled. "I know, but not with this in it." She brought it up to face level and pulled back the cover.

It was such a pleasure to meet you and have you at our teen revival this year! So pleased you enjoyed yourself and plan to return next year.
All the Blessings of Christ.
—Reverend Tim

Eleanor took the leather-bound book in her hands and read and reread the message scrawled in heavy black ink. Mouth open, she looked up into Lysette's eyes. "But we weren't there."

"We were not, but my cousin Betty was there last year, and she was so kind as to make avail her Bible to her favorite aunt."

Eleanor let out a slow, shaky breath, relief washing through her. She understood immediately. This was meant to be backup, should they need it. She hoped it wouldn't come to that, as they'd covered their bases pretty well, but...

"Thank you," she whispered, setting the book on the back of the tank of the toilet before turning back to Lysette and pulling her into a hug, tight due to their confines, yes, but also she needed to feel her against her. "Thank you for everything."

"Of course," Lysette whispered back, her face buried in Eleanor's neck as they held each other. "I'm so glad you agreed to come this weekend."

Eleanor's eyes closed as she felt Lysette's fingers lightly touch the back of her neck beneath her hair, brushed to a shine and left loose. She turned her face inward, as well, the feel of Lysette's soft hair tickling her nose. She inhaled her scent, committing it to memory for later, alone in the darkness of her bedroom at the farmhouse.

She somehow managed not to sigh in surprised pleasure when she felt the softest of lips lightly brush the side of her neck. She did, however, freeze when the door to the bathroom squeaked open. She tried to pull away from Lysette, but she was held fast. Her heart raced as she felt a second pass of those lips as the woman who had entered stepped into the stall next to theirs.

The newcomer let out a small fit of coughs as she readied herself to do her business, the porcelain creaking slightly under her weight as she lowered herself onto the commode. Eleanor's thoughts of their neighbor were interrupted when she felt the fingers on the back of her neck move up into her hair, lightly tugging as soft lips grazed her neck.

On pure instinct, her face moved in the direction of those touches, Lysette's hot breath on her skin inflaming her. Her hands moved of their own accord from Lysette's back down to her hips, gently pulling their bodies just that much closer together.

Eleanor didn't even hear what she would

ordinarily find amusing or offensive noises coming from the stall next door as she felt the sweetness of Lysette's lips find her own. She felt more than heard the sigh that escaped those lips as their kiss silently deepened.

Everything that wasn't Lysette disappeared as Eleanor accepted the gentle strokes of her tongue into her mouth, able to taste the fudge from the sundae she'd just eaten. She marveled at the feel of their breasts pressed together, closer than ever before, their bodies fully flush. Their kiss was more passionate than the other two they'd shared before, and the sensations it sent through Eleanor's body nearly left her dizzy.

The woman in the stall next door finally finished her business with a flush and the squeak of the hinges as she pulled the stall door open. She quickly washed her hands, then left, which seemed to signal a natural end to their kiss.

Lysette left a few soft kisses on Eleanor's lips before pulling away just enough to rest her forehead against Eleanor's, both breathing heavily. She brought her hand out of thick dark hair and cupped the side of Eleanor's neck. "I wanted to be able to give you a proper goodbye." She smiled, giving her one more quick kiss before pulling away as far as the confines would allow. "I know once we reach Brooke View, that's not possible."

Eleanor nodded, reaching up to brush some hair away from Lysette's beautiful lips, a few strands caught in what was left of her lipstick. "I'm glad. You know, us girls can never get enough practice." She grinned, which Lysette returned.

"Never enough," she murmured, giving her another quick peck before grabbing the Bible and shoving it at Eleanor and opening the stall door.

❧❧❧❧

Okay, so April 14, 1865, Appomattox Courthouse, they signed the thingy to end the Civil War.

Eleanor paused in her sweeping as she considered that information for a moment as she leaned on the broom. "April 14," she murmured, "Then April 9 he died."

Rolling her eyes at her own indecision, she reached into the pocket of her skirt and pulled out the cheat sheet she'd created before leaving school to help her study for the upcoming test.

"How would Grant and Lee sign the declaration at Appomattox Courthouse *after* Lincoln was assassinated?" she muttered to herself. "Brilliant deduction, Ellie."

She continued sweeping the sidewalk outside her father's store. Earlier, a child who had been walking by with his mother decided it was the perfect spot to free himself of the stomach bug, and Eleanor was sent out to clean it up. After the mess was cleaned up and thrown in the garbage can behind the building, she decided to tidy up the front of the store. They seemed to be having a break in the cold spell, so she took advantage of the mild, late October day.

"What'cha mutterin' about?"

Startled, she whipped around to see a grinning Gabby standing there, a forty-pound bag of feed slung over his shoulder. "Oh, uh, just going over some facts for a test coming up."

The toothpick that was so often present between his lips bobbed up and down as his tongue played with the end inside his mouth. His gaze flowed over her body like a slow-moving avalanche of molasses.

"Though I like me a smart woman, not sure why you're bustin' your back on this stuff, Eleanor," he finally said, ice cold gaze meeting her own timid one.

She was also trying desperately to hide her disgust and fear. Ever since that night in the woods, she had felt even more awkward and uncomfortable around him while he seemed to be more assertive, even aggressive, around her.

"You're so beautiful," he said, taking a step closer. "There ain't no reason to worry about the school learnin'."

She swallowed and managed to stand her ground and not step back, though she did grip the broom handle so tightly that her knuckles were turning white. "It's okay, Gabby," she said, trying to keep her voice friendly. "I enjoy school."

"Yeah, but when you've got a husband, all the school learnin' in the world ain't gonna do you no good."

She gave him a small smile, turning away to give him the hint she intended to get back to her task. "I'll keep that in mind for a future situation."

Relieved that he continued on to the delivery truck, she spared a glance in his direction as he climbed into the Ford and got it rumbling to life. With a clenched jaw, annoyed and wanting a bath, she hurried up and finished her sweeping. As she was about to head into the store, broom in hand, she heard her name. Turning, she felt her stomach drop.

"Hello, Mr. Miller How are you?"

"Oh, good, good. How are you, young lady?" the friendly mailman asked, offering her his usual smile and tip of his uniform cap. "Mind if I hand these to you?"

"Absolutely, sir. My father won't be in until a little later, anyway."

"Ah, perfect." He handed her a bundle of letters, which she knew was for the business, as well as their personal mail. Her father never let it go to the farmhouse. "You be sure to tell him that supply of lumber he ordered should be coming in later this week, you hear?"

"Yes, sir, Mr. Miller. I sure will," she assured, raising the letters she clutched to emphasize her promise. She watched him head down the sidewalk, mailbag slung across his chest as he whistled a happy tune continuing his delivery route.

Tucking the bundle of mail under her arm, she reached down and grabbed the dustpan she'd set on a small table outside the store and carried it all inside. She left the broom at the bottom of the stairs in that alcove like she did every day before hurrying behind the counter to put the mail where her father could easily find it.

She knew it would be slow for a little while as folks weren't out of work yet, so she decided to continue her cleaning inside the store. As she began to clean the inside of the large front window, she saw the delivery truck pull up and park in its usual spot out front. Gabby climbed out from behind the wheel, a man she didn't recognize from the passenger side.

"Lovely," she muttered as the two men headed to the store.

"We meet again, Miss Eleanor!" Gabby bellowed as he entered, a bit of swagger in his stride.

She glanced over at him, wondering why on earth

he was showing off for the scrawny man who walked a few paces behind him. His hair was strawberry blond, though it was cut so short it was hard to tell. His fair eyebrows and eyelashes gave it away. He had eyes the dull color of her father's, and he walked with his hands shoved into his baggy trousers.

Saying nothing, she simply smiled and turned back to her task at the window. She cringed when the two men walked up to the counter near the cash register where her customers would stand.

"So, Eleanor, this here is my good friend Thomas, all the way from Oklahoma."

She turned and accepted the large, bony hand he offered. "Nice to meet you, Thomas." She figured he was around Gabby's age, mid- to late twenties.

"Gonna head back to the stoop to smoke me a cigarette," Gabby said, pulling the rolled smoke out from behind his ear. "Let me know when your daddy gets back, will ya?"

She nodded for a second time, relieved when he left. She was interrupted again when a panicked Mrs. Gomez hurried inside.

"Oh, honey! I need three yards of this material right now," the frazzled woman exclaimed, looking as though she were about to jump out of her skin.

Eleanor put her cleaning rag down and looked at the swath of material that was thrust in front of her. "Oh, we've got plenty more of that, Mrs. Gomez. Three yards, you say?"

"Yes," the mother of five said with a tired sigh, leaning against the counter. "The cousins decided they wanted to be clowns for their trick-or-treating, too." She gazed at Eleanor with big brown eyes. "I'm going to charge my sister next year."

Eleanor smiled as she made her way around the counter. "Yell if someone needs me," she added, taking the swatch and heading to the back of the store. With Halloween around the corner, she'd set up an extra display of new fabrics for costumes near the back door.

She hummed softly as she dug through the bolts of fabric until she found the one she needed. She'd cut the first batch for Mrs. Gomez a week before, and she wasn't sure it had been touched since.

"So I'm sittin' there behind them bars, right?"

"Right."

Eleanor stopped, glancing toward the back door to the store, the back stoop just beyond.

"Sheriff Barnes comes up to me and says, 'All right, son, y'all sure picked the wrong niggers to string up,'" Gabby continued, his voice muffled through the door, but she could understand his words. "He says, 'I don't give two shits you done kill them darkies, but you done pissed off the mayor, son. One of them niggers worked for his son.' And I'm thinking, 'Ah, hell.'" Gabby laughed, Thomas laughing right along with him. "Hell, of all the damn niggers in the goddamn world, right?"

"Ah, man!" Thomas boomed. "What did you do?"

"Well, sheriff says the mayor's son is all up in arms and may come stormin' the jail. He tells me he ain't gonna save me from no lynch party, but," he added, and Eleanor could almost imagine him holding up a finger to add a bit of drama to his pause. "He says, 'Son, I'm headin' to dinner, be back in about an hour. If'n y'all just happen to make your way outta Texas, can't say my boys will try all that hard ta find you.'"

"No, he didn't," Thomas said, wonder in his

voice.

"Damn straight, he did." Gabby laughed. "Hightailed it the hell outta there! Made my way on up to Colorado."

Horrified, Eleanor staggered backward. The bolt of fabric in her hands caught a coat tree tucked in the corner and sent it crashing against the door and to the ground. Mortified, she nearly threw the fabric as she bent down to grab the coat tree and her father's jacket that fell to the floor with it.

The back door swung open, nearly knocking Eleanor in the head. Gabby stood in the open doorway, looking around with startled surprise on his face. His cold gaze landed on her as she slowly got herself and the coat tree to an upright position.

"How long you been back here, girl?" he asked, his voice low and dangerous.

"Oh, uh, uh, I just came back here to get this fabric," she said, reaching for the bolt, grabbing it up into her arms. "I have to cut some for a customer," she said, hoping her voice wasn't as shaky as it sounded in her own head. With a quick smile, she hurried toward the front of the store, heart in her throat.

⁂

"Thank you so much, Mr. Howell," Eleanor called out, climbing out of the dark green Buick owned by their neighbor. "I really appreciate the ride home." She watched as the car puttered down the road, leaving her at the mouth of the dirt drive that led to the farmhouse.

It had cooled down, no longer the mild day from earlier. She hitched her school bag a bit higher onto her shoulder and tried to bury herself in her jacket as she began the quarter-mile walk up to the house, her feet feeling heavier and heavier with each step. Her father had returned to the store only to quickly leave with Gabby and Thomas, though she wasn't told why. All she knew was she'd be closing the store on her own and then heading home to help her mother cook dinner for five, Thomas their guest.

She considered what she'd overheard from Gabby's conversation with Thomas. She didn't know what to think, whether she should believe what he said. What about the story he told them at breakfast? What about his dead wife and child? Was that the real story and what he'd told Thomas was simply to look big?

She considered when he'd come into the building after the crash of the coat tree. He hadn't looked embarrassed, which she'd think he would if he'd been telling tall tales to his friend. He looked angry; he had looked angry enough to truly frighten her.

She needed to talk to Lysette. It wasn't possible, and she wouldn't see her until the following day, but she desperately needed to bounce the events of the afternoon off someone, and her mother wasn't an option.

The thought of her mother brought a small smile to her face. It was a nice feeling to smile with the heaviness in her heart regarding Gabby. But in the week and a half since their jaunt into Denver, she and her mother hadn't been able to talk about it or share their thoughts on the events, but when they passed each other in the hall or Eleanor helped set the table, they always shared a small smile meant only for each other.

As she got closer to the house, her thoughts were interrupted by the sound of shattering glass inside followed by the crash of what sounded like wood. Her steps slowed as her eyes widened in confused shock. When she heard the sound of her mother scream, she took off, jetting up the drive and nearly flying up the stairs to the front porch. The door was unlocked, and she almost plowed through it to get inside.

"You like making a fool of me?" her father roared, standing over Emma, who lay on the floor among the pieces of the destroyed coffee table, shards of the candy dish that was once atop it scattered on the floor near the wall. "How dare you lie to me!" He reached down and grabbed her, almost using superhuman strength as he threw her across the room where her body slammed into the wall, sliding down to the floor. "How dare you make me look bad?"

"Stop!" Eleanor yelled, storming over to him and grabbing his arm. "Stop!" she cried out as he backhanded her and sent her flying into the remnants of the table. She landed with a grunt and a white hot flash of pain that sliced through her back, the hot, coppery taste of blood in her mouth.

"Don Miller told me!" he bellowed at them both, but mostly his ire was aimed at Emma. "He told me he saw you with that, that...*thing*...in Denver! In some goddamn ice cream shop!" He rushed over to Emma and grabbed her again, slamming her so hard her head bounced off the wall. He lifted her so she was face to face with him. "You lied!"

Oh, god! While his attention was on her mother, Eleanor used every ounce of will she had to pull herself to her feet and run up the stairs to her bedroom. She threw her school bag, no idea where it landed as she hurried over to her dresser. She grabbed the Bible that lay there, the one Lysette had given her, and flew back downstairs. She was about to do something she'd never dare—lie to her father's face.

"Look!" she exclaimed, nearly breathless as she opened the Bible to the signature page and shoved it in front of his face. "Look."

He tossed Emma aside like a rag doll and focused on the Bible he took in his hands, chest heaving from his exertions.

Eleanor knelt next to her mother, taking her in protective arms, careful in case she was badly injured. "We were all tired after the long drive," Eleanor said, shocked at just how believable the story sounded as it fell from her lips. "So we had the idea to stop at the ice cream place on the way home."

Ed glared down at her. "He didn't mention you were there," he growled, doubt tinging his words.

"We were in the bathroom, Lysette and I," Eleanor said, the only truthful thing she had to say. "But," she continued, looking to her mother, her eyes pleading with her to go along with it. "Remember, Mama, you told me you saw Mr. Miller. Remember?"

Emma said nothing, only nodded, blood smeared from her nose across her cheek and trickling from her badly cut lip.

"I'm sorry I forgot to tell you that, Father," Eleanor added, her voice conciliatory even as she was filled with hatred. "I hope you don't mind that Reverend Tim wrote in the Bible you gave me. He just wanted to—"

"Fine," Ed growled, tossing the Bible down to her. He ran a hand through his hair, which hung in sweaty strands in his face. He looked around before moving away from them, stepping over the pieces of the table. "Get this cleaned up," he said before walking out the front door, slamming it behind him.

"Thank god he didn't notice," Eleanor whispered, closing the Bible, which was a different color than hers, before setting it aside and turning her attention to her mother. "Are you okay?" She gently wiped her hair out of the blood on her jaw. "Can you move?"

Emma looked at her, her face deathly pale and eyes wide. She looked stunned and deeply afraid. Without warning, her features crumbled, and the tears came.

Eleanor shoved her own emotions down as she gathered her into her arms as much as she could, holding her as she cried. "It's okay," she whispered. "I'm so sorry."

After a few moments, Emma gathered herself together, sniffling as she pulled out of Eleanor's embrace. "We have to clean this up," she said, wincing as she attempted to push to her feet, stopping and lowering herself back to a sitting position. "Lord, give me strength," she whispered. "He won't be gone long."

Eleanor nodded. "Want to try again?" she asked softly, getting to her feet, hands under her mother's underarms. "Ready?"

Emma nodded, and with a loud cry of pain, they slowly got her standing, though she leaned heavily on Eleanor. She took in several lungfuls of air, seeming to try to work through the pain. Finally, she looked at Eleanor, focusing on her.

"Honey," she said, voice quiet. "Adalyn came by today. Samuel's missing."

Chapter Seventeen

Eleanor sat in the rocking chair, head in her hands. It had taken a moment after she'd gotten the call, but now the full force of what she'd been told was hitting her. The tears were quick and hot, streaming between her fingers. Her chest heaved so much that she was worried she wouldn't be able to catch her breath. She was gasping for air.

Her moment of grief and fear was interrupted by a soft knock on her apartment door. She glanced over at it, doing her best to get herself together as she pushed to her feet and walked over to it. She unlatched it and pulled the door open, her neighbor Gwen standing on the other side.

"Hi," Gwen said softly, looking at her with her large brown doe eyes. "I'm so sorry to bother you, but…um…I think the person who just called thought I was you."

Eleanor used the sleeve of her cardigan to wipe at her eyes and cheeks, blinking away the tears that were sticking her eyelashes together. "I'm sorry."

"No, it's okay," Gwen said quickly, a smile on her young, pretty face, her blond hair brushed back from her face. "Um…the lady said your friend made it out of surgery, and they found the bullet."

Fresh tears assaulted Eleanor, nearly sending her crumbling to the floor. She felt strong arms catch her and caress her back. Eleanor allowed herself to be held for a moment as the relief rushed through her in a wave of emotion. She could hear the soothing words Gwen was murmuring to her, but she couldn't understand them.

Finally, she calmed down, giving Gwen's arm a slight squeeze in indication that she was about to pull away from her. Again, she used her sleeve to wipe her eyes, giving the younger woman a sheepish grin.

"Thanks," she said quietly. "Sorry about that."

"No need to apologize, Eleanor," Gwen said, giving her one last one-armed hug. "Listen, Richard and I are about to have dinner…" Her voice trailed off, the invitation clear.

"Oh, thank you so much. I need to be alone for a while."

"I understand." Gwen stepped back out into the hall. "We're just across the hall if you need anything," Gwen offered, squeezing Eleanor's hand before turning and heading back to her own door.

Left alone, Eleanor closed and locked her door and leaned back against it. Eyes squeezed closed for a moment, she let out a shaky breath before pushing away from the door and making her way back to the handmade rocking chair she'd won in the raffle at school. She wasn't entirely sure what group had put the raffle together, but she knew the money was going to a good cause of providing supplies and food for underprivileged children in Woodland and the surrounding areas.

She grabbed the throw her mother had crocheted her that had been discarded when she'd been summoned to take the initial phone call an hour before, covering herself with it as she curled up in the chair. The gentle rocking motion soothed her.

As she rocked, she stared off into space, the soft murmur from the television ignored as she saw the sweet face of her friend. How could this have happened, she wondered. How, in these early days of 1957, could they be no further ahead than they'd been when she was a kid?

It brought a memory to mind that she absolutely didn't want to think about, so she let out a heavy breath and glanced at the small television set, attempting to find interest in it. She was just getting the gist of the game show when there was another knock on her door.

For the second time, she pushed the throw off her legs and steadied the rocking chair so she could stand before making her way to the door. Expecting it to be Gwen again, she was surprised when it was a uniformed police officer.

"Ma'am," he greeted, removing his hat. "Are you Eleanor Brannon?"

"Yes, how can I help you, Officer?"

"I'd like to talk to you about the events surrounding the shooting of Scott O'Shea and his... *friend*, Ronnie Washington."

Without a word, she stood aside, allowing him to enter. "You can have a seat at the table over there, Officer." She closed the door after he passed and joined him. "Care for some coffee?" she asked, placing her hand on the hand-cranked coffee grinder.

"No, ma'am, thank you." He placed a notepad on the table, opened to a fresh page, and removed the cap from his pen. "I'm Officer Forbes, and I understand you're a good friend of the victim. His girlfriend? Is that correct?"

Eleanor's mind reeled, thinking back to who all in Scott's life believed that about the two: his parents for certain and a few of their coworkers. That deduction meant nobody really outside of that small circle, so it told her likely who the police had spoken to before her. That meant she had to be very careful about what she said. To her knowledge, only a few people knew the truth.

"Scott and I are close, yes," she said, figuring it was the best answer she could give without lying and without making those seem like liars who had previously spoken to him. She had no idea where any of this would go, including to court.

"Do you know Mr. Washington?" he asked, pen poised above the page.

"I do, yes."

"And how would you characterize his relationship to Mr. O'Shea?"

"Well," she said, setting her hands on the table and folding her fingers together so they wouldn't fidget. She could almost feel the eggshells crunching slightly beneath her feet. "They're friends. Good friends."

"What do you mean by 'good friends'?" the officer asked.

"They got along. I know Ronnie had done some work for Scott's parents, some landscaping at their house, that sort of thing. I think Scott helped him."

"Are you aware of anything Mr. Washington may have done to have an enemy that might go after him and Mr. O'Shea?"

She looked at him for a moment, her mind whirling back to every conversation she'd ever had with Scott about Ronnie. Finally, she shook her head. "No. Absolutely not. Scott, either. Both men are clean as a whistle."

"And," he said, plowing on as though he hadn't

heard her last statement. "Do you know of any reason Mr. Washington would take Mr. O'Shea so far out, away from town?" he asked, pen still poised over the page. She realized he hadn't written down a single thing she'd said, obviously he wasn't getting what he'd hoped for.

"Officer, if I'm not mistaken, weren't they in Scott's car when they were ambushed and *both* shot?" She sat back in her chair, arms crossing over her chest. She really did not like what this policeman was insinuating. "I'm assuming Scott went of his own free will then. And no, I have no idea why they were out there." She knew it was essentially a lie, but since Scott had never told her about it, she could call it truth.

He sighed, irritation clear on his face as he closed his notebook. "Anything else you'd like to add?"

"The only thing is that I truly hope you find whatever cowardly person shot two unarmed, *innocent* men who weren't hurting anyone, parked in a car."

He met her gaze for a long moment before nodding as he pushed back from the table, preparing to leave.

❦ ❦ ❦ ❦

"Did you want some more mashed potatoes, Miss Lilly?" Lysette asked, loaded scoop ready. At the elderly woman's nod, she let loose of the scoop, which landed atop the first one on the plate like ice cream.

Eleanor watched, amused yet worried they were going to run out of food as Lysette kept giving seconds before they'd given all the firsts. "Hey," she hissed after the elderly woman had moved on down the line to get her Thanksgiving turkey. "We're going to run out of mashed potatoes!"

Lysette glanced over at her from where they stood side by side in the line of church volunteers who were doling out the early holiday meal to those less fortunate in town. "We'll make more, silly," she said with her special smile, playfully pushing her hip into Eleanor's.

Eleanor returned the grin, way too taken by Lysette's beauty and charm to be irritated. She returned her focus to her ladle and pot of gravy when a man she recognized from around town ran into the church.

"They found a man," he shouted, eyes wide with panic. "In the river!"

Eleanor stared at him before turning to Lysette to see if she had any idea what the man was talking about. When she got a shrug and shake of her head, she turned back to see some of the men in the sanctuary—those who were helping to serve and those who had come for a meal—head out into the cold, snowy late November day.

Without a word, the teens left their respective serving implements in their pots and followed the crowd outside. The Little Red Rock River flowed thirty yards from the small Church of Christ, and often sermons were held out near it during a hot summer day. Now it was partially frozen over, the ice layer too soft to walk on, but within a month, it would be hard enough for ice fishing.

A group of kids stood on the shore in a huddled group, one of them crying as four men knelt in a group at the river's edge. As if in a dream, Eleanor felt compelled to get closer. She felt Lysette's hand on her arm, trying to hold her back, but she had to see. As if choreographed, the crowd parted, leaving a path for her to the water. Two of the four men stood, one looking at her as the other two remained where they'd been.

As she got closer, she saw the body of a man lying on the bank, his legs and feet still in the icy river. One of the kneeling men was in the way, blocking her view of the rest of the man, though she saw a large hand with dark skin lying on the ground.

She swallowed hard as she stood ten feet away, part of her wanting the man who blocked her view to move and part of her wanting him to stay where he was. As though he heard her silent thoughts, he glanced over his shoulder up at her, then moved aside.

"Oh, my god, no!" Eleanor yelled, bolting upright in bed, eyes wide and heart racing. "No. The rope is still around his neck! Get it off!"

Slowly, the images faded, her bedroom illuminated by the gray of early morning taking its place. As realization of where she was filtered in, her heart rate slowed and fear subsided.

"Jesus," she blew out, running her hand through her hair. A dream fueled by a memory she hadn't had in many years. "Ack!" she cried as her alarm clock went off. Hand to her heart, the other reached out to pound on the dismiss button.

⚜ ⚜ ⚜ ⚜

Eleanor had gotten to the school early, not wanting to have to traipse through groups of upset kids in the halls if she could avoid it. She would be more than happy to be there for them and explain as best she could how their beloved Mr. O'Shea had been hurt, but she needed a moment to get her bearings first.

Her lunch stowed away and jacket hung on the coat tree in the corner, Eleanor opened the textbook to the chapter they were on and carried it over to the blackboard to write out some important notes for her first class.

"Hey."

Glancing over her shoulder, she was shocked. Turning fully, she lowered the textbook balanced in one hand and the other that held the stick of chalk. "Hi." She didn't know what to think and felt slightly on edge as the stunning woman walked farther into the room. How could she possibly be perfection at seven twelve in the morning?

"I heard about your friend," Lysette said, her voice soft and kind, if not a bit uncertain, just as Eleanor felt. "Well, Jimmy said he's your boyfriend, really."

Eleanor gave her a small smile and set the book and chalk on her desk before gripping the back of the chair, which she stood behind. "No," she said, her voice equally as soft and quiet, almost worried if she rose in volume it would break the moment and Lysette would disappear. "He is my best friend, though."

Lysette nodded, stopping her advance a few feet from the other side of the desk, eight feet of space between them. "I understand. He was with his... friend?" she asked, none of the edged innuendo in her voice like the police officer, none of the judgment or accusation.

Eleanor nodded. "Yeah." She looked away, emotion rising in her chest. She swallowed and took a deep breath to make it go away. "Just two men going out to the middle of nowhere to be themselves," she near-whispered. "Nothing more, nothing less. Out in the middle of nowhere because they can't be themselves here, amongst their peers and townsmen." She felt the anger rising along with the emotion and took another deep breath. This was not the person she could ever show vulnerability or weakness in front of, not anymore.

"They're going to be okay?"

Eleanor nodded. "Ronnie was barely hit, grazed in the shoulder, I think." She smirked, shaking her head. "I think Scott saw it coming and tried to block him with his body."

"Wow," Lysette whispered, looking down at her hands for a long moment. "He really cares about him."

"He does."

The bell in the hall rang, alerting students and faculty that first period was to begin in three minutes.

Lysette glanced over her shoulder toward the door before turning back to look at Eleanor, who met her gaze. "I'm so sorry. I wanted to tell you that." She again looked down at her hands, which clutched her purse. She took a deep breath before looking up again, seeming to have composed herself back into the woman Eleanor had come to know her as in their limited encounters over the months, a woman of incredible beauty but deeply guarded eyes and cool focus.

Without another word, she turned and left the room, her high heels clicking a staccato goodbye.

❧ ❧ ❧ ❧

The theater wasn't as busy as Eleanor worried it would be, kids already ready to get back to fun after two weeks back in school after the holiday break. Eleanor found a seat she was happy with, a bit farther back than she wanted, but it would certainly work. It was a western, not her favorite, but she didn't care. All she wanted to do was relax and lose herself in fantasy before she headed to the hospital to visit Scott.

She settled in, her purse on the floor between her feet and the box of licorice on her lap. She glanced around as others found seats and chatted quietly amongst themselves. She got a strong whiff of freshly buttered popcorn very close to her. Glancing to the seat to her right, she saw someone sit down and get settled, a bag of the buttery stuff lowered to rest on a lap. A moment later, she found herself looking into Lysette's eyes for just a moment before the other woman turned away, focused on the screen where dancing hot dogs sang their way across it.

Chapter Eighteen

And I have something special for our Christmas meal this year," Ed said, rising from his seat at the table. Emma, Eleanor, and Gabby remained seated.

Eleanor watched him walk out of the room before sparing a glance at her mother, who gave her a nearly imperceptible shrug and shake of her head. Feeling an icy gaze on her, she turned to her left to see Gabby watching them closely. The hard, heavy footfalls of her father on the old plank flooring brought her attention back to his vacated seat.

He carried a bottle about two-thirds of the way filled with clear liquid with a fat cork stopper shoved into the neck. He looked to Emma. "Get glasses. The special ones."

Without a word, Emma did as she was told, hurrying out of the dining room and returning moments later with four cobalt blue glasses that looked like miniature wine glasses.

Eleanor watched this, a sickening feeling in the pit of her stomach. As her father uncorked the bottle, the pungent fragrance that wafted her way told her it was hooch, something that had been illegal due to Prohibition until a few weeks before. Ed filled each glass halfway with the clear liquid, which smelled more like gasoline than liquor, and handed them out.

Taking her glass in hand, Eleanor brought it up

to her nose and sniffed experimentally, instinctively jerking away, blinking her eyes rapidly as they immediately began to tear. She wasn't entirely sure she had any nose hairs left.

"It goes down easy as long as it's quick," Gabby assured with a grin.

She met his gaze before her focus returned to her father, who still stood and began to speak.

"Okay, so we don't drink in this house, but today is a very special occasion, despite it being the day of the birth of our Lord." He grinned. "So glasses up," he instructed, raising his own. "To good news!"

Eleanor looked around the table to see the two men easily down their drink, which told her that her father hadn't abstained nearly as much as he liked to pretend he had. But then, as it had always been: do as I say, not as I do. She watched her mother, who essentially squeezed her eyes shut and downed the potent brew as best she could, a violent shiver rushing through her once it was down.

All of this would've been amusing if there wasn't such a profound sense of foreboding hanging in the air. Looking down into her own glass, Eleanor took a deep breath, sent a silent prayer up, and squeezed her eyes shut, doing her best to down the liquid fire.

"Whoa, there." Gabby laughed, pounding her on the back as she coughed, half her drink spilling down her chin.

"This is not for wasting!" Ed bellowed, banging his fist on the table, making the dishes of their mostly eaten Christmas meal jump.

"Hey, now," Gabby said, raising a hand toward him. "Y'all calm down. This is her first real drink, and it was a doozy." He grabbed Eleanor's napkin and wiped at her mouth and chin. "That rot gut will get'cha right quick," he told her, his hand dipping down to wipe at a bit of the liquid that landed on the shirt covering her left breast.

"I've got it, thank you," she croaked, still coughing as the hooch had burned her esophagus the entire way down, plus her head was already beginning to swim. She took the napkin from him, glaring at him until he moved away from her, a smirk on his lips.

"So," Ed said, getting attention back on him. "Our friend here," he said, reaching a hand down and placing it on Gabby's shoulder, "has asked for Eleanor's hand in marriage."

Eleanor heard the words and understood the meaning, but as she sat there, her world became fuzzy, and the sound of his voice took on a strange, long-distance quality. Her father may as well have been talking to her from the next house over as the sound of her own blood rushing through her veins took over.

"And as her father and head of this household, I accepted on your behalf, Eleanor."

I don't wanna! Eleanor had no idea if she'd actually spoken. She tried to stand but found herself still in her chair.

"And as a special gift to you, Eleanor, I'm going to allow you to finish out the year in school. You'll be sixteen soon, and after a nice summer wedding, your time will be dedicated to learning how to be a good wife." He poured himself and Gabby a second drink. "Congratulations, son," he said, clinking his glass against Gabby's raised one. "And good luck," he added with a wink. "Trust me, you'll need it." The two snickered like little boys before downing their liquid fire, Gabby yelling out dramatically as the liquor hit him.

⁂

After the men had a third drink, the two grabbed the bottle and staggered out of the house, one apparently tripping down the front stairs as their laughter after the thud indicated. Eleanor had done her best to help her mother clean up, but that one drink—nearly one hundred ninety proof—had knocked her on her behind.

Taking it super slow, her mother had helped her to her bedroom. She collapsed in her bed, her pickled brain trying to wrap around the fact that it couldn't quite perform normally but also around the information it had been given to sort through.

"It's going to be okay, sweetheart," Emma said softly, tucking her in under her quilt, her own words slightly slurred. She sat on the edge of Eleanor's bed, a hand resting on her daughter's covered hip. She let out a heavy sigh and stared out the window. "He did this to us on purpose," she murmured, seemingly more to herself than Eleanor, who watched her.

"What?" Eleanor pulled her quilt higher under her chin. She felt chilled and slightly nauseated.

Emma glanced down at her, moving her hand from Eleanor's hip to brush hair out of her face. "Made us take that drink." She smirked, her hand falling into her own lap. "Can't exactly fight back when you can't think straight. Bastard." Her gaze went to the window again.

Eleanor was surprised to hear such language out of her mother's mouth regarding her father. Sure, she knew she felt that way, but they both seemed to feel his presence around constantly, no matter where he was. It was almost as if a bad or mean thought were voiced he'd know about it, somehow.

"I don't wanna marry him, Mama," Eleanor said, her voice sounding more like a young child than a young woman. "I don't want to leave school."

"I know. I know you don't, sweetheart." Emma leaned down and left a kiss to Eleanor's forehead. "Get a little rest. I'll wake you before they get back."

❧ ❧ ❧ ❧

It was two days after Christmas, and the store was open again. Eleanor had thought of nothing else other than what she was going to do to get out of the prison her father was determined to put her in. It was two days after Christmas, and she missed Lysette desperately. The Landons had gone away to visit some family in another part of the state, so they hadn't seen each other or spoken since the last day of school before the holiday break began.

She was in the store taking down some of the Christmas decorations when she was grabbed from behind. Her mouth was covered, which muffled her cry of surprise as she was tugged out of the main area of the store and into the small space at the bottom of the stairs that led to the second floor before nearly being dragged halfway up the staircase.

Pulling away, she whipped around only to go from terrified of seeing Gabby to relief at looking at a grinning Lysette. "Thank god," she almost sobbed as she pulled Lysette against her, wrapping her in a tight hug.

"Hey," Lysette said, holding a trembling Eleanor tightly for a moment before pulling away just enough to look into Eleanor's deeply troubled eyes. "What is it? I mean, god, I missed you so much, it's been a whole week, after all, but what's wrong? You look like you're about to cry." She caressed the side of Eleanor's face.

For the first time in the two days since she'd been told, she felt safe. In Lysette's presence, in her arms and seeing the affection in those beautiful endless pools of compassion and warmth, she felt the tiniest optimism that she may get through this. "I really need to talk to you," she whispered, knowing that at any moment her father or Gabby could come around the corner, either looking for her or to head upstairs for something.

Lysette nodded. "Okay. I need to talk to you, too. Can you come over tomorrow? I mean, school doesn't start for another week..."

Eleanor shook her head. "No. No way. Not now." She looked away, the tears threatening. The way her father was watching her every move now, she assumed keeping her "in check" before Gabby could take over as her owner, she knew there was no free time for her.

"Damn. Okay, um..." Lysette chewed on her bottom lip and looked at the wall, almost as if for inspiration. Suddenly, eyes wide, she looked back to Eleanor. "Sneak out tonight. I'll pick you up in my dad's car over on Overton Road. It's close enough you can easily get to but far enough they wouldn't know I was there, wouldn't hear me."

"God, I don't know," Eleanor groaned, leaning against the wall in the narrow staircase, quickly glancing down to the bottom of the stairs to make sure they were still alone before looking at the gorgeous girl no more than two feet away from her. "If they found out, it would be...I don't even want to think about that."

"They?"

"My father and Gabby."

"Oh. Look, Ellie, we don't really have a choice. I mean, you know I'll be here every single day just to see you, but we can't talk here," she said, indicating the building around them. She moved closer, her hands resting on Eleanor's hips as her body grazed hers. "Please," she whispered, pleading eyes pinning Eleanor to the spot. "Meet me."

Eleanor's eyes fell closed as she felt the soft, lingering kiss, her hands coming up to rest on Lysette's shoulders before they slid down her arms and finally rested at her waist. The kiss never deepened, but Lysette definitely left her wanting more, brushing her full bottom lip against Eleanor's before moving away, giving her a look that told Eleanor Lysette's mind was nowhere in the neighborhood of moving away from her, but they both knew she had to.

"I'll be on Overton at midnight," she whispered, leaving one last kiss on Eleanor's lips before trotting down the stairs and out of the store.

Left alone, Eleanor's body was on fire, pulsing with a need and want she didn't understand and had no clue what to do about. All she did know was Lysette was the only person who could put the fire out.

Letting out a long, shaky breath, she leaned her head back against the wall. "How on earth am I going to pull this off?" she whispered.

❧ ❧ ❧ ❧

The clock ticked, mocking Eleanor as she lay in bed, fully clothed. She'd tried to act as normal as possible that night. She'd helped her mother cook dinner and clean up. That was something new, now that Gabby staked his claim. Her father felt it was time for her to, in his words, stop acting like a child and start learning.

She rolled her eyes at the thought. She'd been offering to help her mother for years. Shoving all that aside, she lay completely still, listening to the sounds in the house. Other than the occasional snort or snore from her parents' bedroom, it was quiet. Everyone seemed to be staying put for the night.

As slowly and silently as she could, she pushed the covers off and got to her feet. She was grateful all the squeaky boards had been taken care of during the remodel, though she felt that was mainly because Gabby had done the floors. If her father had, he would have not only found a way to leave the squeaky spots, but also would have created more.

She spared a glance to her open bedroom door to make sure she was still alone before she put all the components together to create a passable dummy in her bed. She'd stuffed her nightgown with her blanket and positioned it so it looked like a body, at least in passing. Any sort of close inspection would be her undoing.

With her "body" positioned where it needed to be by her pillow, she grabbed a dark-colored knit cap, stuffing it with part of the blanket and placing it as the head. She knew it could pass as the top of her head just barely sticking out of the quilt. Everything positioned, she took a step back, looking at her handiwork objectively. With a shrug of acceptance, she grabbed her jacket and, after glancing to her doorway, shrugged into it. She'd carry her shoes with her and put them on once outside. There was no way she was going to chance the hard sole making too much noise.

Ten minutes and a million heartbeats later,

Eleanor was running in the moonlit night from the farmhouse, her heavy breathing escaping in billowing white puffs of air. It was a strange mix of feelings inside her: fear, panic, total liberation. She nearly cried in relief and excitement when she saw the slow-moving head lamps creep down Overton Road, pulling to a stop at the end of the dirt road she was running down.

"Hurry, get in before you freeze to death," Lysette hissed as she pushed open the passenger-side door from inside the car.

Eleanor nearly dove inside, slamming it shut behind her as Lysette hit the gas and got them moving off into the darkness. The only light in the car was that coming off the dash instruments, painting Lysette's features an eerie green. The two shared a look before bursting into laughter. For Eleanor, it was utter relief and shock that she'd done it at all.

"Where are we going?" she asked, watching as the car headed into the country, the houses getting farther and farther apart.

"Just out to the middle of nowhere," Lysette said, slowing the car before turning left on a random road that led toward a large stand of trees, several miles from the farmhouse. She pulled to a stop, killing the engine and lights. They were essentially in a tunnel formed by the trees, which Eleanor figured completely hid the car. "Is this okay?"

Eleanor nodded. "Yeah. Nobody should bother us here, and we can talk."

"It might get cold," Lysette said softly. "I brought a blanket, but I think it'll potentially draw attention to us if I leave the car running."

"No, it's okay. I agree." She gave her a small smile, suddenly nervous as it occurred to her that they were totally alone together. A little thrill went through her, both excitement and anxiety.

They sat awkwardly in silence for a moment before Lysette turned to her. "I'm freezing. Let's get in the back with the blanket."

Without comment, they quickly abandoned the front seat and went to the back bench seat, the large leather seat cold and slick.

"Holy moley!" Eleanor exclaimed, hugging herself from where she was huddled by the door.

Lysette chuckled, sliding over to her with the wool blanket in hand. "Well, what do you expect, silly goose, sitting all the way over there?"

They giggled as they huddled together and wrapped up in the blanket, which helped break the ice, making things far more comfortable. Eleanor was in heaven as she was in a veritable cocoon with Lysette, the world closing down to just them, a car, and a wool blanket. She could feel every inch of the right side of Lysette's body as they were pressed together side by side. She nearly sighed in happiness as Lysette adjusted her position so she was more facing Eleanor, her right arm wrapped around Eleanor's back and her head resting on her shoulder.

"Are you still covered?" Eleanor asked softly, bringing the blanket back up to cover Lysette's back where it had fallen to the seat.

"I'm good now," Lysette murmured. "I love that you let me be such an octopus with you," she said with a small laugh.

Eleanor smiled, resting her head against that resting against her shoulder. The arm that was wrapped around Lysette's body came up so her fingers could run through the cool, silky strands of her hair. "You're the only person I've ever been this way with."

"Ever?"

"Ever." Her breath hitched when Lysette's hand rested on her thigh. She could already feel a breast pressed against her side. "So what did you want to talk to me about?" Eleanor asked, needing to get her mind off of where she was being touched, as well as stalling in her own news.

"Oh!" Lysette said, lifting her head. "As you know, spring break is coming up. We're going to our house in California, and my parents and I want to take you with us."

Eleanor could see, even in the dimness of the car, the excitement in Lysette's eyes, hear the hopeful tone in her voice. She'd do anything to go, but a lie about a weekend away was one thing, an entire week was a different animal.

"There's no way. I mean, absolutely no way," she said, sorrow in her heart and sorrow in her voice.

"What could he do to you?" Lysette asked defiantly.

She met her gaze, hers deadly serious. "Kill my mother."

Lysette studied her for a long time, different expressions crossing her face. Eleanor could almost read her thoughts: *Is she joking? There's no way he'd do that. Wait, I think she's serious.*

"Lysette, he's making me leave school after this year and marry Gabby," she said, voice void of any emotion as she had none left to feel regarding that.

"What?" Lysette whispered, tears gathering in her eyes. "What? How? What did you say? Did you agree to marry him?" she gasped, moving slightly away from Eleanor.

"Of course not!" Eleanor was stung by the question, by the mere fact that Lysette could even consider that. "What options or choices do you think I have here? Do you think I like having that man in my house? Do you think I like having to duck and weave whenever I'm around him so he won't cop a feel whenever he can?" Her own tears were beginning, angry tears from so much bottled-up frustration. "I hate this! I hate my father, and I hate William Gabford! I hate the fact that the reason he's in Colorado is because he murdered two colored men in Texas, and I hate that I'm pretty sure he murdered Samuel!" Finally, the dam broke and everything she'd kept in came out with her sobs.

"Oh, Ellie," Lysette murmured, pulling Eleanor into her arms. "God, I'm so sorry." She rocked her gently, stroking her hair and back. "I wasn't thinking. I'm sorry."

The initial wave of grief, fear, and anger released, Eleanor lost herself in the comforting touch of the young woman who held her. She returned the embrace as her tears slowed then stopped.

"We'll think of something," Lysette said, looking into her eyes and brushing her hair away from tear-streaked cheeks. "I swear to you, we're going to get you out of this."

Eleanor nodded, using the edge of the blanket to wipe at her eyes. "Yeah," she murmured, feeling hopeless.

"Ellie, look at me." Lysette waited until Eleanor met her intense gaze. "I need you to believe me. We'll make a plan."

Chapter Nineteen

Eleanor let out a heavy sigh, tired. For the tenth morning in a row, she was forced to get up at three thirty to get laundry started, then switch over to help her mother with breakfast. Laundry was something her mother used to do during the day while everyone was at the store or school, but Eleanor was now forced to scrub the farmhouse down to Ed's approval. After that, she would be painting the entire inside, in his words "getting it ready for a nice May wedding."

The painting had been skipped in haste of moving back in the house after the flood the previous August. Though it did need to be done, Eleanor was positive all this was nothing more than busy work for her and her mom. She was still going to school, and she was still working at the store, though now she was closing the store nightly, which got her home between six thirty and seven thirty—depending if she got a ride home or not—then she had to get any homework done, eat leftover dinner, and clean it all up. She'd drag herself to bed and start all over the next morning.

Her saving grace had been seeing Lysette at school. They'd only been back for a few days, but the times they were able to steal away to the bathroom for a lingering hug or when Lysette would steal a kiss or a look across the hall, it made it all okay for just a moment.

"Eleanor."

Yanked out of her thoughts, she turned from where she was cutting up vegetables, amazed she hadn't lost a finger yet. She met her mother's gaze from where she stood at the stove, frying bacon. "What?"

"I need you to take a look at this recipe," Emma said, indicating the recipe card on the counter near her with a nod.

Eleanor's eyebrows drew, and irritation born of exhaustion reared its head; the attitude was evident in Eleanor's voice. "Mama, I've made this same darn breakfast every single—"

"Eleanor, I need you to read this recipe," Emma said again, her tone more forceful. The look in her eyes told Eleanor there was no room for argument.

"Okay," Eleanor blew out, setting her knife down and accepting the card her mother pulled out of her apron pocket, which confused her. She glanced from the recipe card in her hand to that on the counter and to her mother's eyes.

Her mind foggy to add to her confusion, she looked down at the card she held in her hands, surprised to see a handwritten message on it:

Give this note to your school principal, then come home with Lysette.

She studied her mother's face for a long moment but said nothing as the card was taken out of her fingers and replaced with a folded piece of paper. She figured it was the note, so she shoved it into the pocket of her skirt and watched as her mother left the room for a moment, returning without the card. She figured she'd likely set it aflame in the fireplace.

"What's going on?" Eleanor hissed as she was nearly pulled off her feet out the front door of the school, Lysette leading the way holding her hand.

"We've got a meeting," Lysette said, dropping Eleanor's hand only when they'd reached her father's car, which she climbed behind the wheel of.

Eleanor stood outside the passenger-side door, looking around. "Um, Lysette, you're not old enough to drive."

Lysette snickered from inside as she got the car started. "Who's going to arrest me?"

Eleanor considered that for a moment, then shrugged. "True." She climbed inside and closed the door. Realizing they hadn't moved, she glanced over at Lysette. "What?"

Lysette looked at her with such pure, unguarded affection that it made Eleanor's heart skip a beat. She reached across the seat and took Eleanor's hand in hers for a moment.

"I guess I just really want you to know that… that…" Lysette's gaze dropped to the steering wheel, and she let out a soft breath. "Just that I'm here. Always." She squeezed Eleanor's fingers before releasing them and getting the car moving.

Eleanor studied her profile in the light of the morning and was struck all over again by how beautiful Lysette was. Yes, her figure was stunning, features flawless, all the things that had caught Eleanor's attention and fancy in the first place. But now, many months later, it was so much more. The heart she possessed, so filled with seemingly unending compassion and understanding. Her endless curiosity kept Eleanor on her toes, and the passion that lived in those breath-stealing eyes, well, that nearly felled Eleanor to her knees.

So much of what she felt for Lysette, she didn't fully understand nor did she have a word for it all, but she knew it was growing by the moment. Every minute spent with her, every look and every touch drew her in further, deeper. She was a prisoner to Lysette's whim, and she wondered if that would always be.

The car pulled up in front of the farmhouse where Davis Landon's pickup was already parked. Eleanor felt her stomach roil in uncertainty and fear. If her father or Gabby were to drop by the house for any reason, their ship would collectively be sunk, and she had no idea what was even going on.

"Hey."

Eleanor turned to see Lysette looking over at her, the engine turned off and keys in the hand that rested on the seat.

"It's going to be okay," Lysette said, giving her a small smile. "Believe me, okay? Don't be so worried. You're far too beautiful to have such a frown." She caressed Eleanor's cheek with the backs of her fingers. "Come on."

Together they mounted the stairs and entered the farmhouse, the warmth of a healthy fire in the fireplace meeting them, as well as the smell of freshly brewed coffee and coffee cake.

"Mama?" Eleanor called out, shrugging out of her jacket, as did Lysette, in the entryway.

"In here, honey," Emma called out from the direction of the kitchen.

The two headed in there where Emma, Davis, and Adalyn sat around the table, mugs in hand and plates waiting to be filled with the sweet confection.

"Girls, there's boiled water for hot cocoa if you want it, or you can have coffee, your choice," Emma said from where she sat.

Eleanor glanced at the two mugs waiting on the counter, then at Lysette, who gave her a little wink before grabbing her mug and heading to the coffee. Eleanor smiled and shook her head before following suit.

Minutes later, everyone was settled, and Eleanor looked around the table, feeling like she was the only one out of the loop. Hands resting around her mug of untouched coffee, she said to nobody in particular, "So what's going on?"

"Lysette told us everything that's happening, and from what I've heard around town, that Kluxer is beyond bad news," Davis began, accepting the plate with a piece of coffee cake served on it from Emma with a smile of thanks. "There's no way in hell we can allow this, Eleanor, you being forced to marry that son of a bitch."

"Kluxer?" Eleanor asked, handing out the forks from the small pile on the table.

"Damn straight. Word has it William Gabford is part of that Ku Klux Klan nonsense, and he's brought it with him to Brooke View."

Eleanor looked down at the milky depths of her coffee before taking a deep breath and looking over at Lysette's father. "I saw them, in the woods. They had horrible robes on and silly-looking hoods with points." She felt all eyes at the table on her. She met her mother's gaze.

"Why didn't you tell me?" Emma asked.

"How could I, Mama? He watches everything we do, listens to everything we say."

Emma reached over and gently squeezed Eleanor's arm before releasing it. "Did you tell your father?"

Eleanor looked down in shame. "He was there, with Gabby."

Emma's hand came up to clasp in front of her mouth, elbows resting on the table. She said nothing as Adalyn rubbed her back in comforting circles.

"And," Davis said softly, "you know he killed some black men?" he asked Eleanor. "Gabford?"

Eleanor nodded. "That's what he was bragging to his friend Thomas. I don't know if he was telling the truth or not, but he said he…" She looked away, bothered by what she was about to say since the day she'd heard him say it. "He said he 'strung them up.' The sheriff let him go as long as he left Texas."

Davis said nothing for a moment as he sipped his coffee, fingers of the hand not holding the mug tapping lightly on the tabletop. Finally, he spoke, setting the mug down. "I've heard some say Ed has changed. He's said some pretty offensive things in the store within earshot of some customers."

"And Samuel," Adalyn whispered, tears in her eyes.

Lysette hopped up from her seat between her father and Eleanor and hurried around the table to her mother, hugging her, silent tears running down her own cheeks.

Eleanor watched, wanting so much to be holding Lysette. Since Samuel's disappearance and ultimately finding his body just before Thanksgiving, they hadn't spoken about him. She figured it was too painful for Lysette, and for her, in truth, she was deeply ashamed. She'd always suspected that Gabby at least had a hand in it or had information about it. Now for it to come out into the light of a beautiful, cool January day, it hurt.

A moment of silence lasted for several minutes before Lysette released the embrace of her mother but stood behind her, hands on her shoulders. "Daddy, tell them what the plan is."

"Yes, here's what we're thinking," he said, accepting a kiss to the cheek from Lysette as she passed him on her way back to her seat. "As a family, we've been looking at a private school in Paris for her to finish out her high school years. Lysette's Aunt Brigitte runs a fashion design program that she's been wanting to be part of for a while now."

Eleanor felt the blood drain out of her face at the mention of losing Lysette to some French private school. She wanted to scream, then she wanted to cry. She was on the verge of doing both when Davis continued.

"I sent a letter to Brigitte after we heard all this," Adalyn said, indicating Davis and herself. "We heard back." She pulled a letter out of her purse, sliding it across the table to Emma, who took it and unfolded it.

Emma read in silence, Eleanor watching, stomach churning. She looked to Lysette, who was grinning like the Cheshire cat. "What's going on?" she asked her quietly.

"Oh, Eleanor," Emma whispered, a hand reaching out to grab her hand. "Oh, honey."

"What?" Eleanor asked, looking to the Landons. "What's going on?"

"Davis, I could never in a million years pay this tuition," Emma said, her entire soul seeming to deflate as she refolded the letter and set it back in front of

Adalyn. "I couldn't clean enough houses in a lifetime to afford one year."

Adalyn grabbed both her hands in hers on the tabletop. "No, Emmaline. Our gift to little Eleanor and to you."

"No, I could never—"

"Will someone please tell me what's going on?" Eleanor exclaimed wide-eyed, looking at everyone, *any*one.

"Honey," Emma said, reaching out to caress her cheek. "They want to send you to the same school in Paris with Lysette. You've already been accepted for next year."

"There's more, Emma," Davis said. "I told Brigitte about your incredible sewing skills, and she wants to bring you on, too, to help with preparation and things for the students' designs, outfits, whatnot."

Eleanor and her mother both looked to him. "Wait, are you saying you could get Mama out of this?" she asked, barely able to breathe, praying she'd heard and understood right. "That you could get her away from this monster?" she added, indicating the house around them and all that it represented.

Davis nodded. "Yup." He turned his gaze to Emma, his eyes seeming so full of profound sadness. "Emma," he said softly, "I let you down the first time." He ran a hand through his short hair as he looked away for a moment. "We all thought you were in the clear after Earl died, and we never thought that Ed would do what he did. And, well, Josie and I really let you down." He finally looked at her, his expression pained. "I know Josie has never forgiven herself for that, and now that I can try and get you out of this, I'll do everything I can."

"Mama," Eleanor breathed, all the information

they'd just been given beginning to sink in. "You could have your own life! We could start over."

Emma gathered her in her arms and held her almost painfully tight, mother and daughter crying together. She pulled away just enough to look into Eleanor's face. "Yes?" she asked her softly. "I'm only doing this with you. Are we in?"

Eleanor laughed through her tears. "Yes, we're in!"

Davis grinned. "That son of a bitch will never find you there."

Chapter Twenty

"Don't forget to pick up your ribbons, boys," Mrs. Hall called out to the class as they gathered their belongings to head to their next destination. "Let your date for the dance next Friday night wear hers proudly!"

Lysette glanced over at Karl, who sat two rows over and was already looking at her. She gave him a smile and small nod, raising her arm to reveal the pink satin tied around it. He brought up a hand to pantomime wiping sweat off his brow, making her laugh.

"I really appreciate it, Lys," he muttered, stepping up to her as he hugged his textbooks to his side. "The guys'll leave me alone now."

She grinned. "Of course they will, thinking you're going with me," she said with sugary sweetness, twisting the pink ribbon from side to side, making sure he saw the part that had his name scrolled in black ink. He smirked. "I have to say, though, I feel like a branded cow."

A bark of laughter erupted from his throat as he placed an arm around her shoulders. "You know, you really should find a fella to take you to the spring dance."

She scrunched her nose up and shook her head, waving off the suggestion. "I have no desire to go. Besides," she added with a little grin as they left the classroom to the chaos of the hallway. "I have plans. See ya!"

"Do I get to hear about him?" Karl called out from where he still stood outside the classroom.

She turned, walking backward as she called back, "Nope." With a giggle, she turned and hurried on to her next class.

It was March, and Lysette's world was a glorious place. With the end of the school year coming in two and a half months, they were already beginning to sort through things, clothing and such that wouldn't do in France. Unbeknownst to Eleanor and Emma, she and her mother were also gathering a whole new wardrobe for them and a collection of books that Lysette knew Ellie would love to lose herself in during the more than week's journey on the passenger ship they'd be catching out of New York, that is, after the train ride to get there.

As she made her way toward the hallway where Eleanor's locker was, she started as a huge clap of thunder rocked the entire building. The clouds had been gray and pregnant all day, and she'd wondered when the storm was finally going to break.

"Good lord," she gasped, hand to her chest before smiling at her own reaction. She continued on, though she quickened her steps as the sky opened up and the rain fell, pounding on the school roof, echoes of thunder joining in.

She considered stopping at her own locker first, as it was closer, to grab her jacket, but her time was limited with Eleanor as she had to hurry from the school to the store, her father timing her. It gave her such a feeling of peace to know she was going to take the person who had come to mean more to her than anyone away from the hell she was being forced into. To know that somehow she'd won Eleanor's trust and, she hoped, far more.

She greeted a few people who waved or said hello, but her focus was fully on the beautiful girl standing in front of locker twenty-seven. She was looking into the small mirror Lysette had brought for her to mount on the top shelf to make sure her appearance was, as Eleanor called it, "Ed ready." She was buttoning her white blouse to the top and straightening the rounded collar before shrugging into her jacket. She'd already pulled her hair up into a bun before Lysette had reached her. After months of trying, she'd finally gotten Eleanor to take her hair down during the day at school.

As she got closer, she studied Eleanor's profile, taking in the gentle slope of her neck the tight bun revealed. The feminine curve of her forehead and nose caught her eye, as well. She loved the slightly heavy, yet still feminine dark eyebrows that arched slightly over her gorgeous and deeply expressive violet eyes. Such an unusual color but somehow so perfect for Eleanor's brand of beauty.

What she loved most, however, were Eleanor's lips. They were full and soft, a bit pouty in their natural shape, yet could transform into the most magnificent smile, which was aimed at her in that moment.

"Hey," she said. "Rain's really coming down."

"I know," Lysette said, stepping up to her. "Do you want us to give you a ride to work?"

Eleanor let out a heavy sigh, stuffing her school bag full of her textbooks and notebook before slamming her locker closed. "'Want' and 'can,' unfortunately, are two different things." Her gaze fell to Lysette's wrist before it flicked up to Lysette's eyes, anger flashing in their violet depths before she turned and stormed away, quickly getting eaten up by the crowded hallway.

"Ellie!"

Stunned by her reaction to something she knew she'd mentioned that she was going to do, Lysette took off after her as best she could. She spotted her near the doors and was making headway when a group of boys stepped in front of her. She shoved one aside and plowed between two who were in deep conversation and was finally free of the throngs of fellow students.

Pushing the door open, she saw Eleanor hurrying down the walkway leading to the sidewalk. "Ellie!"

Taking off again, she managed to catch up to her, the rain coming down in torrents. It didn't take long before Lysette's hair and blouse were plastered to her skin. She didn't care as she reached Eleanor and grasped her shoulder to stop her.

"Hey, stop. Ellie."

Eleanor stopped and turned, her eyes hard, jaw pensive. She said nothing.

"Hey, what's wrong? What did I do?" Lysette asked, brushing some of her soaked hair out of her eyes.

"You said you weren't going," Eleanor said, her voice angry and hurt.

"I'm not," Lysette responded, baffled.

"Then why are you wearing someone else's ribbon?" Eleanor exclaimed, grabbing Lysette's hand and bringing it up, the ribbon darkening from a light pink to nearly mauve as the rain hit it.

"Ellie," Lysette began, but paused as a couple of their classmates walked by.

She gave them a quick smile before grabbing Eleanor's hand and tugging her over to the side of the building where there was a small supply shed. She knew some of the kids ducked over there to smoke a cigarette during lunch, so she knew they were hidden.

"Ellie," she began again, "I told you Karl had asked me to accept his ribbon so he wouldn't have to go but wouldn't take guff from his buddies for it." She took a slight step forward and lowered her voice. "If there was a way I could wear your ribbon, I absolutely would." She looked deeply into Eleanor's eyes. "Don't you know that by now?" She reached out and tugged playfully on one of Eleanor's pinky fingers. "You don't need to be jealous."

"I'm not jealous," Eleanor muttered stubbornly, making Lysette smile and her heart fill almost to the point of bursting.

"Whatever you say, dear." Lysette chuckled, amused as she didn't know how many times she'd heard her father lovingly say that to her mother. "Are you still wanting to go out tonight for driving lessons?" she asked, brushing her hair out of her eyes again as the rain continued to pound down on them. "We've got to make sure you're proficient to get you and your mama to the train station."

Eleanor's dark mood seemed to break as a smile spread across her lips, bringing the sun with it. "Yes. I'll do my best."

"Okay." Lysette looked around and, sure they weren't seen, placed a quick kiss on Eleanor's lips before scurrying away.

❧❧❧❧

Lysette grinned, watching as Eleanor white-knuckled it all the way down the bumpy lane. In fairness, the rains had caused horrible holes and ruts in the dirt roads, and Eleanor was navigating them as best she could.

"How do you feel?" Lysette asked, a hand reaching out to brace against the side of the door as Eleanor slowed the car to crawl over another set of ruts in the road.

"I feel like your poor father is going to be angry because his car is so out of alignment," Eleanor said, never taking her eyes off the road.

Lysette chuckled. "Let's call it a night on the driving."

With a nod, Eleanor pulled the car to the side of the road, and the girls giggled as Eleanor slid across the front seat toward the passenger side while Lysette held herself up to climb over her.

Finally settled behind the wheel, Lysette felt her heart race a bit as she was going to move on to the next part of her plan for the night. She met Eleanor's gaze across the cab of the car. "Want to go home?" she asked, giving Eleanor the option, as she knew her friend was being run ragged.

Eleanor said nothing, simply shook her head slowly, never taking her eyes off Lysette.

"Good," Lysette said softly, getting the car moving again. She headed to the main road that would take them away from the rural area where they'd been practicing Eleanor's driving and toward town.

"Where are we going?" Eleanor asked, looking around.

"You'll see."

Less than ten minutes later, Lysette pulled the car into town, which was dark and quiet, the light from the head lamps shining on the building as she drove around to the back.

"Lysette, this is my dad's *store*!" Eleanor hissed.

Lysette grinned as she parked the car and cut the engine. "Yes, and it's also my father's *building*." She glanced over at her passenger. "Come on."

Being as quiet as they could, the two went into the main entrance of the building through the back, which led up the narrow staircase and to the scattered rooms, used for storage, as with the Landry store or as apartments, such as where Ed and Emma stayed during the renovation of the farmhouse. Lysette led them to that same uninhabited apartment.

Unlocking the door with the keys she'd snagged from the keyboard in the mud room, Lysette pushed it open, allowing Eleanor to enter before she followed and closed and locked it behind them. It was a little different than the last time she'd seen the tiny space. Last time, it had been rented by a traveling salesman who'd gotten drunk one night and trashed it. Now it had a single bed pushed against the wall with a folded blanket at the end and a pillow resting atop it. There was a small kitchenette area across from that and a window.

"It's chilly in here," Eleanor said quietly, glancing out the window before turning her back to the kitchenette and leaning her back against the small square of preparation countertop. She shoved her hands into the pockets of her jacket.

"Take your jacket off and stay awhile," Lysette suggested, shrugging out of her own jacket and tossing it across the radiator, which wasn't working. She moved the pillow to the head of the bed and plopped down on the mattress on her side.

"Um, what part of 'it's chilly in here' would

be made better by my shedding my jacket?" Eleanor muttered, raising an eyebrow.

Lysette smiled invitingly as she patted the mattress next to her. As Eleanor unbuttoned her jacket and let it slide down her arms, Lysette sat up and reached for the blanket, giving it a violent shake to spread it out and pull it over her as she lay back down on her side. She took the end of it and lifted it in invitation to Eleanor, who made her way to the bed, looking shy.

Eleanor lowered herself to the small bed and adjusted her position to lie on her back, her entire right side pressed against Lysette's front, Lysette's behind and back against the cold, plaster wall.

Lysette rested her elbow into the mattress between the pillow and the wall and cradled her head in it. Smiling down at Eleanor, she brought the blanket up to cover her, tucking the scratchy wool up near Eleanor's chin. Beneath the blanket, her hand rested on her shoulder for a moment before it slowly, deliberately slid downward, fingers grazing Eleanor's left breast. The rounded firmness and the soft gasp that resulted from Eleanor's lips sent a fiery jolt shooting down Lysette's body.

Resting her hand on Eleanor's side—her thumb dangerously close to the rounded side of the breast— she smiled. "Warmer?"

Eleanor swallowed and gave her a small nod. "Getting there."

Lysette smiled at that, her thumb caressing the warm flesh covered by the plain white button-up blouse.

"So," Eleanor said, her voice filled with the nerves that shone in her eyes. "Since we're here, shall we practice?"

Lysette gave her a soft smile, her hand moving up over that breast again to rest on the side of her face. "No," she whispered, shaking her head. She saw the uncertainty in those beautiful eyes from the moonlight that filtered into the otherwise dark room. "No more practice."

She leaned down, the first kiss soft and almost chaste, but she felt it was different. There was no hesitation, no need to seek permission nor to give it. In that moment, it was their time to share, it was their time.

The kiss deepened as Eleanor's hand reached up, fingers burying in Lysette's hair, lightly tugging her closer. Lysette lowered herself to her forearm, her right breast pressed into Eleanor's as her hand once again found the left breast.

Lysette was on fire as she heard and felt the soft whimper that escaped into their kiss as she squeezed the breast encased in a bra. She'd caught herself staring at Eleanor's beautiful body so many times, and she wanted to see her. She wasn't sure if she'd be allowed, but she had to try.

Pulling away from the kiss, Lysette brought up a hand and began to work the buttons on Eleanor's blouse. There was a soft gasp as realization dawned on Eleanor, but she didn't stop her. She let out a slow, shaky breath as pale flesh was revealed a button at a time.

"Wow," she whispered, tracing her fingertips over her throat as Eleanor swallowed, lightly touching the hollow of her throat before continuing down into her cleavage.

She'd never touched another female before so intimately. She'd never touched *anyone* so intimately.

She was mesmerized by what she was looking at, what she was feeling.

"So soft," she whispered.

She unbuttoned the blouse farther until the soft, milky flesh of Eleanor's bra-cupped breasts were fully exposed. She felt a thrill shoot through her when she saw that her nipples were hard, pressing against the stiff material. She could see how Eleanor's chest was heaving slightly, and a look into her eyes told her it was from arousal, not fear.

Leaning down, she initiated a slow, deep kiss as her fingers found one of those erect nipples, lightly pinching and tugging. She marveled at the soft sighs and moans that elicited from Eleanor, beautiful noises and reactions that Lysette ate up in their kiss.

She wanted more.

Breaking the kiss again, Lysette sat up and pulled Eleanor into a sitting position. They shared another shorter kiss as she finished unbuttoning the blouse and pushed it off smooth shoulders before tossing it aside. She reached around Eleanor's slim figure to unclasp the bra at her back, it too tossed over the side of the bed.

Lysette stared at what was revealed, awed. She brought her hands up and ran them over the soft skin covering defined collarbones, Eleanor a bit thin for her height. They followed the hungry trail of her eyes to the fully exposed breasts, cupping them, sampling their weight and firmness.

As Lysette was about to push Eleanor back to the mattress to explore, she was stopped with a hand to her chest. She met Eleanor's gaze, worried she'd taken things too far, but the look Eleanor gave her told her that wasn't the problem.

"Wait," Eleanor said softly, her hand sliding down from Lysette's upper chest to lightly tug on the rounded neckline of her dress.

Getting the hint, Lysette took a deep breath before moving to her knees, gathering the material of the flowing skirt of her dress in her hands before easing the entire garment up and over her head, leaving her in only her panties and bra. She shook her head to get her hair back into some semblance of order as the dress joined the other garments on the floor.

Kneeling there, mostly naked in front of a non-family member for the first time in her life, Lysette thought she'd feel shame or embarrassment or even nervous. But as she looked deeply into Eleanor's eyes, she knew she had no need to feel any of those things. In fact, she could see a deep curiosity and want, yet she knew Eleanor was scared and wouldn't act on any of the desires she may have had.

She lowered herself so she was sitting on her feet and grabbed Eleanor's trembling hands, bringing them around to the clasp of her bra. She had no idea what she was doing as she waited for the bra to disappear, but she allowed her instinct to guide her. In some ways, Eleanor's fear-based hesitation helped her, as it eased her own uncertainty and fears in taking the lead.

Finally, the clasp was successfully unhooked, and the bra was tossed aside. She grabbed Eleanor's hands again and placed them on her own breasts, breath hitching at the sharp pleasure that lanced through her as her nipples came into contact with the lightly calloused palms of a young woman who worked hard every day.

"It's okay," she said, squeezing Eleanor's hands before releasing them. "You can touch me, Ellie."

She watched, fascinated by the sharp contrast of Eleanor's tanned hands against the pale flesh of her breasts as Eleanor cupped her, watching her own hands explore Lysette's softness.

Lysette gasped in surprise, then moaned in pleasure when Eleanor leaned forward and, though slightly hesitant, swiped at one of her light pink nipples with her tongue. She'd never felt anything like it, and her eyes slid closed as her head fell back. Her hand wrapped around the back of Eleanor's head, urging her in closer, which brought a whole new sensation as her nipple was sucked into the depths of Eleanor's mouth.

She felt faint as her heart was racing so fast, speeding blood to all sorts of places that were new and exciting. In a moment of instinct, she grabbed Eleanor and brought her up so she could take her in a deeply passionate, almost possessive kiss that was open-mouthed, sloppy, and wet in her desperation to exert dominance in that moment, as well as express her deep arousal.

Lysette pushed Eleanor back to the mattress and followed. They both moaned at the feel of their naked breasts pressing together as Lysette lay on top of her. Their kiss continued as Eleanor's hands caressed Lysette's naked back, one of Lysette's hands beginning to do a bit of its own exploration.

Lysette broke away from the kiss and explored a soft, warm neck with her mouth as her hand slid down Eleanor's side, over her hip, and finally to a thigh. Her fingers flirted with the material of Eleanor's skirt, tugging experimentally to pull it up. When a hand reached down and covered hers, she stopped.

Lysette left a little kiss of apology where she was exploring on the side of Eleanor's neck, her hand moving away. She knew they had plenty of time for more. It was a single night of many.

She did, however, realize that part of Eleanor's skirt had been pushed aside when they'd lain down after removing some clothing. Needing to touch as much bare flesh as she could, she adjusted herself a bit and tucked her thigh between the legs of Eleanor, who responded in kind, moving slightly to give her more room. This made them both gasp as saturated need pressed against a thigh.

Lysette's eyes flew open at the surge of sensation that shot through her, Eleanor's reaction similar. They stared at each other for a moment before she lowered herself fully atop Eleanor, breasts pressed together as she moved her hips, slowly grinding against the firm thigh pressed to her, Eleanor doing the same.

Lysette wanted to kiss her, but they were both breathing entirely too hard, their moans and heavy breathing shared in a single space as they held on to each other, hips working together to bring them to an explosion of pleasure, which drew a loud cry from Lysette. She felt Eleanor stiffen beneath her, holding on to her in a painful grip, like an iron vise. As the waves of pleasure continued, she buried her face in Eleanor's neck, her own heavy breathing blown back at her as she pressed as hard against Eleanor as she could, milking out every sensation she could.

Finally, she lifted her head, chest still heaving as she tried to get herself under control. She met Eleanor's flushed face, smiling at the look of wonder she found there. She left a lingering kiss on slightly opened lips.

"I love you, Ellie," she whispered against them. "I really do."

Eleanor hugged her tightly. "I love you, too."

Exhausted—and surprisingly sore—Lysette climbed out of her father's car at the curb in front of the school. "Thanks, Daddy."

"No problem, Princess," he called out. "Don't forget we've got Michael's school project to work on tonight. You promised," he added, pointing a finger at her.

"Yeah, yeah," she said, playfully rolling her eyes at him. "Love you."

Slamming the car door shut, she looked around for the only face she'd wanted to see all morning. Eleanor wasn't standing by the huge cottonwood tree where she often was, so she looked to the flagpole. Nothing.

"Hey, Lysette."

She turned to see a boy she thought was named Jethro Howell. She knew he was a neighbor of the Landry family. "Hi."

"Um," he said, fidgeting slightly. "Um, I was told to give this to you." He handed her a folded note, then scurried off, face pink from a hot blush.

She smiled at the freshman before turning her attention to the note. Little did she know, the moment she read the hurriedly scrawled words, a clock began to run, ticking down the hours, minutes, and seconds that would change her life forever.

She turned, frantic to see if her father was still there.

"Oh, god," she gasped as he pulled away from the curb.

Running over to his car, the very car she'd taken

Eleanor driving in the night before, she pounded on the first window she could reach, which was the back passenger one. He screeched to a stop.

"Good lord, Lysette!" he bellowed when she yanked open the front passenger door. "Scared the bejesus out of—" He stopped when she shoved the note into his hands, getting herself settled into the seat she'd vacated moments before.

Without a word, he squealed the car away from the curb and roared into traffic.

❧❧❧❧

"Only pack what you think you're going to need!" Adalyn called out from the bedroom she shared with Davis. "We can replace whatever you forget in New York or France."

Heart racing, Lysette didn't hear her mother. Instead, she saw Eleanor's face again and again in her mind's eyes. She saw her smiling, saw her laughing, and she saw her in sensual bliss. The tears wouldn't stop falling as she packed the single suitcase she said she could take. They had no time for more.

Her father had dropped her off at the house, then had taken off again, to "arrange things." Now an hour later, she heard his voice on the first floor talking to another man whose voice she recognized as Alan Manning, one his many business associates.

"Landon family!" he bellowed. "Five minutes! Let's go!"

❧❧❧❧

Almost two hours later, Lysette sat on a bench

between her mother and little brother Teddy. They sat in the depot of the train station, passengers coming and going as the mighty beasts eased in or chugged their way out, howling their retreat into the Denver morning.

Lysette's leg bobbed nervously as she chewed on her lower lip. Her father was pacing while Adalyn sketched an elderly couple sitting across the way. "Daddy?"

Davis stopped pacing just long enough to glance at her. "What?"

"When do we board?"

He reached into his pocket and pulled out a pocket watch. "Train is scheduled to leave in thirty minutes, so anytime, I'd wager." He let out a heavy sigh as he pocketed the gold piece.

As if on cue, the boarding of the ten a.m. passenger train to New York would commence forthwith.

"Okay, everyone," he said, clapping his hands together to get his family's attention. "Let's go."

Lysette looked around frantically, silently praying, *begging* to see them running through the train station, running late. There was nobody, just an endless sea of strangers. That is, until she saw Mr. Manning.

"Daddy," she said, tapping his arm to get his attention.

As Davis was gathering luggage to take over to the men to load, he glanced over to where Lysette was indicating. "Here," he said, handing her their tickets. "Be right back."

She held the papers in her hand, looking down at them, all seven of them, before glancing back to the two men. Alan had yanked his fedora off and ran a hand through his greased blond hair as he gesticulated wildly, her father listening, fingers stroking his chin. Finally, Davis placed a hand on the man's shoulder and said something to him, Alan nodding.

The two men walked over to the family, Lysette almost feeling as though she would cry. Something was wrong, very, very wrong. It was written all over her father's face.

"My love," he said softly to Adalyn, who stood not far from Lysette. "Alan is going to escort you and the kids to New York. I'll meet you there." He gave her a tight hug and kiss.

"Daddy, wait," Lysette said, reaching for his arm to stop him. "What is it?" she asked, words soft yet serious. "Let me go with you."

He gave her a sad smile and briefly cupped her cheek. "Help your *maman*," he said. "See you in a few days."

She watched him go, wanting to scream and cry, throw a fit like a child, and demand he take her with him and tell her what was happening.

"Come, *ma fille chérie*," Adalyn said, touching Lysette's shoulder. "We have to go now."

Tears in her eyes, Lysette felt like she'd fallen down a rabbit hole, as though reality weren't really reality but a giant mass of confusion.

"Come," Adalyn said again, taking Lysette's hand and tugging her away from the darkness she felt nipping at her heels.

Chapter Twenty-one

Y ou know, I have to say…" Lysette grinned as she tossed her empty popcorn bag into the trash on the way out of the theater. "I really enjoyed that movie. I haven't seen it since it first came out, what, four or so years ago?"

Eleanor nodded, hands tucked into the pockets of her capris. "Yeah, I think it came out in fifty-two, so about that, yeah."

Lysette glanced up at the marquee above the sign. "*Singin' in the Rain*," she read. "I'll be singing those damn songs for the next week, though."

Eleanor grinned. "Well, June at the box office told me they're bringing back some of the older movies. I think *An American in Paris* is coming soon, too."

"I missed that one." Lysette glanced at Eleanor before looking out into the street, Saturday afternoon traffic light. "Well," she said finally, once again sparing a glance at the woman who stood a few feet away. "I suppose I should go." The truth was, she didn't want to, even if she was hesitant to admit that to herself.

"Okay. I'm glad we 'bumped' into each other in there again," Eleanor said, using air quotes, grinning.

Lysette gave her a devilish grin. "You should be so lucky." With a dramatic flick of her head, she turned and headed toward her car, smiling to herself. It felt good to be a bit casual for a moment.

"Hey, Lysette."

Standing at the driver's door of her car, Lysette glanced back to Eleanor, who still stood on the sidewalk. "Yes?"

"Same time next week?"

"I'll be here." Her smile grew at Eleanor's laughter as she climbed in behind the wheel. She glanced into her side mirror, noting that Eleanor had walked away in the opposite direction, seeming to be doing a bit of window shopping. Eleanor stopped and stepped closer to a business that Lysette couldn't quite make out before she entered the shop. For a moment, just one moment, she considered following. She could claim a coincidence or that she simply needed something within the same shop. It wouldn't be hard to find something inside to buy, no doubt.

"Stop it," she whispered, inserting the key into the ignition of her car. She got it started and, checking to see if it was clear, pulled away from the curb and merged into traffic.

She considered the last two hours she'd spent sitting in a dark movie theater munching on a bag of incredibly fattening buttered popcorn and chatting with Eleanor about the picture they were watching and the gossip about some of the actors in it. The theater had been barren, only a handful of people in there with them.

The truth was, the first time she'd shown up three weeks before had been to offer silent comfort as the situation with the shooting of Scott O'Shea and Ronnie Washington had affected Eleanor deeply. How could it not? Scott was a close friend and colleague and, she suspected, the two used each other as very convenient "significant others" to stave off unwanted questions and assumptions.

Wasn't that essentially what Jim represented? The glorified version?

She reached to turn the radio on, hoping music would help clear her head. She rolled her eyes when *Don't Be Cruel* blared through the speaker. Turning the volume down, she made her way through town.

Three weeks earlier, she'd been in the office working on the books, as she had been for weeks now and had once again spotted Eleanor walking up to the box office. She was alone, that blonde who Lysette had seen her with before the holidays not with her. She'd watched her buy her ticket, she'd watched her stand outside for a moment and lean against the building, almost as though Eleanor had been trying to get her emotions under control. For a few moments, Lysette thought she'd been crying.

Once Eleanor disappeared inside the theater, Lysette had packed it up and decided to go in. Almost as though on autopilot, her mind turned off and her compassion turned on. No, they were not friends anymore, no they were not connected anymore. But yes, Lysette could care and could try to be there for her, even if it was with a bag of popcorn.

It was a beautiful day as spring was making its presence known. Trees were beginning to blossom and flowers to bloom. It was a favorite time of the year for her, enjoying time outdoors in her garden and flowerbeds. She and Aunt Josie would work side by side for hours in spring and summer.

Pulling up to the house, she saw that Jim hadn't returned from his afternoon with the kids. He tried once a month to spend time with them, be it with ice cream and roller skating or lunch and horseback riding, as it had been that afternoon.

Parking her car where she always did, Lysette shut it off and climbed out, heading into the house. "Aunt Josie, I'm home," she called out, not sure if she was back from her own Saturday outings.

Hearing nothing, she assumed she was alone in the house, so she headed to the bedroom to change her clothes. It was then she noticed a note resting on her side of the bed. Unbuttoning her blouse as she walked over to it, she picked it up and read.

"Horse-riding ribbons it is," she murmured, crumbling the note and taking it with her to the master bathroom to toss it into the trash there.

She studied her reflection as she brushed her hair out, noting the small crinkle that appeared between her eyes when she was troubled by something. She raised her eyebrows and made ridiculous faces to try to get rid of that crinkle, but it remained, as her internal troubles remained.

Feeling annoyed, frustrated, and generally discontent with so many things in her life, she pushed it all aside and went back to what made sense: being a mother and doing for her children.

❧❧❧❧

Heading up to the attic, Lysette tugged on the chain that would switch on the naked light bulb. She easily spotted her hope chest where she knew Bronte's ribbons had been stowed for the move. Her daughter was a lover of all things horse and pretty much all things nature and animal in general. They'd had her in a riding program in California but had yet to find a decent one in Woodland.

She lowered herself to her knees and took hold

of the underlip of the cedar chest that her parents had given her when she'd returned from Europe. It had once been something that held all her deepest, darkest secrets, hopes, and desires, those that had yet to be fulfilled and those that had been shattered, leaving a trail of tears and confusion in their wake.

Over time, after agreeing to marry Jim and becoming a mother, the hope chest had taken on a new purpose, new meaning. It became that which kept the proof of expectation: baby pictures, wedding album, the veil Jim insisted she keep, and the bronzed shoe that each of her children took their first steps in. It had become a hope chest for others' hopes, for others' dreams.

"Okay," she breathed, moving things aside to find the specific box she remembered placing the ribbons in so they'd remain together and undamaged.

She'd dug through the chest the previous fall to find the pictures Jimmy needed for his family tree project. The photo album she'd hastily stuffed the pictures back into after he'd removed them from the sugar board lay on top. She moved to sit on the dusty floor, placing the photo album on her lap to place the photos back properly so they didn't fall out and get lost or damaged.

Flipping through the stiff pages looking for the correct ones to replace the pictures, she smiled, amused or touched all over again by various shots of the kids over the years, a wonderful photo of her and her father and, her heart hurting, her mother.

"Oh, *Maman*," she whispered, running a fingertip over the smiling face. The picture had been taken four or so years before, but her mother had already been diagnosed with cancer. She could see it in her eyes.

"I miss you. Send some help this way, will you?" she asked softly. She brought the album up and left a kiss to the frozen image, then continued with her task.

Old clothing—some she tossed aside to discard, no idea why it was in her hope chest to begin with—old toys, award plaques from Jim's career highs, and basketball trophies for Jimmy. Finally, she found the small jewelry box and opened it to ensure the ribbons were inside. Satisfied they were, she set the wooden box aside to place everything back where it went.

She was about to close the lid when something caught her eye. It was a small lead crystal jewelry box that her father gave to her one random day when they'd been in Paris for little more than a week. She remembered the look on his face: pensive, sad, and deeply troubled.

"She wants you to have this."

With a simple sentence, he'd managed to break her heart and confuse her all the more.

The ring box-sized jewelry box held a single item that she'd never removed. Lifting it out of the small space it was wedged into, Lysette held it in her hand. She used her other hand to gently pull open the beveled lid.

Reaching a hand up, Lysette scooped out the tiny gold cross Eleanor wore on a simple chain around her neck. She brought it out into the light of the bedside lamp.

"This is beautiful. I don't think I've ever noticed it before."

"It belonged to my grandmother," Eleanor explained. "I didn't really know her, but Mama says I'm a lot like her so," she added with a shrug, "I guess I wear it to feel close to her somehow."

Lysette stared down at that gold cross, partially buried in the nest of chain. Her attention was grabbed when she heard the explosion of noise down below as her family arrived home.

Pocketing the glass ring box, she cradled the box Bronte's ribbons were in, then got to her feet, closing the lid of the hope chest before leaving the attic.

❧❧❧❧

Lysette hummed softly to herself as she gathered everything she'd need to make lunches for the kids for the following day at school. It had been a pleasant evening after everyone had returned home. The kids had gone on and on about their day with Jim, the horses, and how Jimmy had accidentally stepped into a large pile of droppings. Though it was completely inappropriate dinner conversation, it had been amusing nonetheless.

With bags of carrots and celery lying on the cutting board with a knife, Lysette decided to start on their sandwiches.

"There you are," Jim said, wandering into the room, folded newspaper under his arm. "I need to talk to you about something."

She glanced at him. "Yes, that's what your note said. Figured you'd come find me when you wanted to talk." She pushed the cutting board in his direction. "Make yourself useful."

He walked over to the counter and looked down at it and the bagged veggies before glancing at her. "Why do I have to do menial labor in order to talk to you all the time?"

She raised an eyebrow at him. "You find it menial labor to prepare vegetables for your daughter's lunch?"

She faced him, hand on hip. "Am I so low on the food chain that it's fine for me to do while you're too good?"

He tossed the folded newspaper to the counter and put his hands up in supplication. "Sorry, I stepped right into that one."

"Yes, you did, and it smelled a hell of a lot worse than what Jimmy stepped into earlier today at the ranch but pretty much came from the same place." She eyed him. "A horse's ass."

He stared down at the cutting board and contents atop it for a moment, jaw muscle clenching and unclenching before he seemed to let whatever he was thinking go. "What do you need with these?"

"Rinse them and cut them into sticks, about a third of the length of the whole thing."

She watched as he nodded again and did her bidding as she got sandwich makings out. "So what's on your mind?"

"I spoke to an old friend of mine last week," Jim began, using his thumb to rub the surface of the carrots and celery he was rinsing. "He led me to some information."

"Oh?" she said, mildly curious as she spread mayonnaise on the bread slices. "About what?"

"About your friend," he said easily, though the look in his eyes was anything but casual.

"Friend?" She was feeling a bit nervous, wondering if perhaps he'd found out about Toni. Though she hadn't seen the woman since their morning together a couple of years before, she knew Toni was married to a judge who hung in similar circles as Jim. "Which one?" Though she never asked questions in their silent "no questions" agreement, it didn't stop him.

"Born to Edward Russell Landry and Emmaline

Rebecca Landry nee Brannon, Eleanor Rebecca Landry." He met her gaze, his penetrating. "These days better known as Miss Brannon."

Thoughts or concerns about Toni Potter flew out of her mind, and an image of Eleanor replaced it. She felt a slight hitch to her breathing. "Yes," she said, matching the casualness in his tone. "We discussed this, Jim." She glanced over at him.

"No," he said, laying the knife on the cutting board where he'd begun cutting celery stalks. "You lied to me."

"How did I lie to you?" she asked, knowing that was not true.

"You said you hadn't spoken to her in twenty some-odd years."

"No," she said, holding up the mayonnaise-tipped butter knife. "I told you we hadn't been friends in twenty some-odd years."

He crossed his arms over his chest. "You're splitting hairs, Lysette."

"Succinct on the stand gets your man. Isn't that always what you're telling me?" she said, returning her focus to making the sandwiches, even as her blood was beginning to boil.

"Cute. Well, I have to say, since you've known this woman for so long, you *had* to know about her, yet you said nothing!"

She started as his palm slammed down on the counter. "Jim!"

"No. No, you let the woman teach our son. You let that woman make me think she was good people. You let that woman into our *house*!"

"What are you talking about? Jesus! You're making Eleanor sound like some sort of goddamn monster!"

Without a word, he reached for his newspaper and unfolded it, revealing a file folder. Grabbing that, he tossed it onto the counter. "That's exactly what she is." With a steely-eyed glare, he left the room.

❧❧❧❧

To say it had been a rough night was an epic understatement. Long after her family had gone to bed, lights were out, and music turned off, Lysette had sat on the living room floor surrounded by police reports, court records, and newspaper clippings. Many tears and shocked whimpers later, she'd awoken curled up on the couch.

Not ready to answer any questions, she'd quickly gotten herself and the pages that filled the file folder together and had readied for the day. Jim had not said word one to her that morning, and in truth, she was glad, as she had no idea what to say to him.

Now she stood outside Eleanor's classroom door, Eleanor inside and alone. It was the lunch period, and the kids were all in the cafeteria, Eleanor sitting at her desk eating a sandwich and reading a book.

Lysette glanced into the window in the door for the third time, not entirely sure what she was waiting for or what she expected to change. Squeezing her eyes closed for a moment, she took a deep breath and opened her eyes, reaching for the doorknob.

Entering the classroom, she shut the door behind her, taking longer than necessary with her back to Eleanor, who seemed to have changed her position as her chair squeaked. Lysette braced herself, then turned around, noting Eleanor was looking at her, a pleasant, welcoming smile on her face.

"Hey there. No movies playing today."

Lysette made no response, her heart racing as she neared the desk. "Eleanor," she said at length, standing before the desk where Eleanor still sat. "Did you do it?" she asked quietly.

Eleanor's smile morphed into confusion as she set the book aside and rested her sandwich on the dish it had come in. "Did I do what?"

"Please, just be honest with me," Lysette nearly whispered, pleading in her voice.

Eleanor cleared her throat, sitting up straighter in the chair. She looked Lysette directly in the eye. "No."

Rather than feeling relief at the denial, Lysette felt anger and betrayal renewed. "Eleanor, I am asking you to be honest with me. Please. Did you do it?" Her voice was louder, a bit shrill as she felt a strange mix of panic and anger rising.

"No," Eleanor said again, her voice never losing the calm, even timbre.

"Jim showed me the reports, Eleanor!" she boomed. "I saw the records, I saw the picture of you in handcuffs!" Angry tears stung her eyes. She tried to blink them away, but it only made more come. "After everything," she begged. "All that we went through, all that you meant to me…Please don't lie to me now."

Eleanor slowly rose from her seat, letting out a tired sigh, her eyes reflecting that exhaustion that seemed to come from somewhere deep inside. "I'm not lying. The answer is no."

The tears came hot and bitter as Lysette turned on her heel and hurried from the classroom, blindly finding her way out of the building.

Chapter Twenty-two

Lysette's lips were mere centimeters from Eleanor's, both breathing entirely too hard to kiss. Their moans and heavy breathing were shared in a single space as they held on to each other, hips working together to bring them to an explosion of pleasure, which drew a loud cry from Lysette, pulling Eleanor's climax from her as she stiffened beneath her, holding on to her in a painful grip, like an iron vise. As the waves of pleasure continued, she felt Lysette's face bury in her neck, Lysette's hips continuing to grind weakly against Eleanor's thigh, which added continued pressure between her legs, making her gasp as a second, smaller wave hit her.

Finally, Lysette lifted her head. She met Eleanor's flushed face, smiling at the look of wonder she must have found there, because Eleanor felt as though she'd just been taken to the moon and back. She gave Lysette a goofy grin before Lysette lowered her head, leaving a lingering kiss on slightly opened lips.

"I love you, Ellie," she whispered against them. "I really do."

Eleanor hugged her tightly, her heart exploding as her lower body had just done. "I love you, too," she replied, holding Lysette desperately to her that she could hardly breathe. Apparently, Lysette couldn't, either, as she begged for mercy. Giggling, Eleanor released her. "Sorry."

Lysette moved off her; the blanket that had become tangled around them was fully pushed aside. Lying in her original position on her side, she looked down at Eleanor, who lay on her back. Though her breasts were bare, somehow it felt liberating, especially the way Lysette was looking at them.

"That was really beautiful," Lysette said, tracing random patterns on Eleanor's stomach.

"Yes, it was. I'm not sure exactly what we just did, but can we still do it in Paris?" Eleanor asked, hope in her eyes. She grinned at the giggle that question received. "What?"

"You are too adorable, that's what," Lysette murmured, leaning down and initiating a passionate kiss that had them quickly breathing hard.

Eleanor's sense of propriety began to nudge her, as much as she wanted to hit the snooze button. After the kiss ended naturally, she reached up and caressed the side of Lysette's beautiful face. "I need to get home," she murmured. "I have to be up in a few hours."

"I know." Lysette groaned before landing one final kiss on Eleanor's lips.

Ten minutes later, they were parked on Overton Road again, hands in hair as they kissed. Eleanor wanted to do what she'd done in the upstairs apartment again, her panties were so wet, but she knew she couldn't.

Placing her hands on Lysette's shoulders, she gently squeezed, letting her know she was going to pull away. "I love you," she whispered as their foreheads rested together.

Lysette cupped her cheek. "I love you. See you tomorrow at school."

Eleanor nodded before she pulled completely away from Lysette and slid across the front seat to the passenger-side door, letting herself out. She held that beautiful gaze for a long moment before turning away, hiking off into the predawn darkness to the farmhouse.

Eleanor felt as though she'd just laid her head down on the pillow when her eyes blinked open. She lifted her head, a dull ache tapping at her skull. She knew it was a tired headache, too many nights without proper sleep, and the night before certainly hadn't helped her case.

"You bitch!"

She had no time to consider her thoughts when her father stormed into her bedroom, roaring at her like a bear as he grabbed her by her nightgown and yanked her out of bed. She had no time to react or defend herself as he banged her against the wall next to the window. Her head lulled uselessly for a moment as she gripped his hands, trying to make him let her go.

"Who did you tell?" he bellowed. "Who?"

"Ed! Please, stop!" Emma begged, limping into the bedroom, her lip bleeding.

"What did you say? Did you go to the cops?" Ed demanded, ignoring Emma's pleading as he banged Eleanor against the wall again.

She had no idea what he was talking about, her eyes nearly rolling in her head as he banged her again. "Please," she said weakly. "Stop."

"It was you, I *know* it was you." He threw her to the floor, looking down at her with disgust. "Gabby had to leave town this morning because of you. He'll be back tonight, and you're going with him. It's over, Eleanor! No more school, no more Landon whore!"

He picked her up by her collar and shoved her to her bed. "Get dressed and pack your things. This time tomorrow, you're *his* problem."

Eleanor lay on the bed stunned, both by the violent attack and by what she'd been told. She looked to her mother, who stared at her from the bedroom doorway, eyes wide and looking just as stunned.

"By the time I get back, you better be packed!" Ed bellowed from the top of the stairs before trotting down them, heavy work boots thudding all the way down before he shoved out the front door. Moments later, the sound of his pickup could be heard.

Emma shook herself out of her fugue, and she hurried over to Eleanor's bed and dropped to her knees. "We've got to get you out of here," she said, voice hurried. She looked up at Eleanor, who stared stupidly at her from the bed, her own mind still gone. "Eleanor!" Emma exclaimed, clapping her hands together. "Come on! We've got minutes." She pulled out the small suitcase and plopped it on the bed. "Pack."

Eleanor watched Emma run out of the room, and it sounded like to the bedroom she shared with Ed. She shook herself out of her rude awakening and got to work. "We've got to get word to Lysette!" she called to her mother.

The sound of opening and closing dresser doors stopped. "Yes, yes." Emma appeared in Eleanor's doorway again. "Write a note. Does that Howell boy go by the house?"

Understanding what her mother was suggesting, Eleanor hurried over to her own dresser, grimacing as exertion of moving made the pain in her head so much worse. After a few seconds of work, she was able to grab her diary from behind it. She flipped to a blank page and ripped it out. Using the pen next to her Bible to scribble a quick note, she explained everything she could of what was happening. Folding it up, she bolted down the stairs and across the yard toward the Howell house. She knew Jethro fed the animals in the morning.

"Hey!" she called out, just as he was about to toss a pail of feed to the chickens that strutted around the yard.

Looking over at her, he raised a hand. "Hey. Where did your shoes go?"

Confused, she looked down. It was only then that she realized she was in her nightgown and bare feet. "Long story. Listen, you know who Lysette Landon is, right? At school?" she asked, praying with everything she had that he knew at least of her.

A goofy grin spread across his lips. "Yeah. What fella doesn't."

She was in too much of a hurry to be annoyed. She shoved the note into his hand. "I need you to give that to her, Jethro, okay? I mean, the *second* you see her, give it to her. Okay?"

"Yeah, okay," he said, looking down at the folded paper. "You okay?"

She gave him a weak smile before turning and running back home, frozen morning ground on her bare feet be damned. As she ran the half mile back to the house, she saw her father's truck pull back into the yard.

"Oh, god," she whispered, moving to hide behind the outhouse. Hand resting on the rough wood, she peeked around the small building, watching.

He held the same clear bottle he'd had at Christmas and that she'd seen more and more in the months since. She knew it was Gabby's influence on him, making him a meaner son of a bitch than he was before, and she didn't think that was possible. It was like Gabby brought the worst out of him.

"Eleanor," he bellowed, climbing the front porch stairs. At the top, he uncorked the bottle and took a swig, his body shaking as the potent alcohol went through him.

Once he'd disappeared inside, she scurried from the outhouse to his truck, peeking through the window. Sure enough, and as usual, the keys were dangling from the ignition. She studied the steering wheel and gearshift, trying to decide if she could drive it. Would it be any different than Davis's car?

"Eleanor!"

She gasped. As quietly and quickly as she could, she opened the passenger-side door, snagged the keys, and didn't even bother to close the door all the way for fear it would make too much noise. Maybe if they waited him out, he'd pass out and she and her mother could take off.

She tiptoed her way up the stairs and back into the house, hiding the keys in her hand as she had nowhere to put them, no pockets in her nightgown. She looked around for somewhere to hide them when she heard a crash upstairs and her mother cry out in pain.

"You told her to leave, didn't you!" Ed demanded, his words punctuated by what sounded like brutal slaps. "You went against the words of your husband!" Another crash.

Eleanor was about to run upstairs when her parents appeared at the top of them, Emma held in a headlock. She was tugging uselessly against Ed's arm that was wrapped around her neck as she gasped for air. When he saw Eleanor standing at the bottom of the stairs, he threw Emma aside and bounded down to her.

"Where were you, you little bitch?" he growled, the full force of his anger seeming to be leveled at her.

It took everything in her power not to back up or run right back out that front door. She considered the keys she held in her hand, wondering if she could do enough damage to get them out of there.

He smirked when she stayed put. "Think you're real big, don't you?" he asked. "Think you're better than me. Think you're better than Gabby, hanging around your rich whore of a friend."

She was stunned, never in all her sixteen years hearing him talk like that. "No, Father," she said quietly, wanting to try to get him to calm down and realize she wasn't a threat of whatever kind he was convinced she was.

"Liar," he said, voice low and dangerous, the putrid smell of hooch washing over her face.

She gasped as he let loose a brutal slap, which made her head whip to the side as she staggered backward. Her hand came up to rest on a heated cheek as she looked at him with wide eyes.

"I saw your mother was packed, too. You talked her into leaving me, didn't you?" Another slap, which sent her into the wall. "You think you two are leaving?"

Ed grabbed Eleanor by the throat and held her against the wall with one hand as he used the other to grasp the neckline of her nightgown. With an absolutely evil grimace of exertion, he yanked, the loud sound of ripping material filling the small space between them, as well as the sound of her snapped chain and cross tinkling against the wood floor.

She cried out in shock as suddenly her breasts were exposed. She tried uselessly to cover herself, but that seemed to enrage him as he roughly pulled her away from the wall by her neck, whirling her around and shoving her down over the back of the couch, holding her in place by the back of her neck.

"No! Father, no!" she cried, desperately trying to stand up or move away from him, but he was far too strong. The tears came hot and fast when she heard the sound of his belt being unbuckled and pants unbuttoned and unzipped.

"Ed!"

Still pressed into the couch, Eleanor had no idea what was happening behind her. All she knew was the pressure against her neck lightened just a bit and he'd stopped fidgeting with his pants. A moment later… BOOM! BOOM!

Still bent over the couch, Eleanor cried out in surprise and fear. She felt the vibration on the floor as a loud thud hit behind her, her father's touch on her gone. Standing up, she turned to see her mother standing there, her father's double-barreled shotgun in her hands, still aimed at a man who no longer stood.

Heart pounding and chest heaving, she turned to see her father lying where he'd fallen, a hole blown into his chest and his left shoulder and upper arm blown off.

Bringing a hand up to wipe at her tear-streaked face and push her mass of hair out of the way, she absently reached for the tattered ends of her nightgown as she turned to her mother, slowly walking over to her, as if in a daze.

"Mama," she whispered. "You can put the gun down now."

Emma slowly lowered the gun, blinking several times as she met Eleanor's gaze with wide eyes, though she said nothing.

"I think we better leave," Eleanor said, swallowing hard. "Let's just go."

Emma nodded, taking what seemed to be the first breath since she'd pulled the trigger, the scent of gunpowder and blood heavy in the air.

"Ed! Ed, you okay?" was yelled from outside, the voice getting louder and closer. "Emma?"

Eleanor's heart stopped. "Mr. Howell."

"Ed, answer me!"

Eleanor turned back to her mother, who was staring wide-eyed at the front door. She squeezed her eyes shut for a second, then with gentle hands, tried to take the shotgun from her mother. "Let go, Mama," she said softly as Emma's hands fell limply to her sides as Eleanor took the weapon. Their gazes met; Emma's filled with terror as Eleanor gave her a small, sad smile. "They won't hang a sixteen-year-old girl."

Chapter Twenty-three

"Welcome, welcome!"

"Thank you, Mrs. O'Shea," Eleanor said, eyes squeezing shut as she was accosted by Scott's mother with kisses all around and a painful hug that she was pretty sure made her rib creak.

The elderly woman stood back, hands on Eleanor's shoulders. Her lipstick was as red and as slightly smudged as ever. "Why haven't you been coming around as much?" she asked, ushering Eleanor into the house. "We've missed you, and I know my Scotty has, too."

"I know. A few teachers and I have been helping the substitute who took over Scott's classes while he's out," she explained. "Late nights and extra hours."

"Well, we're grateful you came today," she said, coming to a stop before leaving the living room. She turned to Eleanor. "He's struggling, Eleanor. He's been home for two weeks now, and he's really struggling."

Eleanor nodded, letting out a small breath to try to ease her nerves as they continued walking again, heading to the back family room, which Scott tended to make his space.

It had been a month since the shooting and, though the town had rallied around the two men— even if there were whisperings behind closed doors of an "unusual" situation and wonderings why Scott had been with a colored man—Scott hadn't bounced back.

The doctors and medical team had worked wonders for him physically, but mentally and emotionally, he had yet to return to whole.

"Scotty!" Mrs. O'Shea belted out in a sing-songy voice. "You have company!"

"Ma, I told you I don't want to see anyone!" he yelled from the other room, sounding more like a petulant ten-year-old than an educated man in his thirties.

Eleanor smiled at that. Sadly, she doubted that was terribly unusual behavior at home with a mother who had catered to his every whim since the moment she'd found out she was pregnant.

They entered the back wood-paneled room, its goldenrod shag carpeting vacuumed to fluffy fullness with perfect striping to prove it. The heavy drapes were closed, and the television was on. Scott sat in his red flannel robe with his hair messy as though he'd just rolled out of bed, and his unshaven face had blossomed into a scraggly, uneven beard.

"Look at those whiskers," Eleanor said, standing at the center of the room with hands on hips. "I think you need a bath and a shave, my friend."

Scott looked up at her, eyes wide with surprise. "What are you doing here?"

"What, can't a girl come visit her best pal?" she asked, smiling as she walked over and plopped down on the couch next to him, careful not to jostle him too much in case he was still having any pain.

"I'm nobody's best anything," he muttered, tossing the book he'd been reading on the coffee table.

"Uh-oh," she said, teasing in her voice as she lightly nudged him with her shoulder. "Someone's having a bad day."

He glared at her, his eyes the poster child for despair. "If you're here to make fun of me, you can just leave. I don't want to hear it."

She was surprised to hear such words and tone from him but was not offended. She'd never seen him like this before. "So I heard the police were going to release your car back to you. That's good news, right?"

"What the hell do I care?" he asked, slapping his hands to his thighs.

"Here we go!" Mrs. O'Shea exclaimed, entering the room with a tray filled with finger sandwiches, a pot of tea, and two teacups.

Eleanor looked at it all, wondering when she'd left and how on earth she'd prepared all that in a couple of minutes. "Thank you, Mrs. O'Shea," she said, watching as the tray was set on the coffee table. Wadded-up tissues, the discarded book, and a small stack of dirty dishes were pushed aside to make room. The dishes were gathered in her hands.

"Do you kids need anything else?" the elderly woman asked, looking bright-eyed between the two.

"Uh, no. I think we're good," Eleanor said with a smile.

"Just go," Scott muttered.

Not skipping a beat, his mother left the room, leaving Eleanor to stare at him, shocked. She knew he could act like a spoiled brat, but she'd never seen him be so rude to her.

"Scott," she said. "That wasn't nice."

"What do you care? Not like anyone does, anyway." He crossed his arms over his chest, again the petulant child peeking his head up.

Deciding to take a moment to gather her thoughts and her strategy, Eleanor went about pouring them both some tea, making it how she knew he liked it. "Martha told me she came by with some dinner for you last Wednesday," she began conversationally. "She said she made you her Swedish meatballs that her husband apparently howls over." She smiled, handing him his tea, which he took, refusing to look at her. "And through the grapevine, I heard that Carlos dropped off a chocolate cake his wife baked and a scarf she crocheted for you." She took an experimental sip of her tea, making a show of it. It was then she noticed something leaning against the wall where it was placed on the floor, even if half of it was obscured by a randomly thrown undershirt that dangled from it. "And I see you have the card that the *entire* student body made for you and signed." She took another sip. "I don't know, Scotty, I'm thinking lots and lots of people care."

He looked away from her, his arms relaxing a bit from their stiff, stern position, but he still kept up the wall between them. "He left," he finally said, voice quiet.

"Who did?"

His head whipped in her direction, gaze hard. "Who do you think?"

She felt her heart fall. "No. Where did he go? Why?"

"He said it was for my own good," Scott said bitterly. "Like he's me and knows what's best for me. He said the whole thing was his fault, that he brought danger to us, and he could never live with himself if he got me hurt again or worse," he added, sounding as though he were spewing a well-rehearsed speech.

"I'm so sorry." Eleanor reached over and grabbed the closest hand to her, tugging his arms apart so she could hold his hand as it rested on her thigh. "People never know how they're going to react to horrible events in their life," she explained. "Some embrace those around them to get through it while others shut down." She studied his profile as he stared straight ahead in the direction of the television, though she knew he wasn't seeing the game show on the screen. "Where did he go?"

"To his sister's house or something. I think she lives in Illinois."

"Look, I'm not going to give you platitudes or patronize you by saying things like if it's meant to be, you'll be together, blah, blah, blah. We're both adults, and we know life isn't always pretty." She smirked. "Or kind. But you do have to pick yourself up and try and move on and continue the best you can."

He turned on her, yanking his hand from hers. "Do you have any idea what it's like to be attacked by a monster and in that moment, everything you hold dear is taken from you? Then, after all that, you're essentially shoved into a prison of your own body and emotions through no fault of your own?"

She could only stare at him, so much going through her own mind, so much she could say, so many things she could share with him about just how well she understood that, but it wouldn't help him.

"Do you?" he demanded, tears in his eyes when she failed to respond.

"Come here, Scott," she said, gently hugging him to her as he began to cry. Her touch in comfort would do him far more good than any words she may have. She rocked him gently. "We'll get through this," she whispered, leaving a kiss on top of his head. "I promise."

After leaving Scott's house with a promise to return the following day to take him out for lunch, Eleanor decided to stop at the theater. Sure enough, *An American in Paris* was playing.

"One, please," she said softly to the girl behind the glass. She slid her money under the slot, and the girl slid a ticket back her way. "Thank you."

Holding her ticket, she headed toward the door, pausing as she looked up at the marquee, then at those stepping around her to enter the building.

"Sorry," she said, as she was blocking the way for a group of girls trying to get past her. She studied the faces of moviegoers, and she knew she was looking for one face in particular.

It had been a handful of days since Lysette had barged into her classroom, shocking Eleanor. She managed to keep her cool because Lysette deserved to know the truth, a truth she thought Lysette knew. She'd been left entirely confused—and admittedly hurt. Now she hoped Lysette would "bump into her" for the show, but in her heart of hearts, she knew she wouldn't.

She saw a young man strolling up toward the box office hands shoved into his trouser pockets. "Excuse me," she said to him. "Are you going to buy a ticket to this showing?" At his nod, she handed him hers with a smile and walked away.

She walked down the sidewalk and headed home. The thought of sitting in that dark theater with the seat next to her either empty or occupied by a stranger was just too much to take. After seeing her best friend fall apart in his own heartbreak, she couldn't handle dealing with her own loneliness, a loneliness that only one person could fill.

She was about to reach the locked door to her building when she heard her name. Turning, she saw Lysette hurrying across the street after a motorcycle passed, her New Yorker parked at the opposite curb. Eleanor waited at the door, keys in her hand. She wasn't sure what was about to happen, but her nerves were already working overtime.

"Hi," Lysette said, stepping up onto the sidewalk and walking over to her.

"Hi." The surprise was evident in Eleanor's voice.

"I need to talk to you," Lysette said, her eyes troubled. Her body language was fidgety. Though she looked as elegant and beautiful as ever in her designer clothing and perfect hair and makeup, something about her was off. She seemed more like a little girl playing dress-up than a sophisticated woman.

Eleanor nodded. "Sure. Want to come up?" She indicated the building behind her.

"Yes, okay."

Without another word, Eleanor unlocked the outer door and held it open for Lysette before entering and climbing the narrow staircase. She could feel Lysette's presence behind her, and it was equal parts unsettling and comforting. A dizzying cocktail, to be sure.

Reaching the second floor, she led the way to her apartment door, unlocking it and pushing the door open for Lysette to enter before her.

Closing the door once they were both inside, Eleanor tossed her keys and purse on the end table as she watched Lysette walk slowly inside, looking around.

"This is lovely," Lysette said, glancing toward the newest addition. She gave a small chuckle. "So you're the one who ended up with the rocking chair."

"Excuse me?" Eleanor asked, glancing from the chair to Lysette.

"Nothing. You live here alone?" Lysette asked.

Eleanor was surprised by the question but nodded as she walked toward the kitchen. "I do. It's all mine, and most importantly, I can afford it." She offered Lysette, who had also moved into the kitchen, a small smile. "Would you like some coffee?"

"No, thank you."

Eleanor leaned back against the counter, arms crossed over her chest. She felt a bit defensive and cornered. "How did you know where I live?"

"Oh," Lysette said, giving her a small, sheepish grin as she removed her purse strap from her shoulder and placed the purse on the table. "Do you mind if I sit?" She indicated the kitchen chair before her. Eleanor shook her head, and Lysette made herself comfortable. "I must have sat in my car for ten minutes outside the theater, trying to decide if I wanted to go in or not." She looked down at her hands, which fidgeted in her lap. "I didn't know if I'd be welcome."

"Welcome into the theater?" Eleanor asked, deciding she too wanted to sit. She sat in the chair adjacent to Lysette's.

"No," Lysette said softly, glancing at her. "By you." She let out a breath. "I was about to make my decision when I saw you walk up and, moments later, leave. I needed to talk to you, so I followed."

Eleanor nodded in understanding and acknowledgment. Even still, she didn't feel the need to explain her quick departure, and Lysette, for her part, didn't seem to be asking for one.

"Ellie, I'm here today because I owe you an apology. I had no right barging into your classroom Monday afternoon like some lunatic throwing accusations everywhere." She paused, her gaze pleading as she looked at Eleanor. "I had no idea what had happened, and when Jim gave me all that information, it rocked me to my core," she admitted, looking away for a long moment.

Eleanor said nothing, didn't move a muscle. She had the feeling there was a lot more Lysette needed to get off her chest.

"I'm sorry I went off half-cocked, especially at your job. That was irresponsible and beyond inconsiderate of me." Lysette gave Eleanor a small smile. "I hope you can forgive me."

"Of course I do." Eleanor returned the smile.

Lysette took what seemed to be a cleansing breath, her entire demeanor changing as though it had been eating her alive for nearly a week, and now she'd finally said what she needed to say. She looked deeply into Eleanor's gaze, her own unwavering. "You took the fall, didn't you?"

Eleanor nodded and responded verbally with a simple "yes."

"For your mama?"

Another nod and "yes."

"My god," Lysette breathed, slumping in her chair. "Why?"

"Well," Eleanor said, placing her hands on the table. "My mother had been through enough. And as I told her that day, I knew, well, hoped," she added with a sheepish smile, "that they wouldn't execute a young girl." She shook her head. "My mother wouldn't have stood a chance."

Lysette's eyes welled with tears as she looked away. She said nothing, seeming to need a moment to get her emotions under control.

Eleanor pushed away from the table and went to the living room to grab some tissues from the box on the coffee table. She handed them to Lysette with a kind smile before returning to her seat.

"Thank you," Lysette whispered, using one to delicately dab at her eyes. "So," she said at length. "They put you into…"

"Seven years, four months, twenty-nine days," Eleanor murmured.

The tears really began to flow as a quiet sob tore from Lysette's throat. She buried her face in her hands, tissues clutched in her fingers.

Eleanor wasn't sure what to do. She'd already cried all the tears there were to cry over her fate as a teen, and she wasn't sure how to comfort Lysette through hers now. She claimed she didn't know about the killing, seemed to have no knowledge of what happened to Eleanor, so Eleanor couldn't even imagine the burden of all this dumped on her at one time. Part of her wanted to go to Lysette, but somehow, she felt frozen to her seat, unable to offer comfort that she didn't even know would be welcomed.

After several long moments, Lysette calmed, her tears relegated to intermittent sniffles as she wiped at her eyes and nose. "My god," she finally said, looking at Eleanor with pain-filled eyes. "I had no idea. What happened?"

Eleanor got up to grab the box of tissues, placing it on the table near Lysette, though she'd done that more for something to do with the nervous energy that question had spawned than anything else. "Apparently, Brooke View police had begun sniffing around William Gabford, asking questions about his years in Texas," she said, sitting again. "I heard years later that he had a couple warrants out of Oklahoma, too. Anyway, he and Ed decided to move things up. While Gabford went out looking for work in Wyoming, just across the state line, Ed's job was to get me ready to go. Life as I knew it was over," she added, sitting back in her chair, staring off past Lysette as she saw that morning all over again.

"You were supposed to marry him, wherever you two ended up?" Lysette asked.

"I don't know," Eleanor admitted. "I'm not sure that was really part of the worry at that point. I think Gabford and Ed panicked, and I was the possession that Gabby wanted to pack first." She smirked at that thought. "Anyway, Mama and I knew the only chance we had was to get word to your parents, so when Ed left, I ran to the neighbors."

"Jethro Howell," Lysette interjected. "He gave me your note. I'll never forget his name or face as long as I live."

"Yeah, Jethro Howell. Well, when I got back to the house, Ed had returned. Things got…ugly." She let out a shaky sigh, seeing the pure, unadulterated evil in her father's eyes again. "Mama did what she had to do to protect me," she finished softly.

"Who called the police?"

"Mr. Howell came over. He heard the shots."

"And you said you did it?"

Eleanor nodded. "I did. Honestly, my mother was so locked inside her own mind at that point, I'm not sure they wouldn't have tossed her into the asylum, thinking she was crazy."

Lysette looked down at her hand, which rested on the table, a soiled tissue crumbled with her curled fingers. "Nobody told me any of this," she said, shaking her head. "My father told me simply that the plan had changed."

Eleanor smirked. "To put it lightly. I sent you four letters. All of them were returned."

Lysette looked at her surprised, but then her expression relaxed. "You sent them to the Brooke View house?" At Eleanor's nod, she explained, "It was burned down around the time we left for Paris, so around the time all this happened. We never returned to that house. Hell, I didn't even return to Colorado until we moved here," she said, indicating the space around them and the town beyond it.

Eleanor shook her head. "Wonder if Gabford was behind that. I'm so sorry."

Lysette grabbed her purse and set it in her lap, unclasping it. She reached inside and brought something out, resting it on the table. Eleanor stared at the beautiful lead crystal ring box, confused as it was pushed toward her. Taking it, she opened it, gasping softly as she saw her cross.

"Daddy gave it to me," Lysette explained. "He said you told him to."

Eleanor nodded, still staring down at it. "I did."

"How did you give it to him?"

Eleanor smiled. "Well, I did, and I didn't. I guess during Ed's attack, it must have gotten ripped off. I didn't even realize it until later. Your dad arrived at the house when the police were still there. He said he found it on the floor, recognizing it was mine." She let out a long breath, exhausted from the discussion and all the emotions it brought. "He came to see me while I was awaiting sentencing. I hadn't been moved to Canon City yet. He tried to give it back, but I told him to give it to you."

"Why?" Lysette asked gently.

Eleanor met her gaze, closing the small box and placing it back on the table. It hurt too much to look at it anymore. "It was all I had to give you, to let you know I'd always be with you."

Lysette studied the ring box for a long moment before blowing out a breath as she shook her head. "A nightmare. An absolute nightmare. I can't even wrap my mind around all this." Elbows on the table, she brought her hands up to cover her mouth.

"It's a lot to take in."

Lysette's hands fell to the table as she studied Eleanor. "I feel like I abandoned you when you needed me the most."

Eleanor shook her head. "No. You didn't know what was happening, and honestly, I'm glad you got to go on and live your life." She gave her a sad smile. "Find love, have a family."

"I love my kids," Lysette whispered, looking down at her hands. She blew out a long, slow breath. "I need to go. So much to think about and absorb."

Eleanor nodded, pushing back from the table. She was sorry to see her leave, but in a way relieved. She too had a lot to think about. She watched as Lysette gathered her purse and soiled tissues, shoving them into the pocket of her wide-leg trousers before she turned and walked to the door. The ring box left behind, Eleanor palmed it and followed.

The door still closed, Lysette stopped and turned to Eleanor, giving her an apologetic smile. "Please forgive my behavior over these past months. I feel so incredibly childish about that now."

Eleanor chuckled. "Don't sweat it." She reached down and grabbed one of Lysette's hands, placing the ring box inside before wrapping her fingers over it.

Eyes filling with tears once again, Lysette took her in a tight hug, their first since saying goodbye on a moonless March night in 1934. Eleanor's eyes fell closed as she held Lysette to her, so much the same as so much had changed.

Without warning, Lysette broke the hug and hurried out of the apartment, the door closing softly behind her.

Chapter Twenty-four

Eyes as wide as saucers, Eleanor walked in, the second of three female inmates who had been on the bus with her taking the two-hour drive to Canon City, Colorado, where they'd find their new home.

After being held in a closet in the Brooke View jail for three months—they had nowhere to place her in general population full of men and didn't feel she'd be safe—she was exhausted and just wanted a real bed.

From the bus, they had been ushered down cement stairs and into the building to a small square room with exposed pipes overhead, cement at their feet and basic plaster walls around them. The uniformed guard who had escorted them off the bus walked over to the two women who were entering the room. They wore uniforms similar to that of a nurse, though they were light gray. The guard handed them some papers and murmured some unheard words to them before leaving the way they'd just come in.

Both women wore identical uniforms, though the younger of the two, no older than thirty, had a thin, dark blue sash on one shoulder of the long-sleeved garment. Her hair was a deep red and bound atop her head, and brown eyes were sharp and focused. Her companion looked to be in her fifties with the plumper physique of a mother or grandmother. Her light brown hair was streaked with gray and just barely hit her shoulders.

"Good afternoon, ladies," the redhead said, stepping forward, the older woman staying put. "I'm Head Matron Sillis, and that is Matron Hadley," she said, indicating the other woman. "She is who you will be going to for any questions, problems, or help from the hours of three o'clock until eleven o'clock. After she leaves, you will go to Matron Phelps for any problems during the night. I will be in at seven a.m. sharp and will handle any and all issues until Matron Hadley once again appears." She gazed at the three newcomers with a smile that Eleanor noticed didn't reach her eyes. "Now with that, you will follow Matron Hadley. Welcome home, ladies. We're pleased to have you as residents here."

Eleanor watched as the head matron walked back to Matron Hadley. The two spoke a few words before she left. Left alone, the older woman walked up to Eleanor and her two companions, looking each over before bringing up the pages she'd been handed by the uniformed man.

"Hello, ladies," she said kindly. "I know you've had a long day, two of you from one place and the third from an entirely different one." She brought up the page to read from. "When I call your name, raise your hand, then listen for your house assignment."

Eleanor was a bit confused at the "house" reference. She glanced at the woman to her right, but the young Hispanic woman stared down at her feet as she had most of the trip. The other woman, one with dirty blond hair and a glare filled with hatred, looked as though she was trying to kill Matron Hadley where she stood with the sheer power of her stare.

Turning back to the woman before them again,

Eleanor let out a silent breath with a prayer that she'd get through this. At least until she could fall apart in her "house" later.

"Lindsay DuPaul?" Matron Hadley read from the sheet in her hand, glancing up to see the blonde raise her hand. "Miss DuPaul, you'll be in house nineteen. Juana Dominguez?"

Eleanor noticed the Hispanic woman only looked up when her name was called. From knowing so many seasonal workers from Mexico on the farms her entire life, she wondered if the woman spoke any English, especially when she didn't raise her hand. She gently nudged the woman, who looked to be around her mother's age, and raised her hand slightly, nodding at her to do the same.

The woman looked at her with frightened dark brown eyes before her gaze moved down to Eleanor's partially raised hand. Seeming to understand, the woman looked back to Matron Hadley and raised her hand high.

"Very nice, Miss Dominguez," Matron Hadley said. "You will be in house three."

The woman looked to Eleanor, who suddenly felt her palms go sweaty. Her Spanish was minimal at best. "Um," she said softly, "*habitación tres.*" She raised three fingers. It seemed the woman didn't understand what she meant by that, but Eleanor had no way to explain, didn't have the words. So all she could hope for was the number would stick with the poor woman.

Smiling at Eleanor, Matron Hadley said, "And you must be our baby, Eleanor Landry."

"Yes, ma'am," Eleanor murmured, not sure if she was supposed to respond.

"Well, you'll be in house eleven. Follow me,

ladies."

Eleanor shuffled along wearing the same oversized men's inmate uniform she'd been given in Brooke View. There were no uniforms for women or even to fit a teenaged boy, so they'd given her the smallest white wool pants and top they could: dirty white with offset black stripes. It was hot and itchy, and she hoped she'd be given something else to wear.

The three female inmates were led into a washroom with two bathroom stalls like they'd had at school, but no doors were on these. There were two sinks, and at the back was a shower area, which was one giant stall with four shower heads jutting out from the walls, two on one wall, two on opposing walls. The floor was small, white penny tile that slanted gently down to a drain at the center.

Folded neatly on the sink were three stacks of material. "Now," Matron Hadley said, walking to them and looking at the women she'd led inside the bathroom. "You ladies will have two minutes to fully shower and dress." She pointed out which pile belonged to which inmate.

Eleanor was suddenly mortified. She had to be naked in front of these women? Wide-eyed, she looked around at them as she hugged herself. The woman with dirty blond hair quickly shed her dingy gray, shapeless garment, devil-may-care and stepped over the cement lip into the showering area. A moment later, the Hispanic woman did the same, though she was trembling. She glanced over her shoulder to look at Eleanor, almost as if to check if she was doing the right thing. She'd obviously begun to see Eleanor as someone who was trying to help her.

Eleanor gave her the biggest smile she could,

which was nearly imperceptible, and shed her own clothing, relieved to be rid of them. She was cold, exhausted, hungry, and terrified as she stepped over the cement lip to join her fellow inmates. She took the bar of soap Matron Hadley offered her with instructions they were all to share.

Eleanor lathered herself as best and fast as she could, knowing she had to get the soap to the others before time ran out. As long as her hair was, there was absolutely no way she could get it washed—regardless of how badly it needed it—in the seconds remaining, so she simply smoothed it back from her face with the water. She'd put it up later.

"Ten seconds, ladies!" Matron Hadley called out, a stopwatch in a plump hand.

Panic settling in, Eleanor quickly rinsed off, then hurried toward the stack of towels Matron Hadley had placed on one of the sinks while they'd showered. She grabbed the top one, shaking it out to full length, which barely made it around Eleanor's body. She didn't care. All she wanted in that moment was to get dried enough to get dressed.

The uniforms they were given were essentially shapeless cotton dresses of light blue with white piping around the sleeves and collar, which was similar to that on a sailor dress. A long, narrow horizontal white patch was sewn on, their inmate numbers displayed just above their left breast. Eleanor would be Inmate 0024 until she was released, *if* she was released. She had, after all, been sentenced to fifteen years to life with the crack of a gavel. Everyone on her side knew a white man was dead, and for a white, male judge, the reasons didn't matter, especially since a female had confessed to causing his death.

The inmates were led up two flights of stairs separated by a landing until they reached the second floor of the facility. They entered a long corridor with rows of cells on either side. Most the cells' doors were closed and locked, though a few stood open, a gaping hole in the grin of captivity.

It was quiet, yet eerie as Eleanor could feel eyes on her, some seen as a few women stood at the bars of their iron barrio while others were back in the shadows of their "houses." A few disembodied catcalls or greetings could be heard, but what unnerved her the most were the baby cries and "goo goo gaa gaa" that she knew were aimed at her. She kept her head down as she followed Matron Hadley, but her gaze was constantly on the move, surreptitiously taking in her surroundings.

After dropping the blond woman into the cell with a one and a nine painted above the door, which was swung shut and locked, they moved a little farther down the line, Juana Dominguez moving in closer to Eleanor as a woman began to laugh hysterically, startling them both. Eleanor glanced over to the cell where it was coming from but saw no one. It was like a ghost.

"Miss Landry, welcome home," Matron Hadley said, stopping in front of the open cell with eleven painted above.

Eleanor and Juana Dominguez exchanged a small smile before Eleanor stepped through the doorway, so narrow that it barely accommodated an average-sized woman's shoulders, mere inches of space above her head. Once inside, she turned to see Matron Hadley swing the door of iron bars shut, the heavy door clanging loudly. She produced another large key from the key ring she'd held. The lock engaged with a sharp click. Without another glance at her, Matron Hadley moved on with Juana Dominguez.

Left alone in the space that wasn't much larger than the closet she'd called home for ninety days, Eleanor let out a slow, shaky breath. She felt so alone and small. She reached up to wrap her fingers around the tiny cross, always a nervous habit, only to find it wasn't there. In her moment of need, she'd forgotten she'd given it to Mr. Landon. She could only hope that it was with Lysette that night, wherever she may be.

Her hand remained by her throat, balled into a fist almost as though just knowing where that cross once used to rest gave her a bit of comfort. She looked around the space, relieved to have a window, even if it was barred from the outside. The window's ledge would be a good place to line up books, she thought, hoping they were as available to her here as they'd been in the Brooke View jail. The bed was a bit smaller than the one at the farmhouse, but she didn't care. A folded wool blanket sat upon the thin mattress with folded starched linens of white atop it, the flat pillow atop them. Beside that sundae of bed makings was a folded bath towel, identical to the one she'd dried off with not long before, its miniature twin folded atop it in the form of a facecloth.

On the opposite wall was a sink, smaller than the average one, covered in white enamel. Next to it in the corner was a small toilet. Above the sink was a single shelf, empty, waiting to be filled.

That was how Eleanor felt. She slowly lowered herself to sit on the bare mattress, knees together and hands clasped on the opposite elbow, effectively hugging herself. She took it all in, though quickly the images began to swim as the tears came hard and silent. Her head fell, arms rained on by her sorrow and profound sadness.

❧❧❧❧

"Landry! Take a break!"

Eleanor looked up from her place at the steam press, making out the IL, or inmate lead, through the steam that filled the cave-like space the laundry machinery was in. She gave a thumbs-up and turned off her machine.

Blowing out a breath, she brought up her hand to wipe away the loose strands that had fallen out of her bun and were stuck to the side of her face and neck because of the thin sheen of sweat that covered her body.

Rolling her head around, she reached up and squeezed the back of her neck. She was in hour six of a ten-hour day, so grateful it was more than half over. She walked out of the large nook in the lower level of the facility where she worked to the cooler air of a small area that housed the hallway to the restroom where she and her two companions had showered upon arrival, as well as a drinking fountain and ragged old couch to take a break on, donated by a local church. The ladies could also await their turn with Nannette, the only hairstylist in the place.

Nannette's chair was stationed at the opposite end of the small room where she had a cabinet filled with the equipment she needed to do whatever was requested by her fellow inmates. Oftentimes, the women wanted to get primped for visiting day. It was the one small luxury afforded to them.

Eleanor made her way to the drinking fountain, her gaze ever on that chair. She leaned down as her finger pressed the button for the lukewarm water—though it tasted like heaven when working in a sauna all day—and sputtered. So focused on that chair, she hadn't realized the water was aimed right for her forehead.

Across the room, she heard deep, boisterous laughter. Eleanor stood, using the shoulder of her dress to wipe her eyes as she glanced in that direction. Nannette stood behind her chair, large belly and breasts jiggling with her mirth.

Feeling stupid, Eleanor gave her a sheepish look before turning to walk away.

"Why you been givin' me the evil eye for four months straight, girlie?" She placed a hand on her chest. "Is it me? Hmm? Don't like my hair?" She reached up and touched the snow white crown upon the lovely face of the older black woman. Eleanor figured she was probably in her late fifties or early sixties, though the twinkle in her dark brown eyes gave away the youthful spirit inside.

"No," Eleanor said, able to hear the teasing in Nannette's voice. "No, ma'am," she added, remembering her manners.

"Ma'am? Why you call me ma'am? You call me Nannette now, you hear?"

"Yes, ma—Nannette."

"Good girl. Now you gonna answer my question or do I gotta guess? Hmm? Why you always lookin' over here?"

Eleanor heard the question and saw the understanding in those kind, dark eyes, but she couldn't speak. She simply looked down, watching her fingers run together nervously.

"You are such a pretty one, girlie," Nannette said, suddenly standing a few feet away.

Eleanor looked up into her eyes. "Thank you."

Nannette reached out and placed a hand on one of Eleanor's shoulders, gently nudging her to turn so her back was to the older woman. Nannette tugged Eleanor's hair free, allowing it to fall like a shiny brown wave down her back.

"What you want?" she asked, running her fingers through it.

"I-I don't know," Eleanor murmured, even as she knew that was a lie.

"Your mama make you keep it long, hmm?" Nannette asked, gently fingering a tangle free. "Preacher man?"

Eleanor shook her head, stepping away and turning back to face the stylist. "No."

Nannette met and held her gaze. "Your daddy?"

Eleanor nodded, glancing around, half expecting Ed Landry to pop out of the shadows like the boogie man he'd been for seven months.

"What you want, girlie?" Nannette asked gently.

Taking a deep breath and letting it out slowly, Eleanor made herself be strong. "Cut it off."

Chapter Twenty-five

O kay," the man murmured absently, the jeweler's loupe firmly attached to his eye as he looked at the piece from this angle and that. "Yes, yes, I've seen this before."

Lysette stood on the opposite side of the glass counter with wood framing. It was taking a significant amount of willpower to not wander and look at all the jewelry displayed as she waited on the squirrely little man. Her patience, however, was beginning to fade.

"Do you think you can fix it?" she asked, keeping her tone light and friendly, even as she was about to yank the piece out of his hands and take it elsewhere.

"Well," the jeweler finally said, lowering the thin gold chain with its cross pendant that dangled from his fingers. "This is a beautiful and unique piece," he explained, removing the loupe and setting it on the piece of dark purple velvet laid out over the glass top. "This piece is likely circa eighteen sixty, perhaps sixty-five. Definitely Civil War era or just after." He grinned at her, his pencil-thin mustache seeming to smile right along with him. "The Victorian Era was a wonderful time for jewelers. There was so much experimentation going on," he continued. "With the discoveries of ancient artifacts and cultures—"

"I don't mean to be rude, Mr. Ellis, and it certainly is interesting," Lysette interrupted, her irritation coming through in her tone. "But can it be fixed?"

The short man cleared his throat, though Lysette couldn't tell if he was embarrassed or irritated. "This piece isn't as simple as it would appear. If you look through this," he handed her his loupe, "you can see that even in the cross itself, there are nearly microscopic notches, each one put there by hand to make the cross sparkle."

Humoring him, Lysette did as asked, and she had to admit, it was kind of neat to see so up close. "Beautiful. So intricate."

"Indeed," he exclaimed, taking the eyepiece back from her, some of his former excitement returning to his voice. "The problem is, each link on this chain is similarly nicked and notched, all unique to this piece. When it was yanked off or however the clasp was broken," he added, tapping the broken ends with a fingertip, "it took several of these links with it."

"I see," Lysette said, eyebrows drawing as concern filled her. "So it can't be fixed then?"

"Well, it can," he said, laying the necklace on the velvet square not far from where the lead crystal ring box sat. "But it won't be as simple as affixing extra gold links that I have laying around here." He indicated his small store with a wave of his hand. "They'll have to be made specifically for this in the tradition it was initially made. That is," he added, "if you want it all to match. I *can* add random links that may match each other but will not match the lion's share of the chain. Your choice."

Lysette stared down at the necklace, a fingernail tapping lightly on the glass as she considered. "What will it cost?" she asked, meeting his beady little gaze. "To re-create them."

"Oh, goodness," he said, resting his hands on

the glass case as he too stared down at the piece in question. "At least fifty dollars, Mrs. Vaughn."

"Oh, my," she murmured.

"You have to understand, the labor that would go into this alone is extensive and laborious, and the materials—"

"Let's do it," Lysette said with conviction, lightly pushing the velvet cloth toward the man to emphasize her decision.

He looked at her, thick, dark eyebrows shooting up from behind the frames of his glasses. "That's quite a bit of money. Perhaps you should come back with Mr. Vaughn."

"Mr. Ellis," she nearly purred, leaning slightly forward, her eyes hard and boring into him. "Mr. Vaughn may handle the money, but who do you think handles him?"

The jeweler swallowed hard before nodding. "Yes, ma'am. I'll get started on this right away."

"Thank you." She finally wandered around looking at various things as her order was written up so she could provide her phone number and sign it. The bell above the door dinged, and her father entered. "Almost finished here," she assured him.

"All right, how much are you going to have to sneak in past Jim?" he joked.

She smiled. "I was good."

"Ma'am?" the jeweler called to her, holding out a pen.

Moments later, father and daughter strolled arm in arm down a shady street in downtown Denver, glancing in various windows when something caught one or the other's eye. Davis Landon lived primarily in California now, though he did return to the Denver property a handful of times a year, such as now. She looked up at him, noting the gray she could see in the hair and sideburns that were visible beneath his fedora. He was still a very handsome man—the most handsome man in all the world, she thought—but he had aged considerably since her mother died. Her illness had hit him hard, and her death had taken a piece of him with her.

"I'm so glad you're staying for a few weeks this time," she said. "I miss you, and I know the kids miss you terribly."

"I miss you all, too," he said, bringing a hand up to rest over the smaller one at the crook of his arm.

She smiled at that, glancing at a window that had a beautiful dollhouse on display. "Hold up," she said, pulling away from her father and walking over to it. "Bronte loves to collect the little furniture," she explained as he stepped up beside her. "Remember, from that beautiful dollhouse *Maman* bought her when she was a little girl?"

"I do," he said with a wistful smile.

"So," Lysette began conversationally. "I haven't told you about someone very special who's come into our lives." She glanced up at him, meeting his gaze for only a moment before getting them moving again.

"Oh? Don't tell me, Jimmy finally got his way and you got a dog."

She smiled, shaking her head. "No. Are you kidding? Jim would kill me. He doesn't believe animals belong in the house, even though it's Aunt Josie and I who clean up all the messes."

"Of course," he drawled. Lysette knew her father liked Jim overall and certainly respected the kind of provider he was, but she always sensed something underlying with him.

"It's Jimmy's teacher," she began, feeling a bit mischievous rather than just outright telling him what she knew would shock him.

"Oh, yeah? If my grandson is actually listening and doing his work rather than wooing every girl in sight, I'm sorry, I can't see that as a very special teacher," he teased.

"He has straight A's, as a matter of fact."

He looked down at her with a raised eyebrow. "Well, this person *is* special," he agreed.

She smiled, the mother in her kicking in when suddenly a baby began to cry across the street. She watched as a frazzled mother tried to calm the infant. Smiling as she remembered those days, she returned her focus to her father and their conversation. There was so much she wanted—no, *needed*—to know.

"It's Ellie," she finally said, glancing up at him. "The special person is Ellie."

He stopped their forward momentum with a touch to Lysette's shoulder. "What?"

"She lives in Woodland, Daddy," Lysette said. "She's been there for years. I had no idea." She found it interesting that her father's expression was a mixture of concern and elation.

"Why didn't you tell me?"

"Hell, I just found out last fall," she said, getting them moving again and guiding them to a stone bench to sit. "I just found out the truth last week."

"She told you?" he asked quietly.

"Well," Lysette blew out, "someone had to!" She regretted her tone the moment the words were out of her mouth, even if she couldn't quite regret the words themselves. "I'm sorry I got a bit loud."

"Please don't apologize," Davis said. "I deserved that." He looked away from her and seemed to have seen something as he pushed to his feet with a grunt of exertion. "Come on."

"Daddy, I want to talk about this—" Lysette began but then saw what had caught his attention.

Without another word between the two, they headed down the street to the Cathedral of the Immaculate Conception. It was a stunning work of architecture that belonged in Europe somewhere and not Denver, Colorado. It had been a favorite spot of Margaret Brown, later known as "The Unsinkable Molly Brown."

They took a seat in the back pew that her mother always sat in when she needed some quiet introspection time. Perhaps her father needed a place such as the cathedral to confess his sins of omission to Lysette.

They got settled, and she waited for her father to speak, giving him time. Eleanor had told her all she knew from her perspective, so now it was time to hear the rest.

"That morning, I sent Alan to grab Eleanor and Emma and bring them to the train station, so we could all leave together," he began, looking straight ahead into the massive structure that was the nave. "When he arrived alone at the train station," he said, lightly shaking his head as he crossed his arms to wrap around his hat, which he'd removed upon entering the church and placed in his lap, "my heart fell. I just knew something had gone horrendously wrong."

As Lysette listened to his soft, calm voice recounting the events of that day, it was lulling her back into those images and memories.

"So," he continued, "I left you guys there

with Alan to go without me, and I drove to that old farmhouse."

He was quiet for so long, Lysette almost spoke to prompt him to continue.

"Some serious violence had taken place, honey," he murmured. "And I don't just mean the murder. There wasn't a room in that house except maybe the kitchen where there wasn't broken furniture, wall hangings crashed to the floor, someone's blood…" He finished the last in a whisper, his eyes becoming shiny as he seemed to be looking into the past, seeing it all over again. He cleared his throat and took a steadying breath. "The police were already there, and Eleanor had been taken away."

"What about Emma?" Lysette asked.

"They were going to take her to the hospital. She was beat up horribly." Again, he cleared his throat. "Broken teeth, broken jaw and nose. I think she was in profound shock. She didn't even know who I was when I tried to talk to her."

"What did you do?" she asked, nearly in a whisper. She was riveted by his tale.

"I told them who I was, answered some questions." He glanced at her. "That was when I found the necklace." He gave her a small smile. "There it was, lying on the floor surrounded by Ed's blood, yet not a drop on the cross or the chain."

She matched his smile. "Phoenix from the ashes."

He nodded. "Yeah. I put it in my pocket, then went out to find the best lawyer I could for Eleanor."

"How was she? When you guys went to see Ellie in jail?" Lysette asked, not entirely sure she wanted the answer. She thought back to who they both were so long ago, but particularly who Eleanor was. She was a strong young woman, to be sure, but had some deep fragilities, too. The thought of her being all alone, sitting in a cage, was almost too much to bear.

"Well, as you'd expect, she was scared, tired." He let out a heavy sigh, seeming tired himself. "I really didn't want to leave her. Wished so badly I could gather her up, hide her in my coat, and just leave it all behind for her." He shook his head and whistled softly between his teeth. "Tough time for that young woman."

"Why didn't you tell me? Why didn't *Maman* tell me?" Lysette asked, getting down to what she really needed to know. "I assume she knew."

He nodded. "She did. Honestly, sweetheart, we wanted you to live your life, which you had all ahead of you. There was nothing you could do where Ellie was concerned. We didn't want you to stop living or turn away from opportunities." He reached a hand over and placed it on her knee. "In retrospect, maybe we should've done things differently, but at the time, it seemed like the right thing to do."

Lysette allowed those words to mull, though she knew she'd need much longer than their time sitting in the church. She needed to be alone to really consider all that she'd been told.

❧❧❧❧

Lysette glanced at the sign welcoming her to Brooke View as she passed by on her way in. It was the same sign she remembered from when she was a kid, though it looked a bit worse for wear. She hadn't been back since that morning they'd all scurried around to hightail it to the train station.

As she prowled down the main street of the town she spent part of her childhood in, her head weaved from one side window in the car to the other, trying to take it all in. Some of the old buildings were gone while some were still there, though many with different businesses inhabiting them now, some twenty-two years later.

She slowed the car to a crawl as she neared the building her father used to own. A few years after the house was burned to the ground, the Landon family had sold all their stakes in the town, save for one, one she intended to visit later.

The building where the Landry General Store had been was now a record store, posters of the day's most popular artists plastered to the large front windows. She pulled the New Yorker in front of the building and let the engine idle as she took in what the store had become. As she saw some teenage girls giggling in the record store through the window, their hair pulled back into ponytails and held with scarves, she could easily see Eleanor standing behind the register, her hair pulled into the tight bun.

Resting her elbow on the side of her door, she put her cheek against her fist. Not for the first time, she wondered what it would have been like had things been different. What if they'd finished school in Brooke View? What if they'd become women together? Would they still be together?

The door of the record shop opened, and the two teeny boppers giggled their way out onto the sidewalk, heads together as they jabbered like monkeys in a tree over the album one of them held.

Smiling, Lysette watched them for a moment before backing the car out of the space and driving on.

There was no way she could drive to where her house used to be. From what she understood, the acreage had been sold to the town, and a baseball diamond had been built there. Though that was wonderful for the kids in Brooke View, she knew that field was there because of hate, and it wasn't something her heart could take.

The roads were as dusty as ever as she headed out into the farmland, which seemed to be producing well. She noticed the scarecrow that had become a roost for all the neighborhood birds.

When she decided to head out, she was worried she wouldn't be able to find it again, but the worry was for naught. The farther out she got, the firmer her memory became. She remembered riding shotgun next to Eleanor, her heart skipping a beat as the inexperienced driver took the dirt roads far too fast, nearly sending them into an irrigation ditch a couple of times.

She smiled at that thought before the smile slowly slid from her lips. She recognized the Howell house coming up, though now it was a light gray with dark blue trim rather than yellow with white trim, but what caught her eye the most and made her gasp was the sight of the old farmhouse.

"My god," she whispered, a hand coming to her mouth for a moment as she slowed the big car.

She drove to the long drive and turned in, her eyes wide as she took in the weed-choked yard and chipped paint on the house. Out of the five windows she could see on the front of the house, first and second floor, three of them were broken or missing. Many of the shingles on the roof were missing, some mixed in with the weeds from flying off during nasty winds or from damage caused by the snow and the rain.

She pulled the car up as close to the house as she dared. Pulling to a stop, she killed the engine and sat in the confines of the car, listening to the slight breeze that made the weeds and wild grasses shake and shimmy as though trying to lull her inside.

Hands resting on the steering wheel, she took in more of the house. Some of the bricks at the top of the chimney were missing. She chewed on her bottom lip as she studied the house, the dark holes left by the broken or missing windows felt like eyes watching her, a presence around her.

She reached her hand out, fingers wrapping around the ignition key ready to turn it when she stopped again, her gaze drawn to the house. As if of their own accord, her fingers tugged the key free, and she reached to open the driver's side door. She climbed out, immediately the breeze brushing by her, trying to take some of her hair with it as it sent it blowing in her face. She brushed it aside, considering for a moment grabbing the scarf she kept in the car for just such moments but decided against it.

Closing her car door, she took a deep, steadying breath, then picked her way carefully to the house, grateful she was in capris and flats. There was a small path, though extremely overgrown, that had once been the path to the front porch and could be navigated with careful steps.

Curiously, she found a single boy's sneaker halfway tucked into the weeds. "Okay," she drawled, picking her way past it.

Finally reaching the porch stairs, she looked down at the weathered wood, trying to make out visually if they were safe. Raising a foot, she pushed down on the first and second step, satisfied that they felt solid. She did the same all the way up to the porch, noting part of a board was missing near the house, but otherwise, she was sure it would hold her in the few steps to get to the house.

The front door was there, but it had been kicked in; the shoeprint still remained on the wood. The doorknob and locks were missing, as were two of the three hinges. She stepped inside, wary. The walls were filthy, likely from dirt and such blowing in, she reasoned. The couch had been torn to shreds, tipped on its side, the innards visible. She couldn't quite recall what the material had looked like, as she'd only seen it the one time.

Turning away from that, she scanned the floor, noting the liquor bottles, food trash, and debris from the house. She noticed something on the faded wood planks that was partially obscured by a broken table. Walking over to it, she used the toe of her shoe to shove the pieces aside.

Gasping, her hands went to her mouth. The floor had a large brownish stain. She knew instantly what it was. Tears came to her eyes as she lowered herself until she was kneeling next to it. She didn't touch it, didn't dare. But as a tear slipped from her left eye, she knew that had been where Ed Landry had taken his last breath, where his life's blood had flowed from his body, forever a stain on the floor and forever a stain on Emma's conscience. It had changed so many lives irrevocably.

Closing her eyes, she said a silent prayer for the souls of those she loved most, and yes, one for Ed Landry.

Chapter Twenty-six

Th his is absolutely adorable, Mama," Eleanor
said, reaching up to pull open a few cabinet
doors. "Plenty of room for your endless collection of
dishes and cookware." She smiled at the playful swat
that comment earned her.

"I don't know," Emma said, hands on hips as
she looked around the small, two-bedroom bungalow.
"These houses all seem so close together here."

Eleanor glanced out the kitchen window, noting
the neighbor's house just on the other side of the small
fenced-in yard. "Yes, but that's what you're wanting,
right? Not so far out, not so much yard or land to deal
with?" she reminded, opening the icebox to see it was
pristine, like the rest of the house. In her opinion, the
place would be perfect for her mother's needs, but at
the end of the day, it was up to her.

"True," Emma conceded, blowing out a breath.
"I don't know," she said, meeting Eleanor's gaze from
across the small kitchen. "I'm just not feeling this one."

"Okay, no big deal. Janice gave us several to look
at today. We'll just keep going." She smiled and walked
over to the older woman, an arm going around her
shoulder as they headed out of the house, pulling the
front door shut behind them.

Back in Emma's car, Eleanor got behind the
wheel as Emma sat shotgun. She removed the slip of
paper the Realtor had given her, using her pen to mark

off the address they were leaving.

"Okay, the next one is at 242 Campbell Street," she said.

"That's a cute little area," Eleanor commented, getting the car moving.

They drove in silence for a few moments before Emma asked, "How's your friend doing? Scott, right?"

Eleanor nodded. "He's," she hedged with a shrug, "okay, I guess. I finally got him to go to lunch with me a few days ago." She pulled the car to a stop at a stop sign. "I talked him into coming back to school in the fall." The way clear, she pushed on the gas.

"But aren't there still a couple months left in the year?" Emma asked, pen poised over the Realtor sheet as she glanced at Eleanor.

"Yes," Eleanor agreed, meeting her gaze for a moment before returning it to the road, driving along the beautiful and quiet tree-lined avenue. "But he's still incredibly jittery with loud noises and," she smirked, "let's face it, teenagers are very nosy."

"Amen to that," Emma muttered.

"Hey, now." Eleanor smiled. "He's also still having pretty bad dreams, from what he told me. I honestly think it would be a huge mistake for him to go back too soon."

"That poor young man," she said with a sigh. "Have they caught who did it?"

Eleanor smirked, anger instantly springing into her tone. "That would require the police to see this as a crime, Mama," she murmured. "They paraded Scott in front of a few lineups, but honestly, I think it was more to make them look like they're actually doing something than to solve this thing."

"You hungry?" Emma asked suddenly, cheery

tone changing the heavy energy in the car after the short discussion about Scott. "Let's get some lunch before we see the next house. What do you think?"

"Yeah, okay. What are you in the mood for?"

Ten minutes later, they were getting settled in the local diner, seated across from each other in a booth. Eleanor had grabbed them both a laminated menu from the chrome holder that was tucked against the wall by the salt and pepper shakers. She placed one in front of her mother and had opened hers when she was startled as her mother began to bounce excitedly in her seat and knock on the window they sat next to.

"Mom!" she hissed. "You're going to get us thrown out of here."

Emma obviously wasn't listening or didn't care as she flew out of her side of the booth and ran down the aisle between their row of booths and the counter lined with stools.

Head whipping to see what on earth was happening, Eleanor was shocked to see Lysette fly through the door and right into Emma's embrace, both women holding on tightly and the tears flowing and a baffled Bronte watching from the door.

"Look at you!" Emma gushed, pulling out of the hug just enough to hold the younger woman by the arms and take her all in. "You're so beautiful!"

Eleanor wasn't sure what to do. She knew that moment belonged to her mother and Lysette, but was she being rude or standoffish staying by the booth where she stood, or should she walk over there?

There was no need to decide as her mother was finishing a smothering hug of Bronte and inviting the pair to join them for lunch.

"Scoot, scoot, scoot!" Emma exclaimed,

backhanding Eleanor's thigh as she sat back down in the booth when she saw everyone headed her way. She slid across the vinyl, surprised to see Lysette slide in next to her as Emma dragged Bronte to her bench.

"Hey." Lysette grinned at her.

"Hey, yourself," Eleanor responded, the surprise evident in her voice.

"You don't mind if Bronte and I crash your lunch, do you?" Lysette teased.

Eleanor grinned and shook her head. "Of course not." Her attention was grabbed when she felt her hand taken in a calloused one. Glancing across the table, she saw that her mother had reached across with both arms, taking a hand of both women. The look of absolute joy and peace she wore took twenty years off her prematurely aged features.

"Got my girls back," she whispered, tears in her eyes. "As it should be."

Eleanor squeezed her mother's hand, swallowing her own emotion as she glanced over at Lysette, who was already looking at her.

"Well," Lysette said softly, giving Eleanor the sweetest of smiles before turning her focus to Emma. "We're all here now."

As the lunch went on, Eleanor felt like she was having an out-of-body experience. Her mother seemed to have found a new best friend in Bronte, the two giggling like school girls over music and horses. Little had Eleanor known about her own mother, but she'd ridden extensively as a child on the family ranch.

"I think Missy Roberts is going to get jealous," Lysette whispered, leaning slightly into Eleanor.

"Who's Missy Roberts?" Eleanor asked, sparing a glance at her.

"Bronte's current best friend," Lysette responded, meeting her gaze. "You know, because there's a new little girl paraded through my house every other week."

Eleanor grinned. "Were you like that?"

Lysette rolled her eyes. "Are you kidding? I didn't switch out besties when I was Bronte's age, I *collected* them."

A short but loud burst of laughter escaped Eleanor's lips at the image that popped into her mind at the comment, which sent Lysette into quiet chuckles beside her. "I can see them all," she whispered back, using her hands to pantomime her words, "all lined up in a row in that curio cabinet you had in your bedroom."

Lysette gave her the mischievous grin that Eleanor remembered so well. She grabbed her unused knife and spoon, as well as Eleanor's knife, standing them on end on the table. She hummed a little tune as she made the three pieces of flatware dance.

She sang in a quiet, high-pitched voice a horrible rendition of *Singin' in the Rain* that made Eleanor laugh.

Eleanor was torn out of her giggles when she felt eyes on her. Goofy grin still on her lips, she glanced over to see her mother and Bronte staring at them.

"Is this a private joke or can anyone join in?" Emma asked.

Eleanor cleared her throat, smile sliding from her lips as she tried to sober, but Lysette blew out a laugh, which got her going all over again.

※ ※ ※ ※

Eleanor pulled the car into the driveway of the

three-bedroom, two-bathroom house that sat on a corner lot on Beth Sayers Court. She could feel her mother's gaze on her, so she met it. "What? You've been staring at me for two minutes straight."

Emma chuckled. "I liked your rendition better than Lysette's."

Pulling the key from the ignition, she rested her hand on the door handle. "What are you talking about?"

Emma opened her door as she began to sing the chorus to *Singin' in the Rain*, her voice as clear and loud.

Eleanor rolled her eyes and grinned. "Yeah, yeah."

The two women stood in the driveway that stretched out from the single-car garage. There was a small front yard, and it was in fairly bad shape but was ripe for Emma's imagination and magical touch with anything that needed love to grow.

"This is really cute, Mama," Eleanor said, hands on hips.

"It is."

They walked up the stone path to the covered front porch to the wall-mounted mailbox where Janice told them they'd find the key.

"Quite the unexpected interlude," Emma said as Eleanor unlocked the door. "Running into Lysette and Bronte."

"Unexpected is right," Eleanor agreed. She pushed the door open, letting her mother enter before her. "You and Bronte seemed to hit it off, though."

"Oh, she's a wonderful little girl!" Emma gushed, entering the home.

"I actually don't know Bronte that well. Today

is the most time I've ever spent with her, but I agree, great kid."

The living room was spacious and was a good shape to furnish, a beautiful stone wall and fireplace the centerpiece.

"This is great, Mama," Eleanor said, easily imagining her mother's things there, including the old rocking chair by the fireplace on a cold Colorado night. "You could read or crochet by the fire." She walked over to the fireplace and opened the glass doors to look at the condition of the inner hearth.

"This house has good energy," Emma said, standing in the middle of the empty living room with hands on hips. "Let's look at the kitchen."

"Oh, Mama," Eleanor breathed, taking in the expansive space, much larger than most kitchens were popular to have. But what was truly special was the attached greenhouse that jutted off the back of the house with a door off the kitchen for entry.

"Sold!" Emma declared.

Eleanor chuckled, not surprised. "Whether you buy this place or one of the others, promise me you'll take it easy and won't overdo it when packing the old place, okay?" she said, eyeing her mother.

Emma waved her off as she headed into the greenhouse, followed by Eleanor. "You know who you haven't talked about in a while is Anne." She glanced at Eleanor. "Are you still going with her?"

Eleanor shrugged. "I suppose. She's been gone since just after the new year," she said, looking up to check the condition of the overhead panes.

"Gone? Where?"

"Family stuff, I think. She either quit her job or got a leave of absence, I forget which. But funny you should ask, though. She called last week and wants to have dinner Wednesday. So I guess she's coming back to town."

⁂

Eleanor was nervous. She honestly couldn't fully pinpoint why, she just knew that she was. She stood outside of the steakhouse Anne had asked her to meet her at, a hand resting on the lamppost as she stared at the restaurant entry. She still had a few minutes before she was scheduled to meet Anne, and after standing there for five minutes already, she was surprised she hadn't seen Anne arrive, just a steady flow of people coming and going.

Something in her gut was telling her that this was a strange situation. Anne had been gone for more than two months, nearly three with nary a phone call or letter from her during that time. She'd left town before to see her family or for business, and when she'd returned, she'd exploded back into Eleanor's life with rambunctious knocking on her apartment door or stolen kisses in the classroom.

Neither of these things had happened this time. Simply the short phone call a handful of days before, requesting dinner, had been her greeting. Taking a deep breath, she glanced at her watch and saw that she was a minute late.

"Damn it."

Hurrying inside, she was met by the host. She was about to ask for a table for two when she noticed Anne already seated in the dining room. She gave him a polite smile, then walked passed him and toward Anne's table. She was confused when a waiter was clearing off a dirty dinner setting from the place opposite where she sat with her fingers wrapped around a wine glass that had already been half-finished.

For a moment, Eleanor thought perhaps Anne had planted herself at a recently vacated table to claim it for them until she heard the waiter ask her if she or the "gentleman" would be having dessert.

"No, thank you," she said, glancing up at Eleanor. "Unless you want anything."

Perplexed and curious who this phantom "gentleman" was, she shook her head and took the empty chair. "Uh, no. I guess I already missed dinner." The knot in her stomach grew. "You know what," she said, turning to the waiter, who was about to leave, arms loaded with gathered dishes and glassware. "I'll have a glass of the house white, please."

"Yes, ma'am," he said with a small bow before hurrying away.

Eleanor turned her attention back to Anne, who brought her own glass of wine to painted lips, her gaze never leaving Eleanor's. "So how are you? It's nice to see you." She felt awkward, as though she were addressing a complete stranger. Normally, Anne oozed sensuality, playfulness, sometimes to the point of making things uncomfortable. Now sitting across from her, Anne looked at her with cold, calculating eyes.

"Good," she said, placing the glass back down on the table. "How about you? How have things been in Woodland since I've been gone?"

"Okay, I suppose. Scott's doing his best to heal, but he's struggling. My mother finally settled on a house to buy, over on Beth Sayers Court. Real happy for her."

"That's wonderful. What's wrong with Scott?

Did his parents finally throw him out?" she asked with a smirk. She gave the waiter a charming smile as he dropped off Eleanor's glass of wine and a fresh one for Anne.

Eleanor was angry; she could feel her hackles rise. "No," she drawled, voice low. "Scott and Ronnie were shot while parked out past Emery Park. Probably targeted."

"So if Scott's struggling, he obviously survived. Ronnie?"

"Ronnie's fine. Moved away," Eleanor said, eyeing Anne as she grabbed her wine. She knew that, like her, Anne thought Scott should have his own home as a man in his thirties, but other than that, as far as she knew, Anne liked Scott and Ronnie. She was surprised by the indifference she heard in her voice.

"I'm glad they're oaky, but people like that should know better. What do they expect to happen?"

"People like who?" Eleanor asked, her anger turning to confusion. "People like us, you mean?" She indicated Anne and herself. "Are those the kind of people?"

Anne studied her for a long moment before looking away, grabbing her fresh glass of wine, even as the first still had a few sips left. "I invited you here tonight to tell you something, Eleanor," she said, completely ignoring Eleanor's question and changing the topic.

"All right," Eleanor said, sipping from her own wine, feeling she'd need a bit of liquid courage for whatever was about to come.

"Patrick and I got married," she announced. "We just returned from our honeymoon." She gave her a sexy little smile. "He took me on a cruise around

Europe."

Eleanor couldn't breathe, couldn't think, not entirely sure she'd heard her correctly. It wasn't until her gaze landed on the hand that held the wine glass that she noticed the giant diamond that rested there.

"Who's Patrick?" she asked stupidly.

"He's the cousin of my sister-in-law. We met at Thanksgiving," Anne explained. Though her voice sounded strong and confident, she wouldn't meet Eleanor's gaze.

"Anne," Eleanor said, incredulous. "Not only is Patrick a man," she hissed, lowering her voice so as not to be overheard, "but you met him four months ago!"

"Yes, and I want children!" Anne nearly growled, though instantly she looked repentant. She cleared her throat and took a long drink of her wine, finishing half the liquid. "Sometimes, you just know," she added stubbornly. "I knew with Patrick."

"What, that you want him to father your children?" Eleanor gasped, stunned. "What, you sleep with him, let him knock you up, then leave him for women again?"

Anne glared at her. "I don't appreciate how you're speaking of my marriage or my husband."

"And I don't appreciate how you're making a joke out of your life, yourself, and people *like us*." Furious and utterly disgusted, Eleanor pushed back from the table, hitching the purse strap higher on her shoulder that she'd never even removed. She took one last look at Anne before turning to leave. She stopped when she heard her name called. She glanced at the seated woman over her shoulder.

"I tried to get you to give more," Anne said quietly. "I found someone who would."

Nothing more to say, Eleanor walked away, unable to not consider the fact that Lysette had also married a man. Yes, the circumstances between the women were very different and her place in their lives at the time were very different. But still, was it not possible to find someone like herself?

Chapter Twenty-seven

Y ou're cheating!" Bronte exclaimed, shoulders slumping and lower lip protruding as she stared down at the two dice that each sported six dots.

Lysette chuckled as she unloaded the last of her Bakelite discs into their compartment that lined one side of the backgammon board. She eyed the sulking twelve-year-old who sat cross-legged opposite the carved wood and leather game case on the living room floor, the fire crackling merrily in the fireplace on the chilly spring evening.

"Come on, don't get upset. Let's play again," Lysette encouraged, wiping the board clear. "Do you want to be blue again?" At the barely perceptible nod, she reset the board. "See, the problem is, you're so concerned with landing on my pieces and putting them in jail that you're not focusing on getting your own guys home, honey," she explained gently. "It's a game of strategy, not just attack." The board set, she studied Bronte until her gaze met her own. "Okay? Want to try it?"

With only a sullen nod for acknowledgment, Bronte accepted the cup with her two dice in it.

Lysette was amused. Her daughter was a competitive soul and definitely not a good loser. She shook her cup, rattling the dice inside when she heard the return of Jim and Jimmy after a day of fly fishing.

"Jimmy!" Bronte exclaimed, hopping up and

running toward the kitchen and back door where her brother and father had entered. "Come help me beat Mom!"

Lysette chuckled, leaning back on her hands as she waited for the cavalry to appear.

"What, did she beat the pants off you again playing Hearts and that's why you're wearing a dress?" Jimmy's disembodied voice joked.

"Jimmy!"

"All right," Jimmy said, appearing in the living room. He glanced down at Lysette and the game as he cracked his knuckles dramatically. "Backgammon, huh?" He nodded with exaggerated confidence. "I got this."

Lysette rolled her eyes at his theatrics. "Get down here so I can beat you and declare a night of victory."

He grinned, lowering himself to the floor where Bronte had been sitting, his sister joining them to watch.

"You'll be *so* jealous, Jimmy," Bronte taunted.

"Why?" he asked, eyeing the board as Lysette made her opening move.

"We met Miss Brannon for lunch today and her mom, Miss Emma!"

Lysette sent a surreptitious look first to her son, then over to the couch where Jim was getting settled with the newspaper in his hands. She noted that he glanced their way as he noisily shook the daily post open.

"What? How?" he asked, looking from Bronte to Lysette with wide eyes.

"Don't fib, Bronte," Lysette said with quiet warning in her voice. "We ran into them at the restaurant, so we all ate lunch together."

Bronte gave her an apologetic look before continuing with her story excitedly. "Did you know Mommy and Miss Brannon were best friends when they were my age?"

Jimmy looked to Lysette, shocked. "Seriously?"

"Well, we were a little older, but yes, we were close."

"Well, hot dog!" He sat back away from the backgammon game for a moment, shaking his head in disbelief, making Lysette smile. "My whole life, it's all been a lie."

She laughed outright, reaching across and slapping his leg playfully. "It's your turn, drama queen."

By the second declaration of "I win again!" by Lysette, the kids lost interest and wandered off to go work on a jigsaw puzzle together upstairs.

"You are a sore winner as a mother," Jim said from behind his newspaper.

Still on the floor as she cleaned up the game, Lysette glanced his way. "Hey, the contract I remember signing while in labor was that I had to feed them and clothe them, not let them win at backgammon."

Jim lowered the newspaper. "Must have been in the fine print." He folded the paper and set it aside. "You should've seen Jimmy out there today," he said conversationally, crossing his ankle over the opposite knee. "Really did well. He's a natural."

"That's great," she responded with a smile as she closed the game closed and clasped it. "He's been wanting to learn for ages."

"So you and Bronte had a good day today?" he asked, his foot falling back to the floor as he sat forward, elbows resting on his knees.

"We did." She nodded as she repositioned her own body, curling her legs behind her as she leaned over to rest her weight on her hand and hip.

"You made it to the skating rink then?"

She wanted to roll her eyes, hating his fishing expeditions. "Yup," she said, hiding her irritation behind a smile. "Got the bruises on my butt to prove it."

"Listen, I was going to ask you if you wouldn't mind organizing Rita's retirement dinner for next Saturday," he asked, fingers spread out as he lightly tapped fingertips and palms of both hands together.

"She finally decided to do it, huh?" Lysette asked of the woman who had acted as a receptionist to Jim when he took over the firm, as well as the original lawyer. "Good for her and, sure. How many, what time, and where? I told you I was taking the kids to Denver next Saturday."

"Why again?" he asked, seeming irritated at that.

"The man at the jewelry store called and said my necklace should be fixed then, and the kids want to see Daddy."

He nodded, sitting back against the couch. "All right. I think seven is a good time to start dinner, so you'll have to be back in plenty of time."

She hated the tone that had entered his voice. It was one he used with her often when they were first married—that he was the man and therefore knew best. He would, however, humor her but would be watching carefully to make sure she didn't screw it up.

"Jim," she said, wrapping her fingers around the handle to the clasped backgammon case as she pushed to her feet. "Don't treat me like a child. I've kept your ass on time for fifteen years."

With those words, she walked out of the room.

☙ ☙ ☙ ☙

"One, please," Lysette said, pointing at the medium-sized bag. "And yes, lots of butter." She was given her total and slid the coins across the counter. As she waited, she felt her nerves act up. She could feel her heart beat a little bit faster, a few beads of sweat trickle between her breasts.

"Here you are, ma'am."

"Thank you," she said, taking the hot buttery popcorn with a smile. She gathered several napkins and headed to the theater.

There were several people already in the large dim room, but it wasn't hard to find the one person she was looking for. Lysette smiled, her heart once again fluttering slightly. Since the surprise—and absolutely wonderful—lunch the previous day with Eleanor and her mother, Lysette had been on cloud nine. There was something about Eleanor that, as much as she made her heart skip a beat and palms sweat, brought comfort to her. She had such a calm, quiet nature that put Lysette at ease, made her feel she could be herself, but her better version.

That feeling increased when she sidestepped her way down the aisle where Eleanor sat, the two making brief eye contact before Lysette turned her focus on what she was doing so she wouldn't step on any toes or do a header over the row of seats ahead of her.

"Hey," Eleanor said, moving her jacket from the seat next to her. Obviously, she'd been using it to save the seat.

"Hello." Lysette handed the popcorn to Eleanor. "Would you mind?"

"Nope."

Lysette shrugged out of her jacket, leaving her in a fitted sweater in a deep green that she felt did good things for her eyes and for her figure. That was to say, she hoped Eleanor thought so. She knew it was wrong to think that way, and even if she never said the words out loud to anyone else but her own conscience, she hoped Eleanor still saw her as beautiful.

Getting settled, she took the popcorn back. "Thank you. Want some?"

Eleanor grinned at her, producing two bottles of Coca-Cola out of the pocket of her purse.

"Oh, still cold," Lysette murmured, taking one. She laughed outright as Eleanor wiggled her eyebrows when she pulled out a church key.

"I feel like high school kids who snuck beer into class," Eleanor murmured, reaching over to pop the top off Lysette's bottle before turning to her own.

Lysette grinned. "Have you had to deal with that one before? As a teacher?" she asked before taking a cool, refreshing drink.

"You have no idea," Eleanor muttered, tapping her bottleneck to Lysette's before sipping.

They remained silent for a moment, Lysette watching some of the concession advertisements that were flashing across the big screen. She was barely paying attention to the message as she could smell Eleanor's perfume. It wasn't a scent she was used to smelling on her. She closed her eyes, trying to focus on that smell as opposed to the strong scent of buttered popcorn.

"Mama is moving in three weeks," Eleanor said,

unwittingly pulling Lysette from her thoughts.

Lysette's eyes blinked open. "She is? That's wonderful!" Lysette glanced behind her when she was shushed by a man sitting behind them. "It's a dancing hot dog, mister," she said with a raised eyebrow before turning back to Eleanor, leaning in close to continue their chatting. "Is she excited?" she murmured into Eleanor's ear, surprised when she felt a small tremor go through Eleanor.

Eleanor nodded, turning slightly toward her. "Very."

"If she needs help, let me know." They sat in silence for a long moment, each taking turns dipping her hand into the bag of popcorn on Lysette's lap. A couple of times, their hands brushed going in or out. Lysette felt a little charge each time, sometimes unable to withhold her gasp. She felt like a child and had to laugh at herself. Finally, she leaned close again. "What are you doing Saturday?" she whispered.

"This coming one?" Eleanor whispered back. "Nothing," she said after Lysette nodded. "Why?"

"I'd like you to come to Denver with me and the kids," Lysette said, meeting Eleanor's gaze in the darkness of the theater, the vibrant light and colors from the big screen reflecting in Eleanor's eyes. "Please?"

Eleanor leaned in, her hot breath washing against the side of Lysette's neck. "Will the kids mind?"

It took Lysette a moment to bounce back as the heat began to extend far beyond the breath coming out of Eleanor's body. She swallowed. "Yeah," she managed. "They'll love it, I think."

Eleanor looked at her, her gaze holding for a long moment before she suddenly looked away, the hand that had been draped casually along the arm of the chair that separated hers from Lysette's moving to her lap, her hand wrapping around her soda bottle. "Okay."

❧❧❧❧

"How did you know all that stuff?" Bronte asked, trailing her French fries through the blob of ketchup. "You knew more than the museum lady did."

"Well," Eleanor responded, setting her malt down after taking a long, slow sip. "I was a history major in college," she explained. "I specialized in European history."

"I told you I'd bring you back here," Lysette said so softly that Eleanor wasn't sure the kids heard. She met and held Lysette's long, steady gaze, so many emotions passing through her before the spell was broken by Jimmy's voice.

"Did you go to CU in Boulder?" Jimmy asked, his cheek leaning on a closed fist like a little lovesick puppy. More than once that day, Lysette had given him "the look" to be a gentleman. "I'm going to CU," he announced.

Lysette's eyebrows lifted. "You think so, do you?" she asked. "You know your dad wants you to go to his alma mater, Stanford."

"No," Eleanor admitted, shaking her head. "I went to Wichita State University."

Lysette was surprised to hear that. "In Kansas?"

Eleanor met her gaze and nodded, popping her last French fry into her mouth. "Yup."

Lysette knew she needed to be careful, as she was pretty sure Eleanor didn't want the kids to know about what happened. "When did you leave Colorado?"

"In 1942," she said softly, though loud enough not to seem like a secret. "I was twenty-three, and some of the other ladies that were leaving at the same time decided to go to Wichita. There were tons of jobs with the war going on, so we worked making B-52s."

"Wow, really?" Jimmy asked, eyes wide with excitement. "You built those?"

Eleanor nodded. "I did. I worked there while I went to school to become a teacher."

"And then you came back here to teach," Lysette said. She felt so much pride and admiration in her heart, knowing where Eleanor had just gotten out of only to turn around and go into service to educate young people.

Eleanor met her gaze. "Eventually, yes."

"Someday, I want to hear the whole story," Lysette said softly, hoping Eleanor would be willing. She wanted to know more about that time in her life but knew sitting at lunch with her children wasn't the right time.

❧❧❧❧

"Come make this shot for me, Mom!" Jimmy whined, holding his croquet club out to her like an offering from where he stood on the manicured lawn thirty yards away.

"Nope," Lysette called back, shaking her head. "As I recall, you told me you never, ever, ever wanted to play games with me ever, ever, ever again."

"You're missing a couple of evers," he groused, turning his attention back to the game he played with his sister and grandfather.

"I see a lot of Adalyn in him," Eleanor said from where she sat under the tree next to Lysette, watching the trio play. "That same spunky personality."

Lysette tilted her head slightly as she studied him, then nodded, looking over at her friend. "Yes, I can see that. Come on," she said, reaching out to lightly slap Eleanor's knee. "Let's go take a walk."

The afternoon was gorgeous with robin's egg-blue skies above and not a cloud in sight. The grass was returning from winter yellow to the emerald green of spring. They walked in silence away from the game, able to hear Bronte's high-pitched laughter float across the late afternoon.

"It's so peaceful out here," Eleanor said, her voice quiet.

"It is. I don't really come here all that much unless Daddy's here." Lysette gave her a small smile. "No time."

"It's amazing to see him today," Eleanor said. "Thank you so much for bringing me here."

Lysette smiled and let out a contented sigh. She reached out and hooked her arm through the bend of Eleanor's, bringing their casual steps closer together. "So I haven't seen you with the pretty blonde in a while," she said conversationally, knowing full well she was fishing with a pole that bore flashing lights. She hadn't even intended to ask, but the words had fallen out of her mouth. "Do you teach with her?"

The smallest of smiles touched Eleanor's lips before she responded. "No, she wasn't a colleague."

Lysette hoped there would be more, but when there wasn't, she knew she had to cast again. "A friend?"

"Anne and I were more than friends but weren't

exactly on the fast track to forever, either." She spared Lysette a side glance. "She dumped me to become Mrs. Patrick Something-or-other."

Lysette felt that like a stab to the heart, both that they had in fact been intimate, that Anne had broken up with her, and that she'd done so for a man. Her own marriage to Jim had weighed heavily on her over the years, especially when she'd come across the few women like Eleanor and Danny Felts who had remained true to themselves and hadn't taken the easy way out, as she had.

"I'm so sorry," she said quietly, about to pull away, but Eleanor covered her hand with her own, keeping her where she was as they continued to walk. "That must have really hurt."

Eleanor shrugged. "The truth is, I think she's selling herself short, but that's her choice, it's her life. I think ultimately what bothered me the most was how she went about it, sneaking behind my back. I just can't condone cheating like that. If you're not happy, leave," she said simply, unwittingly driving another stake through Lysette's heart.

"Do you miss her?"

Eleanor shook her head. "No, not really. But I *do* miss knowing there's someone out there that thinks I'm special. Someone out there that I know is going to think about me at least once a day and maybe even smile or," she gave Lysette a sheepish grin, "blush a little when thinking about a memory regarding me. That's what I miss. It's not something tied specifically to Anne, but yeah." She shrugged again. "That's what I miss."

Lysette stopped them, deciding it was the right time. "Turn around," she said softly, gently guiding

Eleanor to turn her back to her. She reached into her pocket and withdrew the cross necklace she'd picked up when they'd first arrived in Denver that morning. "I got this fixed for you," she explained, taking the beautiful piece, which had been cleaned and polished to brand new perfection out of the ring box, tucking that back into the pocket. "The clasp was broken, and it was in bad shape."

Taking the ends in both hands, Lysette raised her arms high enough so the chain cleared Eleanor's head, then brought them down and back until the cross pendant was in place before she clasped the chain home.

"I love that you cut your hair," she said, quickly running her fingers through the short strands at the base of Eleanor's neck before turning her back to face her. Her gaze dropped down to take in the cross, which glistened beautifully against the paleness of Eleanor's soft skin. "Looks beautiful," she whispered, looking up to meet Eleanor's gaze.

"I told you to keep this," Eleanor said, a bit of emotion in her voice as her hand fluttered up, fingers immediately wrapping around the cross as Lysette had seen her do a hundred times when she was a teenager.

Lysette nodded and gave her a soft smile. "Yes, but now I have the real thing back. I don't need the cross." She leaned in and left a small kiss on Eleanor's cheek. "And," she added, moving away just enough to look into her eyes. "Tonight when I'm at Jim's dinner party, I'll remember the look in your eyes right now, and I'll smile."

Chapter Twenty-eight

It's wonderful to see you, Jeffry. I think it's been since Mandy's birthday dinner that we saw each other last," Lysette said, turning her head to accept a kiss to the cheek by one of the three partners from the law firm.

"It's nice to see you, Lysette." He took the empty seat next to her at the three tables that had been pushed together in the reserved back room of the restaurant. "I apologize for being late."

She smiled politely at him as he scooted his chair closer to the table. The dinner had been going on for nearly forty-five minutes now, yet only drinks had been served in the open bar that was manned by one of the restaurant employees.

"Would you like a drink? I'm going to grab myself another," she offered, pushing back from the table.

"Aw, that'd be swell. Yeah, how's about a rum runner?" the bespectacled attorney said with a smile.

"Coming right up."

She knew she looked good in her fitted purple dress with a neckline that left the tops of her shoulders bare and gave a peek of her legs, but the truth was, she wanted to be in a nightgown sipping coffee and watching television or reading a good book. Her smile was instant as she pictured Eleanor lying with her head in her lap holding the book high above her face reading aloud, just like they used to.

Walking toward the bar, she saw Jim already there, placing an empty tumbler on the bar top as he grabbed what she'd counted was a third bourbon on the rocks, as well as a mixed drink that she knew wasn't for her.

She watched him, curious where he was off to. He'd been drifting from person to person and group to group mingling, as she knew he would and should be. However, he usually dragged her around with him. He'd been quiet since she'd returned with the kids from Denver to get ready for their night.

Jim scooped up his fresh drinks and headed across the room where there was one of his partners and his wife standing, as well as a lovely young woman with mid-back dark hair and a lovely olive complexion. She looked young, mid-twenties, perhaps. She looked away from the conversation she was having when he approached and accepted the cocktail he extended to her. What really caught Lysette's eye, however, was when the woman allowed her finger to trail over his during the exchange of the glass from one hand to the other. It was a very intimate move and one he didn't even react to, as though she'd touched him a hundred times before.

Shaking herself from her thoughts, she continued to the bar and ordered the rum runner for Jeffry and a pink squirrel for herself.

"Here you are, sir," she said dramatically, delivering Jeffry's drink to him. He thanked her with a smile before returning to the conversation he was having with Rita, the retiring receptionist.

Lysette sat down and sipped the pink drink, made a bit strong. Her gaze found Jim again, but this time, he and the brunette had moved away from the others and were standing in a corner, the woman halfway hidden behind a large potted plant.

Initially, they seemed to be chatting, a little flirty by his expression, the woman's face out of Lysette's view. But within a few moments, things changed. Jim's expression became attentive, then serious, then upset. She could see the woman's hands as they gesticulated wildly, her drink disappearing somewhere along the way.

Jim ran a hand through his hair, anger in his eyes. He said something, words unheard from the distance. He turned to walk away, but she stopped him with a hand to his shoulder. He turned and said something else before he successfully walked away.

∿∾∿∾

"You can put those on the dresser," Lysette said quietly, pointing. Jeffry followed her directions, placing Jim's car keys there while another of the men from the dinner party helped get an extremely inebriated Jim to the bed where he fell with a dramatic groan.

"Are you sure you're okay with him?" Jeffry asked, stepping up next to where Lysette stood by the bed as the second man joined them, sweat beading on his forehead from the exertion.

"Oh, yeah. I'll let him sleep it off, then admonish him in the morning," she said with a small grin, glancing at both men. "Thank you both so much for bringing my drunk husband and his car home."

She walked them to the front door and accepted a quick hug from Jeffry before closing and locking the door behind them. Glancing to the stairs in the dark quiet house, she let out an annoyed sigh and headed back upstairs to take care of him.

To her surprise, Jim was sitting up on the bed, using incredibly uncoordinated movements to try to loosen his tie. One hand shot to the bed to brace his weight as he nearly fell over sideways. A small giggle escaped his lips.

"Let me help you," she said with a sigh, walking over to the bed.

"I can do this!" he exclaimed, shoving her hands away and glaring up at her like a petulant child.

She stood back, fists on her hips as she watched, doing a mental countdown in her head until finally he grumbled—

"I can't do this."

"You don't say," she uttered, reaching out again and untangling the knot he'd made in the fabric as he'd tried to slide the tie knot loose. "How many of those stupid things did you drink?" she asked casually, sliding the tie free from Jim's upturned collar.

"Enough," he muttered, glancing up at her before quickly looking away. "Or maybe not enough."

She ignored the slight, knowing Jim only drank to excess when something was bothering him, and apparently, that something regarded her. She began to unbutton his shirt, but again, her hands were pushed aside. Knowing he at least couldn't accidentally hang himself with shirt buttons, she moved to his shoes.

"So who is the brunette?" she asked, keeping her voice conversational.

He looked up at her with so much anger in his eyes that for a moment it startled her. "Why?" He smirked. "Jealous?"

She dropped the first shoe to the floor as she considered his question. After a moment, she was able to look him in the eye and answer honestly. "No."

"Of course you weren't," he spat, pulling the ends of his shirt apart, not realizing he'd missed the last two buttons, which went flying. "Goddamn it!"

"Calm down, Jim," Lysette hissed. "You'll wake up the kids." She threw the second shoe to the floor far harder than she'd intended to, the leather wingtip thudding heavily. She walked away from the bed and to the closet, reaching behind her to unzip her dress as she went.

"I know she was there with you today," he muttered, climbing off the bed. He braced himself against the wall for a moment before pushing away, shrugging out of his shirt as he did.

Her back to him as she opened the closet door to retrieve her nightgown, she said, "Hardly a mystery, Jim, considering the kids were talking about it when I fed them dinner before we left tonight."

"I don't want her around my children," he said, allowing his shirt to slide down his arms and to the floor where he left it, stepping over it to get to the bench at the end of the bed. He staggered over to it before nearly collapsing onto it, banging his head on the footboard as he nearly slid off the bench. "Goddamn it!" he roared again.

Lysette could only stare at him. Like anyone, Jim had bad days or bad moments, but he certainly wasn't known for the temper he was showing. "Jim, calm down."

"Calm down?" he repeated, looking at her as he pushed himself into a sitting position on the bench. "Why should I do that? As your husband, I've made it clear that I don't want that woman around here."

"And as a woman who thinks for herself, she's

hardly here, Jim," Lysette snapped, her own anger building. She tugged the dress off over her head and, standing in bra, panties, and nylons, hung it on its hanger. "What is your deal with her, anyway? You had such profuse admiration and adoration for her a handful of months ago. What's changed?"

"*You* changed," he said, removing his socks and throwing them wherever they landed. He got shakily to his feet and began to unbutton his trousers. "You, Lysette," he said, glaring at her as she retrieved her nightgown from its hanger. "You're a cold, hard bitch," he spat. "Unmoved, unfazed by anything, even those bitches you've messed around with over the years."

Stunned at the venomous words he was spewing, she turned and looked at him, nightgown forgotten in her hands. "What?"

"Oh, yes," he said with obvious satisfaction. "I know about the other women," he added, obviously misunderstanding the source of her shock. "Even they couldn't bring some semblance of warmth to you." He paused as she took a couple of steps toward him. "But then there's pretty Miss Brannon," he continued. "She enters the room, and either you're so hot you're ready to throw a glass against the wall, or you can't keep a clear thought in your head. Either way, you're ready to roll over with your legs spread."

The slap came so quickly and so hard, the shrill sound startled them both. It wasn't until her hand was falling back to her side that Lysette realized she'd inadvertently cut his cheek with her nails in the process. A tiny thread of blood trailed from the small wound.

Jim reached a hand up, dabbing his fingertip into red fluid and looking at it before rubbing his finger and thumb together until the tiny smudge was gone. "I don't want her around my kids."

"Leave her alone," Lysette said, warning in her voice as she stepped back toward the closet. She would never condone violence, but right now, she just couldn't promise she wouldn't lash out at Jim again if he dared continue his verbal attack on Eleanor. "She paid her debt to society, Jim, and for a crime she didn't even commit. Leave her alone," she warned again.

"Do you think her fellow teachers know about her past?" he goaded, staring at her with hands on hips and feet planted wide. "Does the superintendent know?"

Lysette was in the process of slipping the nightgown over her head as her discarded bra lay at her feet. She whirled on him, jaw clenched. She was about to speak but stopped when Jim beat her to it.

"I could ruin her!"

"Mama?"

Lysette turned, horrified to realize she hadn't closed the bedroom door and Bronte stood there, looking frightened at them.

"Why is Daddy bleeding?" she asked, her voice small and a finger going to her mouth to chew on. It was the nervous habit she'd carried since she'd been a toddler.

Lysette hurried over to her, gathering her against her. "It's okay, sweetheart," she murmured, leaving a kiss atop her head. "Go on back to your room, and I'll be there in just a minute, okay?"

Bronte nodded and glanced over at her father before turning around and padding back down the hall.

Lysette watched her go and waited until she was in her bedroom before she turned to Jim, who still had fire in his eyes. She sauntered up to him, her gaze boring into his. "I've known you almost twenty years," she said softly, her tone belying the danger in her own eyes. "And I've done your books for nearly ten. I know a lot about you, Jim, so don't fuck with me." She held his gaze for a moment longer before she turned and left the bedroom, closing the door behind her.

⁂

Lysette stood outside the door, not entirely sure why but knowing she shouldn't be there, yet there she was. She leaned against the row of cool metal lockers, able to feel the lock on one press into her lower back.

She blew out a breath and glanced at her watch. The bell should be ringing at any time, which it did, startling her in its shrillness. Doors up and down the hall flew open as excited students rushed out of their classrooms to hit the cafeteria for the lunch period. She scooted out of the way as a couple of students needed to get into lockers near where she stood.

"Sorry," she murmured, her gaze going to the classroom across the hall from her.

"Ross, I know it's burger day, but you forgot your books!" Eleanor called out, standing in the open doorway.

Lysette smiled as Eleanor was nearly knocked over by the forgetful student who ran past her back into the classroom. It was in that moment that Eleanor saw Lysette waiting. She walked over to her, dodging a student or two along the way.

"Hey."

Lysette met her gaze and tried to smile, but it failed miserably. "Hi."

"Is everything okay?"

Lysette shrugged as she hugged her purse to her. "Sure," she managed with a smile that was obvious that Eleanor didn't buy.

"Stay right here," Eleanor said, hurrying back across the hall to her classroom. She appeared a moment later with her own purse before closing the classroom door and locking it. She returned to Lysette's side. "Come on."

They drove the short distance to Eleanor's apartment in silence, though Lysette did reach over and squeeze a soft hand briefly before pulling to the curb next to the brick building where Eleanor lived.

"Can I get you anything?" Eleanor asked, letting them into her home. "I can make some coffee, or I think I have some Coca-Cola," she offered, setting her purse and keys on the table before closing the door behind Lysette.

"No, I'm okay. But please, eat your lunch," Lysette said, feeling guilty that she was taking up her time.

"Come sit." Eleanor pulled out a kitchen chair and patted it before moving to the icebox.

Lysette let out a heavy, tired sigh as she entered the kitchen and laid her purse on the table before taking the seat offered her. She was exhausted, both physically and emotionally. She'd spent the night with Bronte and had slept little, her mind solely on the horrible argument with Jim and her feelings about it. She wasn't entirely sure what she wanted from Eleanor in that moment, other than she made her feel so much better about everything. Simply being around her gave her peace.

"I have enough for two," Eleanor said, turning to show a plastic container of egg salad. "Sandwich?"

"No, thank you. Please, Ellie, eat. I really should leave." She pushed up from the chair only to have Eleanor set the container of food on the counter and rush over to her, stopping her with a hand to her wrist. She met Eleanor's concerned gaze.

"God," Eleanor whispered, bringing up a hand to lightly brush Lysette's cheek with her fingers. "What's wrong?"

To her horror, the tears came. She felt Eleanor's arms wrap around her, and she was brought into a warm embrace. She allowed herself to be held and returned the hug, clinging to Eleanor. As she cried, gentle fingers combed through her hair and caressed her back. She realized that she wasn't just crying over the upset of the night before, but of what she'd been feeling since she'd come to realize Eleanor was back in her life. She knew she also deeply grieved over the loss of something so long ago, something only able to be exorcised recently when the truth was finally revealed.

After long moments, her emotions calmed, and she was able to control herself once more. Still, she held on, taking several cleansing breaths, letting them out slowly. "Jim and I had a horrible fight last night." When she felt Eleanor pulling out of the hug, she held fast. "No. I need to say some things, but I can't dare look at you." She smiled at her own words, knowing it was silly. "I just can't."

"Okay," Eleanor said softly, stroking her back. "Tell me."

"Jim said some truly terrible things to me, but he said something that made me think." She smirked, her fingers playing lightly in the soft strands of Eleanor's hair. "He said I'm a cold, hard person, unless I'm around you."

"Lysette, no. That can't be true—" Eleanor protested.

"But it is true," Lysette interrupted. "It is," she whispered against her neck. "Unless it's my children or my father, I'm so closed off, emotionally vacant. I hide, Ellie. I hide behind walls that were built the night I lost you." She squeezed her eyes closed as emotion balled in her throat. She swallowed it down to continue. "Since you've come back into my life, all I want to do is be around you," she admitted. "I want to feel again." She inhaled Eleanor's scent, absorbed the feeling of her warm skin against her face. "I want to touch you," she whispered. "I want to kiss you." She swallowed again and squeezed her eyes shut in shame. "I want to make love with you." The tears were threatening to come back. "I know that I can do none of these things because once I start, I know I'll never be able to stop."

Lysette heard the small gasp at her words, words she couldn't hold back. Now that she'd let herself begin to open again, so much was washing over her. Eyes remaining closed, she pulled back just enough to rest her forehead against Eleanor's. She cupped her face, enjoying the softness beneath her fingertips.

"Forgive me," she continued, leaving a lingering kiss on Eleanor's lips before pulling her back into a tight hug. "I have to go," she said into it, knowing if she didn't she'd allow something to happen that could destroy any chance of their even being friends.

Chapter Twenty-nine

Eleanor looked down at the same container of egg salad that sat on her counter. She wasn't all that hungry but knew she had to eat. After Lysette had left her apartment earlier that day, Eleanor had been left confused and deeply moved by her words.

She'd lost her heart to Lysette Landon the moment she first saw her, and Lysette had selfishly kept it for twenty-two years, unbeknownst to her. Well, come to find out, Eleanor had been just as much of an unwitting keeper.

With a look of disgust, she grabbed the plastic container and headed back to the icebox, deciding she'd rather watch a little television while grading papers, then hit the hay early. Closing the icebox door, she was headed to the living room when she heard raised voices outside her door.

"Sir! I can't allow you to bother Miss Eleanor!"

"Get the hell outta my way!"

She hurried to the door at the sound of the scuffle. Unlocking her door, she yanked it open to see her neighbor Marvell Walker trying to stop Jim Vaughn's approach.

"Damn it! Leave me alone!" Jim growled, struggling against the taller black man.

"Hey!" Eleanor called out, hurrying over to them. It was only then that she realized Jim held a pistol and a bottle of whiskey. "Jim! Stop!"

At the sound of her voice, Jim pulled away from the older man. He shook his arms out to straighten his jacket, which had become hiked up during the scuffle.

"Want me to call the police, Miss Eleanor?" Marvell asked, eyeing Jim.

She looked into Jim's face, and despite the fact he held a weapon, she saw a man in deep pain, not one who intended to inflict pain upon her. Walking over to her neighbor, she placed her hand on his arm. "No, Mr. Walker," she said softly, giving him a smile. "Thank you so much."

He took a long look at Jim before nodding at her and returning to his apartment.

Eleanor turned to Jim, as well. He stood in the center of the hallway, whiskey bottle held between two fingers by its neck while the revolver was held limply in the other hand. She nodded toward it. "What's that for?"

He looked down at it, almost as though remembering he was holding it. He halfheartedly raised it. "You're gonna tell me where my wife is," he declared, taking a step toward her.

"She's not here," she said simply.

"Bullshit!" he exclaimed, holding the gun a little firmer. "Where is she?"

She let out a heavy sigh, heartbroken to see the man standing before her. His suit was sloppy, tie loosened, and shirt partially untucked. His jacket was wrinkled as were his trousers. He looked as though he hadn't shaved that morning, and his hair obviously hadn't been greased that day, the bangs hanging in his eyes.

Walking to her open apartment door, she stood aside, looking at him as she indicated with her hand that he should go look for himself. As he passed her, the smell of Jack Daniels was strong. She followed him in, closing her apartment door softly behind her so as not to bother her neighbors anymore.

She walked into the kitchen, irritation flashing hot as she stood by the table, arms crossed over her chest. She could hear him in her bedroom, opening her closet door and even pushing the shower curtain aside once he reached the bathroom.

She glared at him once he appeared, shoulders slumped and looking utterly defeated. He looked as though he couldn't decide if he wanted to yell or cry. She was very surprised by the gun, but she now saw it as the actions of a desperate man, though she wasn't entirely sure where that desperation lay.

Walking over to him, she grabbed his wrist with one hand and with gentle fingers, removed the pistol from him. "Come on," she said. "Sit down."

She walked over to the counter, took the gun in both hands, and pulled the pin to release the cylinder. She let out a small sigh of relief to find the Smith & Wesson was unloaded. Slipping the cylinder back into place, she set the revolver on the counter and stepped back over to the table where, unbeknownst to him, Jim had planted himself in the very chair his wife had sat in earlier that afternoon.

Taking the seat to his right, Eleanor studied his face, noting he refused to meet her gaze. "What's going on, Jim? Give me one reason I shouldn't have you arrested."

"Lysette," he said quietly. "That's the reason." He sat back and unscrewed the cap on the bottle before taking a swig. Face screwed up with the burn of the alcohol, he offered the bottle to her.

She stared at it for a moment before taking it from him and taking her own swig, a shiver racing through her body as the burning whiskey did. "Yikes."

He grinned, taking the bottle back and setting it aside. "She took off," he said, any mirth gone from his expression. "Figured she'd come here."

Eleanor shook her head. "No." She wasn't about to tell him that she'd already seen her that day.

"If I ask you a question, Eleanor, will you tell me the truth?" he asked, staring down at his hands, which rested on the table.

"Of course," she said, though her stomach lurched. But she'd promised him and would answer his questions.

"Are you and my wife having sex?" he asked, gaze still unwilling or unable to meet her own.

"No," she said simply and honestly. "We are absolutely not."

He finally looked up and studied her for a long moment before nodding. He reached for the liquor bottle again, but Eleanor stopped him.

"Slow your roll there, mister," she said, taking the bottle and getting to her feet. She grabbed two drinking glasses and sprinkled in some ice cubes along with Coca-Cola and finally, a splash of whiskey each, though barely any in her own. She brought the glasses back to the table and set his in front of him. "I have a feeling you need to talk, so let's keep a straight head, huh?"

He gave her a grateful smile before wrapping a large hand around his drink. "Thanks." He sipped thoughtfully for a moment before speaking again. "But you do love her, don't you?"

"Yes, I do," Eleanor responded easily. "I never

stopped."

"And you two weren't in contact in any way all these years, until last fall?" he pried.

She had a feeling these were questions he'd asked of Lysette and was trying to confirm her answers. Lysette had no reason to lie to him, so the truth should suffice for Eleanor, as well. "None. I wrote her a handful of letters when I was first incarcerated, but they went unanswered. That was in…" She glanced up at the ceiling as she did the mental math. "The last was sent back to me unopened in thirty-five, maybe early thirty-six, but she never received them, so it had nothing to do with her."

He nodded, seeming to take her at her word, taking another small sip. "This is good," he said, studying the clear glass of dark liquid. "Never tried it with Coca-Cola before."

She smiled. "Can I ask you a question?"

He looked surprised but nodded. "Shoot."

"How did you meet her?"

His eyebrows raised. "You mean, you guys haven't chatted about all this?"

"I think you have it in your head that she and I spend every waking moment together that she's not in your visual presence. We don't, haven't."

He let out a heavy whiskey-scented sigh as he sat back in his chair, a hand running through his hair. "Well, she'd returned from France. Things started to get really ugly there. She won't talk about it much, but I think she lost some good school friends when those Nazi bastards began clearing Paris of Jews. Bad time," he said, taking a sip. "Her family was in California, so that's where she went. She began working with the accounting office for the factories Davis owned, where

I worked while in law school. God, she was gorgeous," he whispered, staring off into a time where Eleanor didn't want to be. It would have killed her to see Lysette fall in love or get married.

She cleared her throat, forcing herself to ask questions that deep down she needed to know the answers to but didn't want to. "How long did you date before you married?"

"Almost two years." He smirked. "Truth is, I didn't want to wait that long, but she just wouldn't say yes." He glanced at her. "I guess now I know why," he said, a bit of bitterness in his voice. "Did her parents know about you two?"

Eleanor nodded. "They did. But more than that, they knew the incredibly bad place my mother and I were in, so they did all they could to help us get out."

"Until you took matters into your own hands, right? Killed your own father?" he spat.

Eleanor felt anger rising but knew it had no place in that conversation. She knew Jim was angry and hurting, and whereas he couldn't exactly take it out on his wife, she was the next best target. *She* was what stood in the way of the happy marriage he wanted, in his mind. She took a sip of her drink and waited for what he'd say next.

"We had kids right away," he said at length, tone quiet, flat. He smirked. "Hell, for all I know, all I was to her was a baby maker. Not like we had much of a marriage that way." He stared off, a wrinkle forming between his eyes as his emotions rose.

Eleanor felt for him, she truly did. But what she knew of Lysette, she wasn't like regular women. "Jim," she said softly. "Obviously, I wasn't there and can't read Lysette's mind or intentions, but one thing I know is that Lysette is an extremely strong woman with an extremely strong mind." She smirked. "Of anyone, I'm sure you know that. She's not one to settle or give in, as it were. I absolutely cannot imagine Lysette agreeing to share her life with you if there wasn't something about you that drew her to you." That absolutely killed her to say, but she believed it to be true, and in that moment, the hurting man before her deserved the truth.

"Yeah, but after a while, you settle in, get comfortable..." he said, crossing his arms over his chest.

"Jim," Eleanor said, sitting forward to get his full attention. "Unlike most women, Lysette had the financial and emotional backing of her family had she wanted or needed it. She could have left at any time."

He gave her a side glance, studying her for a long moment before relaxing his arms a bit. "I hadn't thought of it that way before," he said with a rueful chuckle. "So she never really needed me per se, but she did choose to stay."

She gave him a small shrug. "Every coin has two sides, good and bad, pros and cons."

He smirked. "Jesus, what a mess," he blew out, running his hand through his hair again. He took a long drink, nearly emptying the glass before slamming it back to the table and staring at it for a long time. The look on his face said he was struggling with something he wanted to say. "I need to tell you something," he finally said, voice not much more than a whisper.

"Okay," she whispered back, not only the whiskey kicking in, but also to try to take a bit of the seriousness out of the situation, hopefully make him feel more comfortable with whatever he was about to reveal.

"Can I…can I have another?" he asked, holding out his glass to her. "I think I need it for this."

"Sure." She got up and quickly made him a second drink, placing it before him. "Here you go."

"Thanks." He wrapped his hand around the glass, almost for comfort. "I got some very upsetting news last night at the dinner party we had for one of my retiring employees," he began, staring down at his whiskey and Coca-Cola. "A gal I've been seeing was there, and she told me that she's pregnant."

The air was knocked out of Eleanor at this one, both the news of an affair and the pregnancy. She fell back against her chair, her own hand reaching out to her mostly untouched drink. "I see. Have you been seeing her long? This woman."

"Almost two years," he murmured, having the dignity to sound contrite.

"Wait, you guys have only been here for—" She stopped herself when he seemed to sink further into himself. "You were already seeing her back in California, weren't you?"

He nodded, clearing his throat as he rubbed the back of his neck. "Yeah."

Anger rose within her. "So let me get this straight," she said, once again sitting forward in her chair. "You've been having a two-year affair with a woman that you moved halfway across the country to continue this affair with, got her pregnant, and you're here waving a gun in my face because you're jealous that your wife may be having an affair with me. Do I have that about right?" When he didn't respond, she shook her head. "Pretty shady, Jim. And selfish."

Again, he cleared his throat and took a drink. "Yeah."

"Look," she said, softening her tone. "Two years and a move is a lot to invest in someone, wouldn't you agree? I mean, if all you're looking for is a good piece of ass outside your marriage, you could easily find that here," she said, indicating the apartment and town beyond it. "Hell, I get propositioned all the time. You men have this crazy idea that women are here for the taking. Sadly, some women do feed that narrative. That aside, you obviously care for this woman."

He nodded. "I do," he agreed, a slight change in his demeanor with those words.

"You love her?"

"How can I answer that?" he asked, hands coming up in consternation before flopping back to the tabletop. "I'm a married man with two kids and a wife that I love very much."

Eleanor studied him for a long moment, considering how to word her next question to get the most straightforward answer. "Are you in love with Lysette, or are you simply trying to keep control of a situation you know you never controlled in the first place?"

He gave her a hard look. "That's harsh."

She said nothing, simply waited him out to consider her words.

Finally, he glared at her. "You're saying all this, trying to get me to think like you because you want Lysette for yourself."

She rolled her eyes. "Deflect all you want, but I'm not the married man who got another woman pregnant." She took a long drink before adding, "Listen, you men like to have the status of the wife at home to raise your kids and give you credit as a good provider and all-American man. Meanwhile, you have your fun on the side that you don't have to be responsible for. We all know what goes on, including the wives at home who have no choice but to put up with it. Well, that's not what you've got here, pal." She continued, "You have a woman who was taught to think for herself, and you knew that before you even married her. Now you hit me as a good guy here, and I can see you're really struggling with all this. So I think the simple question is, does this other woman give you what Lysette can't or won't? As I said before, a sexual fling you could get anywhere with far less complications. Why this woman? Why couldn't you let her go when you left California?"

He let out a heavy sigh as he considered her question, bringing up a hand to rub at the day's worth of scruff on his chin. "She makes me feel like a man," he said. "She makes me feel needed, you know?" He didn't wait for a response as he continued. "She's very passionate, fun. I feel like what I think matters to her. She comes to me for advice, wants my input on decisions."

Eleanor smiled and said with understanding in her tone, "She's not so wildly independent like Lysette, huh?"

He smiled. "I guess not. I mean, don't get me wrong. I absolutely love Lysette's mind, so brilliant and witty. I love that she has such a strong sense of who she is. I respect her."

"But," Eleanor said gently. "It doesn't work anymore for you in the marriage," she concluded for him.

The ironic thing was, as she listened to his complaints of what he didn't feel he was getting from Lysette, she realized those were some of things she loved most about Lysette. And so often, they were of such similar thought, so connected that there was always a conversation—verbal or silent—going on between her and Lysette when they were together, a transfer of thoughts and ideas.

"No. I guess it doesn't."

"Does Lysette know about this other woman or the baby?"

He sipped from his drink. "The baby, no, but she's not stupid. Long ago, we entered into some sort of silent agreement that neither of us was getting what we wanted or needed so, as long as there were no embarrassing situations and our children weren't affected in any way, we've done what we wanted to do." He glanced at her. "It just wasn't talked about."

Eleanor was supremely bothered by that, something Lysette had hinted at with her, as well. But she wasn't going to judge. "I'm guessing falling in love with someone else and having a baby with her wasn't part of that silent deal."

"God, no!" he breathed, followed by rueful laughter. "I think that falls under both embarrassing and affecting the kids."

She smiled. "Listen, Jim, I think you and Lysette really need to sit down and talk all this out. She has a right to know about this woman and the baby, and she has a right to know about your feelings for the woman." She gave him a sheepish grin, guilt still stabbing her. "After all, you know about our situation."

Chapter Thirty

"This is precisely why I rarely drink hard liquor," Eleanor muttered as she padded her way down the hall, hair sticking up in every direction as she made her way to the kitchen. She had coffee on her mind when she had about three years startled off her life by the sudden knocking on the door.

"Ellie! Ellie, are you okay?"

Hand to her chest, she hurried to the door and unlocked it before opening it only to have a frantic Lysette fly into her arms.

"Oh, thank god! I was so worried!"

"What? What's wrong?" Eleanor asked, returning the squeeze before she tugged Lysette into the apartment and closed the door. Her poor neighbors were already treated to enough drama the night before. "What is it?"

Lysette leaned back against the door, relief clearly written across her lovely face, as well as her sagging shoulders. "Jim didn't come home last night, and when I dropped the kids off at school, they said you'd called in sick. Then I got here, and Jim's car was parked outside." She covered her face, rising emotions bringing her voice to a higher and higher pitch with every word.

"Hey," Eleanor said softy, taking the upset woman into a hug. "It's okay." She caressed Lysette's back. "Jim's here."

"What?" Lysette pulled out of the hug and

brought a hand up to swipe at her eyes. "What do you mean he's here?"

Eleanor indicated the couch to her left where Jim was conked out in his trousers and shirtsleeves. One leg hung off the couch, leaving a socked foot to lay flat on the floor as he snored softly.

"I don't understand," Lysette said, turning her focus back to Eleanor. "Why is he here? Did you invite him?"

Eleanor smirked and shook her head. "No. He showed up pretty upset around dinnertime. He was looking for you."

"God," Lysette breathed, again burying her face in her hands. "I'm so sorry to drag you through all this mess."

A snort from Jim in his sleep startled them both. "Come on." Eleanor took Lysette by the hand and led her toward the bedroom so they could talk without waking him up.

"That's Jim's gun!" Lysette gasped, glancing at the kitchen table where the revolver had been placed next to the recapped bottle of whiskey. "Jesus, Ellie. What did he do?" She pulled free of Eleanor's hand and began to arch back to the living room when Eleanor caught her hand again, firmly yanking her back.

"No. Come on, let's talk."

She led the way to her intended destination, closing the door behind them. She was slightly embarrassed as the bed was unmade, covers strewn everywhere and her clothing from the night before tossed at the hamper, most articles missing their mark.

She gave Lysette a sheepish smile. "Just getting up and around after calling the school."

"I don't care. I'm just so grateful you're okay.

Oh, Ellie." Lysette sighed, walking over to the bed and sitting down. "I can't apologize enough. You must truly think we're all a bunch of crazy people who have come in to turn your life upside down."

Eleanor had to fight hard to push the incredibly inappropriate images and thoughts out of her mind as she looked at Lysette sitting on her bed. Clearing her throat, she walked over to her and sat next to her, making herself focus on the situation at hand.

"No," she said softly. "I see you and Jim as two people who are struggling in a situation that just isn't working anymore."

Lysette smirked. "If it ever really did." She turned to Eleanor, giving her an affectionate smile as a hand came up to run through her unruly hair. "You're absolutely adorable in the morning."

Oh, don't do that! I have to be an adult here and stay focused. "And you're absolutely stunning in the morning," Eleanor whispered, berating herself internally for giving in. "It's not fair."

Lysette chuckled. "It takes work. I don't roll out of bed like this." She gave her a sweet smile before her hand fell harmlessly back to her own lap. "Why is Jim here? Did he hurt you?"

"Not at all. I think he had himself all stirred up. I know the gun was scary, but it wasn't even loaded. Honestly, when it was all said and done, he needed to talk." Unable to help herself, she reached up and lightly brushed a soft cheek with her fingertips. "You guys really need to talk. We had drinks together, then I beat the pants off of him in rummy."

Lysette smiled. "Finally, I have some real competition."

"What?"

Before Lysette could respond, they heard loud coughing and a groan from the other room as Jim seemed to be waking up.

"I better get him home," Lysette said with a heavy sigh. She leaned over and placed a quick peck to Eleanor's lips. "Thank you."

The two women got to their feet, and Eleanor pulled open the bedroom door. They were walking down the hall as Jim appeared, looking more like a rumpled teenager than a forty-year-old attorney. He took in the two women entering the room before his gaze settled on Lysette. He gave her a slightly sheepish look.

"Hey," he said.

"Hey, Jim. Come on, let's get you home and out of Eleanor's hair."

He nodded, taking the few steps over to Eleanor and giving her a kiss on the cheek. "Thanks for everything."

She nodded. "Anytime. Oh, wait." She walked over to the kitchen table and grabbed the gun and booze, handing it to him with a small smile.

"Sorry about that." He gave her an embarrassed glance.

To Eleanor's surprise, Lysette walked over to her and gave her a tight hug. "I'll be back later to pick up Jim's car," she said into it.

"Do you want me to throw some clothes on and follow you home?" she asked, returning the hug.

"No. Let me get him settled and in bed, then I'll take a cab over and grab it."

Eleanor nodded, feeling quite surreal as she watched the love of her life and said woman's husband leave her apartment after he'd crashed on her couch the night before.

As she closed and locked the door behind them, she rested her back against the cool wood. "Crazy people, no kidding," she muttered. "We're all nuts in this."

Pushing away from the door, she glanced down to the couch to see the blanket she'd given Jim lying halfway on the floor where it had flowed off the couch. Shaking her head, she walked around to the front of the sofa and gathered the heavy material into her hands to fold it.

As she did her mindless task, she considered her time with Jim Vaughn. She had to admit, she liked him. She could see what Lysette had seen in him. She felt some guilt in her unwitting part in everything, though at the same time, she was so relieved that Lysette felt it, too.

A small smile played across her lips as she considered their all-too-brief history back in Brooke View. Yes, they'd been young, yes, it had all played out in less than a year, but Eleanor knew with everything in her that, had everything played out the way they'd planned, they'd still be together. Even then, they both recognized the connection between them, a connection that apparently had not broken, just stretched across time.

She carried the folded blanket to the linen closet and put it away before deciding to get the coffee percolating while she took a shower. She felt guilty about not being in the classroom, but ultimately, she wasn't sure how long Jim would be there, plus she was still a bit fuzzy with a slight headache.

Coffee started, she shed her bathrobe and nightgown as she walked to the bathroom where she brushed her teeth naked before stepping into the spray, closing the curtain behind her. As the warm water flowed over her body, her hands pushing her hair back away from her face, she thought about the last twelve hours. She considered all that she'd learned, the story of how Lysette had come to be in Jim's life. Doing the math in her head, she assumed Lysette had remained in France until the late thirties, which meant she'd stayed for several years after everything had happened in Brooke View.

As she washed her hair, she thought about what was going on with her in 1938. She was still one of the youngest women there but no longer the baby. For years, she'd been preyed upon by some of the women, some wanting sexual favors, others wanting to beat her into submission. It had been some of the older ones, like Nannette, who had protected her, educated her, and ultimately gotten Matron Hadley to talk to the school system outside the prison system to get her a diploma. She'd been twenty by the time she'd earned it, but it was a proud day, the girls using their time in the kitchen to make her cupcakes to mark the event.

She smiled, thinking about the extreme differences in her life compared to Lysette. One living and learning in Europe while the other lived and learned how to survive in a five-by-eight cell. While one was being wooed and ultimately wed, the other was being released from prison and learning how to be an adult in a very large world of sudden choices.

Finishing with her shower, Eleanor stepped out and toweled herself off. She smiled when the smell of coffee reached her nose. She quickly combed her hair back before leaving the comb on the bathroom counter and turning off the light as she grabbed her bathrobe and slid her arms into the sleeves, the majority of the garment fluttering behind her naked body as she headed to the kitchen.

Humming softly, she reached into the cabinet and pulled out a coffee cup when there was a knock at the door. Looking down at herself, she quickly belted the robe as she padded over to the door.

"Who is it?" she called, not willing to open the door in her bathrobe to just anyone.

"It's Lysette" came the muffled reply.

Without another word or hesitation, Eleanor unlocked the door and pulled it open with one hand, the other holding her robe together. "Hey."

"Oh, I'm sorry," Lysette said, taking in her wet hair and robe. "I can come back if you want."

"No, it's okay. Come on in." Eleanor stepped aside, allowing Lysette to enter before closing the door again. "Is everything okay? Jim still alive?" she asked with a small smile.

Lysette returned the grin. "Barely. He went right to bed once we reached the house. I know he's deeply embarrassed by his behavior last night," she said, where they stood just inside the apartment. "I'm really grateful that you were so kind. I don't know if I could have been so compassionate if the roles were reversed."

"It's okay, honestly. I learned a lot, too. Helped me to understand you, the you of the last twenty years that I don't know. I'm just hoping you're not angry I allowed him to stay to talk let alone crash on the couch."

"Of course not," Lysette said. Her gaze fell to the spot just above where Eleanor was clutching the robe together. Her touch was soft against Eleanor's upper chest as she gently fingered the gold cross. "I'm glad you're still wearing it."

Eleanor could hardly breathe. It was hard enough having Lysette so close to her while wearing nothing more than terrycloth let alone being touched by her. "I didn't realize how much I missed it until it was back," she managed to say, her voice far more breathless than she intended. She met Lysette's gaze before her gaze fell to slightly parted lips. Her heart was racing.

Jim's face flashed before her eyes, but she pushed it aside as, seemingly of their own accord, her hands reached out to rest upon Lysette's hips, so beautifully defined in the dress she wore. She heard the hitch in Lysette's breathing and could see the increased rise and fall of her chest, much like her own.

As if by magic or a magnetic force, their bodies drifted together. She could feel the soft warmth of Lysette's breath against her face as her eyes slid closed. The first touch of Lysette's lips drew a sigh from her. They were so soft, so pliant, but most importantly, it was Lysette.

The first touch of a silky tongue brought out a second sigh. Her hands slid around to Lysette's lower back, pulling her in even more as Lysette's fingers found their way into Eleanor's hair, still damp from her recent shower. As the kiss deepened, Eleanor knew Lysette had been right the previous day: once they started, they could never stop.

It was very clear that this deeply passionate woman was no longer the awkward teenager she'd first been with. This woman knew what she was doing. The way she kissed was nearly bringing Eleanor to her knees, and her hand, wandering dangerously close to the belt on her robe, made her heart stop

Her hands slid over Lysette's extremely shapely

behind, using it as leverage to push their hips tightly together. Her body was being flooded with sensations and a desire she didn't know could exist in a human being.

When her hands had been at her lower back, Eleanor had felt the bottom of the dress's zipper. Slowing the kiss, she pulled away and gently turned Lysette away from her so she was presented with her back. She once again grasped her hips and pulled Lysette back into her, eyes closing as she inhaled the fragrance of her perfume, her hair, and her skin. She could also smell her need, which sent a thrill down her spine.

Her lips found the side of Lysette's neck, and her hands made their way up to cup her breasts, a long sigh escaping Lysette's lips as her behind pushed back into Eleanor, who responded in kind.

Continuing with her exploration of Lysette's neck, one of Eleanor's hands found its way to the zipper tab, slowly pulling it down, creamy flesh revealed with every inch. Leaving her neck, Eleanor watched, her need to touch the beautiful woman before her so great she almost couldn't stand it.

Fully unzipped, she pushed the ends of the deep purple dress apart until it slid off smooth shoulders, Lysette's arms still trapped within the sleeves. Her gaze focused on the black bra strap that bisected Lysette's back, deciding that wasn't a wanted distraction. She used deft fingers to unclasp it, the two ends falling away, kept on Lysette's frame only by the straps and the material caught up in the dress.

Eleanor was in awe of the beauty before her. She ran her fingertips down the soft plane of Lysette's back, marveling at the smoothness. She brought her mouth to that soft smoothness, running her tongue up along Lysette's spine to the nape of her neck as her hands wormed around her side beneath her arms and into the pocket of material the front of the dress made. She loved the groan she got when she cupped Lysette's beautiful breasts. When she tugged lightly on the rigid nipples, Lysette's hands shot out to brace the door as she began to fall forward.

Eleanor was startled as suddenly Lysette pushed away from the door and turned around. The fire in her eyes was downright intimidating as she shrugged out of the top half of her dress, allowing the garment to fall down over her hips to the floor. That gaze was still locked on Eleanor as she reached down and with a simple flick of her fingers unsnapped her garters.

She reached behind her with one hand and turned the lock on the door before stepping out of her high heels and dress, walking the short distance in nylons, garters, and panties to where Eleanor stood. Taking her in a deep and almost possessive kiss, her hand swept the belt of her robe loose, Eleanor completely exposed with a simple wave of Lysette's hand.

Eleanor was nervous, though she had no idea why. She'd always been told she was lovely, but the way Lysette strutted around with seemingly unending confidence in her nakedness, it made Eleanor feel vulnerable and acutely aware of Lysette's every touch, every look.

Once Eleanor was exposed as her robe fell away, Lysette pulled out of the kiss and allowed her finger to trail down from the hollow of Eleanor's throat between her breasts continuing until it slid through the dark saturated hair between her legs, partly wet from the shower and partly wet from the intensity of her arousal.

Eleanor gasped as that finger pushed into her folds, lazily exploring as Lysette again leaned forward, initiating a slow sensuous kiss. Her hips moved with Lysette's finger. That finger found her engorged clit, and a second finger joined it as she rubbed in quick circles, torturously quick as it pulled an orgasm out of Eleanor that nearly made her fall. Lysette steadied her with her other arm, Eleanor's hands gripping Lysette's shoulders with a talon-like grip.

She was breathing heavily, forehead resting against Lysette's shoulder as a chuckle bubbled up. "God, how pathetic."

Lysette left a kiss to the side of her head. "Can we go to your bedroom?" she whispered.

Chapter Thirty-one

Lysette was ready to explode as she watched Eleanor shrug out of her robe, letting it drop to join the rest of the clothing on the floor. Without a word and with nothing but love in her eyes, Eleanor took her hand, and they stepped over the garments as they left the living room and made their way down the hallway to the bedroom.

"Tsk tsk, Ellie," she teased. "Still didn't make your bed."

Eleanor grinned at her over her shoulder. "Hey, I barely achieved a shower before you returned."

"Are you complaining?" Lysette teased, her voice not much more than a purr. She gasped as she found herself shoved to the bed flat on her back, Eleanor on top of her.

"Not even a little bit," Eleanor whispered.

Lysette sighed as they kissed again. She so loved the way Eleanor kissed: so gentle and thorough. Yet with her tongue and full bottom lip, she could instantly set Lysette on fire. She sighed as Eleanor slid her thigh between her legs as their kiss continued, Lysette's own thigh becoming instantly saturated as she returned the favor. She knew she had just as much wetness between her own legs.

As they moved together, Lysette's head fell to the side when Eleanor kissed along her jaw, tongue flicking here and there. She let out a groan as the hot wet kisses moved down her throat and across one collarbone before heading south, the intended destination evident.

Lysette arched her back, offering her breast to Eleanor, needing to feel her mouth on her. Fingers buried in Eleanor's hair, she nearly forgot that the pressure had been removed from where she desperately needed it as her right breast was engulfed with wet heat.

Eleanor hummed into her task, seeming to enjoy what she was doing as much as Lysette was enjoying what she was doing. Her taut sensitive nipple was sucked hard before being flicked with a relentless tongue, which made Lysette whimper. Her body was restless, her arousal nearing a painful stage.

"Please," she whimpered, her hips bucking against any part of Eleanor they could find.

Getting Lysette's none-too-subtle hints, Eleanor left that breast and moved to the other as her hand reached down and nudged Lysette's thighs apart, moving her body to settle between them. Lysette allowed her thighs to fall open, thrusting upward against Eleanor's stomach as she suckled her left breast.

"God, baby, please," she whimpered again, nearly in tears.

Letting the nipple leave her mouth with a pop, Eleanor left a final kiss to the rounded side of the breast before she kissed her way down Lysette's body, drawing a long, languid groan out of the woman beneath her. Lysette was softly asked to lift her hips as her panties and garter were removed, followed by her nylons. Lysette was impressed that Eleanor got them off in one fluid motion. Task finished, Eleanor gave Lysette the sexiest smile Lysette had ever seen in her life before she continued.

Lysette gasped, her hips jerking at the first feel of

Eleanor's tongue against her clit, which was so overly sensitive that it was nearly ready to burst. Eleanor didn't keep her tongue there but instead explored, roaming through her folds, teasing her opening before licking her way back up.

The slow, sweet torture lulled Lysette into a false sense of light, languid pleasure because suddenly her clit was sucked into Eleanor's mouth. Like a pulse, she suckled her as her tongue beat ruthlessly against it.

Lysette nearly jerked to a sitting position at the explosion of sensation as her thighs tried to slap shut. Ahead of her, Eleanor had wrapped her arms around the undersides of her thighs, holding them open for her attack, which didn't end until Lysette's cry of orgasm rent the room loud and throaty. Her fingers tugged Eleanor's hair as her entire body stiffened with the power of her release.

After what seemed like an eternity, Eleanor released her from her mouth, small whimpers still escaping Lysette's lips as her breasts heaved and she tried to get herself under control. A forearm flopped uselessly over her eyes as her brain tried to wrap itself around what had just happened.

She let out a lazy purr as she felt Eleanor crawl up into her arms, the two sharing light kisses. "You are so beautiful," she whispered against soft lips.

Eleanor smiled. "Thank you, but that would be you." She moved off Lysette and to her side, pulling Lysette to hers, facing each other.

Lysette moaned softly when her thigh was pulled up to rest against Eleanor's hip, one of Eleanor's thighs resting between Lysette's, hips pressed together. She ran her nails lightly down the arm attached to the hand that rested on her behind. She loved the closeness she felt to her, loved the feel of their breasts just barely touching yet so intimately connected.

Looking into Eleanor's completely sated, relaxed, and painfully beautiful face, she smiled. "God, I love you," she whispered. "It's crazy, after all this time, it hasn't diminished. Nothing has—my love for you, my need for you. I mean, the intensity of my wanting you frightens the hell out of me."

Eleanor smiled, her fingernails tracing over a rounded cheek before playfully slapping it. Lysette gave her a wicked smile in response. "I love you so very much." She leaned forward and left a soft kiss on Lysette's lips. "What do we do now?"

Lysette let out a heavy sigh, wondering the same thing. "Well, Jim and I need to talk. I know there's someone else where he's concerned. I mean, I've known, suspected, figured for a long, long time. But seeing him with her Sunday night, just a gut feeling, it's not just a fling." She brought her hand up and tucked some dark strands behind Eleanor's ear. "But even if there wasn't someone else, and I have no idea what his plans are with her, the writing's on the wall. It has been for a while, but now…"

"It makes me feel terrible, you know," Eleanor said, so much uncertainty and sadness in her eyes. "I don't want to be at the center of the breakup of a family."

Lysette smiled, the spoken words going straight to her heart. "My sweet, sweet, Ellie," she said. "You may be helping to speed things up a bit, but it would have happened at some point. You can only go on pretending, keeping yourself as busy as possible to not deal, deny yourself for so long. Jim deserves more than that, the kids deserve more than that in their parents and the example we're setting for them and," she shrugged the shoulder that wasn't pressed to the mattress, "I deserve more than that, too." She looked deeply into the violet depths of Eleanor's eyes. "I can't lose you again. I barely survived it the first time when it was out of our control. Now it *is* in my control. Well," she added sheepishly. "I guess I'm seriously assuming here. What do you want?"

Eleanor's gaze traveled all over Lysette's face for so long Lysette was beginning to get nervous. "You," she finally said. "All I've ever wanted was you."

❧ ❧ ❧ ❧

Eleanor let Lysette shower before leaving, although that had turned into yet another round of making love. Lysette smiled thinking about it. She could still hear the wonderful noises Eleanor made far above her as the water rained down on her back as she'd fallen to her knees to explore every bit of what made Eleanor a woman. She could still taste her on her lips and tongue.

As beautiful as those memories were, what made her smile even more was the feeling of holding each other in Eleanor's bed. The softness of a breast beneath her head as they talked was wonderful. Being held after making love, hell, being held at all, wasn't something she usually allowed or wanted. Her views on sex with the few women she'd been with had been extremely focused on the act itself, the release, the temporary feeling of normalcy. She loved Jim, cared deeply about him, and in so many respects, he was the closest person to her.

She drove Jim's car through town, looking at the

buildings and houses, businesses she'd frequented and the school she sent her children to. Everything looked the same, same storefronts, same wares sold within, and same lessons taught, but today, it was all different.

In the few hours she'd spent with Eleanor, finally shedding the last of the armor she'd so carefully erected to protect the damaged person inside, she saw the world in all its brilliance. She saw the possibilities that lay before her and the fact that she could have her Ellie back.

Her happy mood dissipated as she pulled into the driveway of the home she shared with her husband and their children. Cutting the engine, she sat there for a moment staring through the windshield at the house.

"How are we going to do this?"

Tapping her fingers on the steering wheel, she gathered her courage and pulled the keys from the ignition before climbing out of the low-slung sports car, his precious 1955 red Corvette, which only *he* drove traditionally, as opposed to the larger "family" car he mainly drove, but she used from time to time for daily life. It was a beautiful car, no doubt, but not an ounce of practicality in it for a married father.

Letting out a steadying breath, she walked up the path that led to the front door and let herself into the house. She wasn't sure what she'd find, if Jim would still be asleep or if he'd even be there. The sounds from the kitchen answered that question.

Leaving her purse on the couch, she headed through the house until she saw Jim moving around the room going from the icebox to the counter and back again.

"You know," she said, leaning against the archway into the kitchen. "Planning helps. Fewer trips."

He glanced at her before turning his attention back to the sandwich makings he was gathering. He had obviously showered recently; his hair was slicked back from his face, and he was dressed in casual clothing.

"Want one?" he offered, indicating the meat, cheese, and veggies he had spread over the counter in their respective bags and containers.

She pushed away from the archway. "Sure." She grabbed the bag of Wonder bread from the breadbox, placing it on the counter and opening it.

"Uh-oh," he said, giving her a side glance. "Guess we're about to chat. Menial work is afoot." They shared a small smile as they worked together to create their lunch. He cleared his throat and glanced over at her. "Were you at Eleanor's place?" he asked conversationally, though his eyes were guarded.

She studied him for a long moment, trying to read him. Ultimately, she knew she had to be honest. The days of lies, half-truths, and omissions had to be over. "Yes, I was," she said simply. "I brought your car back."

He nodded. "Great."

He took the head of lettuce in one hand and was about to grab a knife when she stopped him with a hand on his arm. "No," she said gently, though with a smile. "You just need to tear some off."

He looked down at the lettuce, then the knife block and finally at her. He grinned. "Good. The less I have to deal with the sharp stuff, the better."

She pulled out four slices of bread and glanced at him. "Do you want to talk?" she asked, knowing Jim would know what she meant. "The kids are in school, and Aunt Josie is with her book club."

He nodded. "Yeah. I was thinking that, too."

He rested his hands against the counter for a moment before turning to her, arms crossed over his white undershirt-clad chest. "Where do we start?"

"That is a great question," she said with a sigh. "I guess, what do you want?" she asked. "Deep down, what do you really want, Jim?"

He smirked, though with affection. "Eleanor asked me the same thing. I want what I honestly don't think is in you to give to a man."

"I don't think I have anything in me to give to anyone."

"Except Eleanor?"

She considered his words for a long moment, then nodded. "Yes. I think you're right, and it honestly wasn't until lately that I've begun to understand that." She leaned against the counter, mirroring Jim's position. "I thought that part of me was gone, to be truthful with you. The sad thing is," she said with a sigh, glancing out the kitchen window, watching as two squirrels chased each other up the huge cottonwood tree, "I didn't know I missed it."

He nodded, looking down at his hand as he picked at a nail. He let out a heavy sigh before finally meeting her gaze again. "I have to be honest with you, too. There's someone else."

The words obviously weren't surprising to her, nor were they particularly hurtful, but they did make her sad. She thought back to when they decided to begin their lives together, already both on different planes and ideas of what they wanted the marriage to be, but they were both filled with hope for some happiness. They had fun together overall and were friends. Somewhere down the line, that split into each of them having their own side life filled with sex and perhaps in Jim's case, love.

"Yes," she said. "The woman from the other night?"

He nodded. "Fran."

"Do you love her?" He looked away and cleared his throat. "Jim," she said gently, reaching across the scant distance between them to place her hand on his arm. "If we can't be honest right now, then we're doomed to move on from this."

"I just have this horrible guilt inside me, Lysette. I made you a promise when I asked you to marry me. I made your father a promise when I asked for his permission—"

"And you fulfilled every single one of those promises," she said adamantly, shaking his arm slightly to emphasize her point. "You're a wonderful father, you've been a good husband, a fantastic provider..." She brought her hand up and lightly cupped his freshly shaven face. "If anything, I'm the one to blame."

He stepped forward and gathered her in his arms, an embrace that was returned. "We both made our mistakes." He left a kiss to the top of her head. "There's something else I need to tell you."

"Okay." She released him as he stepped back, resting back against the stove. Once again, he crossed his arms over his chest. "What is it?"

"God, there's no easy way to say this." He ran his hand through his drying hair. "Fran is pregnant," he finally said. "And the baby is mine."

"Oh, Jim," she groaned, bringing a hand up to cover her eyes. "How could you let that happen?"

"I know," he said, hanging his head. "Trust me, I know. Just complicated things substantially."

"How far along is she?"

He shrugged. "No idea. She hasn't said, but she did ask me to accompany her to the doctor next week."

"You have to do it. You've got to take care of this woman and this child."

"Speaking of," he said, hands on hips. "What do we tell *our* kids?"

"Let's decide what we're going to do, make a plan, then let's sit them down and tell them."

He nodded, looking thoughtful as he glanced over at the unmade sandwiches. After a moment, he looked at her. "I'll never regret us, Lysette," he said softly. "I'll never regret being your husband."

She smiled, touched. Walking over to him, she left a lingering kiss to his cheek. "Neither will I."

Chapter Thirty-two

Eleanor couldn't keep the smile off her face as she readied her classroom for the first hour. After responding to a million and one questions about her incredibly unusual absence the day before, she felt she'd assured her colleagues, as well as her students, that she wasn't dying and that it had simply been a bad headache that had kept her in bed.

She smirked as she wrote the day's assignment on the board. "That and a gorgeous woman." She glanced down at the open textbook she cradled in her arm for the next part of the assignment when she heard the classroom door open. The smile was instant when she glanced over her shoulder to see Lysette walking toward her, her hips swaying just so as she approached. It drove Eleanor absolutely wild. "Hey."

"Hey," Lysette responded, giving her that little smile that took her back to being fifteen with absolutely no weapons to combat such a subtle attack that had a deadly effect.

It was moments like that that Eleanor wondered how every person, male and female, who came into Lysette's sphere wasn't leveled by her natural, raw, and unbidden sensuality.

Lysette brought her hand up to reveal a polished red apple. "I brought an apple to perhaps sway your affections." She walked up to Eleanor, who still stood by the blackboard. "You see, I hear I'm in a bit of competition with my son when it comes to being hot for teacher."

A loud bark of laughter burst from Eleanor as she accepted the apple. "Well, word has it Jimmy found himself a girlfriend. A cute little sophomore named Tabitha." She grinned. "So I think you're in the clear for the win."

"Well, gosh," Lysette murmured with exaggerated dramatics. "I didn't think you'd be so easy." Again, that little smile. "But then, I guess all I have to do is remember yesterday morning."

The blush that flew up Eleanor's neck was embarrassing but worth it. "Yes, yes, I admit it." To her surprise, she decided to give as good as she got as she leaned forward, peeking into Lysette's subtle cleavage, and licked her lips. "Not that you make it remotely difficult."

Lysette lifted an eyebrow, hands going to her shapely hips. "Miss Brannon, are you suggesting I'm dressed inappropriately?"

Eleanor grinned. "No, I'm suggesting you're entirely *too* dressed."

Lysette met her gaze before she broke, an adorable giggle falling from her lips. She glanced behind her shoulder, the two still alone in the classroom, before leaning forward and leaving a lingering kiss on Eleanor's lips. "Good morning," she said against them.

"Good morning," Eleanor responded, accepting the full body hug she got. She knew she needed to be careful, as Lysette was the mother of one of her students. "I missed you," she whispered into the hug.

Lysette left a kiss to the side of Eleanor's neck. "I missed you, too." She pulled back from the hug and caressed Eleanor's cheek, love and affection in her eyes to replace the vixen mere moments before.

Eleanor felt like she was queen of the world in that moment. "I love you," she said, surprised she'd spoken the words she felt so deeply in her soul.

"I love you, my Ellie," Lysette replied, giving her another kiss, a bit quicker than the last as time was running short. "I have a lot to talk to you about. When are you free?"

"How about my lunch period today?" Eleanor suggested. "Starts at eleven fifteen."

Lysette smiled. "I'll be here to pick you up by eleven twelve."

Eleanor laughed. "Okay."

๑ ๑ ๑ ๑

Eleanor was desperately trying to get her breath back as Lysette kissed and caressed her way back up her body, humming in satisfaction as she lay fully atop Eleanor to initiate a deep, lazy kiss. Eleanor buried her fingers in soft auburn hair as she sighed, able to taste herself in the slick warmth on Lysette's lips and tongue.

"I know you said we had to make it quick," Lysette murmured, "but I didn't think it would be three seconds quick."

Eleanor grinned. "You're just too good at what you do." She released a contented sigh as her fingernails trailed down Lysette's back and over shapely cheeks, which flexed in response.

As the kiss began again, Lysette adjusted her hips between Eleanor's spread thighs, Eleanor sighing into the kiss as she raised her knees. They both moaned as Lysette's clit found Eleanor's clit.

Lysette rested her upper body on a forearm, her

other arm reaching back to run her fingernails along the side of Eleanor's thigh as she continued to move against her. Eleanor wormed her hands between them, cupping Lysette's beautiful breasts, tugging lightly on her nipples as they kissed, though as the pleasure grew, their breathing became more labored. Soon, it became too much to kiss, so they simply stayed in each other's space as Lysette moved in tandem with Eleanor, the bed squeaking softly beneath them.

Soon, Lysette lifted herself to her hands and used the power of her body to increase her thrusts with Eleanor, who gripped her behind, urging her faster and harder. The small bedroom was filled with the sounds of their heavy breathing and moans, the creaking bed matching the intensity of her thrusts until finally, with a loud cry, Lysette collapsed on top of Eleanor, even as her hips continued to move, milking every ounce of pleasure for herself and bringing Eleanor to a powerful release as her body exploded for a second time in less than ten minutes.

Lysette buried her face in Eleanor's neck for a long moment, breasts heaving against hers as she warmed Eleanor's skin with each deep, hot breath. Finally, she lifted her head and left a few small kisses on Eleanor's lips before moving off her. She flipped to her back on the mattress beside her for a long moment, her forearm resting over her eyes.

Eleanor straightened her legs, sore from being in such a position for so long. She glanced over at Lysette and reached her hand out, taking Lysette's as it came down from her face.

"I love you."

Lysette met her gaze, a soft, beautiful smile on her lips. "I love you, too." She brought their joined hands to her mouth and left a lingering kiss on Eleanor's palm. "How much time do we have?"

Eleanor lifted her head to look past Lysette at the bedside table alarm clock. "About twenty minutes before I need to start cleaning up." She released Lysette's hand as she moved to her side, facing the beautiful woman. "So you said you have a lot of things to tell me and wanted to talk."

Lysette let out a long, tired sigh, then mirrored Eleanor's position, reaching out to rest her hand on Eleanor's hip to maintain physical contact between them. "Yes." She gave her a happy smile. "Jim and I talked. He's going to do what needs to be done legally this week."

Eleanor eyed her. She had a feeling of what she was talking about, but she didn't want to assume. "Meaning?"

Lysette leaned forward, a hair's breadth away from Eleanor's lips. "We're getting a divorce."

Eleanor gasped. "Really?"

"Yes."

Eleanor's eyes fell closed as she pulled Lysette to her, their bodies flush as they held each other for a long moment. Finally, Eleanor fell to her back, taking Lysette with her until an auburn head lay on her shoulder. "I can't believe it. What about the kids?" she asked, trailing her fingertips over a rounded shoulder.

"We're holding off talking to them and Aunt Josie until things are more final. We don't want this to be any more difficult or make them feel any more unstable than we have to." She placed a kiss to Eleanor's upper chest as she adjusted her head to a more comfortable spot. "Neither of us is contesting anything. For right now, the kids and I and Aunt Josie will stay in the house, and Jim will get an apartment until he finds something, I suppose."

"Well, there's not a place available here," Eleanor said with a grin.

Lysette lifted her head and matched that grin. "If there was, I'd move in."

Eleanor met her gaze, the smile fading from her lips. "What do you want, Lysette?" She didn't want to assume and didn't want to dream or fantasize about what she didn't know.

"I want you," Lysette said simply, no hesitation. "I want to take back what was stolen from us. I want to read the newspaper with you in bed every Sunday morning, I want to go to sleep with you every night. I want to learn everything about you, give you all that you need and want." She ran her fingers through short, dark strands. "I want you to get to know my kids and for them to really know you." She smiled, so much love shining in her eyes. "I want what was stolen from us," she whispered, repeating the words that were tattooed on Eleanor's soul.

"Me too. More than anything," Eleanor whispered back.

❧ ❧ ❧ ❧

As she re-entered her class after her special lunch, Eleanor felt a little pep in her step, not only from the amazing moments shared with Lysette, but also because she felt like a little rebel in her activities. She did feel a bit uncomfortable when Jimmy came bounding into her classroom the last hour of the day and was immediately drawn to the apple that she'd kept on her desk as a little reminder of the woman who had given it to her.

"So," he said, tossing the apple into the air and catching it easily with one hand. "Who's trying to get an A?" He leaned a hip against the side of the desk.

She glanced up at him from where she sat behind it, thoroughly amused, even as she was slightly unsettled. "Who says anyone is?"

"Oh, come on, Miss Brannon," he said, setting the apple down as he leaned in. "Everyone knows it's the best way. 'A is for apple,'" he said in a sing-songy voice, making her laugh. He winked at her. "You know, it was super strange hanging out with you Sunday."

"Oh, yeah?" she asked, truly curious of his answer because, according to his mother, there would be a whole lot more *hanging out*. "Why?"

"Because!" he exclaimed, as though it should be common knowledge. "Teachers don't have real lives. They don't have real homes and," he raised an eyebrow to add a bit of theatrics, "I hear they don't even eat real food."

"Oh, I see," she responded sagely. "So what do us teachers do then?"

"Well, the way I hear it, this desk here," he said, standing to his full height and grabbing the edge, trying to rock the heavy, solid desk. "It folds out into some sort of cot-type structure, and in that closet over there is a television set. You know, you just chill in here and think of ways to torment us further."

She burst into laughter, in an unreasonably good mood. "Go sit down, you pest." She pushed away from the desk and got to her feet as the bell rang alerting that the final hour of the day had begun. "All right, everyone. Take your seats. We've got a lot to get to today." She grabbed her teacher's copy of the textbook and walked to the blackboard when the classroom door opened. One of the seniors who acted as an office aide walked in.

"A message for you, Miss Brannon," she said, handing her a note.

"Thanks, Shelly." Eleanor read over the scribbled message, then read it again, her heart racing. "Uh," she said, a hand coming up to run through her hair. "Guys, read chapters twenty and twenty-one out loud." She hurried over to the coat tree and grabbed her purse. "Jarrod, please start it, then go in order after each page," she said, her voice higher pitched than normal as panic was setting in.

"Miss Brannon? You okay?" one of the students asked, but she didn't even know who it was nor did she respond as she flew out of the classroom and toward the front office.

The office was abuzz as usual with ringing phones and chatting faculty, administration, and students. Eleanor was nearly in tears as she hurried to the front desk.

"Rachel, can I please use the phone?" Without a word, the secretary lifted the rotary phone up to the desk where Eleanor stood. Eleanor quickly dialed the numbers, then waited. "Hello, Mrs. O'Shea, it's Eleanor Brannon. I need to speak with Scott right away, please…yes, please, wake him up. It's an emergency."

❧❧❧❧

They were both silent as the car sped south. Eleanor could feel Scott's gaze on her, but she couldn't take her eyes off the road, watching each passing mile marker and the unending staccato of the white dotted line, her hand clutched around her gold cross.

"It's going to be okay," he said, his voice soft in the near-silent cab of the car. "We'll get there." He reached over and wrapped his fingers around hers where they lay on her leg.

She didn't meet his gaze but simply nodded, praying with all she had.

After what seemed an eternity, they finally reached Memorial Hospital in Colorado Springs. Scott barely had the Packard stopped before Eleanor jumped out, running full speed across the parking lot, him not far behind, unshaven and unshowered and dressed in baggy jeans and a flannel shirt. His longer legs got him there just before her to pull the door open, then follow her inside.

"Can I help you, miss?" the receptionist asked, glancing at Scott's unkempt appearance with contempt.

"I need to find a patient," Eleanor said, breathless from fear and the exertion. "She was brought in here about an hour ago."

"And her name would be?" the woman asked, already flipping open the large patient registry.

"Emmaline Brannon."

Chapter Thirty-three

Eleanor sat in the chair, staring off into space, only to return her gaze to the still form lying in the bed every few seconds. Scott sat next to her, his arm slung out over the back of her chair. She could feel his fingertip graze her shoulder now and then as he gesticulated with whatever he was talking about. She had no idea, his voice not much more than muffled noise to her.

All she could hear over and over again was what she was told by the doctors:

Heart weakened from the virus she contracted eight years ago...heart attack hit her quick...lucky she was found when she was...surgery went well, we hope. Hope for the best.

Emma had been brought back into her room little more than an hour ago, and though she'd opened her eyes and had murmured something to the nurse who came in to check on her every ten minutes or so, she had said nothing to her two visitors. Eleanor wasn't even sure she was aware they were there.

"Do you think that life or the universe or God or whatever would be so cruel as to let her get this far in her life after all that he put her through only to let her die now?" Eleanor asked. She realized silence befell them, so she glanced over at Scott, who was staring straight ahead, his jaw muscles working. For a moment, she thought maybe he hadn't heard her, but then he spoke, his voice quiet.

"You know, if you'd asked me that three months ago, even three weeks ago," he amended, turning to meet her gaze, "I would have told you, hell, yeah. God was that much of a son of a bitch. But," he added, a small smile on his face as he brought his hand up to lightly tap the tip of her nose with a finger, "I don't think so. I don't know why this happened, but I think it was for a reason. Miss Emma is meant to come through this and be better for it."

She met his gaze for a long moment. For the first time since his and Ronnie's nightmare, she saw the Scott she knew and loved in those smiling eyes. She leaned over and left a lingering kiss on his cheek. "Thank you."

"Whew," he said, wiping a dramatic hand over his brow. "I was hoping I was going to say that right."

She smiled. "Goofball." As he grinned that adorable boyish grin, she reached her hand up and lightly patted his cheek a couple of times before giving it a final pat that was much harder than need be, an old tactic she used with him often. "Good boy." They were both alerted that someone was at the hospital room door when soft rapping began.

"I'll continue my 'good boy' status and see who that is." Scott pushed up from his chair and made his way across the room.

Figuring it was the nurse returning with the food she'd promised nearly a half hour before, Eleanor turned her focus back to her mother. Though Scott's words had touched her, there was no way they could ease her fear. Again, Scott's quiet conversation with whomever was on the other side of the door was muffled noise as Eleanor looked at her mother, lying so still, so small in that bed. She was heavily bandaged after the surgery. Eleanor wished so badly that she could have a sign, anything, that everything would be okay.

She was startled at the sudden touch of fingers running lightly through her hair. Her glance to the bed showed her mother hadn't moved. She looked up, and Lysette smiled lovingly down at her. For a moment, she thought she was seeing things, but the fingers that moved down to caress the side of her face were quite tangible.

Shooting up from the chair, Eleanor felt her world right itself, if even just for a moment, as she was wrapped in Lysette's comforting warmth. "God, it's good to see you," she murmured into the hug. "What are you doing here?"

Lysette left a small kiss to Eleanor's cheek before pulling out of the hug. "Jimmy said you were really upset when you left, so he asked the girl he knew in the office, and she told him. We called around until we found the right hospital."

"We?" Eleanor asked, surprised to see Josie already at the bedside, one of Emma's hands held in her own.

"Aunt Josie heard us talking about it, and quite honestly, she was ready to leave me behind if I hadn't thrown myself into the car," Lysette said with a small smile.

Scott joined them, looking from Eleanor to Lysette and back again, a huge question in his eyes at the obvious comfort level the women had in their intimate affection.

"Scott, this is Lysette Vaughn," Eleanor introduced, stepping away from Lysette to an appropriate distance. "Lysette, Scott O'Shea."

"Yes, you're the music teacher, right?" Lysette held her hand out in greeting.

"Choir and band, but close enough." He took her hand and gave her one of his charming smiles.

Eleanor watched the two and couldn't help but think with the charm and natural charisma those two oozed, they could take over the world far too easily.

"I believe you said I don't have either of your kids, right?" he asked, studying her.

"Correct, but my son and daughter both attend Woodland, as you know. I've heard a lot about you from Ellie."

He glanced at Eleanor, eyebrows raised. She hid her smile as she could almost hear his thoughts: *Ellie?*

"How's she doing?" Lysette turned back to Eleanor, her hand resting on her lower back.

"She's still out," Eleanor said, glancing over at the bed. "Doctors sounded positive, but there's just no telling until they see how well the surgery took."

"What happened?" Josie asked from where she'd planted herself in the chair next to the bed, Emma's hand still held in both of hers.

"A handful of years ago, Mama caught a pretty nasty virus. It almost killed her. It went to her heart, which weakened quite a bit. I moved back from Kansas to take care of her," she added. "It was scary for a while, but she recovered and was feisty as ever. But she was warned that she had to take it easy." She let out a heavy, tired sigh, running her fingers through her hair. "That's one reason she sold the place in Colorado Springs. I think it was getting to be too much for her, and she wanted to simplify her life."

Josie looked over at Eleanor. "Where is she moving to?"

"She recently bought a house in Woodland," Lysette said.

"And you never told me about this?" she asked, eyes filled with hurt.

Eleanor was confused as she glanced from Josie to Lysette. She knew the two women had been close friends as teenagers, but Josie's reaction seemed a bit strong. She looked as though she were about to burst into tears.

"Bronte and I literally ran into them one day at the diner when she was looking for houses," Lysette explained. "I wasn't sure it was my news to share."

Eleanor could feel eyes on her and noticed Scott looking at her, questions in his eyes. He was obviously picking up on the same vibe she was. She shrugged. He walked around Lysette to Eleanor's side.

"Hey, I think I'm going to head home for a bit. I feel like a bum," he murmured, indicating the gorgeous woman standing on the other side of Eleanor. "I need to shave and shower. I'll bring some dinner back. Shouldn't be gone long."

Eleanor smiled and nodded. It was nice to see a bit of his old dignity returning. The old Scott she knew was prissier about his looks than she ever could be. "Absolutely." She accepted his hug and kiss to the cheek. "It means the world to me that you were here for me, Scotty," she said. "Thank you."

"I need to go for a little bit, too," Lysette said apologetically. "I had to make sure you and Emma were okay, but Jim is in client meetings tonight preparing for trial, so I have to get the kids." She pulled Eleanor into another tight hug. "I promise I'll be back soon."

"I ain't leavin', Lysette," Josie said, an eyebrow raised in defiance.

"Can I take your car?" Lysette asked.

"Just come with me," Scott offered, looking between the women. "I'll happily drop you off, then bring you back when you're ready."

"Really?" Lysette asked.

"Absolutely." Scott glanced at Eleanor and winked.

Eleanor accepted another quick, one-armed hug from Scott and a lingering one from Lysette after the redhead had gone to Emma's bedside and had left a small kiss to her cheek and a promise that she'd return. Left alone with Josie and her mother, Eleanor was left with so many questions.

She glanced at Josie, amused by her overalls and seeming devil-may-care attitude. That woman was there with purpose, though Eleanor wasn't sure what it was.

"It's really nice to see you again." She pulled a chair up to the other side of her mother's bed. The two women glanced at each other over Emma's sleeping body.

Josie gave her a genuine smile. "You, too, sweetheart. It's real good to see you and Lysette together again. Somehow, I always knew that would happen, you two would find your way back to each other."

Eleanor was surprised and touched by her words. "Thank you. I'm glad she's in my life again, too," she said, not entirely sure what Lysette's aunt knew or what she thought the nature of their relationship was.

Josie studied Eleanor for a long moment, so long that the younger woman felt a bit uncomfortable. Finally, Josie smiled. "You grew up to be a truly beautiful woman. Lysette's lucky to have you. You two certainly make a stunning couple."

Eleanor stared at her for a long moment before smiling as she shook her head. "Guess we're that obvious, huh?"

Josie gave her a side glance and a crooked grin. "Well, for someone who knows what she's looking for, yes."

The words spoken rolled around in Eleanor's mind for a moment as she tried to pair them with the knowing look she was given as they were being said. Finally, something occurred to her. "Wait, are you… like us? Like Lysette and me?"

"You know," Josie said, leaning back in her chair as far as she could while maintaining a connection with Emma. "You could scour the streets for ladies like us and not find a single one. But then, in two families— yours and mine—you have two sets of ladies who understand each other perfectly." She grinned at the end of her declaration.

"You're talking homosexuals, right?" Eleanor asked, making sure they were on the same page. At Josie's nod, she asked, "Okay, Lysette and I and you. Who's the fourth?"

Josie met her gaze, her expression openly confused why Eleanor didn't seem to know that already. "My Emmaline."

"That Emmaline?" Eleanor exclaimed, pointing to her mother's sleeping form. At Josie's nod, Eleanor fell back against her chair, looking to her mother, wishing she'd sit up and either validate what Josie had just said or dispute it.

She thought back to the only other time she'd been with Josie, which had been that wonderful day in Denver. She thought of them together and the instant connection she'd seen between them. In fact, she'd almost felt a bit jealous that day, the fact that her mother seemed to *only* have eyes for Josie. If Eleanor hadn't been so obsessed with Lysette at that time, she would have been outright hurt and confused.

"Well," she said at length, clearing her throat. "I guess that makes sense now why she was always so understanding about Lysette and me." She smirked and met Josie's gaze. "And why Lysette's parents were so good about us, too. They already dealt with you… and my mother." She shook her head, still trying to wrap her mind around it all.

"You know, since your mom never told you about all this, maybe I should just shut up now," Josie said, defeat in her tone as she looked away, her shoulders sagging a bit.

"No, Miss Josie—"

"Aunt Josie," the older woman demanded, pointing a finger at her.

"Aunt Josie. I can tell you since Ed died, there's been nobody for her, not another man, not a woman." She chuckled. "She doesn't even have a dog, though she is intending to get a cat when she moves into her new house," she pointed out. "But the fact that she's stayed alone all this time, maybe that means something, huh?"

The two women glanced toward the door when it opened and a nurse appeared, white uniform crisp all the way to her cap, pinned in place over dark brown hair.

"How's our girl?" she asked, giving the two a quick smile before she set the clipboard she carried on Emma's blanket-covered legs. She went about checking her vital signs, as well as her IV drip. The nurse grabbed her clipboard and scribbled a few things down before tucking it against her side. "Looks good, ladies. She should start coming out of this within the hour." With that, she was gone.

Aunt Josie glanced at Eleanor. "Guess that's good news, right?"

"Tell me your story," Eleanor said softly. The truth was, it was difficult to think of her mother in any sort of sexual way or as a sexual being, but she really needed to know about this shocking revelation. "Does Lysette know?"

Josie nodded. "She figured it out when you girls were younger."

Eleanor let out an annoyed sigh. "I must be the thickest person on the planet."

Josie chuckled. "Don't be so hard on yourself. You two girls were raised in very different environments."

"So true. So tell me."

"Well," Josie said with a sigh, getting comfortable in the decidedly uncomfortable hospital chair. "Davis met your mom first. I think we were all thirteen or so. See, I was always too busy out climbing trees, fishing, whatever. My brother," she waved off the memory with a laugh, "was high and mighty inside. We were close, though, close enough that I actually began to get a little miffed at the time he spent with her. I honestly wondered if maybe she was his sweetheart, but nah, they just really hit it off. Anyway, so finally I met her, and that was it." She snapped her fingers. "Like that, I was a goner." She grinned, and Eleanor could easily see that lovestruck young girl in her smile.

"Did Mama feel the same?" she asked softly.

"She did. Don't know why, but she did. So the three of us hung out together. If you were looking for one, just look for the other. If you were looking for the other, just look for the third." She gave Eleanor a mischievous grin. "Finally, I got up the nerve to kiss her when we were fourteen. Never forget it." She laughed. "Sorry. I doubt you want to hear about all that."

"No," Eleanor said, surprisingly interested to hear about this side of her mother. It was almost like hearing about another person, two strangers she didn't know. "Keep going."

"Well, needless to say, eventually Davis began dating girls, so he was off with them a lot, which left Emma and I together. We spent endless hours talking, giggling like fools." She stopped, her mood turning serious. "When the fella your mom was supposed to marry was killed in the war," she glanced up at Eleanor, "well, we thought that was it. Maybe we could be together forever after all. That was the plan, anyway."

"Best laid plans..." Eleanor murmured.

"Ain't that the truth? Anyhow, the night before she had to marry your father, I snuck into her bedroom at the house, and we, well, we spent the night together."

Eleanor felt the profound sadness coming off Josie in waves. "Was that your first time?"

Josie nodded, letting out a shaky breath. "Yup. That is, until Davis and Adalyn gave your mom the job cleaning the house. She brought you along, and together, we took care of you and Lysette." Her smile was that of a proud mama bear. "For a time, we got to feel like it was our life, our children, you girls." She gave Eleanor a loving smile as her thumb caressed the back of Emma's hand. Eleanor wondered if she realized she was even doing that.

"Ed really seemed to hate Davis and Adalyn a lot. Why?"

"Because he suspected something was up. I

think for a long time he thought Emma and Davis had something in the hopper, but then one day, he caught us."

Eleanor stared, her mouth hanging open. "Ed caught you and Mama?" she hissed. "As in, *together*?"

Josie smiled. "We were only sitting together holding hands while Emma read to you girls who were half asleep in our laps. I'm sure we made quite the picture of a family. He erupted. After that, he got super religious and banished Emma from the house or anything to do with us. We continued to write letters for a while, but then they stopped. I'm guessing maybe he found that out, too."

"He'd never let us get the mail," Eleanor said, remembering how adamant he was about that. "That son of a bitch."

"The day that bastard died was the day the world became a better place," Josie said, her voice flat. She looked at Eleanor. "Sorry, honey. That wasn't right to say in front of you."

"No, it was very right and very accurate. Good riddance. You know, independently, Mama and I dropped his name. She said she wanted no part of him, never had, and when I began my teaching career in Wichita, I was worried some colleague or student would find out about my past. So I dropped Landry and never looked back." She smirked. "Ironically, it was a parent who found out who I was, anyway."

"Yes, but by Jim nosing around, he essentially brought you and Lysette back together, didn't he?"

She met Josie's gaze, and after a moment, a slow smile spread across her lips. "Yeah, I guess so."

Chapter Thirty-four

Lysette let out a tired breath as she directed Scott to her street. They'd engaged in a bit of chitchat on the drive back from Colorado Springs, but Lysette was caught in her own concerned thoughts, and from the pensive body language of the man who sat next to her, she assumed he was worried, as well.

"The one with the circular drive," she pointed out.

"Yes, ma'am." He pulled the car up to the house. "I was here for your Christmas party with Eleanor. We chatted," he added with a boyish grin.

She looked at him, surprised. Then, yes, she remembered. "Oh, lord," she said, smiling at her own silliness. "Sorry. Yes, now I do remember."

Scott chuckled. "That's okay. We may have talked about the weather, but we weren't exactly properly introduced that night."

Still embarrassed by her behavior that night, she turned sheepish eyes on him, though she knew his comment was innocent. "No, we weren't." She leaned over and gave him a quick kiss to the cheek. "Thank you for the ride, and I want to tell you how sorry I am about what happened to you and Ronnie Washington. A lot of us here are pulling for you, Scott."

He met her gaze before nodding as he looked away. "Thank you." He gave her a kind smile and his mother's telephone number to call when she was ready to return to the hospital.

Leaving Scott with a smile and a wave, Lysette heard his car continue on as she walked up the path to the front door of her home. The moment she pushed it open, she heard her kids arguing.

"Stop it! Jimmy, give it back! I'm gonna tell Mom."

"Mom isn't here, little squirt." Jimmy grinned evilly, holding Bronte's sandwich above his head so she couldn't reach it. "You're daddy's little squirt."

Bronte, who had been jumping up trying to grab her after-school snack, stopped and looked at him, confusion in her eyes. "What does that even mean?"

"Yeah, Jimmy," Lysette said, standing in the archway to the kitchen, arms crossed over her chest and irritation in her eyes.

The kitchen was an absolute disaster with peanut butter and jelly smeared on the counter and a thumbprint on the icebox door. Both jars were left open as was the bag of bread. The used knife—still slathered with peanut butter—was stuck to the wall.

Arm frozen in the air, Jimmy whirled around, the classic *busted* look on his face. "Mom! You're back."

"I'm glad you noticed." She walked over to him, her gaze never leaving his as she reached up and snagged the sandwich out of his hand, tossing it to the plate on the table that held his half-eaten sandwich. "Snack time is over," she declared, taking both plates and dumping the uneaten food into the trash and nearly tossing the plates into the sink. "Now you two get to clean this kitchen from top to bottom!" She glared at them both, two pairs of guilty eyes looking back at her. "I cannot believe this. I leave you alone for just over an hour, and this is what you do?"

"We…uh…" Jimmy murmured, a hand rubbing the back of his neck, which bore the flush of the rest of his face. "We were going to have it cleaned up before you got home."

"You asked me for more freedom, James," she said. "You've been asking me to leave you alone more and let you prove yourself to us." She indicated the kitchen around them. "So I do, and this is what you do." She looked at Bronte. "Is your homework done, Bronte? Did you get your outfit ready for your dance class tonight like I asked you to do?"

"No, ma'am," she whispered.

Angry and disappointed, Lysette turned to leave the kitchen. "Twenty minutes!" she called over her shoulder. "This kitchen is spotless when I return in twenty minutes!"

Letting out a sigh of annoyance, she headed toward the stairs when she stopped, her focus on the front door when she heard a key in the lock. Confused, she walked across the living room to the door, unlocking and yanking it open to see an incredibly surprised Fran staring at her on the other side.

"Can I help you?" Lysette asked, arms crossing over her chest once again.

"Uh, I, uh…" Fran looked past Lysette for a moment before meeting her gaze again. "Jim told me to come over and grab a suit for him," she explained. "Um…I was under the understanding nobody would be home now."

Lysette felt a bit of defensive territorialism wash over her as she stared at her soon-to-be ex-husband's mistress, just the beginnings of her baby bump visible through the material of her cotton dress. "Why exactly would nobody be home?" Her voice dripped with sarcasm as her arms fell free only for a hand to rest on her hip. "My children are out of school, and I happen to live here."

Fran's eyes widened, and her mouth worked like that of a fish out of water.

Realizing her concern over Emma's condition and frustration that she couldn't be with Eleanor when she needed her—let alone the situations with her kids—was not this woman's fault, she forced herself to calm and relax. Lysette still was angry with Jim for giving Fran a key to her house.

"I'm sorry," she managed, stepping back from the door. "Rough day. Come on, and I'll show you."

"Mom, who's here?" Jimmy stepped into the room, a dish towel slapped over his shoulder.

Lysette glared at him, not saying a word as she pointed to the kitchen behind him. He glanced at Fran for a moment before turning and disappearing back where he'd come from.

An awkward moment as any, Lysette led Fran up the stairs and down the hall to the bedroom she'd shared with the very man who had impregnated the brunette.

"Did he put you up to this?" Lysette glanced over her shoulder as they entered the large bedroom. Her voice wasn't unkind, but it didn't exactly scream besties, either.

"He did. I'm really sorry." Fran slowed her gait as she neared the bedroom doorway. She looked around, seeming incredibly uncomfortable. "I was assured I could get in and out without bothering you."

Lysette nodded with a sigh. "Sounds about right. He rarely knows what's going on and assumes he does." Nearly to Jim's closet, she realized Fran wasn't following her. She looked at her. "You can come in." She would have been amused if the situation wasn't so sad as the poor woman looked as though she were about to enter the Coliseum and was looking around to see which door the lions would enter through.

"Yes, ma'am," Fran murmured, stepping into the room.

"Ma'am?" Lysette gasped. "I'm not *that* much older than you, darlin'." She turned back to his closet and opened it. "Now," she said, eyeing the woman who timidly made her way over to her. "I'm guessing he's going to want his gray pinstripe." She ran her fingers down the sleeve of the described suit jacket until her fingers reached the cuff, then she pulled it out into view. "He's going into trial against D.A. Runsted, who he can't stand, so he's going to want to feel confident and powerful. This one and the red and black tie are what do it for him." She let the sleeve drift back into the closet before she grabbed the hanger and pulled out the entire jacket, matching trousers already ironed and flipped over the second rung of the double hanger, and handed it to Fran.

"Thank you," Fran said, taking the clothing from Lysette.

"If he ever asks for his 'Superman suit,' this is what he wants."

Fran smiled shyly. "That's what he said, and I was so confused. I wasn't sure if I'd go into his closet and find an actual superhero outfit."

Lysette threw her head back and laughed. She looked at the other woman who gave her a sheepish smile. "Oh, that was good." Still chuckling, she gathered the rest of the pieces of the suit and a garment bag, loading it all in for easy transport.

"Thank you," Fran murmured, taking the heavy bag. She looked down at it, folded it over her arms for a moment before she looked up into Lysette's eyes. "Listen," she began. "I just want you to know that, though yes, I love Jim, I've never really been okay with how things happened between us. I didn't know he was married or about Jimmy or Bronte when we first met, I swear."

Lysette looked down at the shorter woman, stung by her words, which she knew weren't meant that way. She saw Fran was likely a young woman who got in over her head.

"But by the time I found out," she gave a one-shoulder shrug, "it was too late. I was in love with him."

"Yeah, I know how he works," Lysette said with a smirk. "Believe me, I know. Listen, Fran, I'm in no position to judge you as a woman or to judge you and Jim as a couple. I guess all I can say to you is, if you intend to be the stay-at-home wife who takes care of your man," she lowered her head while lifting her eyes, a playful mischief in them, "make him pick up his damn clothes off the floor. You'll thank me for it later."

Fran went from pretty to stunning with the glow of her smile at those words. She seemed to break out of her fear and intimidation a bit, relief in her body language. "Okay. I'll keep that in mind." She lifted her arms with the garment bag on them. "I better go."

Lysette walked her out, watching for a moment as the woman who was having a baby with the man she'd lived with for more than fifteen years hurried down the walk to her car. Her gut told her that Fran was a decent person, and that mattered because she'd be around her children.

"Hey."

Lysette turned to see a contrite Jimmy walking up to her.

"We're done."

She looked at him and let out a breath. Her anger was obviously long gone from the antics of her kids, and the look of self-recrimination in her normally confident son's eyes broke her heart.

"Thank you, son," she said, walking over to him and leaving a kiss on his cheek. "Come on, let's go check it out."

"I've seen her here before," Jimmy said as they walked to the kitchen. "That woman," he clarified with a hitched thumb back toward the front door.

"Here?" Lysette asked. When he nodded, she stopped him with a hand to his arm. "When?"

He looked uncomfortable as he shifted his weight with the shuffle of his feet. "Remember last year when I had that really bad bloody nose? Aunt Josie had to come get me because you were down in Pueblo delivering the school supplies?"

She thought about it for a moment, then nodded. "Yes. Just after school started."

"Yeah. So we get here, and Aunt Josie dropped me off to get some stuff for my nose. We were surprised to see Dad's car in the driveway, but anyway, when I went in, they were in your bedroom."

She stared at him, shocked and embarrassed. No, it wasn't her; no, she'd never done that. But good god, what kind of people had she and Jim become? "What were they doing?"

He shoved his hands into the hip pockets of his jeans and shrugged before bouncing on the balls of his feet. "I don't know. The door was closed, but when Dad came out, he looked pretty surprised to see me.

She came out a few minutes later, and they left."

"Why didn't you tell me?" she asked, hurt.

"Oh, right. 'Uh, gosh, Mom, I kinda need to tell you about the chick that was in your bedroom with Dad today. Cool? Okay, gotta run!'" He glared at her.

"I'm sorry." She took him in a tight hug. "You're right. That's not your problem or your job. I'm sorry," she said again, leaving a kiss to the side of his head. "Come on. Let's check out that kitchen."

❧❧❧❧

Lysette gently set the pillow with hand-stitched wisdom on it on the wing-backed chair she knew Aunt Josie loved to curl up in and read before returning to the bed and pulling down the quilt and folding it at the foot of the bed. She figured it would be too warm for it, especially with the two blankets and sheet Josie used to sleep under. Josie always said she was half-reptile and got cold far too easily.

She let out a tired sigh as she ran her hands through her hair, looking down at her nightgown, which had been tossed over the back of the chair. She reached up and began to unbutton her blouse when there was a knock at the door. It was late, and she knew the kids were in bed, or at least pretending to be asleep, and she'd already spoken with Aunt Josie and Eleanor on the phone. Both would remain at the hospital overnight, and she'd join them after dropping the kids off at school in the morning.

"Come in, Jim," she said, loud enough for him to hear but quiet enough not to disturb Bronte and Jimmy.

The door opened, and Jim peeked his head in,

quickly glancing around the room before his gaze landed on her. "You're alone in here?"

"I am." When he stepped inside and closed the door behind him, she went back to unbuttoning her blouse to ready for bed.

"Why are you in here? Where's Josie?" he asked, stepping just inside the room, hands on his hips. He looked tired, necktie pulled down and collar unbuttoned. From years of living with an attorney, Lysette knew the nights before a trial were long ones.

"She's at the hospital," Lysette said simply, her blouse sliding off her shoulders, leaving her in bra and slacks.

"What? Why? Is she okay?" He moved farther into the room to sit on the end of the bed.

"Yes. She's with Emma, Eleanor's mother. She had a heart attack earlier today, and it was pretty serious. So I knew better than to try and drag Aunt Josie away," she said with a small smile.

He nodded, not asking for further elaboration. "So why are you in here then?"

She let out a sigh, reaching over to tug the nightgown off the chair, and tossed it to the bed. She reached behind her to unclasp her bra, then slide the gown over her head. She didn't want to have to get into this tonight, but she knew it was inevitable.

"Why did you do that to Fran tonight?" she asked in lieu of a response to his question. She looked over at him. "That poor girl looked like she was about to have a damn coronary when I yanked open the door that she was trying to unlock."

He looked up at her from his perch on the bed with confusion. "Tonight was Bronte's spelling bee thing. You guys weren't supposed to be home."

"That was last week, Jim! You were there, remember?"

He threw his hands up and looked away. "Shit." He eyed her. "Well, she didn't mention anything to me."

"What is she going to say?" Lysette asked, exasperated. "Uh, gee honey," she deepened her voice for exaggerated effect, "I kinda ran into your family while trying to figure out what the hell you meant by your Superman suit."

He let out an irritated sigh as he ran a hand through his hair. "Crap. Yeah."

"Yeah. That poor girl is in over her head with you. She's a nice lady, she really is," Lysette said, genuine affection for a strange situation. "But I have to ask."

He looked up at her, expression guarded. She knew he knew that tone of voice from her. He wasn't going to like what was coming. "What?"

"Do you have such little respect for me, for the kids, and for the home we've made for them that you'd bring your mistress here?" she asked. "And then if that's not bad enough, you fuck her in *my* bed?"

His eyes widened, and his face paled. He swallowed before his demeanor changed, a conscious effort on his part. "What are you talking about?" he said, attempting to wave off her accusation. "That's bullshit."

"Is it?" she asked, arms crossed far more casually over her chest than she was feeling.

"Did she tell you that?" he asked, voice sounding far less sure that he could get one over on her.

"No."

He physically relaxed, pushing to his feet. "Well then, that's absurd—"

"Your son did."

He stared at her for a long moment before turning away, again that hand pushing through his hair. "Little bastard."

"Don't you dare blame this on him," she growled. "He only told me tonight, after watching Fran come and go. That poor baby had to hold in the fact that this father is a cheating rat for more than seven months. He was really upset by it."

"I'm a cheating rat?" he asked, turning on her, hand on his own chest. "*I'm* a cheating rat? You cannot tell me that you didn't bring one of your, your floosies into this house to fuck!"

She walked up to him, angry and over all of it. "Don't call them floosies. Any one of those women has more class than you'll ever have. And no, I never did. I didn't have sex with any one of them in our bed, in our home, or even in the same goddamn county. There's a thing called discretion. And even though you and I opted to take the lowest of the low road in our marriage, I wasn't about to do that to our children." She looked him dead in the eye. "Or to you."

"Well, aren't you just a fucking saint," he said evenly.

Deciding enough had been said, Lysette wanted to move on to what she'd been thinking about all evening. "I think you and Fran should take this house. Aunt Josie and the kids and I will find a place here to start over."

"And Eleanor," he bit out.

She wasn't going to take the bait. "If that's what we decide to do down the road, absolutely," she said casually.

"So you expect me to move Fran into our marriage

bed?" he asked, incredulous.

She brought a hand to her hip and looked him square in the eye. "You already did."

He looked away, jaw muscles working as he attempted to control his temper. "Fine," he said at length, heading to the door. "I'll make an amendment in the papers, which should be ready for your attorney to look over by the end of the week."

"Jim," she said.

He stopped, hand on the bedroom doorknob, glancing at her over his shoulder.

"We need to have a proper discussion with the kids. Soon."

He nodded, then left.

Chapter Thirty-five

"Mama, where do you want this? Though I think the better question is, *why* do you want this?" Eleanor held the small knitted blanket up for inspection, her face pulling in mild disgust. "It's definitely seen better days."

"Excuse me, but that was your first baby blanket, thank you very much," Emma said, indignation in her voice where she stood at the counter pulling newspaper-wrapped dishes out of a box.

"Yes, and I'd wager it still has my first diaper change on here, too," Eleanor muttered.

"Yup, and it's right about where your hand is."

Eleanor gasped, her hand falling away as though burned. Realizing by her mother's mischievous grin she'd been had, she rolled her eyes and tossed the blanket so it drifted down onto her mother's head. "You figure it out," she grumbled playfully.

Emma chuckled, pulling the blanket away and lightly setting it aside.

"Hey, now," Josie said, glaring at Eleanor as she stepped up next to Emma, placing a protective arm around her shoulders. "You be good, or I'll take you out back for a good whoopin'. Your mother is in recovery," she said sweetly, her demeanor instantly changing from playfully gruff to tender with adoration in her eyes fixed solely on Emma.

Eleanor stood back and watched. She honestly

couldn't be happier for her mother, as she'd truly never seen joy in her eyes the way it was there when Josie was anywhere near her or was simply mentioned. The only thing that had ever brought her joy like that was Eleanor's own successes in life or when Emma was surrounded by anything green that grew.

Josie hadn't left her side in the entire month since she'd arrived at Memorial and just over two weeks since she'd been released. Even once Eleanor had to go back to school, she'd felt far more okay about it because she knew Josie was with her. She knew that Josie was finally giving Emma everything she'd dreamed of: love, attention, affection, and true acceptance for all that she was.

"Lunch!"

Eleanor looked to see Bronte leading the parade inside. She carried a large paper bag that was filled with Styrofoam containers of lunch orders taken when Lysette had called earlier. A few moments after she entered and headed their way, her mother and brother followed, though Eleanor could tell not all was well.

"Jimmy, your dad told you no," Lysette was saying, a cardboard tray with a few drinks in Styrofoam cups on it in her hands, Jimmy carrying the rest.

"What does it matter what he said?" Jimmy stepped over the threshold behind her. "He's a jerk."

"Jim," Lysette said, turning on him, her voice lowering with warning. "I know you're angry right now with everything going on, but he's still your dad." She leaned in closer to him, their conversation no longer able to be heard.

Not wanting to seem like she was trying to nose in on the situation, Eleanor turned away and focused on Bronte. "Hey, kiddo. Lunch, huh?"

"Yup," she said, grinning brightly as she handed the large bag to Emma. "Mom let me put your order in myself."

"You did?" Emma asked, hands on hips. "And what, pray tell, did you order me?"

"Something Mom said would be nice to your heart." Bronte placed the large bag on the floor and opened it, reaching in and pulling out a closed Styrofoam container. "Salad!" She grinned. "With chicken."

Eleanor smiled and turned to the small kitchen table that the movers had brought in with the rest of the furniture the day before. She was about to start clearing the packed boxes off it when she felt a small touch to her arm. Turning, she saw Lysette standing next to her.

"Hey," she said.

"Hi." Lysette looked tired and a bit exasperated.

"You okay?" She wanted to give her a hug and kiss, but they decided to keep things quiet until school was out, which would be in a few weeks. Eleanor didn't feel right fully disclosing their relationship to Jimmy, considering he was in her class. He wouldn't be next year, and it would be a couple of years before Bronte would be. By then, any and all wrinkles should be ironed out.

"Yeah," she said, blowing out a breath as she set the drinks on the table. "I'll tell you about it later. Do you think your mama would be upset if I kidnap you after lunch?" She stuck bendable straws in the thin plastic covering the hole in the lids on the drinks. "I want to show you something."

"No, that shouldn't be a problem," Eleanor said, accepting her lemonade. "We're down to the kitchen and a few odds and ends now in the unpacking arena. I mean, they're even sleeping here now."

Lysette gave her a devilish grin. "Is that weird for you?"

Eleanor sipped her drink and glanced over at her mother and Aunt Josie. The two were getting everyone's lunch containers out of the bag they'd brought up to the counter, standing nearly hip to hip in their work. "Not weird, per se," she responded. "It's different, for sure, but honestly," she added, glancing at Lysette, "I can't think of two women more deserving of happiness."

Lysette gave her a loving smile. "I can."

⁂

"It is an absolutely gorgeous spring day," Eleanor said, arm resting along the passenger window, which she'd rolled down in Lysette's car.

They drove along the quiet streets of her mother's new neighborhood, which was headed slightly toward the outskirts of town. She felt so content and happy to be with Lysette. She reached over and took Lysette's free hand, Lysette immediately entwining their fingers as the two shared a quick smile.

"So what's going on with Jimmy?"

Lysette let out a sigh. "He's been fighting with Jim nonstop since we told the kids that we were getting a divorce. He's convinced it's because Jim brought Fran home and he told me."

"Oh, man. Baby, I'm sorry. Wow. Couldn't be further from the truth."

"Exactly. So he's on this kick that anything Jim tells him he doesn't have to listen to because obviously

Jim doesn't want to be part of the family anymore."

Eleanor listened, but the rare bumps the Vaughns hit in this road of separating lives always made her feel equal parts guilty and worried. Her worst fear was that Lysette would decide it wasn't worth it and call off the divorce, despite all the endless assurances she got from her that would never happen. She was always reminded that the divorce would be final as of June 1, just over a month away.

"You know, the irony is," Lysette continued, unwittingly breaking through Eleanor's morose thoughts. "I always thought Bronte would struggle more with this. Heck," she said with a smile, "she's super excited to have a younger brother or sister to pick on. You know," she said, glancing at Eleanor before turning left onto a road that took them out into the wooded area that surrounded Woodland. "She's been the baby for almost thirteen years and picked on incessantly by her older brother."

Eleanor smiled, nodding. She'd certainly seen enough of that in the months she'd been back in Lysette's life. "I'll bet."

"Jimmy is such a laid-back kid, you know? I'm really surprised by how he's acting out."

"Well, consider how close you two are. I'm actually not surprised at all that he's doing this," Eleanor said. "I see it with my boys at school, whether it's a younger sister or a girlfriend. They get very territorial when any other boy comes along. I think he's just being protective of you and probably of Bronte, though he'd never admit it."

Lysette smiled. "Isn't that the truth."

The car slowed and turned onto a private lane that began under a wooden gate, ranch-style. A

handwritten sign was stuck in the ground: *Estate Sale.*
"We're going to look at old stuff that belonged to dead
people?" Eleanor asked, confused.

Lysette chuckled. "Sort of."

The New Yorker pulled up the long dirt road
that led to the house, which was about a half-mile
back from the road, patches of trees obscuring much
of the view until suddenly they cleared, revealing the
beautiful property.

The old two-story farmhouse had a wraparound
porch and dormers jutting out from the roof.

"What a darling house," Eleanor said, noting the
tables of belongings that were laid out on the front
lawn, a few people wandering around looking at things.
This was obviously where the sale was.

Lysette pulled to a stop and killed the engine. As
they climbed out of the car, a frail, petite man hobbled
over to them. His skin was like leather while his hands,
far too large in proportion to his small stature, were
that of a man who'd worked hard his entire life.

"Welcome back, Miss Lysette. I see you did
indeed bring your friend to see the house."

"I did, Mr. Oscar. This is Eleanor," she said,
presenting Eleanor to the old man, who held a hand
out in greeting.

"Hello, Miss Eleanor. You gals take your time
looking around now."

"I see," Eleanor said as they headed up the stairs
to the porch and into the house. She winced when the
screen door, with its entirely too-tight hinges, slammed
behind them. "So we're here to look at the *house* that
belonged to dead people."

Lysette chuckled. "Exactly. I guess Oscar was the
caretaker here for about fifty years for the same family.

The last family member died last winter, so now it's time for him to move on." She glanced at Eleanor as they made their way through the downstairs rooms. "So he told me."

"This place is great," Eleanor murmured, noting the original molding and beautiful fireplace in the sitting room. It was obvious it was an old house, the rooms small and plentiful, much like they were a hundred years before.

"So, Miss Historian," Lysette said, leading the way into the kitchen. "According to Oscar, this house was built just after the Civil War ended. Four bedrooms, five acres, and a horse barn."

Eleanor nodded, thinking it would be fantastic for Lysette and the kids. "Sounds great. You could get horses down the road for Bronte."

"My thoughts, too." They took the winding narrow staircase at the back of the house in the kitchen to the second floor. At one time, it would have been used by any servant help. They walked down the hall, peeking into the three smaller bedrooms, as well as a bathroom to be shared. Finally, in the master bedroom with a rare bathroom for the time period, Lysette stood in the center of the room, hands on hips. "What do you think?"

Eleanor took in the second fireplace tucked into the corner. "I think it's unfortunately been neglected, but it's nothing some elbow grease and paint can't cure. There's plenty of space without it being ostentatious or unmanageable."

Lysette nodded, taking in the empty room around them. "And," she added, eyeing Eleanor, "it's only about a fifteen-minute drive to the school."

Eleanor met her gaze. Her mind went to the kids

getting to school, but from the look in Lysette's eyes and the carefully hopeful smile, she knew the kids weren't exactly who Lysette meant by that.

Looking around to make sure they were alone, Eleanor walked over to her, reaching out to place her hands on Lysette's hips, gently tugging her toward her. Lysette's arms snaked up around Eleanor's neck, fingers lightly playing in the short dark hair at the nape of Eleanor's neck.

"What are you saying, hmm?" Eleanor asked, not wanting to assume or hope, regardless of what she felt Lysette was insinuating.

"Well, I know we just started dating about twenty-three years ago," Lysette said, that grin on her lips that Eleanor loved. "I want us to be together, Ellie," she said, her smile replaced by seriousness. "When you're ready, whether it's this house or the other one I've been looking at, I want you with me. Every place I've looked at over the past month, I've had us in mind." She tugged lightly on a strand of hair to emphasize the "us." "I want us to make a new life together. You, me, and the kids." She smirked. "I mean, they already love you, and Bronte and your mama have adopted each other."

"Jeez, isn't that the truth," Eleanor said, leaning in to initiate a slow, deep kiss, though she kept it short, concerned they'd be discovered. "Okay," she whispered against Lysette's beautiful lips. "Sounds like a plan."

Epilogue

The house was filled with loud chatter and laughter amid the crackle and popping of a dancing fire, which Jim sat near reading the paper while Jimmy and Aunt Josie were attempting to teach the new puppy Ralph a few tricks in the grand entryway of the farmhouse. In the kitchen, Fran laughed at one of the endless anecdotes Eleanor was sharing about her students with the ladies as they finished the last few details of dinner. Fran and Bronte were carrying the food into the formal dining room, decked out for the special Thanksgiving meal. Davis was in New Hampshire celebrating the holiday with Lysette's brothers and their families, the entire group expected in Colorado for Christmas.

"Is that it?" Fran asked, hand resting on her massive belly.

"That's it. Call 'em in," Lysette said, carrying the last of the food dishes in.

"Let's eat!" Fran called out, carefully taking her seat.

"Need any help, Fran?" Eleanor asked, standing nearby just in case.

"Nope," Fran said with gritted teeth as she lowered herself into the chair. She let out a loud sigh as her behind made contact with the padded seat. "I've got this." She grinned up at Eleanor, who returned the smile.

"Where are you sitting, baby?" Lysette asked, walking up beside Eleanor. They hadn't used the formal dining room since they'd moved in six months before.

"I don't know," Eleanor said, looking at the filling chairs. "I guess here at the end and you to my left?"

"Oh, I see," Lysette teased, giving her that smile saved only for her. "*You* get to be the 'man' of the house, huh?"

"Bet your cute little ass," Eleanor murmured into her ear, making Lysette laugh.

With everyone seated, Eleanor looked out over the large table, a feeling of absolute satisfaction filling her. She'd never been happier, her relationship with Lysette as strong and fulfilling as she always knew it would be. And though there were a few bumps along the way, the kids had settled in remarkably well with both their parents' new situations.

"Mama, can we go riding tomorrow?" Bronte asked, stealing a quick spoonful of mashed potatoes from the huge bowl at the center of the table.

"Only if you don't do that again." Lysette pointed a playful finger at her.

"Well," Jim said, clapping his hands from his seat mid-table next to his new wife. "Time to carve that gorgeous turkey."

Eleanor grabbed the carving knife she'd set next to her plate and stood, noting Jim was, as well. The two stood there looking at each other, the most awkward Wild West standoff in history before he grinned, laughing at himself before he reclaimed his seat.

"Uh, I think that's your job," he said.

"Okay, gang," Eleanor said, running the carving knife over the sharpening stone a few times. "Who wants what?"

"Uh…"

Eleanor's attention was drawn to Fran, who sat there looking a bit shell-shocked. "Fran? Did you say something? You like dark meat, right?"

"Uh…"

"White?"

"Honey?" Jim reached down to lift the tablecloth as he glanced at her belly. "Are you okay?"

She looked at him, hazel eyes large. "My water just broke."

The room went deathly silent for a moment until there was an explosion of sound and flurry of movement. Jim was helping Fran to her feet while Emma and Lysette hopped up from the table, barking out orders to each other and to Jim. Eleanor, Josie, Bronte, and Jimmy remained at the table, the kids looking as baffled and frightened as Eleanor did. Josie, on the other hand, nibbled on a dinner roll as she watched the hectic activity.

"What do we do?" Eleanor asked, feeling utterly helpless.

"Nothing," Josie said, meeting her gaze. "Stay out of their way until it's time to leave, honestly."

Eleanor pushed back from the table and walked to the front door, which stood open after Jim had helped Fran through it. They were down the stairs at his car. She hurried down to them, unnecessarily holding the front passenger-side door open for him just to feel useful.

"Here's your newspaper, Jim," Emma said, tossing the folded post to the backseat of the car. "You've probably got some time to kill."

He looked at her but said nothing as he got Fran seated. "You okay?" he asked. At Fran's nod, he closed the door, trotting around the front of the sedan he'd traded the Corvette in for. He glanced back at the crowd that had gathered at the bottom of the stairs. "Well, uh, Happy Thanksgiving, all," he said, panic in his voice before he climbed into the car and roared away from the house, red taillights disappearing into the darkness.

"Well," Jimmy said. "That was interesting."

"What do we do?" Bronte asked. "Do we go to the hospital to meet them?"

"Nah," Josie said, placing an arm over her shoulders. "That kid ain't comin' out until tomorrow sometime."

Eleanor glanced at Lysette, who stood next to her. "What do we do?" she asked. "Are we terrible for not going, too?"

Lysette chuckled and shook her head. "Let's eat, everyone. They'll call when he's ready to come out."

"I get the wishbone!" Jimmy called, turning and taking the stairs two at a time toward the porch.

"Do not!" Bronte hollered after him.

Josie and Emma grabbed hands and climbed the stairs together, disappearing inside the house. Left alone in the cold, late November night, Eleanor looked at Lysette again, and their gazes met.

Lysette snaked her arms around Eleanor's neck, clasping her hands behind her neck, their bodies pressed together. She studied her for so long, Eleanor began to feel like a bug scrutinized under a microscope. Finally, Lysette smiled. "My whole life," she said softly.

Eleanor wrapped her arms around Lysette's waist, letting out a contented sigh as she felt the love coming off the woman in her arms. "What about it?" she asked.

"My whole life I've waited for you."

Eleanor chuckled. "Hey, now, I know I stood you up when we were sixteen, but I showed up."

Lysette let out a soft laugh, absolute music to Eleanor's ears. "Yes, yes, you did." She leaned in, leaving a lingering kiss on Eleanor's lips. "Thank you," she whispered against them.

"Certainly my pleasure. I love you," she whispered back.

"And I love you, with all my heart."

Eleanor felt those words to her very soul. She let out another contented sigh before asking, "Hungry?"

"Starving," Lysette announced, trailing a fingernail from the nape of Eleanor's neck down along the side of her neck before her hand dropped away. "Worked all damn day on that dinner," she muttered, grabbing Eleanor's hand and tugging her back toward the house. She glanced over her shoulder and gave Eleanor that look that had first melted a fifteen-year-old girl's heart. "By the way, you're dessert." With a giggle, Lysette scurried through the front door, squealing at the pinch to her behind.

About the Author

Kim has spent her life in Colorado and can't imagine living anywhere else. She's been writing since she was 9 and stumbled into her first book being published in her mid-20s. She's worked in the film industry as a writer, director and producer, but now enjoys the quiet, happy life of a professional author. She can be reached on Facebook and on her website at, www.kimpritekel.com

Check out Kim's other books.

Zero Ward - ISBN - 978-1-943353-19-4

Danny Felts grew up in the heart of the Midwest on a dairy farm, expected to follow in her mother's footsteps and marry a farmer and become a mother. Danny had other ideas. As World War II heats up, she makes a decision that will change her life forever as she becomes a lie, serving with the Seabees in the Navy as Daniel Felts.

Kate Adams is about to graduate high school in her prestigious and elite San Diego neighborhood when she's dragged to the USO for a dance with friends and servicemen. There, she meets the person that will catch her eye and her heart, only for jealousy and vengeance to tear her apart.

Are Danny and Kate strong enough to win the battle within and fight for their love?

Connection - ISBN - 978-1-939062-24-6

Julie Wilson lives a charmed life as a beloved teacher and aunt in the small town of Woodland. Close to her brother and guardian of two adorable Yorkies, she loves her life, the only negative being ex-boyfriend, Ray who can't seem to understand the phrase, "We're done." Believing that's her only problem, Julie has no idea what hell awaits her during a normal summer afternoon.

Remmy Foster is the quirky, friendly drifter who has

never found roots after a difficult childhood, as well as the difficulties her very special gift brings into her life. Though she may call it exploring, the truth is she's running from ghosts that haunt her every step.

After a chance meeting with Julie while hitchhiking, Remmy will be thrown head first into darkness she could never have foreseen, regardless of her abilities. As the clock ticks, life and death is on her shoulders to make the right connection.

Warning - Some scenes may be too intense for some readers.

1049 Club - ISBN - 978-1-939062-97-0

Almost two hundred souls, one plane, six survivors, endless heartbreak.

When flight 1049, headed from Buffalo, NY to Italy falls from the sky, a firestorm of drama, pain, angst and sorrow ensues. Can an author, a business owner, a teenager, good ol' boy, veterinarian and ruthless lawyer survive? Better yet, can those left behind?

1049 Club is a story of survival, love, deep regret and miracles. Can the living make peace with the presumed dead? Can the presumed dead make peace with the lives and loves they thought they had before?

Blinded – ISBN – 978-1-943353-53-8

After a horrible explosion sends local television news reporter, Burton Blinde reeling both physically and emotionally, she walks away from her life and the dream job she was about to start at a major news network.

For six long years she hides out in a small mountain town, working at the local library, though is haunted by the life she had, including mysterious messages and gifts she was receiving before her life was turned upside down, a veritable bread crumb trail leading to the unknown.

Unable to resist, Burton begins to follow the clues, which will lead her into the darkest places of human nature that she may not be able to return from.

Damaged - ISBN - 978-1-939062-45-1

Family. A group of people you are related to by blood or love.

Nora Schaeffer has come home to her family after twenty years working around the world as a photographer for National Geographic. She's welcomed into the open arms of her father and siblings.

Family. A group of people who support you, lift you up when you fall.

Shannon, the youngest of the four Schaeffer siblings, has vanished, leaving her five-year-old daughter, Bella, terrified and alone. To help find Shannon, Nora has no choice but to turn to the dark-haired specter who has haunted her for twenty years. Along the way, she finds her own long-dead heart and uncovers chilling family secrets beyond imagination.

Family. A group of people who will stick together to hide the rotten soul at its core at any cost.

Who will live? Who will die? Who will be the most damaged? And who will learn to love again?

The Gift - ISBN - 978-1-948232-47-0

The dead do speak. You just have to listen. Homicide Detective Catania "Nia" d'Giovanni is the only daughter in a large Italian family of six children. The backbone—a position not applied for nor wanted—she continues to create new glue to hold the dysfunctional group together. For Nia, family time feels more like herding cats than spending time with her brothers and feisty, aging parents. Her heart has always been in her career with the Pueblo Police Department, especially since it will never be okay with her very Catholic mother to openly give her heart to any woman, until she meets a secretive waitress who has her at, Can I take your order? And then it begins… Three murders that are so gruesome, so horrible, they rock the small town to its core. Nia and her partner Oscar are left to piece together a deadly puzzle to find the key to unlock the monster they hunt. Or, are they the hunted? As they dissect the murder scenes where not one shred of evidence is left behind, more bodies begin to show up, each cleaner than the last, the shadowy specter that is the killer vanishing without a trace, making the woman Nia loves disappear right along with it. When there is no evidence to follow, Nia must trust her instincts… or, is she being guided?

Other books by Sapphire Authors

Twisted Deception - ISBN - 978-1-939062-47-5

There are two types of people who can't look you in the eyes: someone trying to hide a lie and someone trying to hide their love.

Addie Blake's life isn't black and white—more like a series of short bursts of color that sustain her until the next eruption. She isn't a ladder-climber in the corporate world. Instead, she works long hours at the office and even at home, something her mechanic girlfriend, Drake Hogan, can't stand. If Addie can't focus on Drake, then Drake finds arm candy that will. After a long week of late nights and a series of text-messaged demands, each one a bigger bomb than the last, Addie has had enough of her Motor Girl.

Greyson Hollister inhabits a world where everything is either black and white, or money green. She's a polished, certified workaholic. As head of Integrated Financial, she has built the ladder others want to climb. Now she intends to attend a business mixer to confront a rumormonger and kill merger rumors involving her company.

Detective Nancy Hill, the lead detective on the Elevator Rapist task force, has just been called in to investigate an attack at Integrated Financial. She can't quite put her finger on it, but something doesn't add up with this latest assault, and Greyson Hollister isn't exactly lending a helping hand.

A storm's brewing on the horizon. Can Addie and Greyson weather it, or will it blow them over?